TITAN
ACADEMY

TITAN
ACADEMY

McKenna Lumley

First edition paperback October 2022

Book design by McKenna Lumley

ISBN: 979 - 8 - 9869582 - 0 - 0
ebook: 979 - 8 - 9869582 - 1 - 7

Published by McKenna Lumley

For 10 year old me.
We fuckin' did it, kid.

CLASS ALPHA ROSTER:

Charlie Whittaker—15, Class Four Marvel:
    Concussive Overpressure
Jack Zelweger—16, Class Three Marvel: Earth Manipulation
Thomas "Tommy" Austin—15, Class Six Marvel: Void
Ethan Wells—15, Class Six Marvel: Glow
Lochlan Garcia—15, Class Four Marvel: Storm Manifestation
Malia Graves—15, Class Three Marvel: Healing
Kai Kelley—15, Class Four Marvel: Water Manipulation
Alex White—16, Class Five Marvel: Self Duplication
Luna Locklear—15, Class Four Marvel: Botanokinesis
Cora Greene—15, Class Five Marvel: Aura Claws
Cecily Day—15, Class Four Marvel: Rock Buddy
Anthony Vargas—15, Class Four Marvel: Warp
Jayne Walsh—15, Class Five Marvel: Black Wings
Luc Nichols—15, Class Five Marvel: Animation
Reese Wilkerson—15, Class Four Marvel: Flash Bang
Joel Briggs—16, Class Six Marvel: Flat Body
Rose Bardot—15, Class Four Marvel: Metal Manipulation
Eric Young—15, Class Five Marvel: Superstick
Dominic Freeman—15, Class Four Marvel: Flay

Prologue

The first explosion doesn't hurt.

It does take Honor by surprise, though. She's standing in line at a pizza joint, minding her own business when she spots the back of her former best friend's head. She hasn't seen him in over a year, and not for lack of trying. After their fight, Colson had just—fallen off the face of the planet, and Honor was a little busy saving the world at the time. She figured they'd see each other again and make up after everything settled down. Not for the first (or last) time, Honor was wrong.

Honor calls his name and watches him turn slowly, carefully, and it puts her on edge. Colson is a bright and sunny personality, like a puppy. But she sees his pale face and sunken eyes and immediately knows something is wrong. She takes a step forward, hand already reaching for him, ready to help in any way she can. But then she's crashing through the front window of the restaurant, glass shattering around her but unable to cut through her Titan skin.

She lands on the sidewalk and rolls messily over her shoulder and up to her feet, stumbling back into a parked car at a meter and narrowly avoiding a pedestrian with a stroller. The car alarm sounds and heads start to turn toward the commotion. All Honor can do for a moment is stare.

It's a warning. Colson knows exactly what level blast he needs to generate to put a mark on Honor. But warnings don't work on Honor, and Colson knows that too.

"What are you doing?" she nearly shouts at him. It's been a long time since Colson hurled an explosion at her outside of training, and the last time had ended up with him in the hospital. Blood drips down his fingers as they curl into a fist at his side. Colson's marvel is the ability to oxygenate his own blood into explosions, and the amount of blood it will take to hurt Honor is dangerously high, but he looks ready to try anyway.

"Don't follow me," he says, but his voice shakes. Glass crunches under his boots as he tries to walk past her. As well as Colson knows Honor, he should already know that isn't going to work.

Honor lunges forward and grabs his arm. For a tense moment, neither of them move. Colson doesn't look at her and Honor's grip is too tight, it's going to bruise. Colson was a professional hero, just like Honor, and after he completely abandoned his life's work, Honor assumed something terrible had happened to him. Not that he's been walking around the streets of Los Angeles this whole time as if nothing was wrong.

"Talk to me," she urges, near desperate. "What's wrong?"

Colson does look at her then. She recognizes the grim determination in the thin line of his mouth. Honor's marvel is the ability to throw tricks, illusions, but Colson knows them too well, they won't work. Especially not in the knock-down, drag-out fight she feels building. She won't need to throw any tricks, though, she's half Titan, and she's got the speed and strength to prove it. Colson knows this too.

"Let. Go."

Suddenly they're eighteen again, standing in the rubble of what used to be their dorm building. The first and last time they really, truly fought. She put Colson in a coma. And it was the first time Honor feared her own power, her own willingness to do whatever it takes. Then it clicks.

"Ravenna," she breathes. Colson's eyes go wide and panicked. He yanks his arm out of her grip and fires another explosion, this one big enough to hurt.

Out of uniform, Honor takes the full brunt of it to the chest. It sears her t-shirt and sends her crashing into a still-moving garbage truck in the middle of the street. The whole thing rocks then topples over sideways, about to crush a small sedan with nowhere to go in the middle of LA traffic. Then it's caught by pro hero on duty, Duchess. She's small and deceptively hardy with a strength marvel dressed in her uniform of a pink skirt and white, armored bodysuit. The Justice Agency logo is stitched onto her shoulder, and she looks to Honor for instruction even though Honor doesn't work for Justice anymore.

"Start evacuations," Honor orders, only coughing slightly. "Ten block radius."

Duchess and Honor move in the same moment in opposite directions. Honor leaps back across the street with all of her Titan strength, clearing the distance between her and Colson in the blink of an eye. She catches his hand when he raises it, turns, throws him over her shoulder and into the intersection. All traffic stops under Duchess's instructions and people get out of their cars, some to film on their phones, others to run screaming in the opposite direction.

Honor's eyes glow pink while she calls her sister for back up, and Colson watches, one of the few who knows what happens when Honor's eyes glow.

Evacuate the district. Colson's gone rogue.

She can feel Verity's disbelief and outrage in her own head. Honor would call Grace too, but she's off world and won't get here in time. Colson raises both his hands this time to take aim at Honor. But there's no way he can hit her and avoid the civilians behind her. For a moment, she thinks he'll fire anyway.

But he changes course, blowing two explosions through his feet, blasting the bottom off his boots and launching himself into the air, onto the nearest rooftop. Honor jumps and follows. She's on him in a second, throwing him to the ground. Colson rolls with the momentum she gives him instead of fighting it and gets smoothly back to his feet.

Honor doesn't want to hurt Colson. She wants to *help*. But it's clear that Colson doesn't want her help, for reasons Honor can probably guess. The mere thought of Colson's mother makes her furious, and Honor's anger is dangerous so she tramps it down.

She follows him from roof to roof, taking the brunt of his explosions and powering through them to slow him down, to keep him from running away again. She doesn't want to hurt him but she's not going to let him get away. This is the Colson who held her when her mom died. Colson, who witnessed her at her worst and followed her into hell just to drag her back out. Now it's her turn to do the same.

Honor pants and lands on a roof across the street from the one Colson stands on.

"Colson, *stop!*" she shouts. He lifts a hand to aim a blast at the building she's standing on. It's already been evacuated with the aid of Verity's marvel, but she still leaps into the air and he takes aim at her directly, instead. His blood ignites and this explosion sends her flying three blocks west and onto a street that hasn't been evacuated yet. People scream and scramble out of the way, toward the safety of the pros in charge of the evacuation. Honor isn't sure where they can evacuate to if Colson keeps throwing her around like this. If she keeps letting him.

Colson's right behind her, having realized by now that Honor isn't going to let him get away unless he takes her out first. She rolls out of the way and he blows a crater in the street. Honor's eyes go wide. It's a massive blast, asphalt and other debris rain down around them, that would hurt even Honor.

But she's faster than him and they both know it. The fact that Honor doesn't want to hurt Colson gives him a huge advantage. It's all she can do to dodge because she refuses to fully fight him, but she's beginning to think he won't stop unless she does.

Her clothes are a blackened and bloody collage from the hits she took at close range. She looks a mess and it's all caught on every cell phone camera that belongs to the idiots that aren't running away as fast as possible. Out of uniform, it's hard for her to get in close without taking too much damage.

Colson propels himself across the street and closes the distance between them. Honor moves under him and takes the explosion aimed at her back, feels it ripple down her spine and singe the thin skin over her vertebrae, so she can wrap a hand around his ankle and throw him through a nearby shop window.

Honor stands, breathing heavy in the street, her mind working a million miles a minute. Colson's not down for the count, she's seen him take harder hits, but she's still at a loss. She doesn't know what to do. She doesn't know why Colson is going to such great lengths to get away from her when he knows she only wants to help. But she can't believe he's turned into a full fledged rogue in the time they've been apart, she can't—

The next explosion blindsides her like she's a rookie. She goes clean through the bed of a truck, the twisted metal scraping her skin open and adding to the mess of blood staining her jeans. She swears and gets to her feet on the other side of the truck and watches Colson extract himself from the storefront. The glass from that window has cut him too, and blood runs down his bare arms. It's just more ammunition for him.

Honor's whole body screams in protest to the beating it's taken. To the beating she's allowed because she doesn't want to hurt Colson. Not again.

Her whole frame is tense to fight and then all at once—it isn't. Colson notices the change and hesitates only slightly before hitting her again. Honor braces for impact with a brick wall painted with a mural of her and her sisters.

"Are you done?!" Colson screams at her. It's not a taunt. But she knows with the crowds and the cameras that it will be perceived that way. Honor briefly closes her eyes and pushes to her feet. Rubble falls around her, off her shoulders. He wants her to be done. He needs her to be done. This is Colson begging.

Please stop.

Fury builds up inside of her, and, if she were Verity, it would be spilling everywhere. Stop what? She hasn't done anything. She's not doing anything besides letting him beat the shit out of her, tearing the city apart in the process. Honor will never stop. She'll never give up. Not on Colson. Not again.

"Am I dead?" she shouts back. The crowd at the end of the street, guarded by three other pros, one of them her sister, screams in answer and Colson's eyes widen a fraction. She feels blood run down the back of her neck and into the collar of her shirt. She feels the emotion of the crowd swell then crest, pushed higher and higher by Verity. It's all just noise to Honor but the answer is obvious.

"THEN I'M NOT FUCKING DONE."

But just as Colson hadn't been taunting her, she isn't taunting him now. She's telling him that if you want me to stop, you'll have to kill me.

Can you do that?

He understands. She knows he does. A language developed over ten years of friendship doesn't vanish after just one.

Colson's frustrated scream is laced with anguish, and Honor didn't think there were any pieces of her heart left big enough to break, but she was wrong. He uses his marvel to propel himself across the distance between them, and Honor lets him come. He doesn't try to engage in close combat with her because he's not stupid, but he does try to blow her up from mid range instead of long and this is going to hurt.

In the blink of the average eye, Honor is behind Colson instead of in front of him. He aims an explosion behind him, blind, but Honor grabs his arm and aims it up, away, then gets a solid hit on his kidney. He grunts and kicks backwards hard enough to make her knee buckle, and then he blasts himself straight up into the air just to get some distance.

Honor goes right after him, wrapping a hand around his ankle to pull him back to earth, back to her. She's momentarily blinded by the sun when she looks up at Colson, and that's why she doesn't see the next explosion coming. She should have anticipated it, but she didn't really think Colson would fire at her, full strength, point blank.

Her violent landing digs her a new grave in the middle of the street. Her skin feels sticky and tight, and she's aware of every single piece of asphalt and rubble embedded in her horrifically exposed wounds. Her breath comes back to her faster than most, but she still takes a moment to lay there, to take stock of her body, broken bones and exposed muscle and seared skin. She needs to end this.

She gets up because staying down is never an option. Colson stands at the other end of the street, watching the hole in the ground with wide eyes. When he sees her head appear first, then her hands as they brace on the side of the crater, his shoulders sag with relief, but his jaw drops when he sees the state she's in. He probably didn't know he could do that to Honor. Everyone always seems to think she's invincible.

Honor's half sure she's going to have to call Verity for backup. She's not up to the task mentally or physically. Someone nearby screams, and Honor clocks it without taking her eyes off of Colson, who still isn't moving as Honor slowly climbs out of the grave she dug herself into. The scream was a name, and there's movement out of the corner of her eye, lanky and skinny, running on legs like a foal. Not a threat, but too close to the fight. Fuck, now she's going to have to save this girl before getting back to Colson, and that could give him time to get away or the opening he needs to send her to the Graveyard of Stars.

She's honestly not sure if he can go through with it either.

Honor reaches for the girl at the same time she reaches for Honor. She can't be older than thirteen. She's probably looking to be saved and that's Honor's job so no matter how much she hurts or wants to cry, she's going to do her damn job.

But when they make contact, a refreshing coolness rushes through her and her skin itches when it stitches itself back together. Her ankle cracks and it doesn't hurt, none of it hurts, not anymore. Honor touches her own face and feels smooth, unblemished skin.

Incredulous and thankful, she turns her full attention to the girl for a brief moment, still painfully aware of Colson in her peripherals.

"Thanks, hero," she says with all the smile she has left to give. The girl opens her mouth to respond, but Honor runs them both back to her family on the street and the pro urging them away. Honor makes sure she's tucked safely back into the circle of her sister's arms, and then she's gone before any of them can say anything.

Honor's a little tired, groggy, like she's just woken up from a nap but it's better than halfway dead by a few miles, so she'll take it. Colson looks more lost than ever, still beaten to hell and covered in blood, mostly his own. Honor's anger flares up again, but she doesn't know what to say. The last time she had said something to Colson out of anger, she'd sent him straight into his mother's arms. She can't make that mistake again.

She jumps. Dangerous, because she can't redirect herself midair, and Colson knows that, but he doesn't take the opportunity to bring her back down. Instead, he blows himself off the ground after her, then into her. He tackles her in the air and they go crashing to the ground in a tangle of limbs and rubble. Honor's shoulder screams when it hits the asphalt and slides, burning a hole straight through her already tattered shirt.

Colson ends up half under her, and she feels his hand on her hip. She rips it away before he can set off another explosion. She's just quick enough, still reeling from their rough landing. The blast hits a nearby house, instead, and smoke curls toward the sky. There are no screams, though, which means this street has been evacuated.

Honor tightens her grip around his wrist to the point where she hears the thin bones grind together. She can see the veins straining in his forearm. He's lost too much blood. He's leveled half the district, of course he's lost blood. He's pale and thin and his chest heaves under Honor's when she pins him to the ground.

"Let me go," he snarls. Honor's grip only tightens and she knows it'll leave a nasty bruise.

"Stop. STOP!" she says. Begs. Her voice is wet even if her eyes aren't, and Colson hears it. He struggles against her, brings his other hand up but Honor catches that one too and feels the explosion singe the shell of her ear before she slams it into the ground above his head hard enough to break them both.

"FUCK! Get off, get off!" His hands spark but he doesn't have much blood left to work with. It's a wonder he's still conscious at all, and Honor chalks it up to fear and adrenaline.

"I'm sorry," she chokes out, and Colson goes lax in her arms for a split second before he struggles with renewed vigor. "I'm sorry! I'm sorry, please." Honor's vision does cloud over then and it's stupid, stupid. Colson dredges up another explosion big enough to blow her off of him and halfway across the street, through a picket fence, onto a well-mani-cured lawn.

Her back hits first, and she rolls over her shoulder into a crouch. She and Colson lock eyes when he sits up, his chest still heaving. His forearms are torn to shreds. He no longer looks wild and angry but lost and heartbroken. Honor's own heart fissures in her chest. She did that. That look is her fault.

"Colson," she says and it's too quiet. There's no way he hears it, but he must recognize the shape of his name on her lips.

"No," he says. He shakes his head and a tear slips down his cheek, cutting a path through dirt and ash. "No."

He raises a hand to his ear.

"Colson, *DON'T*—" Honor screams and launches herself forward but it doesn't matter how fast she is. She won't get there in time to stop him.

PART ONE

LIFE

1

"Bay Area to Rebuild Better After Titan Attack"
—*Heroes Globe*

"**T**here's another Titan in the bay!"

Charlie has seen this video a thousand times, but she'll never get tired of seeing her favorite hero, Honor de Mora, absolutely wreck this Titan's shit. She combines with her two sisters into a single Titan form with three eyes, each a different color for each sister, yellow, blue, and pink. With a sword in hand, they swing as one into the evil Titan in the bay.

"Oh damn!" Charlie's brother, Joshua, shouts out when the Triumverate's sword slices clean through the evil Titan's arm. He does it every time, it's part of what makes it so fun to watch these videos with him. But Charlie is only half paying attention, having memorized every single detail of the video down to the exact shade of pink that Honor's eye is. Tincture #M130712, since renamed "Honor." It's the color of Charlie's sneakers by the door, limited edition, that Charlie had stood in line overnight for. They're right under the framed photo of Honor and a five-year-old Charlie. Honor probably doesn't remember it because she's saved thousands of people—hell, the whole world—since then, but Charlie will never forget.

Charlie can't focus on the video because she's anxiously awaiting a letter from Titan Academy. It's nearing the end of summer, and Charlie had applied to Broadly, another hero school, and been accepted, but she wants nothing more than to get into Titan Academy in its inaugural year.

When word had gotten out that Honor and Verity de Mora were opening up a hero academy, it was met with scores of think pieces and clickbait articles about how qualified they are or aren't, or how it shouldn't be so easy for just anyone to open up a school. Honor and Verity might be the number two and three heroes respectively, but they're still very controversial heroes. Charlie hadn't paid much attention to any of it. She knew she had to go to Titan Academy.

Charlie wants nothing more than to become a great hero. To save people like Honor saved her and countless others. It's the only thing she can ever remember wanting. She never had a veterinarian phase or an astronaut phase. It's always been a pro hero or bust, and she's fully prepared to dedicate herself entirely to the task. These next six years will help prepare Charlie for her future career as a professional hero, just like Honor.

Noticing that Charlie's mind had wandered again, her oldest sister, Kimberly, changes the video to one of a young Honor. Kimberly is like their second mom, but her hair is bright pink so Charlie thinks she'll be a cool mom one day. This video is from before the lost years where Honor and her sisters had all disappeared from active hero duty. It's a shaky cellphone video shot by a bystander as Honor chases down a rogue in what is now called the Titan District.

Honor is wearing her original hero suit. A pink crop top with a high collar and loose black pants tucked into pink boots. Her arms are bare and she only has only one sleeve tattoo. It's a far cry from Honor's much more conservative black hero suit now, with the bullet details attached to her belt and the pink accents built in and pink gauntlets, both of her full sleeve tattoos fully covered. But her original suit will always have a special place in Charlie's heart and in her closet from when she was Honor for Halloween five years in a row.

In the video, a random dude makes a disparaging comment about how Honor could do her job better, and Honor takes a seat right next to him at his table on a restaurant patio and helps herself to their appetizers. It makes Charlie laugh every time.

"You do it, then," Honor says. In the background the rogue is slowly getting to his feet, disoriented from the blow Honor had landed. She leans back in the chair and the dude sputters and turns around to look at the rogue then back at Honor again.

She raises an eyebrow at him. "Well?"

"It's your job!" he says like an accusation.

"Clearly you think you can do a better job," she says, unconcerned with the rogue on the street collecting a bag of jewelry while Honor appears distracted. "So. Go on. Let's see what you got."

"He's going to get away!" he shouts.

"He's not," Honor says and picks up a chip and dips it into some salsa. "Mm. This is good."

"What are you doing?!"

"Everyone thinks they can do a hero's job, always picking apart heroes and their every move as if you could possibly know what it's like to have to make a split-second decision based on a million variables under immense pressure," she goes on, seemingly without a care in the world. "If you think you can do a better job, let's see it, big guy."

The guy can't even stand up from his brunch table. Honor rolls her eyes at him and talks directly to the guy's friend, who's been filming the whole exchange.

"If you can't walk the walk, then shut the fuck up." She takes another chip and in a flash she's gone, pinning the rogue to the street again.

The rogue had a speed marvel and had evaded two other heroes, but even a speed marvel is no match for the speed of a Titan.

Kimberly switches to the next video and, again, it's nothing Charlie hasn't seen before, but it's another one of her favorites. It's more recent, just over a year ago, Honor vs. disgraced hero Incendiary. He'd demolished half the city with his explosive marvel and Honor took him down. Charlie's only half paying attention until her favorite part—

"Are you done?" Incendiary shouts at Honor, a taunt. Honor is clearly tired because she has double the job, she has to protect the people around her and Incendiary and prevent more damage to the city all while taking this guy down. Honor pushes to her feet from where she'd been blasted through the side of an evacuated building and rubble falls from her shoulder. The news helicopter captured the whole thing in decent quality, but shitty audio from a nearby cell phone camera has been layered over it.

"Am I dead?" Honor shouts back, and it gives Charlie chills like it does every time. The crowd close enough to hear roars in response. "THEN I'M NOT FUCKING DONE!"

Charlie's siblings all shout along with Honor, having also seen this video numerous times. Charlie can't bring herself to join in, still too nervous, but she does grin into her knees where she's pulled them up to her chest.

"Mail's here," Charlie's mom calls. Charlie bolts off the stained corduroy couch and runs to the kitchen where her mom is sorting through the mail. Sorting isn't really sorting as everything lands in one pile while she searches for the one thing they all want to see. The whole family, Charlie's parents and all four of her older siblings, crams into the kitchen around the big marble island. It's a small envelope that her mom hands to her, hand-addressed, and the return address is Titan Academy.

Charlie's breath catches. She tears into the envelope and catches the black tile that falls out. Familiar with the new holo technology, she clicks the middle and a life-sized projection of Honor de Mora appears in front of her.

"Hi, Charlie," she says, and Charlie nearly falls over at hearing Honor de Mora say her name. It's not the first time she's heard it, but these circumstances are much better than the last ones. Honor's grin is wide, and Charlie finds herself returning it before she can even get the news. "Congratulations. You've been accepted into the first class of Titan Academy."

Charlie completely misses the rest of the message as her family erupts into cheers. Josh picks her up like she scored the game winning goal of an Olympic soccer match and marches her around the kitchen. Elation fills her chest until her heart feels ready to burst. She did it. *She did it.*

2

"Honor de Mora Testifies Before Congress
for Titan Battle: A Look Inside"

—*Hero Review*

Honor lays on the couch in the teacher's dorm, doing an awful job of pretending she's not stressed about move-in the next day. All of her kids in one place, everyone seeing the fully finished campus for the first time, parents she has to impress somehow. Her sister, Verity, is sitting on the floor, bent over a tablet on the coffee table, making the seating chart for their first and only class of students. In Honor's rush to get the school off the ground, she'd made the executive decision to start with one class and build out as they go on. So Class Alpha will be the only twenty students on campus during the first year.

It stems from a lot of reasons, but Honor doesn't want an impersonal assembly line of heroes like Marvelous, and she doesn't want civilians teaching future pros like Broadly. But the pool of dedicated and active pros who are also willing to teach full time is virtually nonexistent and it mostly consists of Honor's close friends.

"It feels dangerous to make a permanent seating chart before we really know the kids," Verity says.

"We know enough from the entrance essays and practical," Honor insists for the fourteenth time. "And we can always change it later, it's not like they're going to stop us."

"You say that, but I distinctly remember when we were in high school and Track sat you across the room from the rest of us, you stole another kid's seat and then refused to move," Verity points out, and yeah, okay, Honor did do that, but Honor was a menace in high school.

The door to the stairwell opens, and Leo Navarro comes through, pulling the tie of his very expensive and bullet-resistant suit free and looking exhausted. The dark circles under his eyes are a permanent accessory to his dark eyes, but they work with his, frankly unfair, dark lashes. He shucks off his jacket and collapses on top of Honor where she lays on the couch, her feet dangling over the arm. The breath she's forced to exhale sounds like a laugh.

"Rough day at work?" she asks, wrapping an arm around him and letting him hide his face in her shoulder. She notices Verity looking at her with an unimpressed eyebrow raised. Honor flips her off and hides her helplessly fond smile in his black hair.

"Just tired," he says. "Prison transfer today. Two attempted break outs. Lots of shields."

"Wanna help us make the seating chart for your class?" she offers. He grunts and shifts so his arms are wrapped around and under Honor, but otherwise doesn't move.

Leo is the homeroom teacher for their first class. Mostly because he volunteered, but also because Honor trusts him more than just about anyone. He knows how much this class means to her, so she feels comfortable leaving it to him, knows he'll do the best possible job.

She's more grateful than she can ever put into words for Leo's support. They had been thick as thieves in high school. Honor, Verity, their sister Grace, Leo, and Colson. An absolute clusterfuck of some of the most powerful hero students in years. After the incident with their mom and Grace's fake death, Honor had gone off the rails, and Leo had refused to watch when she wouldn't accept help. When she came back with an apology, he had already forgiven her.

"Us?" Verity echoes. "Honor's not helping as per usual." Honor flips her off again. "The girl with the giant rock monster thing— "

"Cecily," Honor supplies.

"Sure, Cecily and her giant rock monster thing that she can control with her brain—is that gonna need a seat too? I saw it at the practical, it's fucking huge, it might need it's own table. And is it sentient? Does it need to be kept entertained? Or does it power off or some shit?" Verity rants. "And where the hell do I put Jack?"

"Zelweger?" Leo asks.

"Yeah, the son of the number one hero in the country is either going to be a huge asshole or subject to bullying and without knowing which one it's going to be, I can't seat him," Verity goes on.

"We didn't take any kids that we thought would be huge assholes," Honor reminds her. "You saw to that." Literally. Verity is very adept at using her marvel to not only see the auras of others around her but to interpret them with a scary level of accuracy. A lot of people mistake her for a mind reader these days, but she's really just good at identifying a person's emotions and then deducing where they come from.

"When you say asshole, you mean an irredeemable shit bag that should never become a hero. When I say asshole, I mean 'kid jerk asshole who thinks they know everything about everything and won't listen to anyone,'" she says.

"So a teenager," Leo says, still muffled by Honor's shirt.

"No one is irredeemable," Honor reminds her.

"Yeah, yeah." Verity waves her off even if Honor knows she agrees. Verity has clearly decided that now is not the time for another emotional confrontation about forgiveness and rehabilitation. She's heard enough of it from Honor in the past year, she could probably give the speech herself. "The *point* is, where do I sit Jack?"

"Next to Charlie?" Honor suggests.

"*God, no*," Leo protests.

"What? Why?" Honor asks.

Verity snickers and writes something on the tablet and Leo says, "Honor 2.0 and a potential Colson Jr.? I don't deserve that."

"He's right, he doesn't," Verity agrees while Honor scowls. "I'm already putting Charlie next to Lochlan anyway."

"They're already friends, we should split them up so they can branch out," Honor says.

"This is why I'm making the seating chart and not you," Verity tells her. Honor rolls her eyes. "Lochlan is a baby Leo, the quiet half of the classic dynamic duo, and if you take the shy baby away from the loud and obnoxious protector friend, what happens?"

"A lot of shouting across a classroom," Leo supplies helpfully, from personal experience.

"Or demonstrative protest seat changing," Verity adds.

"Oh, shut up and make the goddamn seating chart," Honor groans. Leo laughs against her silently so, annoyed as she is, it's pretty worth it.

As much as Verity is stressing about the seating chart, Honor knows she'll do a good job. She got a pretty good read on everyone with her marvel during the entrance exams, and the kids' personalities really shone through in their essays. That's how they already know Charlie is a mini Honor. Never mind the fact that her social media presence is basically a shrine to Honor and all of her exploits, from saving the city from a rogue with a dragon quirk to her latest stint on late night where she played mini sports games to promote her new collaboration with a sportswear brand. But her fiery personality and her single-minded determination to become a hero really sealed the deal.

Honor knows from experience that Charlie stands at the top of a very slippery slope and she wants to help guide her. Given that Honor has never been a direct mentor before, she's not sure she's up to the task. But she *knows* that schools like Marvelous or even Broadly would turn her into another one of the hero machines that they've been churning out for the past decade, and Charlie deserves better than that. When Honor was at Marvelous, she remembers being willing to do anything, *anything,* to be the best. That was all anyone cared about. She competed with her classmates, her friends, her sisters. No one ever wanted to work together, not truly. Everyone wanted to stand out, stand at the top. Honor wasn't the only person who took it too far.

If anything, that only increases the pressure that Honor's put on herself. For this school and these kids to succeed means being a perfect mentor and example, and Honor has never come anywhere close to perfect. Despite what she may have thought of herself in the past when she equated being the best with being perfect. In fact, it's exactly that kind of thinking that sent her down a path of destruction. Of herself and others. A path that Marvelous started her on by fostering unhealthy competition and jealousy between classmates and other schools. The pressure to *win,* when winning isn't the most important thing at the end of the day, and those other schools seem to have forgotten that.

Honor won't forget. But remembering the 'why' isn't enough. She's concerned with the *how.* How her kids will respond to their teaching practices. How to balance letting them learn on their own and giving them the answer. How to be the best mentor she could possibly be while teaching these kids how to be the best heroes they can be.

How?

Honor's phone vibrates at the same time she breathes a heavy sigh. Both Leo and Verity look up at her, Verity squinting while she parses through Honor's aura. Honor knows there's nothing she can do to stop her, so she just answers the phone call.

"Unless the city is burning down, I feel inclined to remind you that I am not on call today," she says. Honor's full days off are few and far between, and they're about to become even more scarce once school is in session, something her boss at her agency is already well aware of.

"The entire insurance department is threatening to quit unless you start filing your paperwork in a timely manner," Dulcet, her boss, tells her. Honor groans, pushes Leo off of her and into the back of the couch so she can roll to her feet.

"Okay, okay, I'm coming in," she says and manages not to whine. "Are you sure the city isn't burning down?"

"If it was, I'd send Maverick," she says.

"Ouch," Honor feigns devastation as she puts on her shoes. "If you keep this up, I'm going to start thinking I'm not your favorite employee."

"All of my favorite employees file their paperwork on time," Dulcet says dryly.

"What if I stop for boba on my way into the office?"

There's a pronounced pause.

"You will not be my least favorite," Dulcet compromises.

"I'll take it!" Honor shouts, and Dulcet laughs across the line. She waves over her shoulder as she exits the dorm and starts to jog down the stairs. Maybe some paperwork is just what she needs to distract her before move-in. That, or maybe the city will actually go up in flames.

Honor can only hope.

3

*L*ife, Joy, Victory!

Those are the school words, the same words engraved on the plate at the base of the statue of the Triumvirate that stands outside of Titan Arena. Charlie stands with the small crowd of her future classmates and their families. Charlie has already seen the arena, but the campus has been closed to the public since it was built, and Charlie is excited for the tour. She recognizes some of the other students from the practical exam milling around. The girl with the large, black feathered wings, the boy that flattens his body, a giant rock humanoid thing that Charlie isn't sure if it's an actual person or a marvel, and their very own resident celebrity kid, Jack Zelweger, son of the number one hero in the country.

Charlie already has him pegged as her biggest competition.

The hot August sun looming over Los Angeles has them sweating already, and there's no covering outside the arena aside from the shadow that the Triumvirate statue casts. Charlie's already taking up most of that with her siblings trying to not-so-subtly push her out of the way to get into the shade. Her mom, on the other hand, isn't subtle in the least and shoves all of her kids out of the way to lean against the base of it. That must be where Charlie gets it from.

A car pulls up to the curb, and Lochlan gets out with his parents. His mom, Tamera, is a pro hero too. She can make herself the size of a large building. Not as big as the Triumvirate, but still pretty big. She makes a mean pasta salad too.

"Hey." Lochlan comes up and greets her, eyes scanning the crowd around her. Their parents all greet each other, and Charlie's brother ruffles Lochlan's hair. Lochlan lets him, like he always does.

"I'm nervous," he says, "are you nervous?"

Charlie considers lying for a moment, just to make Lochlan feel better because if she isn't nervous then he can lean on her, but she nods.

"A little. But I'm mostly excited." She punctuates it with a wide grin that Lochlan can't help but return, albeit shyly because Lochlan does most things shyly. She gives him a little friendly shove, and he rocks back then forward.

"We're *here*."

"Still can't believe it," he says. He glances around at their new classmates and spots Jack. His eyes go wide and his voice drops to a whisper. "Is that…"

"Yeah," Charlie confirms. Jack himself isn't on any social media, but he's photographed with his parents enough that he's easily recognizable. "Gravitas' kid. Look, and his mom, she's even hotter in person."

"Keep it in your pants," her sister, Kimberly, says, then smacks her over the back of her head.

"It's a *fact*," Charlie says as she rubs the sore spot.

"Agree," says Lochlan. Kimberly raises a threatening hand like she's going to smack him too. It wouldn't be the first time, Kimberly's practically his older sister because he and Charlie have been attached at the hip since they were eight. Kimberly spent the most time babysitting too.

Someone nearby gasps then whisper-shouts, "There they are!"

The doors to the arena slide open, and Honor comes outside, flanked by her sister Verity and someone else. Charlie recognizes him from the practical but she doesn't know who he is. He looks overdressed in pressed, navy slacks and a white button down under a matching navy vest, especially next to Honor and Verity who are both wearing jeans and Titan Academy t-shirts. They really are identical, and it's only Honor's sleeve of tattoos that gives her away. That, and the way her eyes briefly flash pink as they walk up.

Honor is one of those people you don't really believe is real until you see her in person, and even then it's hard to accept. Even in regular street clothes, she looks powerful and important. Her biceps pull the sleeves of her shirt taut, a subtle reminder of her inhuman strength. Her colorful and geometric tattoos are smudged in places from scars, evidence from battles fought and won because Honor never loses.

Charlie doesn't think she'll ever get used to the way Honor's mere presence commands attention. All idle chatter ceases, and everyone turns to look at her stride up with her arms spread wide in welcome and a bright smile on her face. She looks more excited than half of the other kids there, but there's no way she's more excited than Charlie.

"Hi, everyone!" she says and comes to stop just five feet away from Charlie and her family. They'd all insisted on 'helping' her move in, but she knows they really just wanted to see everything for themselves. She can't really blame them for that, though.

"I'm Honor, and this is my sister, Verity, and this is Leo. Leo will be Class Alpha's homeroom teacher this year."

It's not going to be Honor? Charlie tries not to let her disappointment show on her face. It makes sense. Honor is probably incredibly busy, what with being a top hero and all. There's no way she has the time to be a homeroom teacher too. That's probably why this new guy is their teacher.

"Thank you so much for choosing Titan Academy," Honor says earnestly. "Training the heroes of tomorrow is one of the biggest honors—no pun intended—and I'm eternally grateful that you've chosen us."

As if anyone sane would choose anyone else, Charlie thinks.

"We'll give you guys a quick tour of the grounds and get your stuff all moved into the dorms. After that we'd love to treat you all to dinner and answer any questions you might have about the school year," she goes on. She looks around to see if anyone has anything to ask before they go inside, but all they can do is stare at her.

One of the top heroes in the entire world, a Class One marvel, a celebrity amongst celebrities standing in front of a bunch of nobodies. Well, mostly nobodies. Lochlan's mom is also a pro and knows Honor personally. Jack is the son of Honor's only real rival, and his mom is a famous supermodel and she's also present. But for the rest of the regular people like Charlie? It's hard not to get starstruck.

"Let's get going," she says and turns on her heel, expecting them to follow, and they do. Charlie tries to crowd in quickly so she can be close to Honor, and her siblings have the same idea, blocking off another family that tries to wedge their way in.

Another girl skips right past from the outside of the group and latches onto Verity in a familiar hug. Verity laughs and hugs her back, and a jolt of panic shoots through Charlie. Of course there are people enrolled who knew the de Mora sisters beforehand, that's probably how they were accepted in the first place. That means Charlie has more competition than she originally thought, because if they know either or both the de Mora sisters, then they're at an advantage, not only just by association, but also because Charlie would expect them to have at least *some* training.

Charlie's already behind. She's going to have to work twice as hard to stand out and make herself known. Maybe even three times as hard. She doesn't even have the advantage of a famous mom like Lochlan. It all depends on her.

As if sensing her spiral, Charlie's sister, Lydia, slings an arm around her shoulders as they head inside Titan Arena to bring her back to the present. Charlie had already been inside for the practical exam but it looks different when it's empty.

There are no lanes for the obstacle courses, no lines for registrations, no crowds of other kids and their parents wearing numbered shirts all hoping to get in. There must have been a thousand kids coming through the exam, but only twenty made it in and Charlie is one of them.

Her siblings look around in awe as they pass through the foyer and head into the arena floor. It's just a wide open space at the moment with raised stadium seating. Everything is sleek and black, from the floor to the dome ceiling with neon blue details, the same color as Verity's eyes when they glow. Honor spins around in front of them to walk backwards.

"This is Titan Arena, completely state of the art thanks to our very own Aurora. She'll be your tech and science teacher this year, and she's the best of the best," Honor tells them.

"The arena is equipped with new nanotech that allows for full-scale training simulations."

"How does that work?" Tamera asks. Lochlan ducks his head as if his mom had embarrassed him, even though she just asked the question they were all thinking.

"I can show you," she says. "Avant? Are you there?"

Aurora is *Avant?* Charlie recognizes her hero name, and Honor wasn't kidding when she said the best of the best. Avant is at the forefront of marvel development and research *and* hero support items. She designed the new marvel nullifiers that are universal so heroes and police don't have to use a different cuff depending on the type of marvel. She's even helped Charlie's dad with his research on how marvels correspond and interact with genetic diseases.

"Am I ever anywhere else?" a voice sounds over the loudspeakers. Charlie looks up like she might see Avant floating there. But it's just a tinted glass dome ceiling.

"Can we get a sim demo?" Honor asks.

"Coming right up, simulation test B," she says.

Next to Honor, a holograph of a punching bag appears. Honor waves her hand through it and it glitches temporarily where her hand goes through.

"As you know, holos are not solid and cannot be interacted with," she says and continues to wave her hand through it. "What we do is create the object out of Aurora's nano tech—" The holo disappears, and from the floor a new punching bag forms, straight from the large square tile. It takes the same exact place that the holo had been, but it's solid black and smooth like the floor it had just come out of. Honor taps it with her knuckles to prove its solidity "—and then layer the holo over it for realism."

The holo reappears, and it looks like a real punching bag again, red leather with a fraying seam and a company logo on it. Honor hits it and it moves like a real punching bag. Charlie catches sight of the weight tag and reads *200 pounds?* She'd barely tapped it and it's swinging like a kid on a playground!

"We have real punching bags, of course," Honor says sheepishly. "But the nanoholos can take roughly the same amount of damage as the real thing it's emulating." She actually winds up this time and hits the punching bag with a right hook. It falls to the ground, nanites spilling back onto the ground, and then they're absorbed until the floor is smooth again. There's an appropriate amount of *ooh's* and *aah's* and a *holy shit* from Charlie's brother. "We plan to use these for the majority of our search and rescue simulations throughout the year to recreate cityscapes and other locales so the kids can use their marvels to the fullest extent without the fear of real property damage."

"A very real fear to have," Verity adds with a huff. That gets a few scattered laughs, mostly from parents.

They continue on through the arena to Aurora's workshop on the second level of the arena. They cram into the big space already cluttered with dozens of expensive-looking tools and computers. Aurora herself stands at a long black table. She runs her fingers over the surface and it pulls up the specs for something as a holo that hovers in front of her. Then she returns to tinkering with the small robot in front of her. It kind of looks like a trashcan to Charlie, but she's sure it's some super high tech trash can.

The lights are low but there's more than enough natural sunlight filtering in through the skylight, and anything cast in shadows has some ambient neon lighting nearby. Charlie's dad ducks out of the way of a moving platform. There's a plant on it, and Charlie has no idea why it's there or what it's doing. She has a feeling that when it comes to Aurora, Charlie is going to be lost a lot.

"Everyone, we'd like you to meet Avant," Honor says, and Aurora looks up, noticing them for the first time.

"Hello! You guys can just call me Aurora." She beams. She's younger than Charlie would have thought, and she's pretty. Charlie wonders if being pretty is a perquisite for being a hero nowadays because Charlie has yet to lay eyes on an ugly one.

Aurora's smile is wide and bright and it makes her eyes crinkle at the corners. Her hair is tied back in a loose knot at the base of her neck and the metal fingers of her right hand gleam when she wiggles them in hello. Behind the table, Charlie can't see the matching prosthetic leg, but she knows that it's there. Aurora's prosthetic tech is revolutionary.

"This is where the kids will have all their tech and science classes," Honor tells them.

"What are you working on now?" Charlie's mom asks, and Charlie suddenly understands Lochlan's reflexive embarrassment. It's a good question! Everyone was thinking it! But why couldn't someone else have asked it?

"These are our groundskeepers," Aurora says. She pats the little robot affectionately. "They maintain the gardens and make sure everything's operating properly because I can't be everywhere at once and it's a big campus."

She pokes the little robot with her pointer finger and it shrinks down to the size of a coffee mug. Then it starts zooming around the table. Aurora spills some of her real coffee onto the table and when it zooms back to her, it rolls right over it and then it's gone. She smiles like it's one of the greatest new inventions of the century when Charlie knows for a fact that Aurora has invented far more impressive things than this little trash can.

"I'm so excited for—oh!" She cuts herself off when an alarm sounds from one of the computers on the wall. It's a loosely outlined map of the Titan District, the district they're in right now, since renamed when the de Mora sisters bought over two hundred acres of land after saving the world from a Titan. "Sorry! Duty calls!"

She bounces out the back door and it slides shut after her.

"That will happen on occasion," Honor says to them. "Since all our teachers here at Titan Academy are active pros, sometimes we'll be on call during school hours, but in those cases we'll always have a substitute ready in the wings so the kids will never miss out."

"Bastian! You too!" Aurora's voice sounds overhead. Everyone looks up again. Leo shrugs and goes to exit through the door that Aurora had just disappeared through.

"Wait, *Bastian?*" a girl next to Charlie hisses.

"Who the hell is Bastian?" Charlie whispers back. The girl looks affronted that Charlie doesn't know who Bastian is.

"He's a pro, Class Two defensive marvel, abstains from the ranking system in the interest of anonymity because his work is mostly underground stuff or security for high profile people and prisoners," she tells her. "But like, if you know, you know."

"How did I not know that?" Charlie asks, mostly to herself but the girl still answers.

"You do now," she says with a shrug. "I'm Malia."

"Charlie," she introduces herself. She pulls Lochlan over by the sleeve of his shirt and he comes stumbling. "This is my friend Lochlan. Lochlan, this is our new friend Malia."

Lochlan doesn't get to say anything in response because Honor is clapping her hands together and leading them out of the arena for the rest of the tour.

They go to the main building with the library, auditorium, and classrooms via bridge from the arena. Then they see the outdoor training area with the Olympic swimming pool and weight room. From there, they get to walk through the gardens, a picturesque mini park on the grounds for fun and recreation and just to look pretty, according to Honor.

The dorm buildings are two separate buildings that share a single stairwell in between them. One is for the teachers and the other is for the students. It's a big building, fitting ten rooms to a floor with a common room and kitchenette. Each room even comes with its own bathroom. It's way cushier than Charlie could have hoped for. She's never had her own bathroom before.

"They get their own rooms?" Charlie's mom exclaims.

"I know, right? We're already spoiling them," Verity says as she holds the door open for Charlie and her siblings. Bringing the majority of Charlie's things up had taken all of two trips with all the help she has. Honor comes bounding out of the elevator, followed shortly by some of Charlie's new classmates.

"We have plenty of room," Honor says even though she was in the elevator when Verity spoke. Charlie wonders just how good Titan hearing is or if it was a triplet thing.

"It's the principle of the matter," Charlie's mom says with her charming smile. Charlie likes to think she has the same smile.

"That's what I said!" Verity cries. "I had the *worst* roommate at Marvelous and it's part of what made me who I am today."

"A giant pain in the ass?" Honor says. Then, "*Wait,* I was your roommate at Marvelous!"

"Exactly," Verity says and goes to the vending machine to get a candy bar. She just has to press a button because the vending machines on campus are all *free*. Maybe they really are spoiling them, but Charlie sure as hell isn't going to complain.

"Oh, Charlie, your pillows are still in the car, do you want to go grab them?" her mom asks and tosses her the keys before she even answers. Charlie jogs back out to the car to grab her favorite pillows.

On her way back, a pillow under each arm, she chooses to walk around the back of the building to get a better look at the pond there. It's pretty. Charlie can't believe she actually gets to *live* here. The sun is just beginning to set, and the warm oranges and pinks slip through the streets and between buildings to dance over the clear pond water and warm the courtyard.

"You turned down the residency for *this?*"

The voice is so incredulous and disdainful that Charlie has to stop.

"Because *this* is what I want to do!"

That's the voice of the girl Charlie met during the tour. Malia. Who is she arguing with?

"I know you want to help people, but this isn't the best way for you to do that!"

This is none of Charlie's business. She knows that in her head, but not in her feet, apparently, because she rounds the corner and finds Malia standing there with an older dude, probably her dad, if Charlie had to guess, but he hadn't been on the tour.

"I want to be a hero! Why is it so hard for you to just support me?" Malia sounds close to tears at this point, and that's when she notices Charlie over her dad's shoulder. Her eyes, clearly wet, go wide, then she wipes at them furiously.

"Honey, I know your heart is in the right place but this is more than about what you *want*, you have a *gift*—"

"Hey, Malia," Charlie says, cutting off the dad. He whirls around with a scowl on his face, clearly irritated that they'd been interrupted.

"Hey," she says and sniffs. "Dad, this is Charlie, Charlie this is my dad."

"Hey, Dad." Charlie nods at him then turns her attention back to Malia. "Uh. Could you help me bring my stuff up?"

Malia stares at her for a moment. "The pillows?"

"Yeah," Charlie says, a bit sheepishly. "They're heavy."

Malia looks at her with a strange mix of confusion and relief, and Charlie doesn't regret inserting herself into something that's clearly none of her business for a second.

"Sure," she says with a huff of a laugh. "I'll see you later, Dad."

"The hospital said you're welcome whenever you're ready," he says. Malia's face shutters again.

"Man, I hope you don't end up in the hospital," Charlie says and she still doesn't have the faintest clue of what's going on, but judging by the way Malia's face lights up again, she said the right thing. "I think Honor said something about having a medic marvel on campus at all times so you should go there."

"I'll keep that in mind," Malia says and takes one of her pillows from her. They go inside, and the lobby is quietly busy with waves of moving crews consisting of families and friends and an actual crew hired by the Zelwegers.

The AC is on full blast and the room smells new, like vegan leather and plastic. The air from the vent skips over Charlie's skin and gives her goosebumps. She shifts her grip on her single pillow as they wait for the elevators in silence until:

"Thanks," Malia says quietly.

"Anytime," Charlie promises.

Charlie selects some sour candy from the vending machine in the downstairs common room. She's all alone during a brief lull in the moving process. No one coming in or out or trying to maneuver furniture into the elevator. It's just Charlie and the occasional and the whir of the vending machine. At least, she thought she was alone. She turns around and sees Honor standing right there with a bright smile. Charlie drops her candy, heart and mind racing at a million miles per hour.

"Hi," is the super interesting opener she ends up going with.

"Hi," Honor says back. She bends down to pick Charlie's candy up for her.

"Thanks," Charlie breathes. Honor pushes a button for a soda on the vending machine.

Honor had been present at the entrance exam, obviously. But she had been in a box with the other teachers to observe from afar. Charlie wants to say something, *needs* to say something. Preferably something cool and memorable. But for all of her knowledge about Honor and all of her hobbies and work, she comes up with absolutely nothing. So she starts from the beginning.

"Um, I don't know if you remember but when I was like, five— "

"I remember," Honor says with a smile. Charlie simultaneously relaxes and gets even more tense. She's standing alone in a room with her hero and she's going to blow it. There are no words for what Charlie feels for Honor. For what she's feeling in this moment. It's too much. Too big.

"Well, uh, thanks," Charlie says, then laughs awkwardly.

"I'd say anytime but—"

"But I have no plans on getting caught in any more house fires," Charlie assures her.

"You know what they say about the best laid plans," Honor says with a shrug, then grins to let Charlie know she's only joking. Charlie opens her candy but doesn't eat any.

"Can I ask about your tattoos?" Charlie asks, and Honor looks down at her own arms, surprised.

"Sure," she says and puts a hand on Charlie's shoulder to gently direct them both toward the elevator. She cracks open the can of soda she'd picked out from the vending machine with one hand and the carbonation sizzles.

"How do you get them?" Charlie asks. "I mean, do they have to use special needles because your skin is so thick? Not like, literally thick—I mean, I don't think so—but you've said before that it's tougher than average and considerable force has to be applied to break through, right?"

"Right," Honor says with a conspiratorial smile, and Charlie finds herself held captive in her gaze. When her eyes aren't glowing pink, they're a warm shade of brown, deep and rich. "They're technically not tattoos, not in the traditional sense. Not for lack of trying, though, I broke two needle guns before realizing that it wasn't going to work. A friend of mine has a marvel that allows her to apply ink permanently to any surface, so she did them for me, even designed them herself."

"But they're not permanent," Charlie points out. "You had them redone after your fight with Incendiary."

"They are permanent on the skin," Honor says, "but the skin, apparently, is less permanent."

Charlie makes a silent 'O' with her mouth, she'd never even thought about that. It sounds more painful than a traditional tattoo, that's for sure. Honor just chuckles like it's no big deal.

"But Calliope touches them up for me every time," she says. Charlie immediately pulls out her phone to write that name down so she can stalk her across all social media channels later.

"Does it hurt?"

"Not at all," Honor shrugs. "But then again, I'm probably not the best control group when it comes to pain."

"True," Charlie agrees, then giggles. "I think if someone threw me through a building, I'd cry."

Honor's hand lands on her shoulder as the elevator doors open up to Charlie's floor. "Just between you and me? The first couple of times? I did."

"Really?" Charlie's eyes go big.

"Yeah, I mean, I was nine and Verity did it on purpose — "

"Are you talking shit about me to the kids?" Verity's voice carries through the hallway and several heads turn their way.

"You mean telling the objective truth?" Honor fires back, and leaves Charlie after one more smile.

"So," says her brother Josh, who's been loitering by the elevator this whole time, *not* helping Charlie unpack. "Did you tell her about your shrine?"

"Shut up!" Charlie hisses and punches his shoulder. "It's not a *shrine*."

"Josh, leave your sister alone," their mom chastises before going back to her chat with Gina Zelweger.

"*Yeah, Josh,*" Charlie says petulantly and shoves him. They both head back to her room, right next to Jack's. Her sisters are sitting on her bed, and her dad and Garrett are nowhere to be found, probably off exploring something they shouldn't be.

"Charlie talked to Honor," Josh says to their sisters.

"Did Charlie talk to Honor?" Lydia asks, dubious. "Or did Honor talk to Charlie while Charlie had stars in her eyes?"

Charlie chucks a pillow at Lydia. "You're all the worst. You're never allowed to come visit me on campus ever again."

Kimberly looks offended at that. "I didn't do anything!"

"Okay, only Kimmie is allowed to visit me on campus," Charlie amends. "And for your information, I *did* talk to her. I thanked her for saving my life and asked about her tattoos."

"Real hard-hitting stuff," Josh says, and Charlie punches his arm.

"She's not a reporter, Josh," Kimberly comes to her defense.

"*Yeah, Josh,*" Charlie snipes and hits him again. He shoves her back hard enough that she falls on the bed, into Kimberly's lap. Kimberly wraps her arms around her to hold her there in a hug and Charlie allows it.

Charlie's room is all set up because as annoying as her siblings are, they know her pretty well and they know how she likes her stuff. She decided on a warm, fall color palette for her room. Her room at home is already black and pink, so she took this opportunity to branch out. She has umber and tawny as her base colors with accents of orange and yellow and a pop of blue here and there. She especially likes the way her russet blanket looks with her multicolored pillows.

The whole room feels warm and welcoming, pictures of her friends and family already taped up to the back of her door and displayed in frames on her desk. She brought a stylized sepia Triumvirate poster because she wants to wake up every morning and see an example of what she's striving toward.

Charlie looks up at the poster. It looks like Honor, it looks like all of the de Mora sisters' because they're identical, but when they're combined into their Titan form, they have three eyes. All three eyes stare back at Charlie and she still can't seem to wrap her mind around the fact that the most powerful people on the planet are her teachers. Not only are they her teachers, they chose *her* to be one of their students.

There's only nineteen other kids in this building, and there are thousands of others all over the world that would kill to be where she is right now. Charlie made it through. Honor believes in her, and she's not going to let her down.

Excited chatter drifts in through the open door, and Charlie's eyes sting. She's fine. She's not sad or upset, just a little overwhelmed and her siblings notice immediately. Kimberly tightens her arms around her and Lydia tackles them both onto the bed, cooing something about how cute her baby sister is and how she's going to be a great hero and that only makes Charlie cry more.

Josh joins them next, laying on top of all three of them and ruffling Charlie's hair.

"Okay, okay," Charlie grunts and tries to push them off, but they don't move. Then Lochlan comes into her room, followed closely by Garrett's lumbering form, and they join the pile, no questions asked. There's a loud shutter sound because Charlie's dad can never put his phone on silent.

"Dad! Get me out of here!"

"No can do, kiddo," he says, and even though Charlie can't see him, she knows he's smiling. Her bed creaks ominously.

"If you guys break my bed on move in day, I'm gonna blast each one of you through the wall," Charlie threatens, and then they're all scrambling off of the bed. Once free, Charlie flops back onto her rumpled pillows and breathes out a sigh of relief. She wipes at her eyes discreetly, but Lochlan still clocks her. He only grins, though, and she grins back.

4

The sun starts to hide behind the skyscrapers and the late afternoon light warms Honor's skin when she steps up to the floor-to-ceiling windows next to Jack's mom.

"The windows are one-way mirrors," Honor tells Gina. "So the kids can see out but no one can see in, and it reflects our lovely Los Angeles skyline."

Gina snorts at that, but it's still somehow attractive. Supermodels.

"Um," Jack's voice comes from behind them. They're standing at the edge of the common room the kids will use as their living space. There's a kitchenette for late night snacks, some comfy seating around a decently sized television, and a large table enough to seat half of them at a time. They're out of the way on this side of the room, but they can clearly see all the hustle and bustle moving in and out of the stairs and elevator to the rooms down the hallway.

"Hi."

"Hi, Jack," Honor says with a bright smile. It had been almost a pipe dream to get Jack Zelweger to pick Titan

Academy over literally anywhere else because he had his first pick of any school in the country. Hell, the world.

She hasn't actually gotten a chance to speak with him yet, but she's met Gina on more than one hero occasion, and she thought it might've been Gina's pull that got him to decide on Titan Academy. But now, looking at him with his wide sparkling eyes and his limited edition Pink Triumvirate bracelet he thinks Honor hasn't noticed, she knows it's because he's a fan. Honor is always flattered when someone is a fan of her, when someone looks up to her. But to have the son of the number one hero idolize her? She feels like she won a competition she didn't know she was participating in.

"I—could I steal my mom for a sec?" he asks. Honor knows that the tabloids and gossip blogs say Jack is the spitting image of his father. It's the blonde hair and blue eyes, but looking at the elegant slope of his nose and his defined cheekbones? All Gina, no doubt about it.

"She's your mom. Technically, I'm the one who stole her," Honor says and throws her arm around Jack's shoulders to walk them all back to his room. He's right next to Charlie in the dorms, and Honor is sure that's bound to be a disaster. "Did you know that your mom is my own personal hero?"

"What?" Jack looks behind them at his mom, surprised. Gina shakes her head fondly.

"Yes, every AHA gala, party, fundraiser, or whatever— they're all so *boring*," Honor says. "To the point where if your mom doesn't go, I'm not going. I would die of boredom."

"But, wait," Jack stutters out.

"What's the AHA?" Alex, another student, asks. She's all the way at the end of the hall just fluttering around because hadn't had very much to move in at all, clearly nervous, but still trying to get herself out of her comfort zone by inserting herself into another conversation.

"American Hero Alliance," Jack answers.

"Jack, meet Alex, Alex, meet Jack," Honor introduces them to save them the awkwardness. It doesn't really work, though, since they both do an awkward little wave thing because teenagers don't shake hands.

"Um, Honor? I had a question," Alex says, and Verity's head pops out from Luna's room across the hall. Honor knows from that alone that some sort of emotion in Alex spiked. Honor releases Jack with a gentle nudge toward his own room and walks with Alex back to hers at the end of the hall.

"What's up, kid?" Honor asks.

"You, um, mentioned that there were extra blankets and stuff?" she says.

"Yeah! Yeah, they're in the closet right here, hang on." Honor ducks out of the room real quick. There's a small cabinet built into the wall, designed to be seamless so it's practically invisible. One small press and *pop*, it's open. Honor grabs a set of sheets and a thick blanket embroidered with the Titan Academy logo. She leaves it open for now so the kids will all see it and be able to find it later.

"Need any help putting the sheets on?"

All the rooms have their own personal bathroom because in Honor's opinion, communal bathrooms should be declared a war crime. They have a bed, a desk, and a comfortable chair, along with a small closet and dresser. They're free to move anything out or bring furniture from home in, but Honor will make sure that they have everything they need. She doesn't wait for Alex to respond before she starts pulling the corner of a fitted sheet onto the mattress.

Alex enrolling in Titan Academy was sheer luck. On both their parts. Honor remembers finding her while on patrol one day—

"Hey," Honor said as she approached the kid. At least, she assumed she was a kid. Small and scrawny and awkward pointed to teenager more than anything else. Honor squatted down on her heels across from her in the cramped alley, as far as she could to make sure she didn't accidentally present herself as a threat. She does that a lot, she's told.

The sobs had stopped when she spoke, but the kid didn't look up.

Are you okay? was the question they were trained to ask in situations like that one. It's meant to differentiate between regular tears and the kind of tears that required hero clean up, but Honor deemed it a stupid question and has never asked it.

"Do you need help?" she asked instead. The kid sniffed, then all of a sudden, there's another person standing in front of Honor.

Honor pushed to her feet out of instinct, but it's just another kid, eyes red and puffy, tears streaking down her face—wait, it's the same kid. In the same ratty jeans and black hoodie.

"Leave me alone!" she shouted, but Honor just peered around her to the kid still on the ground with her face buried in her knees and her arms wrapped protectively around her head.

"Is this your marvel?" Honor asked. "That's so cool!" On a whim, she reached out to poke the kid in front of her, and she smacked Honor's hand out of the air. There was a slight sting to it, but Honor allowed it. Not an illusion, then, those are always extra flimsy against Honor and that was definitely a real touch, not a fabricated one. So this kid made copies of herself.

"What do you want?" the Copy (Honor assumed it was the Copy), asked.

"I wanted to make sure you got help if you needed it," Honor said, disarmingly honest. "Still am because you didn't answer my question with a no, just an emotional teenage outburst, but I'm also super interested in your marvel now. Can you make more than one? Where do they come from? Do you feel anything they feel?"

"Who are you?" the copy asked, brow furrowing in confusion. Honor briefly wondered if the kid on the ground was making the same face or if they're completely independent.

Honor doesn't put a lot of stake in being one of the top heroes in the world but damn if it's not a blow to her ego when someone doesn't recognize her in uniform.

"My name is Honor," she answered. "What's yours?"

"Alex," she answered warily.

"Well, Alex, do you need any help?" She leaned around the copy to talk directly to the actual kid. She sniffed again and when she looked up, Honor saw the bruise blooming across her cheekbone and her eye swelling shut and answered yes for her. Without letting any of her anger at the state of the kid show, lest it be mistaken for anger directed toward her and not the person who did this to her.

Alex tentatively accepted Honor's offer, but then refused to go to a hospital or to Honor's agency.

Honor eyed her up again, the damage, her clothes, her approximate age. She was a minor for sure, which meant that any place Honor offered to take her would call her parents. The pieces clicked together, and Honor cursed her habit of never being able to follow the rules like she was supposed to. She's trying, okay?

"Alright," she said. "What about to my place?"

Her eyes went wide.

"Your place?"

"Sure, I can call a friend to come take a look at you, get you fixed up like new," Honor promised. *Alex thought about that, searching Honor's face for any sign of a lie.*

"And no one else?"

"No one else," Honor promised.

Honor learned later that it wasn't her parents but her foster parents who hurt her after they accused her of stealing their food out of a locked cabinet. Honor arranged immediately to pull Alex out of that home and into a new, decent one for the time being. Then, Honor broke a few more rules.

Two steps forward, one step back, but Honor can make the whole journey that way.

When she offered Alex the spot at Titan Academy, she leapt at it, and now she's here, under Honor's care, with only a single backpack stuffed full of clothes. Her new uniform is spread out on the freshly-made bed, and Honor spared no expense for her kids. She wants them to be able to have their individuality while also looking like a team whenever they're on campus or at an off campus school event. They can mix and match the dozen different items they'd provided and it makes it easier for kids like Alex to not have to worry about that kind of stuff.

"Anything else?" Honor asks. Alex looks around her sparsely decorated room and shrugs.

"Don't think so," she says.

"Okay, then get out there and see if anyone else needs help moving, make some friends." Honor beams and pats her on the back, probably a little too hard. Alex drags her feet but still leaves the privacy of her dorm room to mingle with her new classmates.

Honor steps into the hallway after her and surveys the organized chaos happening. Charlie comes down the hall, talking with Malia. Tommy and his dad try to maneuver his big chair through his doorway. Luna is handing out small potted plants to everyone.

Honor may just be a little bit in love with all of them already.

"*Woah*," Verity's voice carries through walls with ease and then her head pops out of another room to stare at Jack where he's just standing in his doorway, staring across the hall at Tommy. He flushes bright red when everyone turns to see what's happening.

Honor doesn't know what Verity sensed but it was a lot of something to make her react like that. Honor looks back and forth between Jack and Tommy and makes an educated guess. Tommy drops his chair on his dad's foot and stares back at Jack. He cocks his head to the side.

"Do I know you?" he asks, genuinely trying to place him.

"No," Jack says and slams his door shut.

Honor is officially the proud guardian of twenty teenagers. This should be fun.

Once the kids are all mostly moved in, they all gather in the spacious lobby common room on the student side. There's plenty of seating for everyone between the tables and couches and pillow seats and the parents lead the mingling way, dragging their kids behind them to introduce them to others. Except for Charlie, she bounds from person to person, making sure to introduce herself and ask everyone's name.

Honor gets the front row seat when she approaches Jack, who has been glued to his mom's side. Gina is talking to Tamera, but they both pause when Charlie walks right up to them.

"Hi, I'm Charlie," she says to both Jack and his mom. Tamera grins wryly, already familiar with Charlie and her bright personality.

"Hi, Charlie, I'm Gina," she says.

"Jack," he says roughly.

"Oh, I know who you are, Boy Wonder," Charlie says with a competitive glint in her eye. After reading her admissions essay, Honor expects nothing less. Charlie is probably the most determined to prove herself out of all of her classmates and that's saying something because not a single person who is enrolled in Titan Academy is there just for a good time.

Jack grimaces at the nickname, but Charlie's been handing them out all day like candy, so Honor doubts he'll be getting away from it anytime soon.

They'd ordered a variety of food from the promenade across the street for the kids to sample. Leo comes back from his call in with Aurora, and he responds to Honor's questioning look with a shrug. Not a big deal, then.

"Okay, any last questions before we officially conclude move in day?" Honor asks, and everyone starts to gather around. She stands in front of one of the tables, and Verity sits on it next to her. Leo leans against it on her other side.

"I didn't know the dorms were coed," a mom says. Luna's? No, Luna has two dads. Rose. Honor is almost surprised to see her, she hadn't been there during the tour or move in, but she's busy as the CEO of Auxilia, one of the leading manufacturers and designers of pro hero support items.

"Not a question, but I'm so glad you asked," Verity answers, and Honor sighs. "Dividing sleeping arrangements by 'gender' or whatever is superfluous because we recognize that our kids might not identify as a gender at all or the gender assigned to them at birth. Not only that, but we're also not stupid enough to assume every student enrolled in Titan Academy is heterosexual, in which case dividing the dorms by 'gender' or whatever would be rendered obsolete anyway.

"I'll assume it's sex you're worried about. We are not your kids parents nor are we trying to be, but we will educate them. Adrian, specifically, our in-house medic will be handling the sexual education unit and then we trust these kids to make the decisions that are right for them. After all, if we can't trust them to make choices about their own bodies how could we possibly expect them to make the right choice when it comes to saving someone else's life?" she asks to ringing silence. Rose's mom looks irritated at being called out like this, but that's what she gets for asking Verity something she deems a stupid question. She's not even done yet.

"That being said!" Verity looks pointedly at their kids. "The dorms for the students and the dorms for the teachers are connected by the stairwell. It's so we can keep a close eye on them while also giving them a chance at independence. The entire dorm buildings are roughly two hundred and forty feet end to end. I can sense any sudden spike of emotion within a one mile radius. So. Keep that in mind."

"Like… any emotion?" Anthony asks. His hair is soaked in so much gel it looks like it would be crunchy to touch, and Honor has heroically resisted the urge all day.

"Any. Emotion," Verity repeats with a pointed look. A faint blush dusts his cheeks. "Of course, I won't be on campus all the time, but I do sleep here. So please. For all of our sakes, keep that in mind." She says the last part with an exaggerated, wide eyed look that makes some of the kids giggle.

"Will we be meeting the other teachers as well?" Gina asks.

"Quite possibly," Honor answers. "We have no concrete plans for parent teacher conferences or anything of the sort, but there will be open training days throughout the semester that all family are welcome to come and watch. Teddy, Rae, and Adrian will be at a few of those."

"There's only six teachers?" someone else asks, Honor doesn't quite catch who, but it sounds like a dad.

"There's only one class," Honor says with a grin. "As more students enroll, more teaching staff will be hired. I was very selective about who I chose to teach here and that won't be changing anytime soon." Honor answers a few more questions about open training days and off campus passes.

"Do you have any information about the year end tournament?" Charlie's mom asks. The year end tournament is when all of the schools in the region compete by class, but only the first three grade levels compete. The older years are too busy with internships and provisional licenses. Honor is very familiar with the tournament, having won it three years in a row with her sisters. It's because of that familiarity that she has no plans to sign them up.

"We will not be participating in the tournament," she answers, and several of the students sound dismayed at that.

"How will we prove we're better than those other schools?" Charlie asks.

"Being a hero isn't a competition," Honor answers with a shrug. "And we don't have anything to prove to anyone."

One of the kids eventually asks about their 'lost years.' The years that Honor spent as an special agent and Verity spent as a small business owner after 'The Incident.' Honor can't tell them about her time at the Homeland Hero Division because that's classified, and she's not proud of it.

"Our mom passed," Honor says, with a small, sad smile. She's not going to divulge her and Verity's shared inability to deal with that emotional fallout. "In an accident. We took some time off to deal with that and the reality that, even as heroes, you can't save everyone."

"Are we allowed to ask about your marvels?" Charlie asks as she raises her hand, not after, unwilling to let the silence settle and morph into awkwardness. Honor likes that about her.

"Of course you are," Honor says.

"Why don't you throw more tricks in combat?" Jack asks Honor. Charlie lowers her hand and scowls at him.

"*I* wanted to ask a question," she says.

"You can ask after," Jack says simply, and Honor knows he doesn't mean to be rude, knows Jack is a sweet kid. But she also knows that Jack is a little awkward and a bit dry and paired with the assumptions made about him based solely on the fact that he has famous parents, he comes off as a bit of an asshole.

"It's a good question," Honor interjects to diffuse the tension. She makes a mental note to get Charlie's question right after this one. "Tricks take a lot of brainpower," she admits and rubs the back of her neck. "People think it's easy because it looks easy, but that's not the case at all. I have to focus to get details right because if I mess up details then it's easier for a person to realize it's an illusion and break from it.

"Add all of that attention and detail to the chaos and danger of combat and it's nearly impossible to juggle both at the same time. I used to use tricks a lot, but after putting a lot of thought into it, I made the decision that it would suit me and my abilities best to develop the physical aspects of my marvel more and prioritize using those for the job. I still throw the occasional trick in a fight just to open up a window or give myself time too, because that split second of distraction is sometimes all you need."

"Verity throws tricks all the time," Tommy points out.

"It's not called throwing tricks when I do it," Verity says with half a smile, amused. "Honor uses that name for her illusions and Trick was her original call sign, so it fits. My marvel is technically aura manipulation and it doesn't take the same kind of brain power that Honor's does. I don't have to think so much as feel, and then it's a push or a pull. Even though it's simple, it's still difficult to do. But, like Honor, I thought long and hard about what would suit me best on the job and knew that manipulating the energy of crowds or rogues would be far too useful to not develop further. So I did."

"So who wins in a flat out fight?" Charlie asks.

"Me," the sisters speak at the same time.

"If Honor focuses more on her close combat skills then it would make sense that she has the upper hand," Malia says.

"Yeah, but don't forget to take into account that even without using our marvels, we're still sisters," Verity points out. "We've been sparring since we were kids, and Honor gets predictable when she's tired or provoked."

"And if anyone knows how to provoke me, it's you," Honor mutters. Then turns her attention back to Charlie. "What was your question Charlie?"

"Oh," she seems momentarily flustered with Honor's full attention. "I just wanted to know more about Leo's marvel."

Leo looks surprised by the attention but he'll have to get used to it. He's going to be the center of their education for the next six years.

"I have a shield marvel," he answers.

Everyone stares.

Honor shoves his shoulder, but he hardly moves, actually expending the energy to remain upright which tells Honor he *does* want to look cool in front of the kids. Cute.

"I gave a detailed analysis of my illusions and all you have is 'shields'?"

Leo sighs, long suffering as Honor de Mora's best friend. It's a familiar sound.

"I'm Class Two. The strength and size of my shields are directly related to my energy levels so I try to conserve as much as possible in any way I can. I can move them too, but that takes physical strength. These are the kinds of details and nuances of marvels that we hope to help you learn and develop here at Titan Academy," he says.

Honor is utterly endeared that Leo turned an opportunity to brag into a teachable moment for their kids.

"They're invisible to the average eye but some marvels can trigger a sort of rainbow reaction? Some people can see them, others can't. I can always see them. They are breakable but at this point, very few things or people can break them."

"Can we see?" Charlie asks.

Leo raises an eyebrow. He casts a shield in between the teachers and everyone else. Honor has always been able to faintly see them, dancing streaks of rainbow light but she doesn't see them in full the way she knows Leo does.

"Can you?" Leo asks.

"What?" Charlie asks. "You're doing it? I can't see shit!" Charlie's mom smacks her over the back of her head. "Ow! What was that for?"

"Watch your language in front of your teachers," she chides.

Shortly thereafter, the parents start to head out, and Honor does her best not to intrude on the tearful goodbyes.

Verity is even worse at the swell of emotion in the room and has to excuse herself. The kids can go off campus whenever they want as long as they submit a form. All of them are from in state too, so no one has too far to go if they want to see their parents again but it's still rough.

Honor remembers when her mom dropped her and her sisters off at Marvelous. Honor had been so excited, but also worried about her mom, who was going from having a full house with three rambunctious triplets to being by herself for the first time in fifteen years. Verity had outright bawled. So she understands the flurry of emotions and leaves them be.

She resists the urge to hover over the kids to make sure they get settled in okay. They'll be alright, she assures herself, and if they're not, they know where to find Honor. She slips into the stairwell. It's quiet. The quietest place Honor's been in all day. She takes each step slowly, savoring it. She's on call tonight but their district has been so calm lately, she doesn't expect to be called.

For a brief, blissfully ignorant moment, she thinks she might get a nice, relaxing night. But then she opens the door to her apartment and finds Verity chucking leftover pasta at Leo's head in the kitchen. He casts a shield, probably more out of habit than anything else, and it hits it with a *smack*. Leo straightens up to his full height with wide, disbelieving eyes.

"Are you serious?" he asks, incredulous.

"Don't say stupid shit in my presence!" Verity says, deathly serious.

"I was gonna eat that," Honor says, a bit dejected. She loves fettuccine alfredo. Verity bursts out laughing, but Leo still looks irate, which means whatever he said wasn't actually stupid, it just annoyed Verity.

"Why don't you cook us something?" Verity asks.

"Because I'm tired and we have a metric fuck ton of leftovers?"

"But we don't have *cookies*," Verity points out, even Leo rolls his eyes at that.

"That's baking not cooking," he says.

"You and your fucking technicalities," Verity snaps at him but there's no real bite to it. "I will throw more shit at your head. Say somethin' else."

"I think today went well," Leo says, changing the subject and ignoring Verity.

"Yeah," Honor agrees. "What was your call? Is everything okay?"

"Yeah, just containment," he says and leans against the counter. "Nothing major."

"Containment for what?" Honor asks, taking a seat at the bar. Verity makes an unnecessarily loud noise of disgust and marches herself fully into the kitchen.

"Fine, I'll make them myself," she says and dramatically yanks the fridge open. A bit too hard, as the handle comes off in her hand. She stares at it for a moment while Honor struggles to contain her laughter. "Well. Fuck."

"This year is gonna be fun," Honor says through her giggles. Just then they hear something crash across the hall.

"Super fun," Leo says.

5

Charlie's uniform is a little too crisp, but she hopes it'll wear in with time. She pulls at the collar again and almost wishes she had worn the pink polo like Lochlan, but the black button down looks better with the pink skirt and she wants to wear the polo with the plaid pants tomorrow and she can't wear the polo two days in a row.

"We should have had breakfast," Lochlan mutters. There's a small cafe situation in the downstairs lobby area of the school building run completely by Aurora's robots, and if Charlie were being honest, she'd say that freaked her out a little, but she's not, so she thinks it's totally cool.

"I had breakfast," Charlie points out.

"You had a candy bar from the vending machine," he retorts. "That doesn't count."

"My stomach's not growling, is it?"

He scowls at her and she laughs, some of her first day jitters eased by the familiar banter with her best friend. Charlie's glad Lochlan got into Titan Academy with her, she's sure she would have hated to do this without knowing anyone else, even if it seems like that's how most of her class-mates have to do it.

Really, she just wishes Noah had gotten in. He's at Marvelous, so it's not like he had to give up on his dream or anything, but Noah was their third musketeer, and Charlie and Lochlan are almost off balance without him.

"Hey! Wait up!"

Charlie is pulled from thoughts about old friends by new ones. Malia jogs to catch up with them on the lawn between the school building and their dorms.

"Do you think we'll be the first ones there?" she asks.

"Probably," Lochlan grumbles as they approach the large geometric glass building. It looks like it could be an art instal-lation rather than a school building. They'd been informed on the tour that all the glass had been reinforced by Aurora and was one-way.

"Charlie would have been there at the crack of dawn if she could have dragged me out of bed."

"I *could* have dragged you out of bed," Charlie points out. "But I didn't out of the kindness of my heart. You're welcome."

"Oh yeah, thanks for acting like a normal human for once in your life, it's greatly appreciated," he says dryly. Malia laughs at their exchange. Charlie opens the door for them and moves to put Malia in the middle of their little walking pattern so she doesn't feel left out, and they wait for the elevator like that.

They got to walk through the building yesterday, but it was perfunctory and they didn't even get to see the classroom they'd be using. It's nice now, in the early hours of the morning and without twenty families all crammed together in the hallway.

Charlie peers around the elevator to the courtyard in the center of the building, an outdoor area for lounging between classes, Honor had said. It's cute, assorted plants and a picnic table and a bench off to the side. A good way to get out of the classroom for just a few minutes and get some fresh air and sunlight.

The elevator comes and takes them to the third floor. When they get off, they find that they are *not* the first ones there, and Charlie scowls at Lochlan in an 'I told you so.' He makes a face back while Malia greets their classmates.

"Hey Jack," she says. "Hi Ethan."

Jack glances up from his phone and gives an awkward little wave. Ethan does the same, but he doesn't go back to looking at his phone like Jack does. Charlie still can't tell if he's an asshole or if he's just painfully shy. After he rudely interrupted her question at the Q&A, she's inclined to believe the former.

Jack even looks like a rich, preppy asshole with the way he's tucked his black button down into the plaid pants, and he's added a pink tie. It must be his own because Charlie doesn't recall seeing a tie with her other uniform things, but she's definitely going to double check later. He's also wearing a blazer which is just asking for heatstroke during LA summers.

"Morning," Ethan says with a yawn. He's wearing the blue polo and the black pants. There's an even number of blue and pink items, but the number of black pieces greatly outnumbers the white in their uniform bundle. She heard some parents talking yesterday about how it's smart because white gets so dirty so fast, but Charlie secretly thinks it's because white is one of the main colors for Marvelous, their rivals. Well, their rivals as decided by Charlie.

"Okay, where do I know you from?" Charlie asks. Ethan looks startled at the sudden assault. Charlie means it as a genuine question, Ethan looks super familiar, but she speaks aggressively and that's off-putting to a lot of people. Or so she's been told. She hasn't found a fuck to give about it yet.

Ethan blushes. At least, Charlie assumes it's a blush that his marvel alters because his cheeks *glow* a bright golden color that's kind of adorable, and then Charlie snaps her fingers, remembering.

"You make videos!"

"Pro Rescue," Jack says the name of his channel without looking up from his phone, and Ethan flails a little at that.

"Oh yeah, you do the analysis on pro hero rescues," Lochlan says. Malia pulls her phone out to look it up.

"You have t-shirts? Cute," Malia says as she scrolls through thumbnails. "Can I have one?"

"Well—I mean," he stutters out, flustered by all of the sudden attention. His gaze flickers to Jack who seems unconcerned, but it must be an act because he knew the name of the channel off the top of his head. Charlie would put good money on him watching regularly.

"My siblings and I watch your videos together," Charlie tells him. Ethan's face glows brighter, and she pokes his cheek. "Is this your marvel?"

"Um, yeah. It's—I glow," he says.

"Like a glow stick?" she asks. He sighs and Charlie feels kind of bad. She knows that sigh. That's the 'everyone says this same thing to me and thinks they're the first one to say it' sigh.

"Yeah, just like that," he answers.

"Why are you guys just waiting outside?" Malia asks.

"The door's locked," Jack answers once again without looking up. Charlie's half tempted to snap at him, but she settles for narrowing her eyes for the moment.

"That might be because we're a *half an hour early,*" Lochlan says and slants a look at Charlie.

"We weren't even the first ones here," Charlie points out. "So, I think your complaints are now invalid."

"Doesn't mean you won't hear them," he mutters, shier than usual because there are other people around, but unable to back down from Charlie teasing him.

Leo comes around the corner, holding a tablet and looking surprised to see them. There's a twitch at the corner of his mouth, and then it all smooths out in the blink of an eye and his face is impassive, but still gentle. Charlie wonders how he does it because she has mad resting bitch face. He walks through their little group to unlock the door. He doesn't have a key and there's no keypad for a code. All he does is knock. They all hear the loud *snick* of the lock.

"Will that work for everyone?" Charlie asks as they file into the classroom.

"No, just teachers," he answers and takes a seat at the teacher's desk in the front of the classroom. They all pause to take a moment to look around. "Your seats are assigned, just look for your name."

Not only are their seats assigned, but they also have little presents on them. Charlie doesn't have to look far to find her seat, the second desk back in the middle row. All the desks are tables of two, and Lochlan is her table mate. They high five when they sit down. Malia sits directly in front of Charlie, and Jack and Ethan move to the third row, the one closest to the windows. Jack sits in the front desk and Ethan is right behind him.

The dual-pane windows are floor-to-ceiling. They have a view of the Los Angeles skyline. Which, in Charlie's opinion, is the worst skyline, but there's not much she can do about that. The new Auxilia building stretches up above the rest, sharp curves snaking around and casting shade onto the floors below. It looks threatening compared to the rest, but it's Charlie's favorite building.

Charlie inspects the gifts that have been left for them. It's a fancy tablet like the one Leo has and the one all the test proctors had at the practical exam. It's not a model that Charlie's seen in stores yet, a thick black handle on one side for grip with a hidden stand for propping it up in various places and a clear screen when it's powered down. She guesses Aurora designed them, which means they're extra special. Charlie feels giddy.

She powers hers up and immediately starts fiddling with the color settings. Lochlan has already managed to make his font green, and he teaches Charlie how to change hers to a deep yellow color so it's vibrant but visible. Lochlan picks the stylus up and starts doodling something while Charlie sets up her tablet so it projects a keyboard onto her desk.

She's so caught up in her new gadget that she nearly forgets she has Leo practically to herself before class starts since her other classmates are also absorbed in their new toys.

"Leo?" she tries, leaning forward on her desk. Leo glances up from his own tablet, expression still smooth. "Why do you abstain from the hero rankings?"

He shrugs. "Not my thing," he says simply.

"But you'd probably rank so high," she says. "Especially because you're friends with Honor. Any hero who teams up with her or is seen out with her even in a casual setting sees their public approval rating skyrocket."

She notices Jack looking at her out of the corner of her eye and very purposely does not look at him.

"I don't need public approval to do my job," he says.

"But you need it to get better endorsement deals and better pay because the government stipend is hardly enough," Jack points out and while, yeah, Charlie knew that in theory, it's still incredibly weird to hear it coming from the son of the current number one hero. Jack's dad is sponsored by all the big name brands.

"I don't need the money, either," Leo says but doesn't elaborate. Charlie thinks he might come from money and that's why he doesn't need it from brand deals. That would also mean that he's a hero solely because he wants to be and she finds that kind of admirable. Charlie knows herself well enough after fifteen years on this earth that she wouldn't be able to forgo credit for her heroic acts, but she can still respect it.

Their other classmates start to file in, surprised to find some of them there already. Luna, the girl who can make plants appear out of thin air, flounces into the seat across the aisle from Charlie. Tommy is right behind her. Charlie still doesn't know what Tommy's marvel is because it can be rude to ask sometimes and it hadn't come up naturally yet, but he's a nice enough dude. Charlie likes him.

"Good morning," Tommy says with a bright smile. His teeth are so white.

"You have a beautiful smile," Charlie says honestly. Tommy stops short on his way to his seat, which turns out is right behind Charlie. His cheeks darken, and he looks at her funny.

"Thank you," he says with sincerity, "but I'm gay."

Charlie can't help the little laugh that bubbles out. "I wasn't hitting on you," she promises, although people do seem to think that a lot. "Just complimenting you."

"Oh God," Tommy says and lifts a hand to the back of his close shaven head. He looks sheepish. "Sorry, then."

"No worries," Charlie says and turns to keep facing him while he takes his seat. "It's good to get that out there early. I'm bi, *by* the way."

"I told you to stop saying it like that," Lochlan groans.

"Cool," Tommy says with that same easy smile.

"Save it for the ice breaker," Leo tells them and there's a collective groan at the mention of an icebreaker.

The class fills up quickly after that, and Leo does a quick head count before standing up at the front of the classroom.

"Good morning and welcome to your first day of homeroom," he says. "We'll do a quick ice breaker where everyone goes around and introduces themselves with their marvel and a 'fun' fact, and then we'll review your schedules before first period. Any questions?" He doesn't actually put air quotes around *fun* but Charlie hears them loud and clear.

They start with Alex, who sits next to Jack, closest to the windows.

"Uh, I'm Alex, my marvel is self duplication, and my parents are dead," she says.

"Yo, he said a *fun* fact." Charlie doesn't even give the horribly awkward silence time to settle in.

"Yeah, well, this way I don't have to deal with explaining it nineteen times when people ask me about holidays or something," she snaps back. Charlie pauses, then leans back in her seat.

"That's fair," she acquiesces. Alex seems a bit thrown by the sudden shift and settles back in her own seat.

"I'll amend the rules," Leo says when he's sure they're finished. "You can share anything you'd like your classmates to know. Jack?"

"Uh, I'm Jack," he says as if they don't all already know that. "My marvel is earth manipulation, and I'm gay."

"Subtle, Boy Wonder," Charlie says and Jack glares at her while his cheeks go bright red.

"I'm Anthony!" The next guy jumps in. He's got entirely too much hair gel in. "My marvel is—" he pops out of existence and back into standing at the front of the classroom next to Leo, who does not jump in surprise, unlike the rest of them "—warp, and my favorite hero is Jack's dad."

Jack sinks low in his seat at that, and Charlie scoffs. Honor is the clear choice when it comes to favorites, and Charlie doesn't want to say anyone is wrong for favoring another hero, but she'll still think it. Malia goes next and says her marvel is healing and her favorite hero is Honor. Charlie leans forward to high five her for that.

Charlie also files her marvel away for later. It makes that conversation she overheard make a lot more sense. Soon, it's Charlie's turn to introduce herself.

"I'm Charlie," she says with a little wave. "My marvel is concussive overpressure, and Honor is my favorite hero. I even have these sick limited edition sneakers," she adds and puts them up on the desk for the class to see.

"That was more than one fun fact," Jack points out.

"You're welcome," is Charlie's response.

"I'm Lochlan," Lochlan says loudly before they can start fighting. "My marvel is storm manifestation and my favorite hero is my mom."

"You're adorable," Charlie says and pinches his cheek. He swats her away halfheartedly, and they listen to the rest of their class introduce themselves. Charlie learns that Tommy is a void and a total sweetheart because he reiterates the fact that he's gay with a nice smile in solidarity with Jack.

Charlie finally gets to learn what the giant rock monster is. His name is Rock Buddy and that's his name because Cecily made him when she was ten and it's the only thing he'll respond to now. Rock Buddy has his own table in the back of the classroom and he's… coloring? Sometimes Charlie thinks nothing can surprise her anymore when it comes to marvels, but the world continues to prove her wrong.

When the class has finished with their ice breaker, they goad Leo into doing it too, and he caves quickly if it means they can move on.

"I'm Leo, my marvel is physical shields, and I like naps," he deadpans.

Leo outlines their schedules for them. They'll stay in this one classroom and the teachers will come to them except for Aurora, for whom they'll have to go to the stadium, but those sessions are at the end of the day so they can transition straight to physical training anyway. They're free to go off campus for lunch as long as they're back on time. They don't actually get to start physical training this week because they have to wait until after the safety seminar that they'll be attending on Friday.

"Any questions?" There are none and Leo moves to stand behind a teaching window. Charlie's old school had these. They work so the teacher is never blocking anything on the board from any angle since the board is in between the teacher and students. Whatever they write appears on the other side, right way around so they don't have to worry about writing backwards and they can even project videos onto it.

"Let's get started with your hero theory class, then."

Charlie sets up her tablet to take notes, anticipation curling in her gut. She's always wanted to go to hero school, but she didn't think even the classes would excite her like this. It's a good sign, since she plans to be at the top of their class in every conceivable way.

Leo takes them through the syllabus for Hero Theory, and the time flies by without Charlie checking the clock once, a far departure from her educational experience thus far. Leo leaves them and their history teacher walks in. He's slimmer than Leo with a wrinkled button-up shirt rolled up to his elbows. He has sleeve tattoos just like Honor does, but his are all in a different, more traditional style with a color scheme that matches his skin tone beautifully. His hair is curly and tousled with a small white patch in the front.

"Good morning, my name is Teddy," He greets them. "I know Leo already tortured you with an icebreaker so I'll spare you. Today we're going to dive right in. We'll be learning about the emergence of Marvels."

Most of them already know this. Charlie definitely knows this. It's the first unit of modern history at every grade level. Marvels were considered genetic defects until they weren't and regulations for marvel usage was put in place posthaste, blah blah blah.

Charlie's hand shoots into the air to save them all from their boring fates for just a little while longer. She starts speaking before Teddy calls on her. "What's your marvel?"

"Oh!" Teddy says like he completely forgot he even has a marvel. "It's phasing. I can manipulate my own atomic density to either phase through solid objects or make myself pretty much indestructible, although it works up quite the appetite to do that one."

He walks straight through the teacher's desk in the front to demonstrate before they can even ask. Charlie and her classmates make the appropriate 'oohs' and 'aahs.'

"Are you an active duty hero?" Jack asks with a squint.

"I'm on reserve," Teddy tells them, which does explain why Charlie has never even heard of a hero with this marvel before. "I used to work similarly to Leo. I work when I'm called in, but I don't patrol."

"That's an option?" someone mutters under their breath from somewhere behind Charlie.

"Be sure to ask Leo in hero theory," Teddy says with a smile that crinkles the corners of his eyes. "He'll take you through all the ways you can be a pro hero. You might be surprised by the sheer volume of answers. But let's get started with class!" He claps his hands together and uses his tablet to put an infographic up on the board.

"People today are much sturdier than they were two hundred, a hundred, even fifty years ago. It used to be so that a twelve-story fall would be enough to kill the average person. Now, just about everyone can walk away with moderate injuries. This evolution is believed to be a direct result of marvels. We'll begin with the first ever recorded case of a marvel. Can anyone tell me what it was?"

Everyone can because they all *already know this*. Charlie feels her mind start to wander and doesn't even try to rein it in. Jack raises his hand to answer like the golden boy he is, and Charlie, still not listening, props her chin up on her hand to at least maintain the illusion of attention.

The first officially recorded marvel was Tanya Newman, a Boston native, who gained the ability to fly on her sixteenth birthday, like, two hundred years ago. There were several other cases before that, but they were all written off as rumors until Tanya flew from Boston to New York with nothing but the clothes on her back. After that, there was no denying it, no keeping it a secret. She was hailed as a 'medical marvel' after it was revealed that her genetic code actually slowly shifted overtime into a unique code that allowed her to fly. Now, every single genetic code is colloquially referred to as a marvel.

Tanya wasn't actually the first marvel ever, historians everywhere are uncovering evidence of marvels dating back to long fallen empires, but hers was the first case that marked change for the future. Several other countries revealed that they had people with marvels working for them all along, but those aren't regarded as the first official record of a marvel, either.

People would claim to do things they couldn't really do, or use juvenile tricks to get people to think they had a marvel when they didn't. It didn't really matter, though, just two generations later, eighty percent of the population had a marvel. Tanya's marvel manifested when she was sixteen, but as years go on, the presentation age gets lower and lower. Charlie got her marvel when she was twelve. She's heard rumors that Jack got his when he was *six*.

Of course, there are all sorts of rumors surrounding the Triumvirate, but Charlie wouldn't be surprised in the slightest to find out that they really were born with their marvels, with their eyes glowing straight out of the womb.

Before the revelation that the triplets are half Titan, before the revelation of Titan existence at all, it was widely believed and generally accepted that the emergence of marvels was just the next step in human evolution. Now, though, there are thousands of theories that link marvels directly to Titans. It makes sense to think that the Triumvirate got their marvels directly from their Titan mother, but there's no way everyone on earth is directly descended from a Titan. There's no way.

Besides, Honor and her sisters haven't said anything about it and wouldn't they be the ones who know? Especially since they work so closely with Aurora, who is the leader in marvel development research? Even *she* hasn't stated a connection between the two. It makes sense that humans would develop marvels naturally to catch up with the rest of the universe, apparently.

Shortly after the emergence of marvels, came the classification system. There are six classes of marvels, six being the lowest, one being the highest. There are only, like, a dozen or so Class One Marvels worldwide and the Triumvirate make up three of them. Jack's dad is another. He can manipulate gravity and, if he wanted to, could alter the literal course of the planet. Jack's marvel must be a result of his mom and dad's marvels combining. She isn't sure what Gina's marvel is, though. Charlie is a mix of her parents, she thinks. She's not exactly sure.

Charlie is sure that she's a Class Four, though, with a naturally destructive, offensive, physical creation marvel. She's not entirely sure what all that means, but it's what it says on her classification card. Everyone is required to obtain a classification card within one year of marvel presentation by taking a special test. It's optional to renew after that for the general public, so Charlie hasn't taken the test again.

They're required for pros and hero students, though, and Charlie's already looking forward to getting tested again before the start of the next year. Class Three is the lowest a pro can be, and she's fairly certain she could snag it right now if she really went for it, but she's willing to wait until she has a year of training under her belt. Maybe she'll even bypass

Class Three completely and get Class Two. That's what the majority of the pros have.

Imagine that, Charlie on par with *actual heroes* as a first year. She's not so arrogant as to assume she's as good as those heroes but she'd be just as *powerful*. Charlie's got her eye on that Class One classification like a dog with a ribeye. She wants to be able to stand next to Honor and be regarded as an equal. Wouldn't that be fucking something.

Charlie smiles to herself just imagining it, being presented with her shiny new classification card by Honor herself. The fantasy lingers in the back of her mind throughout the day during all of her other classes. She's going to make that fantasy a reality no matter what.

"Lochlan and I are going across the street for lunch," Charlie announces to class. "Does anyone wanna come with?"

"I'll come," Malia stands up immediately. Beside her, Luna gathers her things to come too. Then Rose, the rich girl with all of the jewelry, decides to come too.

"Sounds fun," Tommy says and moves to stand, which means Cora is coming too. Charlie throws a quick glance to Jack to gauge his reaction. If Charlie's as good at reading people as she likes to believe she is, she'd say Jack looks tempted to tag along too. But then he catches Charlie staring at him, and he scowls at her, sinking down further in his seat. Charlie looks away and glances over Kai in his seat next to Tommy, literally twiddling his thumbs.

"You're coming too," Charlie says, grabbing a fistful of Kai's shirt. She knows his name because he'd introduced himself during the ice breaker but she hadn't seen him talk to anyone during move-in or at all yesterday when the majority of them spent time settling in with their doors open so they could all get to know one another.

If he's shy or private, Charlie will let him be shy or private. What she won't let him be is friendless. She's good at making friends with shy kids. It's almost her brand at this point. Lochlan once said she was the extraverted friend to all introverts, and she didn't hate it.

Kai looks startled but offers no resistance when he stumbles out of his seat and walks out with their little group. They walk quickly to make it to the shopping center across the street from campus and, after coming to a general consensus that they don't want to risk being late, settle on the place closest to campus.

In theory, Charlie is well aware of the fact that Titan Academy opening up is a big deal. Even to people who don't really care about or follow heroes. *Everyone* knows who the de Mora sisters are and here they are, a group of teenagers waltzing into a pizza joint wearing their Titan Academy uniforms like a giant neon beacon.

They get a lot of stares. But Charlie's used to that because she's loud and draws a lot of attention in public spaces, anyway. So she's the one to pick a booth big enough for all of them. The server approaches nervously, but Charlie puts on a bright smile and orders waters all around and two large pizzas right off the bat so they can get back in time. One plain cheese, one with everything.

Charlie has always been good at leading a conversation, and she does so all through lunch, learning about her classmates and competition. As a whole, though, she likes them. The more she talks to her classmates who are also next-level stoked to go to Titan Academy, who are also determined to be top heroes, who also love the Triumvirate, the more she starts to think that this year might be the best year ever.

6

Honor strides into Ameliora like she owns the place, because she does. The facility, a rogue rehabilitation center that Honor staked her career on, had cost nearly as much as the entire Titan campus to build, though it's only the size of the dorms. It has all of the same state of the art protections, courtesy of Aurora, but on the inside as well as the outside.

Heroes only save good people. When Honor had first heard those words, she didn't expect them to break her heart. Anyone who knows Honor would have said that she would have agreed. *Honor* thought she would've agreed. But when she'd been sent on a mission to take out a rogue, she couldn't do it. Seeing Moone standing there, half out of his mind, standing at the edge of a nuclear reactor pool, truly believing that no one was ever going to save him—her whole heart shattered.

Because Moone wasn't good. He's hurt a lot of people and there have to be consequences for those actions, but Honor knew right then and there that *not being saved* is not one of those consequences.

Heroes save anyone who needs saving, she had said. Then she threw her whole weight behind that statement because Honor de Mora doesn't half ass anything, especially not being a hero.

Moone had been the first Ameliora graduate, sponsored by the widely revered pro hero Spectra, Honor's own mentor, who had done it as a personal favor to her. Since not many people knew about Moone or what he had done, it didn't cause much of a stir with the general public. Colson, though, is another story entirely

She walks into the lobby. It's sleek but modest. Black chairs and wood floors with custom art pieces serving as low tables make for a nice waiting room for visitors. Honor's design direction for Ameliora had been "as long as it doesn't look like a goddamn prison," and she let Verity run with it.

The front desk is another installation art piece that Verity found, large and blue and… some sort of shape. Honor isn't good at this kind of thing, that's why she has Verity. The woman working the desk, though, Honor had hired herself. She's a pretty unassuming lady, straight hair, thick rimmed glasses, wearing the standard Ameliora uniform of navy slacks and a white button down. But her marvel is immobilization on sight. She can stop anyone in their tracks with a single look, and they wouldn't be able to move again until she takes her eyes off them.

She looks up when Honor walks in. "Hi, Honor," she says with a smile.

"Hi, Lisa," she says and leans on the counter.

"Colson's ready for you," Lisa tells her.

"Awesome, thanks," Honor says with a parting pat to the counter. The automatic doors slide open as someone else comes out, the one and only *Candor*. Ursula Knight, call sign Candor, has a compulsive truth telling marvel that was absolutely instrumental in getting Ameliora off the ground. Honor hit roadblock after roadblock and pushback from every conceivable direction from people saying that rogues can't be reformed. They belong in prison. They don't regret their actions, they're just saying that to get out of prison. They'll just do it again.

Enter Candor.

Any question she asks must be answered with the most truthful answer. There are no exceptions, and as of yet, no one is able to resist. Not even Honor, who had tested it extensively, and now Ursula holds more of her embarrassing secrets than Verity or Grace. The entrance exam for Ameliora is an interview conducted by Candor herself, and she asks the standard questions Honor had come up with.

Why did you do what you did?

Do you regret what you did?

Do you want to be better?

Do you need help?

Honor's been in the room for several entrance interviews. The way someone will crumple, a strangled *yes* leaving their mouth when Ursula asks the last question will always tear a hole in her chest, but it also assures her that they're doing the right thing. These people need help, and Honor is going to provide it along with her rockstar team.

Colson's interview had hurt her almost as much as it had hurt him, watching through the window as Ursula asked, *"Do you need help?"*

"Yes," Colson choked out and laid his head on the table between them. He wrapped his arms around his head and started to cry. It was just trembling at first as he tried to hold it back then a sob—"Please."

It hurts just to remember it.

"Hey, Honor," Ursula says with a tired smile.

"My saving grace! My hero! My partner in anything but crime! My tall drink of truth serum!" Honor cries out, and Ursula shakes her head with a laugh and accepts Honor's hug, which is really just Honor throwing herself over her dramatically. "How's work?"

"It's work," Ursula says with a shrug that moves Honor. "But it's good work."

"I don't think I'll ever be able to thank you enough," Honor tells her. "Are you sure you don't want an all-expenses paid vacation to the Bahamas? Hawaii? Do you like snow? I know some cool places in Iceland."

"I told you I'm good," Ursula says.

"What about a house?" Honor says, and Ursula laughs. "I'll buy you a house!"

"You already pay me enough," Ursula insists.

"Enough isn't enough, how about a raise?"

"You're ridiculous."

"Okay, okay, lunch? This weekend?"

"I'll agree to that," Ursula says.

"You done for today?"

"Not quite," she says. "I'm assisting on some interrogations in Pointe. But I'll call you about lunch. Get in there before he starts to freak out that you're late."

Honor lets her go and heads through the automatic doors. The hallway is long and well lit, and she doesn't have to go far to get to the room she's looking for. It's the second door on the right that leads her to an open visiting room. There are some nice leather couches with a television in one corner and a kitchenette stocked with teas and coffee and some snacks. Colson sits at one of the tables strewn about the room, all from some dining room collection Verity had raved about for days and how the designer used her marvel to construct them from trash. They don't look like trash, though, and that's all Honor cares about.

"Hi," she says with a bright smile. Colson looks up from his cuffed hands and his eyes brighten, but his smile barely takes. It makes her heart ache a bit to know that Colson had once been so loud and brash and his smile had been so big and bright.

Next to him is Bobby, one of the usual guards. The guard uniform is the same as the other staff, not meant to be imposing or elicit an immediate negative response. Bobby chose the gray slacks with a white button down for the day. He has a power augmentation marvel so he appears average, maybe a bit of a beefcake, but Honor has seen him muscle up to the size of a tow truck.

"Hey," Colson breathes, and it sounds like it's laced with the barest amount of relief. He stands to return her hug. She wraps him up too tight every time but he never complains. It's nice to have the reminder that he's here, he's okay, he's alive. Sometimes it's hard to remember when he isn't in front of her.

"What's up, Bobby?" she asks as she lets Colson go. She sits down across from them, and Bobby makes to stand.

"Hey, Honor," he says in a low baritone. She's always tempted to invite him to karaoke. He nods to Colson who nods back, his white blonde hair falling into his eyes. He needs a haircut. Does he want a haircut?

"They feel alright?" Honor nods to Colson's hands. His thumb digs into the palm of his other hand, and she knows it's because he's trying to resist the urge to tug at the cuffs themselves.

"No," he admits with a small huff of humorless laughter. She knows what he means. Nullifiers *suck*. They make her feel foggy and slow, not to mention the constant jab of needles in her skin. "They said that once I get a sponsor I can switch to blood transfusions full time, though."

That was another condition of Ameliora. Everyone who graduated from the program had to do so with a sponsor signed up. Honor had already been planning on it, but then the commission told her that it had to be a pro hero or no one, and that made things harder.

"And you'd rather do those?" she asks. He raises an eyebrow at her.

"Yeah, they don't make me feel like I'm sleepwalking," he says. "They've already got the numbers on file for them. I'd have to get them once a month. Around then is when I can start to use my marvel again, but nothing big enough to do any real damage."

Honor nods along. Colson presents the information as fact and it is, but she knows that it hurts him to not be able to use his marvel freely. That's another condition of Ameliora, restriction of marvel use for at least a year after graduation. There are exceptions, of course, at the discretion of the committee that Honor is not permitted to sit on, but they both know that Colson wouldn't be one of them.

"Well, I can tell Aurora to stop designing fashionable nullifiers," she tells him, and that earns her a real laugh.

"Oh man, I can't wait to wear my own clothes again," he says, and Honor grins, remembering how precious Colson had been about his appearance in high school. He'd never admit how much he cared out loud, but after the third time she caught him fixing his hair in the closest reflective surface, it couldn't be denied. Ameliora reformers wear sweats in black, gray, or navy. Colson has on the navy set right now, and he looks comfy, cozy, with his wide shoulders swathed in soft cotton, like he used to when they would lounge around their apartment at the agency. But they're not at the agency. There is no agency. So much is different.

"How are the kids?" he asks. "All settled in?"

Honor can't help the fond smile that surfaces. "Yeah, yeah, they're good. Still finding their footing a bit, but they're going to be sore as hell tomorrow after their first day of weight training with V."

"Oh man," Colson says with half a laugh. "I hope she goes a little easy on them, they're babies."

"You know she won't," Honor says, and Colson bows his head to hide a small grin. He knows just as well as Honor that Verity never goes easy on anyone, but it'll make them stronger in the end. In every sense of the word.

"Then I wish them luck," he says.

Thinking about the first days of her first year of hero school makes Honor's gut twist. That's when she met Colson and Leo. Friendships for a lifetime. It's a miracle all of them are still alive, let alone still together like this. But it's not a miracle that was freely given. They've worked for this. They've shed blood and tears for this. It makes her nervous for her kids, but she keeps reminding herself that the only thing she can do is train them to be the best they can be. She takes a deep breath.

"Got a date for your hearing," she tells him, and his head snaps up to look at her. "May 2nd."

She watches him deflate a bit at that. That will put Colson in Ameliora for just under two years, probably a little more since he won't be released the day of the hearing. It's not even really a hearing, more of a performance review where the committee meets with his potential sponsor and outlines the duties and guidelines and emphasizes the risk they're taking by sponsoring a rogue. A sponsor will be charged as an accomplice in any crime the rogue commits after release.

Honor hates the committee. It had been forced on her as a requirement for her program, but there are some good people on it and they haven't had any major issues so far with other graduates. Still, they've never had someone as high profile as Colson before. Getting him into Ameliora had been a battle in itself, and the only reason Honor had won that fight was because of Ursula and her marvel. Getting him out is going to be another fight, and they both know it.

"It doesn't matter, really," he says.

"What do you mean?" she asks, dread creeping over her slowly.

"Can't graduate without a sponsor," he says with a shrug and looks down at his hands. He massages them in turn out of habit. "And who's going to sponsor me?" His smile is deprecating and sad but resigned, like he's already accepted that he's never going to graduate and get back into the real world because of the mistakes he's made.

"Colson," she says and waits for him to look at her. He avoids eye contact now, she's noticed, but she wants to make sure he hears this. His eyes meet hers, and she says, "I'm going to sponsor you."

Immediately, his eyes are wet with tears, and Honor starts to panic even though she knows Colson is a crier. He's an angry crier, a happy crier, a sad crier, a laugh so hard you cry crier, but seeing him cry in here with those nullifiers around his wrist and realizing that he truly believed he was never getting out makes those tears hurt a little bit more.

She yanks him out of his seat with too much force, but he doesn't resist her hug, just buries his face in her shoulder and holds her back, shaking.

"Why are you crying?" she has to ask because it could be a hundred different reasons and she doesn't want to assume the wrong one.

"I'm not," he says with a gross, wet sniff. She snorts and his next tremor is one of laughter.

"Colson," she says as sternly as she can. She pulls back enough to cup his face so he can't hide from her.

"I guess… I didn't really let myself believe that you had forgiven me," he admitted. He looks away then back at her. "After—after everything and Honor, I almost *killed* you. I just don't understand how you can—I'm really grateful for you, you know?" He wipes furiously at his face and Honor feels tears prick the backs of her eyes.

"First of all, of course I forgive you," she says with every ounce of seriousness she can muster. "I almost killed you too, that one time, so I think we're even." He laughs then, remembering the ridiculous trajectory their friendship has taken over the years. It's honestly a miracle they've made it this far. "Second, you couldn't kill me if you actually tried so don't go getting a big head, okay tough guy?"

"Yeah, okay," he says, voice still thick with tears. Honor pulls him into another hug because she knows he needs it. They both do.

7

Charlie bounces on the balls of her feet. Today is marvel assessments and she is *stoked*. They haven't had much chance to use their marvels at all, and now she gets to show her teachers exactly what she can do. The entrance practical was only a small taste.

They're all dressed in various versions of their gym uniforms, all black with Titan accents in pink and blue. Some people have gone with the baggier options of joggers or sweatshirts, but Charlie is in the compression leggings and one of the brighter options in their new closet, a vibrantly pink shirt with moisture wicking whatever. All of their uniforms are made from high tech fabric that Aurora invented, which allows all of their clothing to act as partial armor. In her matching, limited-edition pink sneakers, Charlie looks good, and she feels good because she looks good.

There are multiple stations set up for their evaluations. Adrian is performing physicals, Verity is testing their strength and agility sans marvels, Honor and Leo are testing their marvels, and Aurora is compiling that data to help them come up with a development plan. Charlie's group is with Honor and Leo first.

"Alright, guys," Honor claps her hands together. "You'll be testing your marvels against me and Leo and, in some cases, just demonstrating your upper limit."

Charlie gets to watch some marvels in action for the first time. Rose's is metal manipulation. She can turn metals into a fluid-like substance and then reshape them to her will with a wave of her fingers. Charlie watches her rings dance around her knuckles then form a puddle in her palm. Honor has her test her distance of application and the size of the objects she can manipulate. Small things like her earrings or the blade of a pocket knife are easy. Bigger things cause her some trouble.

Kai's marvel is water manipulation, and Honor makes it a point to ask him if it's just water or all liquids. It's another testament to her intelligence, because Charlie never would have thought to ask something like that. Kai is a Class Four, like Charlie, but she wonders when he was tested last, because the control he demonstrates while manipulating the provided tub of water is astonishing.

"Are your physical movements necessary for your marvel activation?" Leo asks. Kai makes big, sweeping motions with his arms and sometimes even his legs in order to move the water, and even Charlie knows that that puts him at a disadvantage in a fight because all someone has to do is restrain him.

"Yes," Kai says like it's the wrong answer, but he doesn't have another one.

"Don't sweat it," Honor assures him. "That's what the development plans are for. We'll either see if you can activate your marvel without them or train you to be faster. Either way, you'll get better and stronger. You all will."

Luna creates a few trees, and Charlie thinks that she might be bigger competition than she originally thought. The trees sprout from the ground where there's no soil, just the nanite flooring and probably solid concrete underneath, but the trees break through easily, roots crawling along the ground and branches shooting outward and almost taking Charlie's eye out. Luna seems sweet and doesn't appear to care about class rankings, but she has advanced control of her marvel and already knows that if she overuses her marvel, it gives her a migraine that can last for days. It's as impressive as it is beautiful.

Next is Lochlan, and Charlie gives him an encouraging punch to the shoulder.

"Go ahead and make a storm, the biggest you can," Honor says. Lochlan blanches.

"But we're inside!"

"Don't worry about it," Honor says, waving him off.

"Easier said than done," he mutters.

Charlie feels the familiar stirrings of one of Lochlan's storms. The way a natural storm will darken the sky and thicken the air, Lochlan's storms will send a shock through the stadium like static. Charlie's closest, so she feels it the most, but she's also used to it. Lochlan's been making storms since they were ten.

It starts as a single dark cloud above his head, and then as it grows outward, it also lifts up, higher and higher toward the ceiling. There's a loud clap of thunder, and then the downpour starts. Charlie immediately laments the fact that she didn't bring an umbrella, but the raindrops don't hit them. They hit the shield Leo conjured around all of them and roll off the dome.

"Wow," Luna breathes and gets closer to the shield to get a better look. Charlie looks around in their little safe haven while Lochlan's storm really starts to rage in the stadium. It's sturdy enough. The shield and the stadium. The high winds kick in and the tub of water Kai had used knocks over completely, spilling water everywhere. Honor punches something into the tablet she's holding, and it beeps back at her. She looks impressed for a moment before she turns back to Lochlan.

"Can you bring it back in?" Honor asks.

"I—I don't know," he admits.

"Try for me," she encourages.

Lochlan can create storms from nothing, but to bring them in, he has to use his arms. He lifts them now and nothing happens, but Charlie can see the veins in his forearms bulging while he tries to call the storm back to him.

"I can't," he says, sounding dangerously close to panic. "I can't. I'm sorry."

"It's alright," Honor promises.

Charlie looks at the size of the storm and how it's been contained by the arena roof.

"I can," she volunteers.

Lochlan sags with relief, and Honor looks at her, surprised. It wouldn't be the first time she's broken up one of Lochlan's storms with her own marvel, and she's certain it won't be the last. Honor gestures for her to go ahead. Leo drops the shield, promptly soaking all of them. Rose cries out in protest, but Charlie acts fast, clapping her arms together and spreading them out wide.

Her marvel generates between her palms and rips outward and upward. Charlie can see the golden outline of it, like the reflection of sunlight on metal as it races toward the clouds. Charlie's marvel tears through the clouds with so much force that it disperses them completely. The roof rumbles taking the second hit, but it ultimately holds.

"Oh, wow," Honor says, and Charlie flushes with pride. She lets her arms fall to her side, still tingling with recoil. "Do you do that often?"

Charlie shrugs. She doesn't want to embarrass Lochlan, but, yeah, she kind of does.

"Try it out against a shield," Honor says, and Leo conjures up a shield between them and Charlie. "As hard as you can."

Charlie shakes out her arms and claps her hands together in front of her again. The force of her marvel shoots forward again and breaks the shield.

It broke the shield.

Holy shit, it broke the shield.

She can't see it, but she can *hear* it. It sounds like shattering glass, and Charlie can picture it fracturing and falling to the ground. She gapes and can feel the shock of her classmates around her. Even Leo looks surprised. It's only the raise of a single eyebrow, but it's a lot more than anyone else has gotten so far.

"Wow," Kai breathes.

"It was impressive," Honor says, "but don't go getting a big head. That wasn't Leo's strongest shield."

"Sensors catch it?" Leo asks.

"Three pounds per square inch," Honor answers, looking at the tablet. Leo holds up a hand and another shield appears, flashing with a glittery rainbow briefly.

"Try again," Leo says.

"I need a second," Charlie says. Her arms are practically vibrating with recoil, and there's no way she's going to be able to get them to come together again so quickly. "Every time I use my marvel, there's some recoil and I can't do it again straight away."

Honor types that information into her tablet. "Can you do it anywhere on your body?" she asks.

Charlie nods. "Anywhere I can make skin to skin contact with myself. I can do it with my feet too, but it's awkward."

Honor cocks her head to the side, thinking. "And can you control the size and direction?"

"Kinda," Charlie answers honestly. "The direction is pretty much straight out from wherever I make contact with myself and the size depends on how hard I hit."

"So you have to smack the shit out of yourself to get a really big one in?" Rose asks.

"Please watch your language in class," Leo sighs, having said this a dozen times already even if it's only the first week.

"Basically," Charlie answers. She shakes her arms out. "I'm good to go again."

Leo nods, and she claps her hands together. Once again, the force rips out of her and the shield doesn't budge. Not that she can see the shield itself, but she can see the way her own marvel residuals make contact and flatten out, useless. Leo doesn't look happy about it, though, squinting at his own shield like it personally offended him. Honor looks like she's holding back laughter.

"You were up late last night," she says. Charlie looks back and forth between them, confused. Leo just scowls at her and mutters something under his breath that Charlie can't catch.

"Is the recoil the only adverse side effect you experience of your marvel?" Honor asks.

"Yeah," she answers. "Too much recoil makes my limbs numb, though. It's super uncomfortable."

"Has anyone else experienced adverse side effects from your marvel?"

"Oh, yeah, I think I've accidentally given my brothers two or three concussions each. Would be my sisters, too, but Kimberly is an external void, and Lydia has the same marvel as me, so it doesn't affect her as much."

"You have a sister with a void marvel and a sister with the same marvel as you?" Honor asks, incredulous. "What are your parents' marvels?"

"Mom's an external void, and Dad's is aerokinetic blasts," she answers.

Honor just blinks at her.

"Huh," is all she says, and Charlie feels like she failed somehow.

"Lydia's marvel is more like Dad's though," she goes on. "They both generate the blasts from blowing through their lips, but Dad's is only ever air and Lydia's is… whatever ours is, so it's not exactly the same."

"That makes sense," Leo says. "Do you know your grand-parents' marvels?"

Charlie shakes her head no, but now she wants to find out. All of her grandparents had been dead by the time she was born, so she never really thought about it but she's thinking about it now.

"Well, I think we got everything," Honor says. "You guys can move onto Aurora's station now. You remember where it is?"

When they all nod that they can find their way, they head out and the next group filters in behind them. Charlie glances back at Honor and Leo who are bent over the tablet together. Charlie knows they'll all be receiving the results of their evaluations later, but she's anxious to get hers.

Aurora's lab is just as sleek and cool as it was the first time they were all in there, only now they get to really take it in with only five of them instead of all twenty plus their parents. Aurora taps at something on her main table and beams when they come in.

"Hello!" she says cheerily.

"Hi!" Luna replies. Charlie thinks Aurora and Luna are a lot alike in personality, if nothing else.

"How did assessments go? Wait! Don't tell me, I already know," she says and projects their individual results in holo squares over the table. They gather around the table and check their own scores.

Charlie's not exactly sure what to make of it. She understands that her blasts create ten pounds of pressure per square inch, but not much else. It's only raw data so far, meant more for Aurora than for them, so hopefully they'll get some help interpreting results later.

"As for preliminary developmental plans—" or now, apparently "—The basics apply. If your marvel depends on your physical strength, then you focus on strength training. If your marvel depends on your energy levels, make sure you're getting an adequate amount of rest. When you receive your reports, you'll also be given resources into how to best attain those goals. We'll be compiling that data until after the safety seminar, so I don't have too much for you now, just the informational packets that I've already sent to your tablets.

"While you're here, though, I will have you test these out," she says and raps on the table with her knuckles. A slot slides open and she pulls out three sets of nullifying handcuffs.

"These are standard use nullifiers. All heroes use them, they're a part of arrest protocol. You're going to try them on."

"Really?" Rose asks dubiously and eyes the cuffs like they're venomous snakes. Charlie holds her hand out, and Aurora gives her one. "Wait, you're really going to do it?"

"Why not," Charlie says. Her teacher says to do something, so she'll do it? She doesn't get the fuss, either. It's just a nullifier. She slaps it on her wrist and four needles jam into her skin, and she gasps.

"That's why," Rose says, but she's not smug about it, only concerned for Charlie.

"The needles pump a special sedative into your system," Aurora explains. "It won't knock you out, but it will slow the processes that are responsible for activating your marvels and render them ineffective. Even just one will do the trick, though both are used just in case. There are different classes of nullifiers for the higher classes of marvels too. But these will work on Class Three and below. Go ahead and try to use yours."

Charlie taps her pointer finger and thumb together to generate a small blast but nothing comes. She feels heavy, like she's just waking up from one hell of a nap. The normal rush of power to her fingers is completely absent, and it's disorienting enough to make Charlie's heart rate pick up.

"I don't like it," Charlie says, which is a huge understatement. Aurora laughs but not unkindly.

"No one likes it," she says and uses the flat key to unlock the cuff. It falls to the table, and Charlie massages her wrist. The needles are so thin that there's only a small speck of blood that wipes away easily. Aurora has each of them try on at least one nullifier so they know how it feels.

"It's important for many reasons, but the top two would have to be—you should never submit someone to something you aren't willing to do yourself. Within reason, of course. And the fact that some rogues have been known to fashion nullifiers into weapons, and if you don't know what it feels like, you may not know what it is and get yourself, and possibly others, into danger."

"I'll also be developing your gym uniforms to account for your marvels," Aurora says. "If you have any special requests you can submit them to me directly but no designs, everything will be in Titan Academy colors as they are still uniforms, but we want to help you develop a taste for what will or won't be useful for you later on when you're designing your pro suits."

Charlie thinks about all the suits she's designed over the years and how different they all are. Most of them are pink and all of them show a lot of skin because that's how Charlie activates her marvel. If she's covered from head to toe, she's going to be wasting precious seconds fumbling with baggy clothes. She wonders how much she'll be able to get away with as her uniform.

"Any questions?" Aurora asks them. Charlie listens closely because she doesn't have any questions, but that doesn't mean someone else hasn't thought of something she hasn't, and she's determined to learn as much as possible as quickly as possible.

Honor pulls up the profiles for Jack's group when Charlie's group moves onto Aurora's station. Jack, an earth manipulation marvel. Tommy, void. Alex, self duplication. Ethan, glow. Malia, healing. Honor's already seen three of them up close, and she's pretty familiar with the other two so she doesn't think there will be any major surprises, just compiling data for Aurora.

"Hey, guys," she says as they walk up and wait for instructions. "How'd it go with Adrian? All good?" She gets the affirmative and explains the process to them. Jack will test his marvel against Leo's shields. Tommy will test his on the both of them. Alex and Ethan will max out their marvels. Malia is a little trickier. They'll need something to heal.

"Let me break your arm," Honor says to Leo.

"Absolutely not," he says, entirely flat and unsurprised.

"It's for the children," she says. Leo is unimpressed, but she catches the twitch of his lip that gives away his desire to smile.

"Then you do it."

"Fine. Give me a table top," she says. Leo creates a shield around table level for her. Honor's eyesight is better than the average human, and they've found that she can see more of the shield than everyone else but not as much as Leo can. So she can see the edge, glimmering under the stadium lights. She lifts her hand and brings it down over the edge, hard.

"What—?" Jack starts, shocked. Malia gasps, hands flying up to cover her mouth, and the others have similar reactions to the hard *snap* her wrist makes.

"*You just broke your hand!*" Ethan shouts, then shudders.

Honor bites down hard on a curse and presents her wrist to Malia, who is quick to reach out and take it, cradling it gently in a palm. A soft golden glow encases their hands as Malia activates her marvel, and Honor's wrist mends. It's cool and refreshing, like jumping in a pool on a hot summer's day, and not at all painful.

Honor remembers this feeling from the fight with Colson. When she had let him blast her into a crater in the street and it had *hurt*. Colson's Class One rank isn't overblown. He's powerful, powerful enough to fuck Honor up even with her Titan blood.

Honor had climbed out of that crater with a nasty burn in her side and more than one broken bone. She doesn't remember the physical pain, only the raw emotional pain because if she kept taking hits like that Colson was going to get away from her *again.*

But then Malia, sweet, strong, brave, thirteen-year-old Malia broke away from the crowd of onlookers and got her hands on Honor before she could protest and send her back to her family. Honor felt her marvel wash over her then like she does now, warm and comforting and oddly refreshing like jumping out of a warm bed the morning of a field trip.

"Thanks, hero," Honor had said with as much of a smile as she could muster in that moment.

Honor flexes her wrist and tests the efficacy of her marvel. Her wrist is completely healed and there's no residual pain.

"How do you feel?" Honor asks her.

"Fine," Malia says with a shrug. As far as they know, there's no limit to Malia's marvel. But Honor knows better than anyone that just because the limit is so far off it seems invisible, doesn't mean it's not there at all.

"How do you activate your marvel?" Leo asks, taking up the tablet and inputting the answers in Aurora's system.

"I just, I touch someone and I think *better* and then they are," she says. She's starting to fold in on herself under the attention, which Honor finds odd. She wraps her arms around herself, hand sweeping up her bicep like she's cold, but it's peak summer months in Los Angeles, no one's cold.

"Have you ever experienced any adverse side effects to using your marvel?" Honor asks. Malia shakes her head. "Have others experienced any adverse side effects?" Malia looks surprised at the question then shakes her head. "So, as far as you know, there are no limitations to your marvel?"

"That's impossible," Jack interrupts, eyeing Malia.

Malia shrugs again. "Sometimes it just doesn't work. I don't know why, but those injuries were all pretty severe and the people didn't recover. It also doesn't work on sickness, only physical injuries."

Leo nods along as he inputs all the data.

"So maybe there's a point of severity that you can't overcome," he muses. "Maybe that point will change with training."

"That sounds like something for Aurora to figure out," Honor says with a cheeky grin because they both know that Honor is going to obsess over all twenty marvels of her students and try to figure out the best way to help them improve into the best heroes they can possibly be.

Next is Alex, who makes as many copies of herself as possible. She gets to three before she taps out. She details how she can see through any of their eyes if she wants to, but they're pretty independent, thinking and talking and acting like her. They're not very sturdy, though, and as soon as they meet their damage threshold, they suck back into her like she's a vacuum. Honor and Leo ask her the standard questions and find that she gets physically weaker when she makes a copy because that copy takes a fraction of her strength.

"I feel weird about punching a fifteen-year-old in the face," Honor says as she surveys one of the copies.

"We need to see it," Leo says, also sounding a little uneasy about it.

"I'll do it," Jack offers. Honor knows Jack's been trained by his father or his father's trainers or whatever, maybe even his mom. Gina looks like she can throw a mean haymaker. So she doesn't feel too awful about letting him do it, especially since she knows Alex feels any and all damage her copies take and anything Honor would dish out, even at her softest, would *hurt*.

Jack faces off against a copy and throws a right hook without hesitation. Copy Alex dodges. He looks over at Real Alex like *what the hell?*

"What, I'm supposed to just stand there and take a hit?" she asks. "Besides, that was all her. I can't move them."

Jack scowls at her but moves back into position.

This time he goes in like a real fight and not expecting to land a real hit. His form is picture perfect but stiff, and Honor is a little impressed. Alex, with absolutely no training, doesn't stand a chance. Honor watches the Real Alex flinch when Jack lands a punch to her copy's jaw. Said copy sucks back into her like Alex is the center of a blackhole and her copy is caught in the irresistible pull of her gravity.

They measure Ethan's glow radius by shutting off the lights on the floor and having him max out his marvel. He gets pretty bright, but Honor bets he can get even brighter. A marvel like his would be incredibly useful during search and rescues, which she knows Ethan wants to focus in. When the lights cut back on, his cheeks stay a faint yellow, and he looks to his classmates to see their reactions. Tommy smiles brightly at him, and Ethan seems to relax a bit, but it's clear to Honor that he feels at a disadvantage because of his marvel. Having a cool marvel isn't everything in this line of work, but it's hard for people to see past that single aspect, especially the kids who are just starting out. But Ethan has a great head on his shoulders and that will take him farther than he could imagine.

They have Tommy test out his void marvel on Ethan, Leo, and Honor in turn, three different classes of marvels to see the disparity between each. Tommy already knew that the duration of his marvel's effects is directly relative to the duration of contact he has with a person. They learn that that length varies depending on the class or strength of the marvel as well. Honor doesn't feel anything when Tommy first touches her. It's just a simple handshake. Tommy's skin is smooth and without callus, unlike Honor's. Then, she feels *nothing*. Which is different and worse.

Honor has never truly been without her marvel before. Nullifiers make it harder for her to use it but not impossible. Tommy's marvel cancels hers out *completely.*

She feels oddly disoriented, unable to contact Verity or Grace in her head. She also feels lighter, without her marvel, like a piece of her is missing and it was the piece that kept her anchored to the ground. But Tommy's marvel has a time limit and it wears off for Honor first.

When she snaps her fingers and throws a small trick, a hummingbird flies through the air. Her weight settles around her bones again. Her marvel is back. She heaves a sigh of relief. Her strength and speed are her own and were unaffected because those things come from her Titan blood, not her marvel. A fact she already knew after testing out the new Titan class of nullifiers for Aurora.

Leo *hates* it. His face is largely impassive, but Honor is close enough to see the way the muscle in his jaw jumps. His hands stay flexed, trying to summon a shield, and when he finally can, he represses his relief and puts on an impressive front that the experience didn't freak him out at all.

Ethan, on the other hand, yells the entire time.

"This is weird! This is WEIRD," he shouts and clenches so hard trying to activate his marvel that he looks constipated. Honor claps a hand on Tommy's shoulder because the kid looks a little stricken at Ethan's overreaction. She knows from Verity that Tommy's pretty insecure about his marvel.

"If I could temporarily void marvels, I wouldn't have 'PROPERTY RISK' stamped in my profile," she tells him, and he huffs a laugh.

"Do you really?" he asks.

"Sure do, the insurance department at Divine has a picture of my face taped to a dart board," she tells him. After the longest time yet, Ethan finally makes himself glow again, and he goes out like a light with a heavy sigh of relief.

"You're being dramatic," Jack tells him even though he had very obviously *not* volunteered to have his marvel voided.

Jack is last. Honor has seen his marvel firsthand too. When she had just arrived on the scene of a bank robbery, Jack was already there across the street. He'd put up four-foot-thick walls around the bank robbers, pulled up from the street. Crumbling asphalt had almost hit a civilian, but Honor was there to catch it. His ability to repair the ground with his marvel so it was as smooth and seamless as before was the only thing that kept him from getting slapped with a hefty fine for marvel use without a permit. That, and who his dad is, probably. He was only fourteen, but his raw power and marvel application was above par and Honor knew he'd received training but he was young, still is, and it shows.

He's overconfident, which is saying something because he has a lot to be confident about. But to overestimate his already-excellent abilities is a recipe for disaster that Honor knows all too well. She watches him tear up the stadium floor with movements that resemble a modified martial art with stiff and severe motions. Large muscles flexing and out of place on a still-developing body. He hurls rock after rock at Leo's shields, and Leo's single, raised eyebrow is impressed.

The way Jack manipulates the ground or any solid surface made out of rock is fluid. He prefers to be barefoot when using his marvel, claiming that it connects him better and allows him greater control. The whole stadium shakes with the force of it, of Jack's push and pull. Being able to change the landscape like this warrants a Class Three classification right out of the gate. Jack and Malia are the only two in the class with a rank that high, and Honor knows it's going to jump by the time the test rolls around.

Leo puts his strongest shield up first this time and Jack can't break it. It takes incredible force to break one of Leo's shields, and Honor's only aware of three other people who can do it at all. But Honor would put good money on him being able to break through by the end of the year.

Leo inputs the data from Jack's assessment and the kids move on to the next station with Aurora. While they wait to get the next group from Adrian, Honor thinks about Charlie's marvel and the raw power it emits. The warble of Leo's best shield under it would have been imperceptible to Charlie and her classmates, but Honor noticed. If Charlie had received the same training as Jack at a young age, she might've already been on par with the rooks at Divine. Maybe even the pros.

Jack and Charlie both, with their ridiculously powerful marvels paired with their matching determination and competitive spirits will pull ahead of the pack, Honor has no doubt.

8

"Titans Among Us? What We Know (And Don't Know)
About These Foreign Beings"
—*The Marvel Spectator*

Charlie fixes the collar on her blue polo shirt, pulling her matching Verity blue eye necklace out so it's visible while Leo powers up the board at the front of the classroom. Sitting in uniform, surrounded by classmates in a building that still smells new makes Charlie feel important. There are thousands of other people who wanted to sit in this seat. But here Charlie is.

"Your application essays were only one question: 'why do you want to be a hero?'," Leo says at the start of hero theory. "We read every essay thoroughly because while there is no one right answer, there are certainly wrong answers. Without the right motivations, this career is not sustainable for your body or mind and we want to make sure we're setting all of you up for success. That being said, I have another question for you."

He writes it on the board.

In a world where everyone has a superpower, what makes a hero?

Everyone writes the question down, but no one offers any answers. Charlie feels like she should say something, she should stand out, step up, but she doesn't know what the right answer is and she doesn't want to be wrong. Leo surveys the class.

"This is a discussion," he tells them. "If no one wants to speak, Aurora made a fun little app with all your names in it that will choose one of you for me." He queues the app up on the board and the first name there is a girl named Jayne, the girl with the black feather angel wings.

"Uh, pass," she says. Leo looks unamused, but Charlie raises her hand and saves them both.

"Someone who uses their strength to help those weaker than them." She takes a shot. It doesn't feel like *enough*, but it's a good place to start. Leo looks thankful for a brief second, and Charlie does an inner victory dance. She knew she was right to speak up.

It sparks a shy discussion since no one really knows anyone yet, but no one is surprised when Jack and Charlie get into it over the socioeconomic impact of the hero profession and whether or not taxpayers should pay for heroes because they're the ones being protected or if the government should take it out of the military budget. It's off-topic, but one that's much easier for Charlie to argue because she has a clear stance. She doesn't know how she would even begin to argue an answer to Leo's question. Every answer she thinks of seems wrong and right at the same time.

Leo eventually interrupts them when the class ends and assigns the same question as homework. They have to write an essay, due Friday. Charlie jots down her ideas on her tablet. But it's not until later after class that she really tries to dive into them.

They're in the dorms and Malia and Charlie are both sitting on the floor in front of the couch, working on homework. Rose and Luna are adding to the photo wall since Rose brought a fancy mini printer with her that lets her print photos from her phone straight away. It's a messy combination of the few memories they've made so far and a vision board. There's a picture of Charlie and Lochlan already up, but it's old, from the entrance exams. They have their numbers on the front of their shirts, and they're all sweaty but proud.

Someone had cut out the list of the current rankings. Gravitas is still squarely at the top followed by Honor and Verity. Someone else had taped up the Titan Academy logo in the center, and they've built out around that instead of the first few photos that were left for them by their teachers. Photos of said teachers from when *they* were in high school. Seeing visual proof that Honor and the others were once where they are right now makes it just a bit easier for Charlie to wrap her mind around.

Ethan is watching something on the television, and it's at a low enough volume that it doesn't distract Charlie from her essay. It's just a blank page so far, so Charlie decides to word vomit until she can figure out a decent answer.

"What makes a hero?" Charlie mutters aloud. Malia sighs next to her, also stumped.

"Every answer I come up with feels wrong," Malia says.

"I was *just* thinking the same thing," Charlie groans. She wonders if it's like the entrance essays, where there wasn't one right answer but there were plenty of wrong answers.

Someone who uses their strength to defend those weaker than themselves. Charlie's answer from earlier stares up at her from her tablet. She's going to run with it. Charlie may not be confident that she has the *best* answer, but she can argue the hell out of her point with the best of them.

Jack comes and sits in the big chair next to Malia. Charlie keeps staring at her tablet, determined to find the *right* answer. Searching the internet hadn't helped, and Charlie doesn't think she's allowed to ask Honor for the answer, either.

"Shouldn't you be a doctor or something?" Jack asks Malia and Charlie's head shoots up. Charlie narrows her eyes at him while Malia flushes pink. Charlie isn't sure if it's embarrassment or anger, though.

She can tell Jack's worked himself up for this. He's wringing his hands like a worried mother but the set of his shoulders scream—*I'm just saying*. Charlie already wants to hit him. He didn't hear Malia's dad yelling at her on move-in day, but Charlie had and she's not going to let her go it alone again.

"Mind your business, Boy Wonder," she snaps and hopes that will be the end of it.

"I'm just saying—" There it is "—that your marvel would be better suited to that kind of work. It's kind of selfish of you to not use it to the best of your ability. And! Doctors are heroes, too. In a way."

"I *want* to be a *professional hero*," Malia says through gritted teeth. Charlie abandons all thoughts of homework and leans back onto the couch, arm braced over the seat cushions casually but in a way she knows is intimidating because her siblings used to do it to her all the time. This was usually the moment she braced for a chase.

"Yeah, but does that mean you *should* be?" Jack fires back. Charlie glances at Malia. She can't imagine what it's like to not have your parents' full support, and Charlie knows she's not a substitute for a parent but she'll support the hell out of anyone she thinks might need it.

"We all want things but that doesn't mean we get them," says Jack.

"Who the hell are you to tell someone what they should and shouldn't be?" Charlie asks.

"I'm just saying—"

"*I'm* just saying," Charlie cuts him off, "that I don't think you should be such a raging dickhead, so it looks like we all lose today."

"Can you ever make an actual argument?" Jack asks, focused on Charlie now instead of Malia. "Or do you just resort to insulting people?"

"You want an actual argument?" Charlie pushes to her feet and steps over Malia. Jack rises out of the chair immediately so they're toe to toe.

"No matter what Malia does with her marvel, what *anyone* does with their marvel, there will always be people who say they're not doing the right thing. Because opinions are like assholes and everyone has shit to say. She could be the most world renowned doctor in the world tomorrow, probably, and there would still be loud assholes like you telling her that she should be somewhere less privileged, helping people somewhere else. Using her marvel how *they* deem acceptable without pausing to consider that she's an actual fucking person with her own thoughts and feelings and not just whatever superpower she was lucky enough to be born with."

"Oh, now *I'm* the loud asshole?" Jack asks, incredulous.

"I thought we were making arguments, but here you are focusing on the insults again," Charlie says.

"Guys," Tommy tries to interject. He's been working quietly with Cora at a table in the back, but now Charlie and Jack have captured the attention of the common room. Tommy's too hesitant, though, and Charlie isn't going to back down until Jack admits he's wrong and apologizes to Malia.

"No one asked for your opinion," Charlie goes on. "What? You think because you're some hot shot son of a hero you can say whatever you want and you'll automatically be right? Think again, Boy Wonder."

"God, you are *so* arrogant," Jack snaps and gets in her face. They're roughly the same height so he can't tower over her like he probably does everyone else he tries to intimidate.

"*I'm* arrogant?" she asks, and it's her turn to be incredulous.

"Yes, you walk around this school like you own it when you've only been here a week like the rest of us!"

"At least I don't tell people what they should or shouldn't do with their lives and try to fucking guilt trip them like some sort of holier than thou, all knowing, douche bag!"

"That's exactly what you're doing right now!"

"Because you came at my friend *unprovoked*," she snaps. "If you could just mind your fucking business like I said, we wouldn't have a goddamn problem."

"No one was even talking to you in the first place so it sounds like you're the one who should be minding your business," he snaps back.

"You come for my friend, you make it my business," she jabs a finger into his chest. "So if you don't want to deal with me, do us all a favor, and stay the fuck away from my friends!"

He smacks her hand away and it *stings* and that's it.

Jack looks shocked when she lands her first hit, like he didn't expect her to actually do it, but he recovers quickly enough and hits Charlie back, throwing a right hook she's too slow to dodge. She feels the capillaries burst under her skin and her eye immediately begins to swell, but he's close enough that she only needs one eye to aim for his throat.

It's obvious Jack has had real combat training. He even puts his hands up by his face in proper form or whatever, but Charlie grew up being the youngest of five kids, so she knows how to scrap. They scuffle around the room and slam into the table, knocking over all of the homework papers and books that had been on it, and the people who had been sitting at it scramble to get away.

They roll around on the floor, and Jack makes a frustrated noise when Charlie proves hard to pin. He still manages to grab one of her wrists and twist it around her back, pushing her face first into the floor. His mistake. Charlie taps her forefinger and thumb together and the force sends him up into the ceiling. It doesn't even dent, a testament to the sturdiness of the building, built to house hundreds of teenagers with powerful marvels. Jack's nose was not built the same way and it cracks under the force of Charlie's marvel, blood spewing down the cupid's bow of the lips he got from his mom.

Charlie rolls out of the way when he comes back down, but before she can get her hands back on him, Tommy grabs her arm and pulls her back. She feels it the moment he activates his own marvel to void hers. It washes over her like a cool wave and then she's just—empty.

She fucking hates it.

She rips her arm from Tommy's grasp. Jack sits up slowly, still recovering his breath, and glares at Charlie, who glares just as fiercely back. She can feel her face pulsing in what's going to be quite the shiner, but Jack's lip is swollen and split open so at least she's not alone.

"Are you two done?"

Leo's voice has them all whipping around. He stands just inside the common room, the door to the stairwell still open. He looks over all of them, expression still blank, but Charlie can still feel the disappointment coming off of him in waves. Hot shame creeps up her neck, but she won't take it back. She'd even do it again.

She briefly considers trying to make her case, but she's been in enough fights to know that adults don't ever care who started what or why. All they care about is the behavior they see. She sighs as she resigns herself to her fate, propping her elbows up on her knees. Leo gives her an odd look she can't decipher before his gaze flickers to Jack and then back.

"Detention, both of you, Monday morning before homeroom," he says.

"I didn't even use my marvel!" Jack says, trying to get out of it.

"You hit me first!" Charlie fires back.

"Tell it to Honor tomorrow," he sighs. Then he turns and walks out.

They both go still at that. It's one thing to have Leo catch them acting like this, but with the competition for Honor's favor already so fierce, neither of them can afford to lose face. From what Charlie knows about Honor, too, she's not one of those people that will just say no fighting no matter what. Charlie knows from rumors that Honor used to pick fights all the time, so she can't even imagine what Honor would have to say about fighting now.

Malia offers a hand to Charlie to pull her to her feet and at the same time, activates her marvel so the throbbing in Charlie's face abates. She prods at it with careful fingers and finds it's not tender at all. She grins at Malia who returns it.

"Thanks," she says.

What makes a hero?

Charlie feels right. She feels vindicated. She doesn't feel sorry for defending her friend or for fighting Jack. But she doesn't feel like a hero, either. Charlie realizes, for the first time, that all of her life she had equated this feeling of *victory* with *heroism*. And they're not the same.

They're not the same at all.

9

"Does Honor de Mora Think She's Above the Law?"
—*Titan Source*

"**P**artner punishment?" Charlie repeats what Honor had just told her. Honor had pulled them both aside before they all leave campus to go to the annual safety seminar. It's mandatory for all hero schools in the district and no one can use their marvel in training until they've completed it.

"Yup," Honor says. "You two will sit next to each other on the bus, at the seminar, and at lunch," she tells them. "Just for today. If this happens again, though, I'll move your class seating arrangement permanently until you two learn to get along."

"Christ," Jack mutters under his breath. Charlie clenches her jaw and resists the urge to snap at him. That would only make this whole thing worse.

Charlie and her classmates all pile onto the bus first thing in the morning. It's the first time they're seeing the bus, and it isn't the average, run-of-the-mill yellow school bus. Which, Charlie supposes, she really should have seen coming. It's a fully-customized luxury travel bus, all black with neon pink lettering on the side that reads TITAN ACADEMY on the side in a diagonal slant. The academy logo is on the door and on the back.

The windows are fully tinted so they can't see inside until they load on. There are individual double seats on either side of the aisle with plenty of legroom and a seat back pocket in front of each one. There are even cupholders in the armrests. The seats themselves are a nice, supple leather that Charlie runs her fingers over while she starts down the aisle toward the back of the bus.

"I want to sit at the front of the bus," Jack says from behind her. She rolls her eyes and turns around.

"And I want to sit in the back," she says. "So, what? We compromise or some shit? Sit in the middle?"

"I *have* to sit in the front," he amends. "I get motion sick."

"Oh, for the love of—fine." She pokes and prods him back to the very front of the bus where they sit in the second row with Jack closest to the window. "If you throw up on me, I will break your nose again."

"Then we'll just be stuck with each other even longer," he grumbles and searches for a seatbelt because he's somehow the biggest nerd and her biggest competition at the same time.

"Then don't throw up on me," she returns and settles into her seat. Lochlan, her best friend in the whole wide world, sits across the aisle from her because he loves her. Charlie puts her back to Jack to talk to him and Luna on the way there while Jack closes his eyes and presumably does his best not to vomit on Charlie.

They get to the convention center and check in. It's really not much out of the ordinary, save for the few obvious anamorphic marvels. Charlie thought Rock Buddy or Jayne would stand out the most, and she was kind of right, Rock Buddy stands head and shoulders above everyone and people don't bother to hide their stares. But there's also a fucking raptor? Charlie isn't sure if it's a pet raptor or if the raptor is a person or creation like Rock Buddy, but Charlie thinks they should all, collectively, be a bit more concerned that dinosaurs are once again roaming the earth.

They pass by one of the classes from Marvelous, in their gray blazers with the white piping, and Charlie tries to see if she can get a glimpse of Noah. Instead, the teacher catches her eye, a shorter, slender woman with ethereal hair, bright red and flowing like the magma she can control. *Magmaid.*

Charlie and half of her classmates watch with dropped jaws as Magmaid walks straight up to Verity with sultry familiarity. Jayne fans herself with a black feathered wing and Charlie has to agree. Magmaid is *hot* in every sense of the word. She gets up on her toes to say something in Verity's ear, and Verity still has to lean down a bit to hear her properly.

The smile that blooms on Verity's face makes Charlie break out in a sweat.

"Aren't teachers supposed to be... less hot?" Malia asks in a whisper. "This seems criminal."

Charlie agrees with a distracted nod because Magmaid is extracting herself from Verity's personal space and backing away with a grin. Verity watches her walk backwards until she turns around then watches some more. Honor punches her arm.

"What do you *do* to these women?" Honor asks her.

"There are children present," Leo reminds them.

"I would also like to know," Charlie says before she can think it through. "For... science." Lochlan snorts from somewhere behind her, and she makes a mental note to hit him later.

"She was asking about a joint training," Verity says.

Absolutely no one believes her, but they all let it go anyway. Malia is right, it should be a crime to have teachers this hot. Like, Charlie already knew that Honor and Verity are hot, even Leo, despite how tired he looks all the time. She's pretty sure Honor was half of her sexual awakening, but to see them flirting in action? Even action as tame as whatever the hell that just was? Life changing.

There's a gasp then some rushed murmuring, and Charlie turns to see what the new commotion is. A trio of students in red, white, and blue Broadly uniforms shuffle up to Ethan. His cheeks glow bright when he realizes they're asking for a photo because they recognize him from his channel. He stutters out a hello and throws up a peace sign as they crowd around him for the photo. The small interaction attracts some big attention and then someone shouts the name of Ethan's channel. Suddenly, more people are crowding around him.

Another, less hot, woman comes up to them as Honor, Verity, and Leo are herding them all into the theater. She looks severe from her sleek bun to her pencil skirt to her practical, but still-sharp heels.

"Honor, Verity, would you mind coming with me for a moment please?" she asks. Honor exchanges a look with Verity and Leo.

"Take the kids in," Honor says to Leo. "We'll be right behind you."

Charlie takes it upon herself to grab Ethan by the back of his uniform collar and pull him along with the rest of their class toward the auditorium. She slings an arm around his shoulders that sag with relief.

"You should really start charging for photos," she tells him, and he huffs a laugh.

"My channel is monetized," he replies.

"Good man," she says with a grin as they walk through the doors.

Honor and Verity go to a meeting room in the convention center, already set up with two long rectangular tables side by side into one big table. Several school board officials fill the seats and a sense of impending doom washes over Honor. These are the same people that she had to petition to open her school minus a few key players that had allowed her to do it at all, like the governor and the secretary of education.

Honor and Verity take their seats next to Spectra, who is still headmistress of Marvelous. Her sleek silver hair is pulled into an elegant updo and she wears her trademark white suit when she's not in uniform. On their other side is Charlie's mom, Leanne, who is an elected school board official. She had been one of Honor's most vocal supporters even before her daughter was accepted into Titan Academy. Charlie looks a lot like her mom in height and stature, but she obviously gets her hair from her dad, unless Leanne dyes it that deep red color.

Honor waits for someone to speak. They're obviously waiting for her to ask what's going on. Verity kicks her feet up on the table and settles in.

"Miss de Mora," Rafferty starts. Verity gags. Rafferty is the superintendent of hero schools in their district and their most vocal opposition. His bushy mustache hides his lack of upper lip but his smile is still smarmy.

"Just Honor is fine," Honor says with a forced smile.

"Honor, then," he says. "It's come to our attention that you do not plan on enrolling your students in the end of the year tournament."

Honor says nothing because there's no question to answer and what he said is true.

"We are afraid we must insist that you enter."

"Insist all you like," Honor says. "That tournament fosters a toxic, competitive environment in-house, and I don't want my kids to fester in that."

"There's nothing wrong with competition," Rafferty says.

"You're absolutely right," Honor agrees, and he looks surprised like they always do when Honor agrees with them. "But there is a difference between friendly competition and whatever the hell goes on at Marvelous."

"Excuse me?" Oculus asks. As a tenured teacher at Marvelous, of course he'd be offended, but Honor isn't wrong.

"I went to Marvelous," she reminds him. "I know what it's like. How much pressure comes from that stupid tournament and the pressure to win it. It divides the students who will eventually have to work together as pros, but instead of encouraging them to work together, it's divisive as each student is coached into being the best individually and not together. And for what? There's no prize, no real worth to the tournament other than being able to say that you won it."

"As someone who also went to Marvelous *and* won that tournament three years in a row, which is still the record for consecutive wins by a single class, I believe, I concur," says Verity.

"The tournament allows us to assess the students," Rafferty goes on.

"I plan to assess my students, in house," Honor says.

"Unfortunately, the tournament has already been declared mandatory."

"Mandatory," she repeats. She glances at Spectra next to her and the grim set to her mouth tells her that she knew about this, but not for very long. "Since when?"

"Irrelevant," he says with a dismissive wave of his hand, "What matters now—"

"I'd appreciate it if you'd answer my question, Mr. Rafferty," Honor says coldly. He pauses, and Verity snorts quietly.

"Oh, he's nervous now," she says, just loud enough for Honor to hear.

"It must have been recently," Honor goes on. "Because for the past year and a half, I've been building my school and it hasn't been brought to my attention once. Not before, during, or after our accreditation, nor our entrance exams, nor the full week of school we've been in session. So tell me, Mr. Rafferty, when did the tournament become mandatory?"

Honor is well aware that from the outside, it looks like Titan Academy just sprouted out of the ground, ready and raring to go. But she decimated her savings, used all of their mom's life insurance with support from her sisters, and secured multi-million dollar brand deals just to pour one hundred percent of those earnings into her academy. She'd had little outside support because she didn't want anyone else sticking their greedy fingers into her business and claiming her success or her kids' success as their own. She had to petition the school board multiple times, and she has the personal cell phone number of the secretary of education because each step had been a battle fought and won. It seems today is another battle, and Honor doesn't feel so confident about winning this one.

"This morning," says Spectra. "The vote was ten to two."

Two dissenters. Spectra and Leanne, if Honor had to put money on it.

"Unless, of course, you would rather myself and two other board members as a part of your administration," Rafferty says.

"No," Honor says as firmly as she can without snapping. If she wants to make Titan Academy *different*, she has to keep it out of the clutches of people who are hell bent on keeping everything the same.

"Right, then, what matters now," Rafferty bulldozes on, "is that we have your school register for the tournament. Otherwise, I'm afraid we'll have to strip your school of accreditation. You, of course, may continue to teach, but your students will not be permitted internships or be allowed to take the license test without recommendation from two pros. One of whom must not be an employee of your institution."

"I'm aware," Honor says. This is stupid, *stupid*, but it isn't worth losing her cool over. So they'll do the tournament. It's really not a huge deal, and Honor will make sure that she and the other teachers take every precaution to guard against in-house hostilities to avoid recreating the atmosphere at Marvelous. It helps that they only have one class, so they'll all have to work together anyway.

Then, Rafferty adds, "It's also stated that new schools must come in first place."

First place.

Out of eight schools, approximately eighty classes, with an average of thirty students per class. Marvelous is notorious for stacking their classes in favor of winning the tournament, and they usually secure two out of the top three spots with Broadly and Providence battling it out for the other.

Sometimes an underdog will slip in there, but it's incredibly rare, and now Honor's kids have to win their first year?

"You're fucking kidding," Verity says.

"You won it three years in a row," Rafferty throws it back at them, "which is still the record, I've heard. I don't see why you wouldn't be able to train your kids to do the same."

"It should be a top three finish at *most*," Leanne protests, and by the frustration in her voice, Honor can tell it isn't the first time she's said it. "If a school has to win this tournament in their first year, we'll never have any new schools which will almost certainly stunt progress. Not to mention all of the money wasted from having schools in session for a single year as well as displacing students so frequently that it will never give them time to settle into a routine learning environment which will almost definitely have a negative effect on their education. Which, I feel inclined to remind everyone here, is our main goal. To educate these students in the best way possible."

"I agree," says Rafferty. "Which is why the tournament is necessary. So the students can be evaluated by outside, qualified educators and to ensure that any new schools are up to snuff. We can't have just anyone opening up a hero school because they have the money and means." He says the last part with a pointed look at Honor.

"Just to be clear," Verity says and drops her feet from the table to lean forward, "because I've never been very good with veiled insults, when you say 'just anyone' you meant us?"

"No," he backtracks quickly. Verity squints while she tracks the lie in his aura. "I'm just thinking about the precedent it might set for others with similar means."

"You mean like another top ten hero opening up a school?" Verity asks. "Because I don't think *just anyone* is going to look at the number two and three heroes do something and think, 'Oh, I should do that too, just for shits and giggles.'"

She's just doing it to be a dick, Honor knows. They're not going to change the outcome of this meeting, not when it had already been decided before they even got there. But if Verity wants to push some buttons, Honor's not going to stop her.

"I, for one, think it would be a brilliant idea for more pros to open up schools," Honor adds on because she's pissed and there's not much else she can do either. "All the theory in the world will never compare to the real thing, and pros are in the best position to teach the next generation of heroes. Having someone teach something they've never actually had to do seems a little—what's the word?"

"Stupid, idiotic, ill-informed, unwise, illogical, a recipe for disaster," Verity supplies.

"Sure, one of those," Honor says with a shrug.

"Regardless," Rafferty says, irate now even though he's technically won this round. "The rule stands for this school year. If the rule needs to change, it will be done so for the future."

"I would once again like to make it known," Spectra continues, "that in the past decade, three other schools have opened up in our district and not one of those has had to jump through the hoops that have been set forth for Titan Academy."

"Titan Academy is the first *private* hero institution in Los Angeles. They have full control over their curriculum and enrollment and other processes, but when it comes to evaluating the heroes of tomorrow, we cannot afford to take any risks, and they must be evaluated with their peers."

"Noted," Honor says. "Is that all?"

"Yes," he says.

She gets up and walks out without a word, Verity right behind her.

They stop in a quiet hallway where they can hear the beginnings of the seminar in the auditorium, but no one else can hear them. Honor puts her hands on her head and breathes, deep and even.

"I'm very proud of us," Verity says. Honor just looks at her. "Back in the day we would have handled that much worse."

"I don't think we handled it *well*," Honor says.

"I think we did. All things considered, we were just fucking ambushed and no hands were thrown. That's a win."

"I can't believe we have to *win* the tournament."

"We've done it before," Verity says with a shrug.

"That was different and you know it. This stupid tournament is the root of that fucking superiority complex that Marvelous has and breeds. We can't let that happen to our kids."

"We won't," Verity says, like it's simple.

"Verity, what if we *lose*?" Honor asks. Everything Honor has worked toward building for the past two years, the future she had envisioned, turned to dust just like that.

Verity says it again, still simple, but with more steel. "We won't."

Back in the auditorium, Charlie settles into the seat next to Jack by virtue of their punishment, with Lochlan on her other side. Thankfully, it's over after today. She sits down before she realizes who's behind them. Lochlan nudges her and she turns her head to see—Noah!

Charlie's face breaks out into a smile, happy to see her friend from middle school, but then one of the Marvelous kids sitting next to Noah jabs his finger into Noah' side. Noah flinches and kid snickers.

"What do you even do? You haven't talked about your marvel once," he says, and Charlie's brow raises.

"Oh jeez," she hears Lochlan mutter under his breath. She ignores him.

"How did you even get into Marvelous? Today after this stupid seminar I wanna see what you can do," the asshole continues.

Charlie wants to let Noah handle this. She really does. They don't go to the same school anymore and she can't protect him so he *needs* to but his meek, "I don't have to prove anything to you," isn't going to cut it. It's true, but there's no confidence behind it, and the guy just laughs at him.

"Hey *asshole,*" Charlie snaps and turns around in her seat. She gets up on her knees for better leverage and jams her finger into the chest of the guy sitting behind her. He looks mildly surprised and outrageously offended at the same time. "Who the fuck do you think you are?"

"Who the fuck are *you?*" he bites back.

"Charlie Whittaker, pleasure to meet you," she sneers. "Aren't you in the hero course? What kind of hero bullies people? Never heard of a hero picking fights with unsuspecting classmates."

"You pick fights all the time," Jack points out. Unhelpful. The rows around them are paying attention now because Charlie is *loud*, never bothered to learn how to be quiet.

"I pick fights with *you*, Boy Wonder," she snaps before turning back around. "Picking fights with people who don't fight back makes you a piece of shit. If you want to be a hero, then you have to fucking act like it."

The guy opens his mouth to respond but next to him, Noah peeps out a small, "Hi, Charlie."

"Hi, Noah," she says with a genuine smile before returning to glare at the guy.

Noah, of course, can fight back. But despite Noah's unerring drive to become a hero, he doesn't like to fight if he can avoid it. Enter Charlie.

"You know this bi—"

He gets cut off by Charlie's fist. Well, the threat of it. She pulls it back, fully prepared to break his pretty nose, when an arm wraps around her waist and lifts her clear off her seat.

"The seminar hasn't even started yet," Leo sighs from behind her.

"Well, yeah, I wouldn't *interrupt* the seminar," she says, still glaring at the asshole. Leo sets her down on her feet, and she straightens out her uniform.

"All that shit about picking fights and you take a swing at me?" the guy sneers at her.

"You want me to believe you can't fight back?" she challenges.

His face colors and his fists clench, but then one of his teachers comes down the aisle and that's enough for him to slump back in his seat.

"Hey, Leo," the Marvelous teacher greets. Charlie recognizes him. He's another pro because Marvelous also has a reputation for getting some of the best to teach their kids too. They don't have *Honor,* but if Charlie remembers correctly, this guy is ranked like fifteenth overall in the country, which isn't too bad.

She doesn't remember his name but she remembers his marvel; the ability to convert the negative feelings or emotions or whatever of others and turn it into energy that he can use offensively. She wonders how much he could pull from the pair of them right now. Probably enough to nuke the entire seminar.

"Khalid," Leo replies.

"What's going on?"

"Looks like our kids were just getting acquainted," Leo drawls. Khalid looks resigned, not surprised and he sends the asshole a withering look.

"Beck? What happened?" he asks.

"She's crazy, she just attacked me out of nowhere," he says.

"I wouldn't say nowhere," Jack says because he can never mind his own business.

Khalid glances at him. Then does a double take when he recognizes him. Boy Wonder really does look just like his dad which is a shame because his mom is way hotter.

"Glad to see that Marvelous is keeping up the tradition of graduating assholes into *super* assholes," Charlie spits. The whole Marvelous row bristles at that, which makes the Titan Academy row start to tense up.

"Hey now, I went to Marvelous," Leo points out.

"This guy was being shitty to my friend," she says, "and not a single one of their classmates was going to say shit, so I did."

Khalid looks his row up and down and by the way everyone avoids his gaze, he seems to take her word for it. He sighs.

"Beck, we talked about this," he says.

"I didn't actually do anything!"

"Because Charlie didn't give you the chance," Jack says. Charlie's known Jack for exactly seven days, but that's more than enough to know that if there's anything *heroic* about a situation, Jack will want to insert himself. He might not have cared about actually stepping in, but now that Charlie is getting noticed for it, he wanted a piece of it.

But he's not wrong.

"Nobody asked you," Beck snaps at him. Leo and Khalid sigh in tandem this time.

"Apologize to Noah," Charlie snaps. Khalid looks at her, surprised. Beck glowers at her. "I said *apologize*, asshole!"

"Or what?" he snaps.

Leo mutters something under his breath and then turns Charlie by her shoulder and pushes her further down the aisle, toward his own seat.

"Make sure he apologizes," she snaps at Jack on her way past because as much as she loves Lochlan, he's not built for confrontation like Boy Wonder. Jack sits up a little straighter and half turns in his seat, expectant. Charlie lets herself be pushed to the end of the aisle where Cora has to move down a seat to make room for Charlie to sit next to Leo.

She sits down and cranes her head to glare down the aisle where Khalid is still talking to Beck, but she can't hear what's being said.

"Charlie," Leo draws her attention back to him. "I know your heart is in the right place, but that's not how you handle that situation."

"Yeah, yeah, I'm supposed to tell an *adult* or whatever," she says and slumps down in her seat, crossing her arms over her chest. "Not that *that* ever does any good."

Leo looks at her, quiet and expectant in that heavy way he does when he's waiting for them to be quiet in class. Only this time he's waiting for her to speak.

"When we were little, Noah, Lochlan, and I went to the same elementary and middle schools," she says. "They were bullied and I wasn't but I wasn't their friend, either, so I minded my business, told a teacher and thought that would be it. But then Lochlan came back from lunch with a black eye. The teacher didn't do *shit*. So I did and it worked. People stopped bothering them because they knew that if they wanted to pick a fight, then it would have to be with me, and I don't lose a fight."

Didn't, her brain supplies helpfully. She didn't lose fights back then, but since she'd seen her competition at the Academy? She's less sure.

"Standing up for your friends was brave," Leo commends. "Doesn't mean it was right. You saved Noah and Lochlan from being bullied, but do you think you changed those kids for the better? Do you think they decided to stop acting that way because they were scared of a fight? Or do you think they grew even more resentful and took it out on other people in other places?"

The lights dim as the seminar begins, and Charlie's blood goes cold. She wraps her arms tighter around herself and watches Leo get comfortable in his seat like he's going to take a nap, legs stretched out in front of him and crossed at the ankle and hands folded neatly on his stomach.

"You're a lot like Honor used to be," he says, and it warms her up a bit because of course she wants to be like her favorite hero, but Leo doesn't say it like it's a compliment.

She doesn't get to ask why before he says, "Wake me up when they play the infomercial video."

"Infomercial?" she echoes, confused.

"You'll know it when you see it," he says.

But Charlie doesn't see it. She's too far in her own head, turning Leo's words over every which way. How can someone be brave *and* wrong? Only heroes are ever painted as brave, she's never heard anyone refer to a rogue as brave. But of course, Leo wasn't trying to imply she's a rogue. Right? Right. There's no way. They wouldn't have accepted her into their hero academy if they thought she was a rogue. She'd probably just be put on some sort of watch list or whatever.

Then why did he say it at all? Charlie was convinced up until five minutes ago that she had been doing the right thing all those years. She was defending her friends! She was even praised for it, lauded as a good friend, a future hero. She was defending people who couldn't defend themselves, and that's what heroes do, what Honor has always done, so she fails to see how she could have possibly done the wrong thing. But Leo had said it. *That doesn't mean it was right.* And if it wasn't right it must have been wrong.

It hadn't felt wrong at the time and it doesn't feel wrong now, not really, but Leo's words leave a sour taste in her mouth. She glances over her shoulder and down the row. The kid that had bullied Noah is now seated on the far other end of the row, next to Khalid. Noah catches her looking and gives her a small smile then does the sign language for *thank you*. Charlie winks back.

It *can't* have been wrong.

Why is it Charlie's job to change those bullies for the better? It's a hero's job to *save* people. That's it and that's what she did. She refuses to feel badly for it.

PART TWO

JOY

10

Charlie stands with her classmates in front of the Titan Arena. It's a Friday night so they technically shouldn't be in class, but Honor said it was training, so here they are at eight o'clock sharp, awaiting instruction. She's aware of Jack looking at her every so often, and she wonders if he's going to pick another fight. Not that he really picked the last one, but that's semantics. Charlie will throw hands any time, any place. Detention doesn't deter her.

Anthony's over-gelled hair glints when he nudges Jack, who rolls his eyes.

"Hey," he says, clearly to Charlie.

She considers ignoring him but ends up snapping, "What?"

"Jesus," he mutters. Then, "Look. We fought and you—I was an asshole. To you," he says, turning to Malia, who's inserted herself into the half circle they've formed at the base of Honor's statue. "So. I'm sorry. Can we not…"

"What Jack means to say is that it's very tense for the rest of us when mom and dad fight," Anthony supplies helpfully.

"*What?*" Charlie and Jack cry.

"What?" Anthony asks while Charlie and Jack eye each other like they each carry a highly infectious disease. "Let's face it. If there were class elections. It'd be between you two for president."

"Bold of you to assume we wouldn't vote for Tommy," Malia says dryly, and Charlie would almost agree with her if she didn't like the way President Charlie sounded so much.

"It's only been a week, how would anyone know who to vote for, really?" Lochlan asks, and Charlie turns to him, betrayed.

"We've been best friends for how many years? And you're telling me you wouldn't vote for me for Class President?" she asks with a hand over her heart.

"You're annoying," Lochlan tells her flatly. It's a good thing she loves him.

"I think it'd be cool if you guys were like co-presidents," Anthony chirps.

"Ugh," Charlie grimaces. Then says to Jack, "We're cool but only if you get him away from me."

"Done and done," he says and hauls Anthony off.

"You really wouldn't vote for me?" she asks Lochlan.

"I didn't say that," he says.

"You didn't say you *would* vote for me, either!"

"We don't even have a class president!"

"It's the *principle* of it, Garcia!"

"Bite me, Whittaker! I'm voting for *myself!*"

Charlie starts laughing then, because her and Lochlan's mini stand-offs always end in laughter, and Lochlan grins along with her. She's not actually pressed about it, but it's always fun to give Lochlan shit. Malia gasps next to them.

"That wasn't a real fight? It sounded like a real fight!" she says, sounding on the verge of distressed.

"No," Lochlan promises. "It's not a real fight unless Charlie throws a punch."

"Like with Jack," Malia says, getting it.

"*That* was a real fight," Charlie agrees.

Their teachers finally come out of the arena. Verity guffaws at something Rae says and shoves Leo so it's safe to say it was at his expense. Rae, AKA Voltage, is a really low-key hero and teacher. She can manipulate electricity and store it in her body. She once powered a whole hospital by herself during a blackout.

Even Leo is out of his usual suit, looking completely different in dark jeans and what Charlie knows is an expensive shirt from the collaboration Honor did with a luxury brand a few years ago. Honor herself is wearing one of the Titan Academy hoodies with the sleeves pushed up. Charlie *wishes* she looked that cool in just a sweatshirt.

All of their teachers are present for this one, a rare sight, Charlie's sure. Honor, Verity, Leo, Teddy, Rae, Aurora, and Adrian. Adrian, AKA Remedy, has a head full of ginger curls and looks like he'd be more suited to teaching kindergarten in the loud prints and colors he likes to wear.

They look like something out of a movie montage, dressed in casual clothes but radiating power even as they laugh and joke with one another while they wait for stragglers

"Are we all here?" Honor asks. When she receives the affirmative, she goes on. "Before we get to the exercise, I have an announcement to make," she says, voice going tight the way it does in interviews when someone asks a rude question. Charlie would say she's hearing things, but she's watched every single one of Honor's interviews. She knows what she sounds like when she's pissed and trying to hide it. This announcement can't be good.

"I know we already told you guys that we weren't going to enter into the end of the year tournament, but some things have changed and we have officially entered."

This is *great* news, Charlie thinks and starts pushing Lochlan. He moves away and comes back easily, used to Charlie's affectionate abuse. They're going to get to kick those Marvelous kids' asses. Sure, they're only one class, but that means all of their power hitters are in one place! Those other schools don't stand a chance.

Charlie watches that tournament every year with her family. They have their favorites from every school that they root for every year like it's a professional sports league. A three day event, one day for each grade level that competes. The older grades don't compete because they have internships, but sometimes Charlie will keep tabs on her favorites until they become pros. She's always imagined herself in the tournament; what she would do in a certain situation or how she would beat a specific opponent. Her and her siblings will argue about it for days after the tournament is over, and now she's actually going to be *in it*. She's already so busy envisioning what it will be like to stand on the podium, that she completely forgets the astute observation she made about Honor just a minute ago.

"It's search and rescue sims for first years, right?" Ethan asks.

"Yes," Honor says. "We'll be sending the information out to your parents this weekend, and Leo will go over more with you guys Monday in homeroom. But now let's get started with tonight's real event."

A scavenger hunt.

"Well," she amends. "Sort of a scavenger hunt. It's important for pros to know their districts inside and out.

All the turns, the nooks, and the speed bumps. You never know what might come in handy or what might get in your way so you want to eliminate as much of that guesswork as possible. Tonight, you'll be divided into teams and dropped off at different locations throughout the Titan District. Your mission is just to get back to campus. You may not use your phones except in the case of emergency. You must go on foot. You may ask locals for directions and maybe even get to know them a bit. First team back here wins."

Each team would be traveling with a teacher to a random location at the edge of the district and would be keeping an eye on them from a distance. A little creepy, in Charlie's opinion. Is stalking a part of hero training? Maybe a part of stealth, Charlie supposes.

"This is our district," Honor says and splays her arms wide. She's so fucking cool. "And we do know it. We know it backwards and forwards, top to bottom. We know how to run through it and we know how to hide in it, so it's extra credit if you can find one of your teachers on your way back."

Charlie is teamed up with Lochlan, Rose, and Ethan. They're not allowed to use marvels in public spaces, not without a license, so they're neither at an advantage or disadvantage there. Ethan's smart, analytical, she knows that and she'll be able to use it. She and Lochlan grew up together in the Mountainside District which is above Emerald, nowhere near Titan and they're not overly familiar with the area yet. That's probably the point.

"I think we should stop and talk to people along the way," Charlie mutters to Lochlan while they're on their way to their location. Leo is their assigned teacher, and he sits in the front of an otherwise empty public bus. Charlie's low observation catches the attention of her other teammates, and Ethan and Rose lean across the aisle to hear better.

"It has to be more than just getting back to campus. Titan Way runs the length of the district. All you have to do is follow it. It's too easy."

"Honor did say the point is to get to know the District," says Ethan. "Maybe we're supposed to map out the area we're dropped off in?"

"She also said it's a competition so speed is important," Rose points out. "Would we even have time for something like that?"

"First one back is the winner," Lochlan agrees. "We want to win… Right?" He looks to Charlie for confirmation, and she nods firmly. Of course they want to win.

"She specifically mentioned talking to locals too," Ethan says. "Maybe that leads to some bonus points?"

"Almost definitely," Charlie agrees. "Not a problem at all."

"Speak for yourself," Lochlan says.

"We'll handle it," Rose says with an easy smile for Lochlan.

"Um," Ethan says.

"We, as in, me and Charlie," Rose clarifies for him. He sighs in relief. The bus comes to a stop and Leo stands at the front of the bus.

"This is our stop," he tells them and gets off.

They follow, and Charlie realizes she should have been paying more attention to the drive there because they're being dropped off at the border of the Titan and Pointe Districts. This is exactly where Charlie didn't want to be.

"Where are you guys from?" Charlie asks.

"Emerald," Rose answers, because of course she's from the luxury district.

"Titan, but over by Blue," Ethan answers, which is also not helpful because they're inland and nowhere near the ocean.

"They probably did this on purpose," Lochlan points out. "No one is going to be dropped off in an area they're already familiar with, what would be the point?"

"Well, shit," says Charlie, knowing Lochlan's right. They linger on a well-lit street corner near the bus shelter. There's a small bookstore that's closed and dark, a dive bar thumping with music and green light slipping under the door, and a coffee shop that's still open and lit with a few late night patrons.

"Come on," she says to her team and starts to cross the street to the coffee shop.

She hits a shield immediately. She swears and stumbles back a step, steadied by Lochlan while she rubs her nose.

"Not yet," Leo says. "We have to wait until everyone's in position."

"Okay, so here's the plan," she says to her team. "We're going to get as many names as possible on our way back to campus, stay along the main road, and walk *fast.*"

"How do we even know which way to go?" Rose asks.

"Well," Charlie says, doing her absolute best not to sound like an asshole, "the bus came from that direction, so I think that's a pretty good place to start."

Maybe she didn't do such a great job at that, but Rose doesn't seem to take offense.

"You're good to go," Leo says. "Don't do anything stupid."

"I resent that implication," Charlie says as she turns to face him.

But he's not there.

"Holy shit," Ethan breathes.

"Wait, what?" Lochlan looks around but their teacher is nowhere in sight. "People actually *do* that? He just disappeared!"

"Focus! We're losing time," Charlie shouts back at them, already halfway across the street. She barges into the coffee shop and puts on a big smile. "Hi! I'm Charlie, what's your name?"

"Uh, Ricky," the barista says, looking apprehensive. He looks to be about college age, eyeing Charlie and her team warily. "What can I get for you tonight?"

"Oh, nothing," Charlie says as Rose opens her mouth to order. She scowls at Charlie. "We were just looking for some directions. We're a little lost. Can you tell us where we are?"

"You're in Titan District," he says slowly, waiting for some sort of punchline. "Close to Crescent."

"Okay, cool, do you by chance know where the Titan Academy campus is?" she asks. His eyes go wide, and he does a slow rolling observation of all of them from head to toe. They're in street clothes, not uniform as per their instructions, and they look like quite the rat pack. What with Rose in her little slip dress and dripping in metal jewelry next to Ethan's ratty old t-shirt and jeans that are too big. Then there's Lochlan's unassuming jeans and hoodie and Charlie's loud oversized jacket hanging past her shorts with her combat boots.

"You're the Titan Academy kids?" he asks dubiously.

"Expecting something different?" Charlie challenges.

"No, no," he says quickly. "Just—uh, what was your question again?"

"We need directions back to campus," Charlie says, quickly growing impatient.

"Oh, yeah, sure, just make a left on Willow and you'll hit Titan Way in like three blocks," he says.

"Thanks!" Charlie beams and stuffs a twenty dollar bill in the tip jar.

"Wait, I want a cappuccino!" Rose says, but Charlie grabs her wrist and pulls her outside.

"No time," she says. "Ricky works at Oh My Coffee and he was wearing a Cal State sweatshirt, so let's just say he goes there."

"Works for me," Lochlan says with a shrug. They walk quickly down to the corner and turn left onto Willow Street. They look at their surroundings, trading observations of what's where, how many people are on the street on a Friday evening, what kind of cars are on the street, and what assumptions they can make based on all of that.

"We also need to find Leo," Charlie says when they finally make it back to Titan Way. It's a straight shot back to campus along this street, but it's also one of the busiest streets in the whole city. It's lined like a boardwalk with shops and apartment buildings with four car lanes, an express bus lane on either side, and pedestrian walkways wide enough that the four of them can walk side by side.

"Yeah, the dude disappeared from right in front of us, I don't think we're gonna find him," Lochlan says.

"We have to at least *try*," Rose says, craning her neck to look behind them. She nearly runs into another person, but Charlie grabs her arm and pulls her out of the way.

"At least we don't have Honor or Verity," says Ethan. "I bet they'd be *impossible* to find."

"I'm sure if Leo's close enough to listen, he's offended," Lochlan says. "His whole job is staying under the radar while Honor and Verity are the exact opposite."

"Oh, shit," Ethan ducks his head down and starts looking at rooftops. "Do you think he's close enough to listen?"

"Must be if he's keeping an eye on us," Rose whispers back, doing the same. Charlie looks around. There are plenty of people out, but half of them are drunk already, and Charlie doesn't really want to talk to any of them. By the scornful looks they're getting, no one really wants to talk to them, either.

Charlie is well aware of the fact that they're teenagers and they probably look like it, but she thinks it's a little much. There's a restaurant up ahead with a host stand outside on the patio. Charlie skips up to it, and the host looks up at her.

"Table for four?" the host asks, looking behind Charlie at the others.

"No, thank you," Charlie says. "I was just wondering if you guys were hiring?"

"What?" Lochlan asks. Charlie swings her heel back and kicks him in the shin.

"We're always accepting applications, you can apply online," she says, clearly bored now.

"Awesome, what was your name?"

"Alice," she drawls.

"Thanks!" Charlie says, and then they're off again. After that, Rose starts doing the same. The boys don't talk to many strangers, but that's okay, Charlie and Rose can handle it.

They're about halfway back with a dozen names in the bag already when Charlie spots none other than Jack Zelweger across the street. Anthony, Cecily, and Cora are on his team, and if they're going the same pace with Rock Buddy trailing behind them, then Charlie and her group aren't going fast enough.

She grabs Lochlan first and pulls him into a department store. Rose grabs Ethan when she sees what Charlie is doing, and they hide behind the mannequins in the front window to peer across the street.

"Shit," Charlie breathes. "We need to speed up."

"Why are we hiding?" Ethan whispers.

"Because if they see us, it'll become a foot race," Charlie explains. "They're not going to start rushing unless they know they have to."

"But we know," Rose adds. "So let's get going. There's a back door that you can use to get into the parking lot. Then it's only, like, five blocks back to campus. We can run, we have enough names, and there's no way we're gonna find Leo anyway."

Charlie looks around at the expensive department store they're in and how the employees eye them distrustfully and, yeah, that tracks that Rose has been here before. But Charlie isn't going to complain when it comes to great insider knowledge. She's also right, so they start walking as quickly as they can to not look suspicious down the aisle.

Then they hear the screams.

They're coming from the street and it's really not anything out of the ordinary. Charlie could open her window any day of the week and hear someone shouting, but these screams are different. They're not joy or surprise or even anger. They're screams of fear.

All four hero students stop in the middle of the store and look back out of the windows.

"We shouldn't—" Lochlan starts to say, but Charlie is already moving.

"We're going," she says and leaves no room for argument.

She bursts back out onto the sidewalk amidst chaos. People are screaming and running in so many directions that she can't tell where the real danger is. Someone bumps into Charlie, and she tries to steady them but a second before she puts her hand on him, he's gone. She startles and realizes that he's not gone, he's shrunk. She crouches down to look at him and finds him not only shrunk but a … doll? A soft fabric doll.

"Holy fuck," she breathes and straightens up. All over the block, people are getting turned into little plush dolls. What kind of marvel is this? What's their motivation? Charlie can't even guess at this point.

"What do we do?" Lochlan asks.

"I don't know," Charlie admits. That's when she makes eye contact with Jack across the street. "Fuck." But neither of them make a run for it. They have to find the rogue and fast before any more people get turned into dolls. Is it even reversible? Charlie sure as hell hopes so.

Then all at once, everyone stops moving. Not because they want to, but because they have nowhere to go. Someone runs full speed into the shield they can't see. Blood spurts from their nose and smears over it. Charlie reaches out and touches the shield in front of her. It's like a pristine window she can't see but can feel. Leo leisurely strolls down the street with his hands in his pockets.

Charlie watches him go, mouth open. Not only had he identified the rogue in the midst of all that chaos, he forcibly halted the chaos and panic by giving everyone on the block their own shield. Charlie will admit that she doesn't know a lot about Leo's marvel, or defensive marvels in general, but she knows that's fucking insane.

She hadn't really thought about Leo in comparison to Honor because no one really compares to Honor, but it makes sense that Honor's friends would also be the best of the best. She inspires people with her mere presence, elevates everyone who comes into contact with her. She's inspired Charlie to be better, stronger, faster, her whole life. Of course she could inspire her friends to be the same and Leo is no exception.

She had overlooked him before because he isn't as showy as Honor or even Gravitas. He doesn't have major brand deals or magazine spreads and for some reason Charlie had correlated those things in her head with expertise but now she can clearly see that that isn't the case at all.

He walks straight up to a specific person, the person responsible, probably. The rogue looks worse for wear, panic written clear across his cherry red face, clothes in disarray. Charlie wonders what happened to him, wonders if she'll ever get to find out. Then Rae is there, behind the man who is focused on Leo, and when Leo drops the shield, Rae slaps the nullifiers on one hand. He looks down at it in shock then raises his other one, no doubt to activate his marvel point blank in Rae's face, but she doesn't even flinch and the small burst of green light hits a shield.

Rae points a finger at him, like she does when she's scolding them in class for talking, except this time, a teal volt of electricity shoots out of her finger and shocks the rogue square in the forehead. He jumps, more surprised than anything which means it was probably just to momentarily stun him while she cuffs the other hand and that's when all of the shields on the street drop.

Charlie runs into the street to stand next to Leo and Rae. "That was," Ethan pants, catching up to her, "That was…"

Charlie understands the sentiment. She hadn't even kind of figured out what to do and Leo and Rae had it covered in seconds. Charlie can't even fully fathom the amount of skill and experience and sheer talent that would take. It's almost overwhelming. Is it even possible for her to achieve something like that?

"Is the scavenger hunt still on?" Jack asks, running into the street with his group. Sirens start to blare as police cars weave in and out of traffic to try and get to them.

"Why wouldn't it be?" Rae asks.

Charlie and Jack exchange a glance, and then they're all running.

Charlie and Jack get the jump and lead the pack, but Charlie can hear the others panting right behind them and the ridiculously loud sounds of Rock Buddy denting the pavement as he brings up the rear. Does the whole group have to make it back first? Just one person? It doesn't really matter at this point because Charlie will be damned if she loses to Jack.

But fuck if he isn't fast as hell. He runs so efficiently too. She can see his perfect posture out of the corner of her eye and he does that dumb little controlled exhale noise thing, and Charlie's tempted to trip him. She probably *would* if there weren't so many witnesses.

Titan Arena looms in the distance, and Charlie keeps her eye on Honor's statue while she pushes her legs further and faster. Her advantage is that her legs are longer than Jack's, and she uses every inch to gain the lead at the very last second, vaulting over the curb and onto the sidewalk and touching the base of the statue in victory, lungs screaming.

"I win," she gasps out. Jack glares at her, but is breathing too heavily to respond. Their teams catch up to them shortly after that, no less winded. Rose has even torn her dress at the seam to run better which Charlie respects.

"Actually," Charlie whirls around to see Tommy and his team of Alex, Jayne, and Malia. "We won."

"What?" Charlie gasps.

"How?" Jack asks.

"Alex knows the back alleys," Tommy says with a shrug. "We went through like a maze, but got here in no time."

"No fair!" Charlie gasps. Jack doubles over with his hands on his knees. "We were attacked!"

"You were *what?*" Honor asks, coming out of the arena. How had she heard Charlie from so far away? Does she also have enhanced hearing? That would be a new fact, even for Charlie.

"They weren't attacked, there was a rogue on their way," Leo clarifies. Charlie does a double take when she sees him. He's standing not far behind them on the curb, not a drop of sweat on him. He's not breathing even slightly unevenly. How had he made it back so fast? "Rae's taking care of it."

"Is everyone okay?" Honor asks, looking them all over.

"I'm gonna throw up," Lochlan says. Then does.

Charlie catches her breath while she pats him on the back and wrestles with the realization that she had lost. She wasn't able to do anything during the rogue attack. Not that she had to, because Leo and Rae obviously had it covered. But she didn't even get the chance. The gap is so utterly cavernous between students and pros but Charlie can't really fault herself that. She's only fifteen, of course she's not on that level.

But her classmates are her age. If she can't even best them at something so simple as a scavenger hunt, then how is she supposed to compete with them when they all become pros? She can't fall behind now, she'll never catch up. She'll never rank. She'll never come close to becoming a hero that means to someone else what Honor means to her and to so many other people.

Charlie is nothing if not stubborn. She's not going to let herself fall behind. She's just going to have to work harder.

11

Charlie is almost late to their first official simulation because she and her classmates are crowded around the television in the locker room lounge, watching the coverage about the rogue attack from the Friday before. None of the reporters mention the Titan Academy students that were present but why would they? They were just as helpful as the rest of the civilians, watching the pros handle it. The reporters also don't mention Leo even though he's in the shaky footage they play. They don't say his name, but they do talk about Rae and use her as a segue into their next segment on saving power.

They all scramble out to the arena in their gym clothes when they realize the time. Seeing a whole city block *inside* Titan Arena is definitely a trip, Charlie thinks. The buildings are overlaid with meticulous detail and if she didn't know any better, she would definitely think they're outside. She cranes her head to look around as she walks in, down a perfectly paved street, to the middle of the arena where Honor said she'd be waiting for them.

The tournament simulations aren't even half the size of this one. That's good, though, Charlie supposes, because if they train on a larger scale with less people, then winning the tournament on a smaller scale with all of them together will be a breeze.

This is their first real exercise since the safety seminar, so they're cleared to use their marvels for training. Charlie can feel her marvel building beneath her skin. She feels heavy, sturdy, ready to *do something*. As she looks around at her classmates, she can see many of them feel the same. Jack has a confident set to his shoulders. Malia is skipping, excited more than anything else. Ethan looks around with an analytical eye. Charlie wonders how they'll be graded.

"Hello!" Honor greets them cheerfully when they arrive in what looks like it's meant to be a town square. It's got a cute little fountain spewing real water. "Welcome to Titan Village!"

"Cute," Charlie murmurs to Lochlan.

"For your first rescue simulations, we'll be doing building collapses," she tells them. Ethan's hand shoots up and he's talking before Honor even calls on him.

"But there are so many different causes for building collapses!"

"Yes," she says with a patient smile. "As part of your training, you'll have to figure out what the cause is. Most of the time when you show up on scene, no one knows what's going on so you have to proceed accordingly. We'll give you the groups and get you started. First up is Charlie, Ethan, Luna, and Malia. Everyone else, up in the stands."

They've already studied this kind of disaster in class with Leo drilling them over and over about procedure. Honor doesn't give them much in the way of direction, telling them that the best way to learn is from their mistakes and not to worry because their victims are dummies, not real people, and Adrian is on standby. That piece of information gets Charlie's blood pumping a little bit faster, the mere possibility of real injury means they're doing something serious. It really is the big leagues, even if they're only first years.

Honor directs them to a small-ish building. The holo layered over the nanotech is a three-story department store. Charlie can already see the way the front of the building has collapsed, no doubt trapping their dummy victims inside. Concrete walls and hardly any windows means extraction is going to be difficult, but the floor plan should be straight-forward enough. The buzzer sounds for them to start, and Charlie is grateful for the full city block simulation because the buildings block their view of the stands and Charlie can't see all of the eyes on her in that moment.

"Okay, we need to stabilize an exit and get everyone out," Ethan says.

Ethan has a huge head start when it comes to these simulations, he's been studying them for years and his marvel is well-suited for search and rescue. Charlie is going to have to work twice as hard to keep up.

Charlie hates the way her hands shake. Her marvel isn't well equipped for search and rescue missions, it's a naturally destructive marvel, and usually the point in a search and rescue mission is to *not* destroy any more things. Having known this, Charlie has spent *hours* studying procedure for this kind of thing. If she isn't going to be able to actually help with anything, she's going to help those who can to the best of her ability.

"Okay, Luna, can you make sturdy trees that could hold up a collapsed roof?" Charlie asks, ready to take charge in order to stand out.

"Yup!" Luna says.

"And Malia, you should lead triage and help anyone who needs—"

"No," Malia cuts her off, and Charlie resists her fight reflex after being interrupted. "Don't pigeonhole me because of my marvel."

"Don't be so sensitive, damn," Charlie says. "You can sweep for survivors and lead extraction and heal anyone who can't move or be moved until we can get them out."

"So I'm still stuck being a healer?" she snaps.

"So you're just gonna walk past people who need healing just to prove a point? What kind of hero does that?" Charlie fires back. Malia settles into a glare that Charlie, for one, thinks is entirely unreasonable. "I will lead triage."

"I can do it," Ethan offers.

"You need to go in and sweep with Malia, you'll be able to see if the power is out, my marvel is pretty useless for this," she says.

"Your marvel can be used to clear rubble and other obstructions if you can control it," Ethan points out.

"I can control it," Charlie says, defensive now. "What? You too scared to go in or something?"

Ethan's cheeks glow. "*No.* I just think that since you're physically stronger than I am that you should go. If you find something inside that requires light just radio us and I'll come in."

"Alright, fine. We'll sweep top to bottom and meet in the middle," she says, only a little peeved that Ethan's plan is better than hers. "Let's go. Luna can you push me up to the top with a tree or someth—*woah!*"

Luna launches Charlie up to the roof of the half-collapsed building with a large redwood that shoots out of the ground. Charlie barely has enough time to brace to jump, but it turns out she doesn't have to because Luna can make the tree *bend*. She steps off the redwood when it gently lowers to a safe ledge on the roof.

That's incredible. Charlie looks back down at the ground where the tree had broken through the floor because, of course, Luna had given the tree real roots for stability and then curved it exactly as she wanted. She has such an amazing grasp on her marvel already, and Charlie is still learning about hers.

"Luna, that was amazing!" she calls down. Luna waves up at her, bouncing on the balls of her feet.

"Thanks!"

There's only three floors, so she searches the top floor while Malia takes the bottom. The dummies look like dummies and not real people, a little detail that Charlie is extremely grateful for. She's seen those hyperrealistic ones and they freak her out.

She collects the first one, marked with a broken leg, and slings it over her shoulder. Instead of heading down, she heads back up to the roof. Usually unadvisable, but Charlie is confident in Luna's ability to secure the building. Once on the roof, Charlie sets the dummy gently down on the tree that had lifted her up. Vines wrap around it, securing it, before the tree shrinks back down to ground level and Luna retrieves the dummy and delivers it to Ethan at triage.

Some of Aurora's mini bots make their own way out to Ethan to simulate survivors that could move themselves.

Ethan awkwardly asks them about the injuries, to which they reply with various things; I hit my head, I broke my arm, and others then record Ethan's response.

"These are *dummies* and I can't actually heal them," Malia says as she picks up a third dummy when Charlie meets her on the second floor. Charlie shoulders her own dummy.

"It's the *principle*," Charlie tells her with a grunt as the very real weight of the dummy settles on her. "Completely shunning your marvel even in hero work isn't the solution you think it is."

"What do *you* know about it?" Malia snaps.

"Damn, nothing I guess, but I thought we were cool," Charlie says and she makes her way back to the stairs. Malia starts to say something, but Charlie doesn't hear it over the loud sound of something cracking. She pauses.

Crack.

The staircase collapses. The full weight of the dummy lands on Charlie, mostly because if this was a real person she'd want to shield them, but it causes her to land on her own leg at a wrong angle. She feels the bone break.

"FUCK!" Charlie shouts, followed by a litany of other swear words that she's sure to get docked for, but she doesn't care. She's broken her arm once before when she was little and diving off of things she was too small to be jumping off of, but her brothers were doing it so she did too. She doesn't remember it hurting like *this*, though. This fucking sucks.

She shoves the dummy off of her and looks around at the collapsed staircase. It had just dropped them to the first floor, but she can see out of the front where Luna had made a safe tree tunnel for exits. At least the secondary collapse hadn't boxed them in. Now that Charlie thinks about it, she remembers learning something about secondary collapses;

how to see them coming, how to prevent them or something, but she can't remember it right now because the pain radiating from her ankle to her hip is taking up all of her consciousness.

"Charlie?" Malia calls.

"Yeah?" Charlie bites out. She looks at her leg and nearly gags at the way she can see her own bone trying to poke through her skin. "Fuck me sideways, *ugh*."

"Charlie, are you okay?"

"Nope!" she shouts back.

"Shit, hang on," Malia calls and the dust starts to clear. Charlie can see where Malia was dropped behind her, falling from a slightly higher height but she seems fine, her landing had probably been a lot less painful. She gets a look at Charlie's leg. "Oh."

"Yeah," Charlie bites. Tears sting at her eyes, and she looks up to keep them from falling. The dust in the air isn't helping, either. "You good?"

"Yeah, I heal too fast for any injuries to really take," Malia tells her as she squats down next to her.

"Lucky bitch," Charlie says, mostly because she's in pain but partly because she means it. Luckily, Malia laughs so Charlie probably won't have to apologize for it.

"Just the leg?" Malia asks, hand hovering just above where the bone is jutting out. Charlie nods and Malia touches her hand to her leg, right under her knee.

Malia's marvel is warm and tingly. Charlie feels like her leg is just waking up instead of mending completely. There's a soft, golden glow around her hand that lingers around Charlie's leg even after she pulls away. Charlie rolls her ankle around, feels it pop and finds that her leg moves just fine. She breathes a sigh of relief.

"I take it back, you're an angel," she says dreamily. Malia snickers again and helps Charlie to her feet. "We should probably still get the dummies."

"Ugh, you're right," Malia says and marches back to find hers. Yeah, they're definitely going to get marked off for this, but Charlie thinks she should at least save some points for prioritizing her dummy over herself and breaking her own leg for it.

The building rumbles again and they try to make a break for the tunnel but the roof collapses in front of it. Charlie briefly wonders if Aurora is doing this on purpose or if the simulation is random. It doesn't really matter because either way, they're stuck.

"Are you guys okay?" Luna asks over their comms.

"We're fine," Charlie answers. "We've got two dum—uh, civilians?"

"Patients," Ethan supplies.

"Sure, we've got two patients with us, but the rest of the building is clear," she tells them. She looks over the rocks and rubble that have collapsed in front of their exit.

"Can you use your marvel to get out?" Ethan asks.

"Not without bringing the rest of the building down too," Charlie says.

"I thought you said you can control your marvel," Ethan says.

"Listen glowstick," Charlie snaps, "I can control my marvel just fine. What I *cannot* control is how the rest of the building will be affected regardless of how small my blast is."

"I can dig you guys out!" Luna interjects. "Don't worry! Just sit tight, okay?"

Charlie grumbles her assent and sits herself down to wait. She's aware of Malia watching her as she sets her dummy down and does the same on an old display cube. This can't be good for their score, and Charlie already feels like she should have done more, been better. She should have volunteered to sweep the building instead of Ethan suggesting it. She's always liked taking action, anyway. She should play to her own strengths, right?

They probably won't fail. At least, Charlie hopes not. She's never fully failed an assignment before, and she doesn't know how she'd react if Honor was to hand her her first 'F.' They're the first group too, so Charlie decides not to overreact about possible failure until she sees how the others do. It might be selfish, but she finds herself secretly wishing for someone to do worse than her.

She can't rely on that forever, though. She can't count on being the best by simply not being the worst. No, it has to be because she's the best. It has everything to do with her and nothing to do with anyone else. She'll just work harder, a small price to pay for pursuing her dreams.

"What's your deal anyway?" Malia asks after a long bout of silence.

"*My* deal?" Charlie repeats, brows shooting up to her hairline. "What the hell are you talking about?"

"That," she says and gestures to Charlie's whole person. Charlie's not sure if she's supposed to be offended. "You're so combative."

"You try being the youngest of five," Charlie mutters back and lets some of the fight seep out of her shoulders. She scrubs a tired hand over her face, smearing dirt all over it.

"Yeah, but I'm not your sister," Malia points out.

"Obviously," Charlie says, toeing the edge of too sharp. "Listen, just say whatever you're trying to say, I don't have the patience to sort through social cues and nuances right now. Or ever, really."

"I want to be what I want to be," Malia says. Charlie looks at her and waits for her to elaborate but she doesn't.

"A hero," Charlie supplies instead. Malia nods firmly. "Okay? I knew this. Why are you telling me now?"

"Because earlier you tried to put me back into the box I was born into."

"I didn't put you in any box," Charlie starts but Malia interrupts her.

"You did! Just like *everyone* else does," she nearly shouts. It disturbs the dust around them and some of it drifts down from the part of the ceiling that's still intact. There's a rumble from outside, but nothing else moves.

"Malia," Charlie starts, "I'm sorry that I made you feel like every other shitty person in your life, and I hate to be the one to break it to you but you have a *healing* marvel. Using it in a hospital and using it in the field as a pro hero are *two different things.* I refuse to believe that you enrolled in this academy and honestly thought you wouldn't be using your marvel at all."

"Of course not," Malia scoffs.

"Then what's the big deal about asking you to use it in a simulation?" Charlie asks.

"I don't want to be stuck doing triage every time just because I have a healing marvel, it isn't fair."

"Your marvel is your strength," Charlie says. "Everyone needs to play to their strengths whether they're alone or on a team."

"I have more strengths than just my marvel," Malia says coldly. Charlie opens her mouth then snaps it shut again. Okay, point Malia.

"Then instead of telling people what you *aren't*, how about you tell them what you *are*," Charlie suggests. Then she takes a breath and swallows her pride to say, "But I'm sorry," with full sincerity.

Malia looks down at her hands, perfectly smooth, no scars and no calluses. "It's okay." Charlie throws a small rock at her and she flinches before looking at Charlie like she's crazy.

"Don't say it's okay if it's not okay," Charlie says with a small grin. Her mom taught her that one when Charlie and her siblings would fight.

"Then *I forgive you,*" Malia says with just enough exaggeration to make Charlie laugh but to also let her know she still means it.

Luna finishes clearing a path for them, long vines and roots clearing away the last of the rubble. They walk out together with the last of the dummies between them and find Honor and Adrian already waiting for them outside. Luna is sweaty and panting and leaning on Ethan, but she smiles at them when they emerge. Honor looks Charlie up and down.

"You good, kid?" she asks.

"Yeah," Charlie says as she drops the dummy to the ground. "Malia got me."

"That's convenient, I would have killed for a classmate with a healing marvel," Honor says. "You sure, you're both good?"

Charlie and Malia exchange a look.

"Yeah," Malia says.

"We're good," Charlie adds.

Honor hates the anniversary of her greatest victory. The whole country commemorates it, and other big cities around the world join in too. California goes all out, though, for their hometown heroes, their resident Titans. Everything is painted pink and blue and yellow. Triumvirate merchandise sales skyrocket. Some people even paint a third eye on their forehead.

All it does is remind Honor of the people that died. Because of her. Reminds her of her mom too, because she can't remember Krewa without remembering how she was the Titan who killed their mother. Their mother had been more powerful than she ever let on to the three of them, powerful enough to cloak herself across space and go undetected for years. Honor misses her everyday, and her death led directly to the worst few years of Honor's life. She spiraled, hard, unequipped to deal with so much grief. They had no idea that their mother's death wasn't an accident until Honor, desperate to change, to be a good person, freed Krewa without knowing who or what she was. Her first decision after being determined to be better was the wrong one. Honor wishes she could say she was surprised.

Honor walks her patrol route and more people than usual stop her. She poses for pictures with a bright smile and excuses herself as quickly as possible to avoid answering too many questions. She passes a toy store selling Triumvirate and Krewa action figures in a bundle. Her stomach rolls.

Freeing Krewa had sparked the fight between her and Colson, he had begged her not to do it and when she did anyway, tried to stop her. She said horrible things to him that drove him away and straight to his mother. Then the immediate death and destruction Krewa wreaked in the Bay Area was also a direct result of Honor's poor choice. Hundreds of civilians and two pro heroes, dead. Countless more injured.

You don't think these things through, Colson had said to her. He was right. She hasn't admitted that to him yet. Maybe she should.

Alex's parents were among the casualties of the Titan Battle. A fact Honor learned only after she was admitted into the Academy and she finally received her unsealed files from the state. Some of her classmates are going with her to the candlelight vigil tonight. Honor will not be in attendance

The only bright spot in that mess of Honor's making was Grace. Honor and Verity thought she had died in the same accident that killed their mother, but she hadn't. She was living just across the country, without her memories or her sisters or friends or her career as a pro. The second she regained her memories she leapt into action alongside them, their strongest sister, the one who taught them how to combine into a single Titan form. Without her, they might've lost. A thought that Honor doesn't allow herself to entertain.

But Grace doesn't get to stay. The more powerful a Titan presence is on a planet, the more it attracts other Titans who seek more power for themselves. Honor isn't sure how it works, she can't sense other Titans, but she knows that with her and her sisters all on the same planet, they make for a bright beacon. So Grace lives on Viasyre with the man who helped her regain her memories. She visits every now and again, though, and Honor takes comfort in knowing that she's alive at all.

She gets back to the agency and is thankful no one really pays her any more mind than usual. The receptionist greets her, cheery as she always is. The insurance department glowers as she walks by to her shared office. Verity is already in there, filing her paperwork on time like a good employee. The other two pros they share with are either off or out on assignment.

"How was it out there?" Verity asks without lifting her eyes from her computer screen. Even though their suits are so similar, Verity's is two pieces and Honor's is a jumpsuit. Verity's jacket is slung over the back of her chair, leaving her in just a blue tank top from her own merch line.

"Same as it was last year," Honor says and sinks into her desk chair. "Don't take Route Four if you patrol today, there's a street fair."

"Ugh, noted," Verity says and sits back in her chair. She looks around her computer monitor at Honor who retracts her gauntlets and massages her wrists. "How are you holding up?"

"Fine," Honor answers.

"Don't bullshit me," Verity replies. "I hate today and I know you hate it more."

"It feels gross to let everyone celebrate when they don't know it's my fault," Honor says.

"It wasn't your fault," Verity says like she does every year.

"It *was.*"

"It *was not.* You did a good thing. There's no way you could have known she would have gone on a rampage instead of fucking off back to wherever she came from. And you did the *right* thing because your old black ops buddies were up to no good. Even if you did everything right and reported the agency and it got shut down Krewa either would have been transferred, which is also bad or someone else would have freed her and this would have happened anyway," Verity's words spill out in a rush like she's been waiting to say this all day. She said a variation of it last year too. Maybe it will sink in this time. Maybe Honor can convince herself to believe it.

"I still don't feel good being celebrated when, at the very least, it should be a wash," Honor says and stares at her blank report. "I feel guilty every time Alex looks at me, you know? I wonder if I should tell her that it's my fault that her parents are dead."

"You most certainly should not!" Verity snaps and pushes to her feet, hands on her desk.

"I'm *lying* to her!"

"What? Did she ask 'Do you know who's responsible for freeing the Titan who killed my parents?' to which you replied 'Nope, not a clue'?"

Honor slates her with a look that says 'you know I didn't.'

"Then you didn't lie. Don't tell her. I mean it," Verity says and jams a finger in Honor's direction.

"Isn't being honest the right thing to do?" Honor asks.

"Listen, being honest in this situation will only help you. It will ease your guilt and validate your need for punishment for something that *isn't your fault*. So you tell Alex that you set Krewa free. Then what? A sixteen year old with no living family has to reconcile with the fact that her *new* family, one of her heroes, is responsible for something that neither of you can change. You make it up to her by doing right by her, not by causing her more pain."

"What if she finds out anyway and feels like I lied to her?" Honor asks, genuinely distressed by the possibility.

"How would she find out? There are eight people alive who know what really happened. You, me, Grace, Colson, Aurora, Spectra, the Secretary of Defense, and the President. So, if the President of the United States tells classified information to a teenager then we'll burn that bridge when we come to it. Or cross it. Whatever."

"I don't like it," Honor says and it's all she really can say. Verity makes for a good argument and Honor doesn't want to hurt Alex more than she already has.

"You don't have to like it," Verity says, and that's true, too. Annoying, but true. "Come on."

"I have paperwork," Honor says because she doesn't want to venture back into the outside world for the rest of the day.

"Like you ever do your paperwork on time?" Verity asks. "We're going to change into our incognito clothes and go sit in the back of a dark movie theater and watch the dumbest movie out right now while eating every overpriced snack they sell at the concession counter."

That... that sounds like a good time. The best time Honor can remember having for a while. It's Saturday and there's no school to worry about, Leo and Aurora are both on campus. Honor already went on patrol and neither of them have any scheduled appearances.

"Okay," Honor says and gets to her feet. Verity does a little victory dance and leads the way to the agency locker room. This may be Honor's least favorite day of the year but it's just another day. It will pass and tomorrow will be better. Honor will be better.

12

"Last Surviving Hero From World War,
Red Bullet, Dies at 142"

—*Heroes Globe*

Charlie is woken up by the sound of screaming. She flails and falls out of bed before she realizes that it's not screaming, it's an alarm. A loud, blaring alarm going off at—she checks her phone—*four o'clock in the morning.* Then Aurora's voice cuts through the alarm.

"This is a drill," she says, and Charlie relaxes. "Report to the main lawn for further instruction. You have sixty seconds."

"SIXTY—" Charlie shouts at no one before shoving her feet into some shoes and bolting out the door. Her classmates are in a similar state of panic, *they're on the top floor.* There's no way the elevator would make it in time and even then they would never fit, especially not split between two floors.

Charlie is first out the door and into the stairwell, but her classmates are right behind her. The whole stairwell shakes when Rock Buddy makes his way in, running on Cecily's heels. Jack catches up to Charlie, but she blocks him off when she grabs onto the handrail and uses it to swing herself around down the next flight. She's not entirely certain this is a competition, but better safe than sorry.

She bursts out the door and runs through the common room to find Honor waiting for them, looking at her watch, no doubt timing them. Leo is also there, looking more exhausted than Charlie's ever seen, and *Anthony*.

"Dick," she says without heat. If she had a warp marvel, she'd use it too. He grins and pulls his hood down further over his head. That's right, he's got a thing about his hair. Charlie tries to put him in a headlock to pull the hood down, but he warps away. He smooths it down to make sure it's in place over his unstyled hair, but Jack is behind him and pulls the hood down before he even notices he's there.

Charlie laughs at Anthony's squawk before she realizes that means laughing *with* Jack. He seems to realize the same thing at the same time and the smile that had been building on his face drops immediately.

"Welcome to the world of midnight calls," Honor says, much too loudly in the quiet night, but who is Charlie to judge? Leo looks asleep on his feet. "All of you managed to be down in less than sixty seconds, but none of you are in uniform, and I'm going to chalk a lot of that up to panic since you didn't know what was going on."

They have to be in uniform too? Charlie resists the urge to groan. Of course they would, a hero can't go out saving people in their pajamas. Well, Honor did that one time, but the rogues had crashed into her building and she hadn't been on call. She looks around and finds a startling majority of her classmates in some sort of hero merchandise. Charlie loves that for all of them. But then she sees she and Jack are in the same Triumvirate shirt.

Jack notices at the same time. He scowls and crosses his arms over his chest.

"We will have these drills throughout the year and you will be expected to be in uniform and on time," Honor goes on. "They will be graded assignments and points will be docked accordingly. Your assignment tonight is simple. There's three holotiles that project your name. Find all three before your homeroom to pass. The faster you find them, the faster you can go back to sleep."

"What's the search radius?" Jack asks, sounding like a dick.

"The Titan District," Honor says with a casual shrug like she hadn't just told them that their assignment is to find minuscule tiles hidden literally anywhere in the biggest district in Los Angeles. "The tiles will be hidden along the previous routes you took during our first scavenger hunt. You've been assigned pairs and they are as follows; Charlie and Tommy—"

Charlie stops listening and finds Tommy leaning on Rock Buddy, nearly asleep on his feet. She jostles him.

"Rise and shine, we've got some holotiles to find."

"Where do we even start?" He yawns and rubs his eyes. Charlie runs through her rough mental map of the Titan District. It's still very limited after their first scavenger hunt and a few weekends exploring with Lochlan and some of the others.

"There's no way it's random," she says, keeping her voice low because Honor hadn't said it was a competition, but assuming it isn't is a surefire way to lose. Around them, their classmates start to link up and strategize. Honor and Leo are a little ways off, keeping an eye on them. Honor says something that Charlie can't hear, and Leo smiles when he huffs out a laugh.

"If this is another way to make us learn the district, it doesn't seem right that they would be places we've already been," Tommy says. Charlie continues to survey their classmates. Lochlan is paired with Luna. Kai is paired with Ethan. Jack is paired with Malia, and Malia sends her an annoyed look over his shoulder. Charlie winces in sympathy back.

No one is paired with someone from their original scavenger hunt group.

"Hey, Tommy, did you stop anywhere on your way back to campus during the scavenger hunt?" Charlie asks.

"We stopped at two places, I think," he says. "Why?"

"I think we might be supposed to show each other our routes," she says.

"Weren't we dropped off at opposite ends of the district?" he asks. Charlie takes another look around at all of the pairs, catches Honor's eyes on her.

"Yeah, that sounds like the point," she sighs. Honor turns around to answer Rose's question. "Come on, we can take the bus to my starting point first, then work backwards through your route."

"Sounds good," Tommy says with another yawn and a stretch that has his rumpled sleep shirt riding up. Charlie immediately looks for Jack, who has predictably been staring the whole time, probably. His face goes bright red when he realizes he's been caught. Charlie rolls her eyes at him, then grabs Tommy and tows him to the edge of campus where the bus stop is.

The bus is completely empty at this hour and the driver is playing his own music over the speakers, but neither Charlie or Tommy protest to the relaxing classical music. They sit side by side in the middle of the bus and settle in for the ride to the southeast end of the district.

"Can I ask you a question?" Charlie asks after a while. Tommy looks up from his phone and the game he'd been playing mindlessly to pass the time. Tommy nods. "How do you know Verity?"

Tommy laughs and it's so clearly uncomfortable that Charlie almost takes it back. He lifts a hand to brush over the back of his closely shaven head. "Um, a few years back, she actually saved my life." Charlie almost opens her mouth to say 'same' but with Honor, but then he's barreling on and she doesn't want to kill the momentum he's clearly building up. "I don't know if you heard about the rogue named Jester and how he was kidnapping people to steal their marvels, but, uh—I was one of them."

"You were *kidnapped?*" Charlie can't help the little outburst. Tommy looks awkward but still earnest.

"Yeah, me and Cora both," he tells her. *Cora too?* Jesus Christ. But then Charlie remembers how she had hugged Verity at the tour. It spoke to familiarity, for sure. "Verity saved us."

"Wait, wait, wait," Charlie says, "Start from the beginning. Tell me everything—but only if you're comfortable!" she tacks onto the end because she doesn't want Tommy to think she's an asshole, she just genuinely wants to know now.

Tommy tells her about how he would visit Verity in the shop she used to own in Orange County and how she was, like, his gay mentor. He didn't think much of his marvel back then. Charlie can understand, she has a sneaking suspicion that her mom feels the same way about hers, which is essentially the same category of marvel as Tommy's. But Jester targeted Tommy specifically for the ability to void others.

It turned out that Jester could only steal marvels for a certain amount of time, but there was no limit to how many he could take at once, so he kept all of his victims in cages in a secret location until Verity, who was largely unknown in that community and effectively retired from being a pro hero at the time, got herself kidnapped on *purpose* to save them.

Tommy gets more animated when he talks about how Verity fought Jester after she woke up, even miming some of the movements Verity made with such fluid grace that Charlie knows he's acted this out a hundred times before. Her chest gets tight just thinking about what it would be like to have witnessed all of that firsthand, to be a part of it. Jester used Tommy's marvel to void her, but it turns out that Tommy's marvel isn't super effective on Titans because it wore off faster than Jester expected. Verity bent her cage out of shape, crawled out and fought Jester one on one. But it wasn't really one on one because Jester had the marvels of twelve other people and Verity had to fight them all.

At one point, Tommy's chest puffs out a bit here, Jester's back was to Tommy's cage, and Tommy was able to get a hand on him long enough to void him and give Verity the edge she needed to win.

"I still can't believe it really happened sometimes," Tommy admits. "Before that, I had never considered becoming a hero, it just didn't feel like a possibility, but after playing even the smallest part in taking Jester down, I just—I had to ask. I went up to Verity while the police were loading Jester into a truck and asked Verity if she thought I could be a hero." He laughs then, a nervous habit, Charlie's noticed, his wide, perfect smile is almost enough to distract from the way he lifts his hand to run it over his head again. Then he gets a little misty-eyed and *oh no* if Tommy starts crying there's a very good chance that Charlie will start to cry too.

"She just looked at me and I remember she was so confused," he says. "And I was confused because she was confused, but then she said, 'Tommy, you're already a hero.'" He looks down at his hands as he says it, like he still doesn't quite believe it, but he still wanted to say it. Wanted Charlie to hear it. She doesn't blame him. There's no feeling Charlie can relate to more than the desire to become a hero and having *your* personal hero tell you that of course you can, that's life changing stuff.

Her own story sits on the tip of her tongue, untold. Her story is nothing like that, it's not as good.

Charlie's story just happened to her. She didn't make anything happen. She didn't put herself on the line to save anyone else. All she has is this intense desire that seizes every muscle and sinew when she thinks about it for too long.

They arrive at their spot right after, so she doesn't have to do much more than commend Tommy and give him a hearty slap on the back. They get off the bus in the crisp morning air, and it's still dark enough that the street lamps are on. But Oh My Coffee across the street is lit up and ready for business, 24/7.

Charlie doesn't fight the grin, sure she's right as she pulls Tommy across the street, unafraid of nonexistent traffic, and into the coffee shop. The bell above the door rings. Ricky is behind the counter once again, leaning on the counter with his head propped up in his hand. He doesn't even look surprised to see them, and then he holds up a holotile.

"Ricky!" Charlie cries like she's greeting an old friend. Ricky does not return the sentiment, but that's okay with Charlie, so long as she gets that tile.

"I don't go to Cal State," he says, as she skips to the counter and plucks the tile from his fingers.

"Huh?" she says eloquently.

"Your teacher asked if I went to Cal State and I don't," he clarifies. "I assume you told him that."

"Uh, you wore the sweatshirt," she points out. So that's why she was marked off points for that on the reports they had to turn in. Her group still got the most points on their reports overall, despite losing the race back to campus, so it's safe to say Charlie was right and that talking to people was a key part of their first assignment.

"Does wearing that shirt make you a de Mora sister?" he fires back and, okay, Ricky brought his A-game today and is clearly more awake than Charlie is.

"How much caffeine is in your chocolate roasted marshmallow shaken espresso?" Tommy asks, reading it straight off the menu overhead.

"A lot, but I can add an extra shot, if you want" Ricky says, sounding bored.

"Two, please," Tommy says and then pats himself down. "Wait, I didn't grab my wallet."

"I don't have mine, either," Charlie says and then immediately feels naked after the realization. Ricky sighs, long suffering.

"Tell you what, you get me an autograph from Honor de Mora and it's on the house," Ricky offers.

"Deal," Charlie says without hesitation. Ricky sets to making their drinks, and Charlie clicks the holotile. Tommy's name is projected between them in shimmering electric blue letters. Charlie groans. "It's just your name."

"Which means it's three *each*," Tommy says and hangs his head, leaning heavily against the counter. "I'm so tired." Charlie feels that and accepts the sugary drink from Ricky with the utmost gratitude.

Charlie leads Tommy to the restaurant on Titan Way where they'd spoken with the hostess. Alice isn't there because nothing is open yet, but the host stand is nailed to the ground outside and the holotile sits right on top. This one has Charlie's name on it.

The third tile on Charlie's route is a bit harder to find since they didn't get a chance to stop anywhere else before the rogue incident and the race versus Jack and his team. But the tile turns out to be on the sill of the display window of the store they tried to cut through. This one has Tommy's name. Charlie hadn't realized how closely Leo had watched them. She wonders what his report would have looked like if he had written one. Maybe she could ask.

"You guys were attacked by a rogue, right?" Tommy asks as they continue to amble down Titan Way. He shoves his hands in his pockets and looks around the empty road.

"Well, not directly," Charlie admits sheepishly. "It was this big commotion when this guy started turning everyone into *dolls*." She recounts how they'd tried to charge into action, but everything was so crazy they didn't do much more than stand there before Leo stepped in and saved the day.

"What happened to the people who were turned into dolls?" Tommy asks.

"I… don't know," Charlie admits. It opens up a hole in the back of her mind that she's gonna itch to fill with information. She should know that. She should have asked. Leo would know.

"But, wow, Leo shielded everyone on the street?" Tommy gives a low whistle. "I don't know much about his marvel but that seems crazy impressive."

"Yeah," Charlie mutters in agreement. Then a laugh nearby has her jumping out of her skin and setting off her marvel out of reflex, just two fingers worth, but it would still do a decent amount of damage if it hit a person. Luckily, it just hits Leo's shield. "You *scared* me."

"I see that," Leo says, and even though Charlie swears she just heard him laugh, there's no trace of a smile on his face. He'd appeared behind them out of nowhere on the empty street, no sound, no warning, no nothing. "Using your marvel against a pro is illegal, you know."

"It was an accident," Charlie insists indignantly, although she's not sure that's helping her case.

"I know," Leo says.

"How did you shield all those people?" Tommy asks.

Leo shrugs, "It's easy if they're all within my field of vision, but I can't shield anyone I can't see." Tommy nods like he does when they're in class. Charlie will hold onto that information like she does with all of her pro trivia, but she's not sure what use it will be to her later on. "I just came to tell you guys that if you want to be back by homeroom, you need to get a move on."

"Oh, like we're the furthest behind," Charlie scoffs despite the real fear creeping up on her that they're falling behind. Leo just shrugs then turns to walk down an alley between a closed cafe and a luxury brand store that has Honor's face on a poster in the window. Charlie turns to Tommy. "How do you feel about an early morning jog?"

Tommy, a true team player, is up for anything, and they jog the rest of the way back to campus. They take a minute to catch their breath and grab some water from inside the stadium before they backtrack through Tommy's route to find the rest of their tiles.

"Can I ask you a question?" Tommy asks as they walk through the deserted corridor inside the stadium.

"Shoot," she tells him.

"Why do you want to be a hero?"

"Ah, shit, can I just send you my essay?" she jokes. Kind of. She hates this question. She hates that she doesn't have a profound answer to it. Yeah, sure, Honor saved her when she was little, and that really sparked her obsession with heroes and Honor, especially, but whenever she cites that as a reason to be a hero people seem to be left wanting. Like her answer is inadequate. But she doesn't have another answer.

I want to help people. It's what I'm meant to do. My parents are heroes and I want to carry on the legacy. Those are all reasons for others, but they taste like lies to Charlie so she doesn't say them. Even having the expectation of being a hero thrust on her like Jack would be better, but all Charlie has is her own desire. Charlie *does* want those things but nowhere near as fiercely as she wants to *be* a hero and no one seems to understand the difference except Charlie.

"I get it," Tommy says, and he probably does, but Charlie still feels like she let him down, somehow. She sighs again.

"I've never wanted to be anything else," she tells him honestly and hopes that's enough. Even if it isn't, he doesn't have to accept it for it to be true. But Tommy just beams at her.

"Me either."

Fortunately for them, Tommy's memory is excellent, and during their first leg of the scavenger hunt, he had been thinking about all of the places that tiles could be hidden. They hadn't stopped to talk to anyone during their race so the tiles are hidden in obscure places like taped to a pedestrian crossing sign and under a dumpster behind the flower shop where Kai had used the bathroom.

Tommy hadn't been kidding when he said Alex knew all of the back alleys because it's a maze of brick walls, and they run across two dumpster divers before they make it back onto a main road near the original start of Tommy's route.

The sun is rising and crisp. The dawn air is refreshing. Charlie takes a moment to take a deep lungful. Tommy notices, but he doesn't make fun of her, just smiles that pretty smile of his and holds the door open for her to the twenty-four hour corner store he'd started at during the last exercise. It's a popular spot for students to grab breakfast, Tommy tells her. From the nearby university and from Marvelous which is right across the district line in Blueside.

"Oh, great." A too-loud voice breaks the peaceful silence of the early morning. Charlie scowls and turns to find the source of the voice. It's Jack because of course it's Jack, he's partnered with Malia who was in a group with Tommy. But Jack isn't talking to them.

Charlie and Tommy cross to the candy aisle where Jack and Malia are and find them in a weird standoff with some kids from Marvelous.

Jack goes on, "A bunch of haughty wannabes telling us where we can and can't go."

Charlie sighs, disappointed, and Jack whirls around, surprised to find her and Tommy there.

"We'll work on it, Boy Wonder," she promises and he scowls at her. She looks past him and at Noah, who's with the other three Marvelous kids, including the one Charlie had threatened at the safety seminar. "This guy giving you a problem again, Noah?"

"No," Noah answers, strongly enough that Charlie believes him but coldly enough that she's immediately alerted to the fact that something else is wrong. She shoulders her way between Jack and Malia.

"What's going on, guys?" she asks with faux cheer. Beck? His name was Beck. He sneers at her in greeting.

"Well if it isn't Hot Hands," he says.

"Oh, wow," Malia says, struggling to choke back laughter.

"Do I need to hold an insult workshop?" Charlie asks. "This is pitiful."

"No one needs to insult anyone," Tommy tries, and it's sweet, but Charlie isn't going to listen to Tommy just because he's sweet.

"Definitely not like that," Charlie says. "If we're gonna talk insults we're gonna talk those ugly shoes that are definitely too big because you're wearing three pairs of socks. Did you steal those from Daddy's closet?"

Beck flushes angrily. Too easy. "Get the hell out of here."

"Uh, I'm gonna have to go with a good old fashioned, 'make me,'" Charlie says with a shrug. She looks at Noah, who won't make steady eye contact with her. Her mom had said something about friends drifting apart when you start at a new school, but she didn't think she meant like this.

"It's not like you own the store," Malia points out. "Why don't you just run back to Blue so you don't miss class."

"Might as well," Beck scoffs. "Our classes are too important to miss."

"'Intro to How to be an Asshole' must require a lot of in class participation," Jack says. Charlie resists the urge to wince.

"Yeah," Beck says, smiling in a way that is already pissing Charlie off. "Given our *superior* education, it's not surprising you don't know what classes a real hero course has."

"Superior?" Charlie echoes and raises a challenging eyebrow. "You don't have a single teacher ranked in the top ten in *California*, let alone the country."

"We have people fully committed to our education," Beck sneers. He takes a step forward, and Charlie matches him, unwilling to give up any ground. "Six of the top ten heroes graduated from Marvelous. We're next."

"What kind of argument is that?" Charlie scoffs. "Titan Academy is in its first year, of course no ranked pro is an alum."

"You'll see the difference between us at the tournament, after we kick your ass," he promises. "I just hope it doesn't crush you so badly that you drop out. I'll need a sidekick when I go pro."

Charlie's temper flares and she's hyper aware of her marvel thrumming right beneath her skin. Before she realizes what she's doing, she's stalking forward down the aisle. Beck meets her halfway and she shoves his shoulders so hard he goes stumbling back a step.

"Why wait?" she goads. "Let's settle this right now."

"Let's not," a new voice says. Charlie feels a rush of cold followed shortly by calm and all of the fight drains out of her at once. Indignation tries to rise in its place but it's quickly snuffed out, replaced by a serene peace Charlie's half sure she's never felt before in her life.

Verity.

Charlie turns slowly, deliberately, currently incapable of the proper level of surprise. Verity's marvel is incredible, indescribable, Charlie feels hollow and whole at once. Filled to the brim with emotions that she knows, logically, do not belong to her.

Verity holds her phone in one hand, against her ear, and a half drunk iced coffee in the other. She's done up, not in uniform, in a white satin dress and a vibrant cobalt coat. That's right, she was on one of those early morning talk shows today. Charlie's brother Garrett had promised to record it on the home TV for her.

Her expensive heels click against the dingy corner store floor as she approaches the candy aisle.

"Names," she says to the Marvelous kids. Beck opens his mouth, "Do *not* lie to me." His mouth shuts with an audible click. Noah reluctantly mumbles their names, and Verity repeats them into the phone then bids the caller goodbye. "Your teachers are expecting you."

The Marvelous kids shuffle back out of the aisle and leave the store via the chip aisle. Verity sucks down the last of her ice coffee while she stares them down. No one says anything. The cashier behind the counter yawns.

"Well," Verity prompts. "Find your tiles. Apparently you need an escort back to campus."

They find their tiles and embark on the walk of shame back to campus. It's tense because Verity doesn't give them a warning or punish them outright, leaving them in suspense. They make it back before homeroom, though, so at least they don't fail the assignment.

Verity leaves them when they get there, dismissing them to their dorms to dress for class. It's not until they get to the classroom that Leo addresses it in front of the rest of the class.

"They were talking shit about the Academy," Charlie tries to argue even though she knows it's pointless. "Said they'll kick our asses at the tournament and make us sidekicks."

Several of her classmates make appropriately outraged noises, and Charlie gestures around as if a jury of her peers will exonerate her for a fight she didn't even get to start.

"That doesn't matter," Leo says. "Fighting in the street with other schools will give people reason to talk badly about the Academy that *you* represent."

"I don't know why you're only looking at me when Jack was the one who started it," Charlie says. Leo's eyes flicker to Jack who sinks low in his seat.

"He tried," Malia pipes up. "Charlie just happens to make for a better trigger."

"All fight, no flight," Lochlan mutters. She kicks him under the desk.

"Regardless, all four of you will serve detention after school for the rest of the week."

"Wait!"

"*After* school?"

"That's during training hours!"

The only one of them who doesn't protest is Tommy, resigned to a punishment that he didn't really earn.

"Tommy doesn't deserve detention," Jack advocates for him. "He tried to stop us."

"Not very hard," Charlie says but she agrees. Tommy didn't do anything wrong, it seems unfair for all of them to have detention during training hours but especially Tommy.

"Let this be a lesson," he says and glances at Tommy, "Convince your classmates to do the right thing or walk away. Standing by doesn't excuse you."

"Collective punishment is a war crime," Charlie points out.

Leo raises an eyebrow. "We're not at war, Charlie."

"You and me, sure," she says, leaning forward. "But we're definitely at war with those Marvelous assholes."

"Hear, hear," Malia says. There are enough murmurs of agreement that Leo sighs.

"Enough," he snaps. Well, snaps in his Leo way, which is anything slightly sharper than his normal, bored tone.

"Nothing actually *happened*," Malia tries.

"Because Verity was there, not because you wouldn't have done anything. Any more arguments will be met with an extra week of detention during training hours." He lets the silence settle before he starts class, and there's no way it's a coincidence when he asks, "Who can tell me when the occupation of 'sidekick' was terminated."

Charlie sinks down in her seat and Lochlan pats her hand.

13

"Pro Hero Spectra to Retire from Active Duty"
—*Marvels Today*

Honor is sitting on the floor, grading the latest Korean essays when Leo gets back from patrol. They're messy and rudimentary but at least they're getting the word order right. Korean was an odd choice for a first second language, Honor knows. But she also knows that most of these kids are already passable in Spanish, and if they're passable in Spanish, they'll grasp the basics of another love language relatively easily. She wanted to introduce them to the Asian languages early and they're starting with Korean because that's Honor's best language and she feels confident enough to teach it. Next year, she'll have to hire someone to teach another language too.

"How was the sim today?" Leo asks, stripping his jacket off.

"Fine," she says without looking up. Leo crouches down next to her at the coffee table and tilts his head to get a better look at her face. He glances at the Korean papers he doesn't understand, then back at her.

"Is something wrong?" he asks.

"Why would something be wrong?" she asks, genuine. The sim went fine and finals are coming up. Then they'll have a break, and Grace is coming with Cal. Honor is excited to see her sister again.

Leo takes a moment to answer. "Because you haven't looked at me yet."

Honor pauses. She hadn't been ignoring Leo, but she also hasn't read a single syllable of hangul since he walked in. What has she even been looking at? She doesn't know. So she looks at him now, turns her head and finds him close, looking her directly in the eye and her ribs constrict around her lungs.

"Why haven't you been to see Colson yet?" is what comes out of her mouth. It surprises Leo, and it even surprises her. Leo hasn't seen Colson since he was discharged from the hospital and admitted into Ameliora. Colson asks about him every so often, but Leo never mentions Colson, not anymore.

When he first pulled back, Honor thought he might've just needed some space at best. At worst, he regretted helping Colson at all. She had been too afraid to ask back then, and they were so busy it was easy to just—not talk about it. But it's been long enough. If Leo doesn't want anything to do with Colson, then he needs to come right out and say it. No more dancing around it. No more avoiding. No more excuses.

"I've been busy," he answers. Leo is the first to look away, and he pushes to his feet. Leo's a runner. Honor's always known this about him, and she's always given chase, which is really something he should know by now too. Honor gets to her feet and watches the muscles of his back shift under his shirt while he picks up some of the errant clothing lying around the living room.

"We are the same amount of busy," she says, calling his bullshit. They have the same jobs and they're in the same social circles. They're *family*.

"What do you want me to say, Honor?" He sighs, and she narrows her eyes at him.

"I want you to tell me the fucking truth," she snaps. "Why won't you go see him?"

"Maybe I don't want to," he snaps back. Leo's voice hardly ever rises but it does get sharp. Sharper than broken glass, but Honor isn't afraid to tread forward barefoot. "Did you consider that?"

"I did, actually, yeah," she says then snaps her fingers.

An illusion of Colson appears in front of Leo, hunched over in his Ameliora sweats, but with the sweet smile that he always gives Honor when she shows up on his face. She can make him say anything. She can make him ask why Leo isn't coming to see him himself. She can make him ask if Leo thinks it was a mistake helping him. She can make him ask if Leo wants nothing to do with him anymore. But she doesn't want to project through Colson. She wants to show him Colson as he is. So she pulls the memory up, and Colson's lips move and his voice comes out.

"How's Leo?" he asks.

"Good," Honor answers, and her real voice is a touch heavier than her illusion. Leo whips around to look between the two of them with wide eyes. He knows Colson is an illusion. Knows all of her tricks. But it's always so much harder to remember that when you're face to face with one. "He's busy but he's great with the kids."

"I'll bet," Colson says with a wistful smile.

"I can tell him you said—"

"No," Colson cuts her off. Honor's eyes remain fixed on Leo as she carries out this conversation crafted from her memory. "No, you, you don't have to do that. I don't want to... bother him."

"You're not bothering him," Honor assures him and her voice nearly cracks. Leo closes his eyes.

"It's okay," Colson says and looks down at his hands. "You don't have to lie to me."

"I'm *not*." Honor insisted at the time, insists now.

"Then why doesn't he come?" Colson's whisper is painful, and Honor releases the trick. Leo opens his eyes and stares at the spot Colson had been standing. His expression is so often closed and unreadable, but he's not hiding now. He looks like someone just broke his heart. Honor would know what that looks like.

"It's hard," he says eventually, voice hardly louder than Colson's had been.

"I know that," Honor says softly.

"I miss him," he admits, still staring at the empty spot. "But he's not him anymore."

"Are any of us?" she asks. Honor is grateful everyday that she's changed and that she continues to change, but change is hard. It's hard to do, and it's hard for people to watch. It's especially hard with Colson, though, she knows that. She feels that.

"I don't know how to do this," he admits. "When it was the hospital, it was—fine. Familiar. We've all been in the hospital so many times we should get a goddamn stamp card. But when he moved to Ameliora and it... it was real. What he did became real. What he did to you. What he tried to do to himself. All the things he did with that *bitch*. And I didn't—I don't know how to—fuck."

"No one knows how to do this," she tells him.

"You do," he says with a scoff.

"The fuck I do," she says.

"Please," he says, and it's so close to a sneer that Honor is taken aback. Leo faces her fully then, gesturing widely with his arms. "Look around us. At all of this. That was all you. Colson being in Ameliora and not in the Matchbox was all you. You always know what you're doing and it always works out the way you want!"

"Oh," Honor says as she pauses to feel the vortex of rage and grief that's building in her chest. A soft exhalation, the first screaming wind. "You don't know, do you?"

"Know what?" he sighs.

Honor hasn't told anyone other than Verity and Grace about what happened. Aurora knows because she was there. Colson knows because he had tried to stop her. But Leo doesn't know.

"I was the one who released Krewa," she tells him.

Disgust is notably absent in his initial reaction and that calms her nerves a little. He's clearly shocked and confused, looking around the otherwise empty room for some sort of evidence that it's Honor's fault hundreds of people are dead and Titans are now known to roam about the galaxy.

"What are you talking about?"

"Um, the short version?" she starts. "I found out the agency I worked at was keeping her hostage in the basement, and I set her free. Colson tried to stop me and we fought about it. It got ugly, really ugly, and he left. Went to his mother."

"You never let anyone leave an argument until you win," Leo points out. Honor flinches. "What happened?"

"I was going to go after him," she tells him. "But then… then Grace came back. In my head. I heard her voice for the first time in a year, and I thought she was *dead*. So I figured I could wait to find Colson until we had both cooled off and Krewa would fuck off to wherever she came from and I could have my sister back. But I was wrong on all fucking counts." Her eyes sting as she remembers the absolute avalanche of events that had swept her up in less than a week. "Krewa was the Titan who killed my mom. I don't think I told you that, either. We thought she had killed Grace too. But it turns out our dad had taken her to New York and wiped her memories so she wouldn't look for us because when we're together we're a beacon for other Titans, apparently.

"So, it was a shit show. Krewa wanted revenge on the people who held her captive, and Colson was gone, and Grace doesn't get to stay because my asshole dad was *right* and all of that because I didn't know what the hell I was doing. All of those people are dead because of me. I put us on the cosmic map. All of that was my fault. But you know what? After all of that, I found you again. We reconnected and I was so happy to have you back that just being around you made me feel better. You didn't know any of that, wouldn't have known what to do about it if you had, but just you being there was more than enough for me and it will be more than enough for Colson."

She pauses and gives Leo time to respond but he doesn't. His face is once again impassive, and she hates that but if he needs to hide behind a shield right now then she won't call him on it.

"I'm just making shit up as I go along," she tells him. "I do it with an absurd amount of bravado so that's probably why I look like I always know what I'm doing... but I'm *terrified* of making the wrong decision again. Please don't hate me."

Leo's expression softens at that. "I don't hate you," he says immediately. "I don't hate Colson, either. I just—I don't know if I'm ready."

"That's okay," she says and wipes her eyes. "Take all the time you need. I just think that maybe we should talk more because apparently this was something that was bugging me and I didn't even realize."

"We should definitely talk more," he says with just enough emphasis to make her giggle. "Because it's been two years since the Titan Battle and I'm just now learning all of this."

"I didn't keep it from you on purpose," she says. "I just didn't know how to tell you."

"This worked," he says with a little shrug. He takes a hesitant step forward. "And I guess I can say more things too."

"Okay," Honor says with a snotty laugh. The second Leo reaches like he might want to touch her, Honor launches herself at him in a hug. Leo has always been sturdy, and today is no exception. He catches her full weight easily and hugs her tight. "I don't like when we fight."

"All things considered, I think our fights are pretty tame, I mean, look at you and Colson," he says, and she pinches him. She feels his lips on her shoulder through her thin t-shirt and wraps her arms around him so tight his spine cracks in a few places. But Leo doesn't ask her to let go.

14

The kids are gaining momentum. Honor can see the way they feed off of each other with every exercise, whether it's a rescue sim or maxing out in the weight room. It's heartening to Honor, to see them so dedicated and determined. They're not perfect, of course, because they're still kids. Charlie does too much herself. Jack can't communicate well. Ethan is too timid in sims. Lochlan is too hesitant to develop his marvel. But those are all things Honor and her team can help them overcome, so she's not stressed about it. Well, she's trying not to be.

Honor seems to exist in a constant state of stress. Part of it is a side effect of the job, both of her jobs, as a pro and a teacher. She's been taking night patrols almost exclusively so she can be available during school hours which is hurting her image according to the agency PR team. The people need to see her, apparently. Honor isn't a fiend for the spotlight, but she's hot and it pays the Academy's monstrous bills, especially since half the kids are on 'scholarship,' which is really just

Honor letting them in for free. Jack's parents made a sizable donation, though, which she appreciates.

Any second of free time she has is spent at Ameliora with Colson, which admittedly, isn't as much as she would like. But Colson understands. Verity doesn't, though. Verity visits Colson maybe once a month, then makes judgey eyebrows at Honor whenever she comes back from her weekly visits.

She's doing it right now, across the coffee table in their living room while they have progress reports for the kids strewn between them. Honor is heroically ignoring it even though she's sure Verity can see her irritation in her aura perfectly clear.

"Charlie says the strength of her marvel correlates with how hard she hits, but given the stats that Aurora compiled, I don't think that's true," Honor says. Verity hums. "I think it might be mental, and since she assumes the size will be bigger if she hits harder, it is. But it could probably work without her beating the shit out of herself."

"You should tell her that," Verity says. Honor slates her with an annoyed glare.

"I will," she replies. "You got something to add?"

Verity pretends to think about it. "No, I don't think I do."

"Okay then. I think we need to start having the kids classified before the start of the school year," she continues.

"I said that during the entrance exam," Verity points out.

"You did," Honor acknowledges. "You were right."

"I'm right a lot," Verity says modestly with a considering hum. Honor's eye twitches.

"Yeah, like about Jayne's wings and how she doesn't have muscles strong enough to support them in her back and shoulders," Honor diverts. "She said the supports that

Aurora made for her are helping, but how's her strength training coming?"

"Well enough," Verity says. "She's too scared to add weight on her own. I usually have to tell her to do it." Honor writes that down in her development plan. They've already received their initial plans from Aurora, but they'll get new ones at the end of the semester. Honor wants to stay on top of it so she doesn't accidentally leave anything out.

"What about Tommy?" She asks.

"What about him?"

"Has he been able to find another time slot for his therapy appointments?"

"Not yet," she says because Tommy still tells Verity everything. "He says he still texts her when he really needs to, but he doesn't have time for regular appointments."

"Did you tell him—"

"That he can take some time at the beginning or end of training to do it? Yeah. He doesn't want to do that," she says. "Cora takes off early on Tuesdays, though."

"Good," Honor says and means it. She considers working in a free period into their schedule for the future so the kids can have time for self care like that. Most of them would probably use it to sleep, but Honor wouldn't mind. Sleep is important for growing kids. She knows a decent few like Charlie and Jack, would just use it as extra time to train. That wouldn't necessarily be a bad thing. She just doesn't want them to overdo it.

"Rae said she could cover me on the next midnight drill," Verity says, thankfully focusing fully on work again. "I'm going to New York to assist on a case with a sensory manipulation marvel."

"Why wasn't I tapped for that?"

"You took yourself off of the loan list," Verity reminds her. The "Loan List" is the nickname for the volunteer list at their agency for team ups and consultations. Of course, if something is directly up Honor's alley, they can still ask her, but she won't be the first stop.

"Okay, give my love to Anders," she says, distracted once again by the papers in front of her. She searches for the one that outlines the details of their next midnight drill and crosses out Verity's name when she finds it.

"Anyone else I should give your love to?" Verity asks. Honor glares at her.

"Just fucking spit it out or leave it alone," Honor snaps.

"Awful defensive over a simple question," Verity says. Honor resists the urge to give into her frustration and fight her sister. Verity doesn't play these kinds of games with anyone else. Says they're too tiring, unless it's her. And Grace, but Grace isn't *here*, so Honor is left as Verity's sole victim.

"What, Verity? *What?* I don't know what it is that you want from me!"

"You know I can see your aura whenever you come back from visiting Colson?" Verity asks, and of course Honor knows that, that's how both her sisters' marvel works. She knows it almost as well as her own. "Do you want to know what color it is?"

Honor freezes.

She hadn't considered that. *Stupid.* She's not even sure what color it is, but it must be some shade of incriminating if Verity is pulling a stunt like this.

"It's awfully similar to the color it is whenever you're with Leo," she goes on without waiting for an answer. Honor continues to say nothing. Verity is too good at twisting words for her to try and defend herself now. She doesn't even know what she's defending. She's woefully unarmed. Verity looks around her, at the space by her ear, above the crown of her head, even around her hands. Where Honor sees empty air, Verity sees the innermost makings of her emotional center. She can't imagine it's very pretty right now.

"And?" Honor prompts. Verity notes her lack of response and continues to scan her aura. Honor's never really been jealous of her sister's sight, either of them. They can't turn it off—well, Verity can, but not without consequence. They have no choice but to experience the world through their own personalized filters that often reveal too much to them, but damn if Honor wouldn't like to see what Verity's thinking right now.

"You love them?" Verity asks, uncharacteristically soft.

"Yes," Honor answers without hesitation. Partially because it's true, but also because she knows Verity would be able to see a lie. Then she adds, almost defensively, "So do you."

"Yeah," Verity says quietly, still looking somewhere over her shoulder. "I do too."

When it becomes clear that her sister isn't going to elaborate or push her buttons further, she returns to the development and lesson plans in front of her. She's got some resumes buried under there somewhere too, because they're definitely going to need to hire some more help next year. They're barely making it by as it is. They'll sink for sure if they add forty new students to the mix with just the six of them.

Leo gets home from patrol before the silence gets too thick, and if he notices anything amiss, he doesn't comment. He just flops down on the unoccupied couch and pouts.

"I'm hungry," he says.

"Then eat," Verity replies without pity.

"We should hire someone so we can have a twenty-four hour caf," he says. "Like the one my agency has. We can't cater every meal forever."

"Think you can filch the chef from your agency?" Honor asks him. He picks up his head to look at her.

"I could work some magic," he says. Verity snorts.

"You got a marvel we don't know about? One that makes you magically charming instead of tired and cranky?" she asks.

Leo pushes a shield at her and it knocks her and the chair she's sitting in over backwards.

Verity just cackles and picks herself up. "I'm gonna go pack. If you guys order something let me know."

Honor hums her acknowledgment.

"Honor," Leo yawns. "Will you cook?"

"Sure, what do you want?" She makes the mistake of looking up and finds Verity staring at her from the edge of the hall.

Fed up, Honor snaps her fingers. Verity yelps and jumps back when an old rogue appears in front of her, one that could grow teeth from his skin. He had really freaked Verity out.

"Oh, I'm gonna fuckin' remember that!" she shouts as the trick disappears. "You suck so hard!"

"Love you too!" Honor calls after her as she storms down the hall.

"I want chili beef bowls!" she shouts back. Honor will make the chili beef bowls and they'll be fine like they always are.

"Something I should know about?" Leo asks.

"Nothing you should worry your pretty little head about," Honor says with a smile convincing enough for him to fall back to the couch and close his eyes. She grabs the front of his vest and yanks him back up. "Nu-uh. You're helping. Get to chopping." Leo groans but does as he's told.

Honor's glad she can't see her own aura. It makes it easier to ignore.

Hero school turns out to be a lot like regular school in the sense that, in Charlie's opinion, there is entirely too much homework. The Titan Academy faculty doesn't believe in the typical multiple choice tests, so everything is short answers and essays, and Charlie finds herself typing thousands of words each week just for homework.

What makes a hero?

Should the death penalty be abolished? Why or why not?

What came first, the hero or the villain?

Pick one of the original ten pro heroes. Do you think they were successful? Why or why not?

It's not enough to just memorize facts. Charlie has to string her thoughts together in a coherent manner and present it in writing, all without swearing. It's not even just hero theory that's like that, it's history and tech and language arts too.

There are some fun assignments, though, the quirky ones that Charlie had apparently spent too much time imagining because they don't happen all that often. They learned how to fly evac helicopters with Aurora. They spent a whole class hotwiring various vehicles. Honor covered for Leo one day in homeroom and gave them an extra credit assignment to make Leo smile because part of being a hero is making people feel safe and happy. The class took the challenge on with heart, but after weeks of nothing more than a mere twitch, their outlook is pretty bleak.

Charlie has never been this sore in her entire life, either. Verity is kicking their ass in weight training, and while Charlie has gone from being able to snatch only the forty-five pound bar to one hundred and sixty pounds in just three months, she feels like her arms are going to fall off on a daily basis. Then she has to carry two hundred pound dummies during training with Honor, from whom she receives no sympathy.

Then, because Charlie is quickly learning that she must be some sort of masochist, she also does early morning training sessions before class by herself. Until Tommy starts showing up to do the same. They run through their exercises separate and silent for the most part. Tommy doesn't seem to harbor any bad feelings at all, let alone any toward Charlie for landing him in detention. Charlie would still insist that it's all Jack's fault, anyway.

They won't do much combat training at all during their first year since it's so search and rescue-focused. It's also to deter people from applying to hero courses if they're just in it to look badass and not to actually help people like they should be. But Charlie doesn't want to start so far behind her biggest competition, and for the time being, she's sure it's Jack and Tommy.

The rest of the class seems sure too. They've divided into factions. Charlie wouldn't call them cliques, per se, because there's a lot of crossover and almost all of them get along. But there's a clear divide between people who would align themselves with her, Tommy, and Jack given the choice.

Obviously Lochlan would be on Charlie's side in this imaginary competition, and she's fairly certain Malia and Kai would be too. Luna might, but she also might side with Tommy, who has Cora squarely in his corner. Rose is another wildcard between all three of them, but Charlie is constantly inviting her to hang out, mostly because she likes her, but also because her mom owns one of the largest hero support tech companies in the country and it couldn't hurt to have a hook up.

Anthony had practically glued himself to Jack's side, with whatever industrial strength hair gel he uses, and Jack seems to tolerate him. Alex also gravitates towards Jack, and Charlie, for the life of her, can't imagine why. Boy Wonder's social skills rank in the negatives on a scale of one to ten. But to each their own.

One day during training, Charlie asks Tommy to void her. He seems taken aback by the request.

"Well, we should also be training our marvels, right?" she asks. They received their development plans, and while they work on them sometimes with Honor during training hours, their training is still mostly focused on search and rescue exercises.

"Shouldn't we be, I don't know, supervised or something?"

Charlie shrugs. She gestures around the empty arena. "There's cameras everywhere, I'm sure. Aurora's probably supervising right now."

Tommy looks around as if to confirm.

"Come on, it's not like you can hurt me," Charlie goads. Tommy doesn't rise to the bait. Sometimes Charlie wishes she could be that patient.

"But *you* could hurt *me*," he points out.

"You can't void externals?" she asks, surprised. Her mom can. Any external force generated by a marvel doesn't touch her. She could void Charlie's blasts, but she wouldn't be able to do anything if Jack hurled a giant boulder at her because that already existed. Her mom can't void a whole person just by touching them, either, so Charlie supposes she shouldn't have assumed.

"I—I've never tried," he says. "I try to avoid getting hit by other people's marvels as a general rule."

"Good rule," Charlie says and grins. "Why don't we give it a try? You void me and I'll try to fight it off, or whatever. Then I'll hit you."

"With your fist?"

"*No,* my marvel!"

"I think this is why we need instruction," Tommy sighs.

"No, come on, Honor just gave me some new notes and I want to test them out," Charlie says, bouncing on the balls of her feet. Tommy notes her genuine excitement and acquiesces. He grabs her hand because it's as good a place as any, counts to ten, not out loud but he mouths the numbers, then lets her go.

Charlie feels it the second he touches her, the way her marvel sloughs away. It's disorienting, and she feels bereft for how much lighter she feels. Tommy watches her carefully.

"Woah," is all she can manage, and she flexes her hand, watches the tendons in her wrist slide. When she curls her fingers into a fist, her marvel doesn't gather at the points of contact. She clenches her jaw.

"I'm sorry," Tommy says.

"What are you sorry for?" she asks, bewildered.

"You don't like it."

She furrows her brow and tries to activate her marvel by rubbing her thumb across the pads of her fingers. It doesn't work. It's not the first time Charlie's ever been voided. It's not even the first time *Tommy* has voided her, but she's not sure she'll ever get used to it.

"Of course I don't like it," she says. "But why would you be sorry about that?" She watches Tommy open his mouth then close it. "I'm not sorry when I use my marvel, and you shouldn't be sorry when you use yours. *Especially* when you start to use it on rogues. What? Are you gonna apologize to them too?" Tommy winces a bit at that. "Your marvel is cool as hell. And I do like it. But not when you use it on me."

"That's fair," he says with a soft laugh. Charlie's marvel comes back and she feels it rush under her skin like electricity.

"Ready?" she asks.

"Already?" he asks, surprised. Charlie can't help but feel a bit smug about that. He takes a step back and holds his arms out. "Hit me, I guess."

Using only her fingertips, she focuses on the size she wants, already intimately familiar with the baby blast her fingertips can produce. This time, she visualizes a bigger blast, the kind that usually comes from a full clap but urges it out of her finger tips. If Honor is right and she can control the size of her blasts by sheer force of will, then it's a total game changer.

She releases her fingers, and the recoil that shoots through them is strong enough to make her wrist ache. The glimmering force only she can see rips through the air toward Tommy and hits him dead on, knocking him flat on his back.

"Oh." He coughs and struggles to breathe. Charlie dashes over to him and offers him a hand up.

"Did you even try?" she asks, sounding like an asshole, but meaning to be genuine. He takes her hand and lets her haul him up to his feet.

"I don't know how to try," he admits, rubbing his chest where he'd taken the brunt of her marvel.

"How do you activate your marvel?" She asks.

"Um, when I touch people, I can feel their marvel. Sort of like a low vibration. Everyone is a little different, but I just focus on making that stop," he tells her.

"Can you feel the vibration when you don't touch?" she asks. He shakes his head. "Hm. Well, maybe we do need instruction."

"I probably just can't do it," he says with an affable shrug. "It's okay."

"Yeah, well," she says and slings an arm around his shoulders. He's a bit taller than her so he has to hunch to allow it. "I think you can. Ask one of the teachers. They might have some ideas. You hungry?"

"I could eat," he says. "But we'll be late to homeroom." Charlie waves him off.

"Let's bring Leo some too and see if he smiles," she says, voice low, like they're conspiring even though most of their classmates are probably still asleep.

"Let's give it a shot," he says and brings an arm up around her shoulders too. They walk like that back to the dorms to clean up and then snag breakfast. They are late, but not by a lot. Leo is grateful for his breakfast burrito, but he doesn't smile.

In fact, he seems even more tired than usual. The bags under his eyes are more pronounced and his countenance so grave, Charlie half expects him to tell them that someone died. But no, they're just getting to study exclusive footage from the Honor vs. Incendiary fight. Charlie is as excited as the rest of the class but something else is off. She just can't pinpoint what it is.

15

"Is Rogue Reform a Suitable Alternative to Prison? Experts Weigh In"

—*Hero Review*

Charlie has been looking forward to this all week. She's watched every angle available on the internet but to see Honor's point of view first hand, an exclusive that was never released to the public, has Charlie buzzing. Leo plays the video without introduction.

The video starts earlier than Charlie was expecting. Honor stands in Rizzo's and waits in line. She's the one who calls out to Incendiary first, and when he turns, he's clearly anything but friendly. He sets off an explosion that sends Honor crashing through the front windows of the restaurant and rolling into the street.

The camera was hidden in the necklace Honor was wearing. They lose sight of Incendiary sometimes, but the quality is so crystal clear that Charlie can see the stray thread on the sleeve of his t-shirt when he gets close.

"What are you doing?" Honor's voice is loud and not at all distorted or distant like it is in every other video Charlie

has seen. She gets chills just thinking about what's going to happen later on in the video.

"Don't follow me," says Incendiary. But Honor grabs his arm to stop him from leaving. Charlie's never seen this part before because people didn't realize what was happening just yet. But she can see in the background people are starting to take notice.

"Talk to me. What's wrong?" Honor asks. Begs. Charlie shifts in her chair. She's never heard Honor sound like that. So desperate and worried. She looks around at her classmates, who are all watching the screen with rapt attention. They also look vaguely uncomfortable. This is not the famous brawl they were expecting. Charlie glances toward Leo and finds him watching the class, turned fully away from the screen, with his mouth set in a grim line. He meets Charlie's gaze evenly, and Charlie looks away quickly, back to the video.

"Let. Go," Incendiary says. It sounds like a warning.

Then, Honor says, *"Ravenna"* and Charlie is lost. Who is Ravenna and why is Honor invoking her name now? But then, Incendiary panics, blows Honor up, and this is where Charlie gets a fresh view of everything she's seen before a thousand times.

The way Honor flies through the air and into a garbage truck makes Charlie nauseous, from the motion and from the realization that if that had been anyone else, they'd probably be dead. Another hero helps Honor save the nearby civilians and start the evacuations, and Honor's hero voice gives Charlie chills. It's different from her teaching voice, from her regular, everyday voice. It's tight and controlled and carries so much authority that no one would dare go against her.

The next part they've all seen, but watching it like this, from Honor's point of view, from a first person point of view, makes Charlie dizzy. Every time Honor's chest heaves with breath, the camera moves. They get a view of the sky when Honor is rocked by another explosion and goes flying. They see Honor get knocked down and get back up over and over and over.

When it reaches the part they've all been waiting for, everyone leans forward in their seats, their chairs scraping across linoleum floors and desks creaking under the weight of elbows.

"Are you done?" Incendiary shouts.

"Am I dead?" Honor shouts back. Charlie's shoulders hunch up against the sudden rush of chills that hit her in anticipation of what's coming next. *"THEN I'M NOT FUCKING DONE."*

Her voice cracks.

Charlie's never heard that before. Honor is too far away from the crowd to truly be heard. All the cell phone cameras pick up is an echo. Just the words and not the feeling behind them, and suddenly Charlie feels ill.

When Honor is blasted into the ground, creating a crater, Charlie watches the girl separate herself from the crowd and come running to save her. The first time Charlie ever saw that, she was equal parts shocked and jealous. She wants to believe that she would have done the same thing, jumped to the aid of her hero given the chance, but she wouldn't be able to help the way this girl does.

Wait.

The way *Malia* does. It's Malia who heals Honor in the video. She'd been too far and small to really see before, but she's standing right in front of Honor, and it's clear as day with her butterscotch hair and cheeks still full of baby fat even though it was only a year ago. Several people whisper with the same realization, and Malia sinks lower in her seat in the front row.

Honor returns Malia to her family and then takes Incendiary for a ride. This is where the other videos cut off because Honor and Incendiary disappear. It was later announced on the news that Incendiary was in custody and Honor was already fully recovered from her injuries.

But now they get to see.

They land in a neighborhood that looks a lot like Charlie's, and Honor pins Incendiary down. He shouts and snarls at her and struggles to get away, but he can't. Honor is too strong. Charlie expects Honor to arrest him or knock him out cold or something.

She doesn't expect Honor's anguished, "STOP!" Charlie can't see her face, but she sounds on the verge of tears. Incendiary's eyes go wide, and Honor's necklace swings between them when she catches his other hand before he can use it to blow her up.

"*FUCK! Get off, get off!*" Incendiary cries, and Charlie's gut twists into an ugly knot. He's all bloody and his face is twisted up like he could cry at any second.

"*I'm sorry,*" Honor chokes the words out, and Charlie goes completely still. *Honor* is sorry? "*I'm sorry! I'm sorry, please.*"

This time he does manage to blow her up and she goes flying across the street. When Honor and the camera settle, Honor breathes a soft, "*Colson.*"

Charlie gets the feeling something bad is about to happen. Somehow worse than what's already happened. It's the same feeling she gets when she watches movies, knowing that there's no stopping whatever is about to happen, that she's helpless and these poor people are already doomed to their fates.

Incendiary shakes his head and says something inaudible. Then he lifts a bloody hand to his ear.

"Colson, DON'T—" Honor's scream shakes her chest and the camera, and she dives for him, but he's all the way across the street. Even Honor can't beat a point blank explosion.

Incendiary screams and his own hand takes the brunt of his explosion. It takes Charlie too long to figure out what exactly happened. She watches Honor scramble over to Incendiary, crying now, and Charlie has never heard Honor cry before. It breaks Charlie's heart.

It's not until Leo comes into the frame and leaves it just as quick that Charlie realizes it was him who stopped the explosion with a shield. He'd stopped Incendiary from hurting himself, killing himself, probably. Honor is still crying and it's hard to hear. For the first time, Charlie is grateful that she can't see her.

"Why? Why did he—"

"I don't know," Leo's voice is unmistakable even though they can't see him anymore. Not in the video, at least. He's still seated perfectly still in the front of the classroom watching them stoically. *"But he's going to be okay."*

"How do you know?" Honor asks and sniffs hard. The only thing they can see is Incendiary's prone form on the ruined lawn. Soot and dirt cover his face, and his own blood stains the grass underneath him. Even out cold, he doesn't look peaceful, but pained. For the first time since seeing this fight, Charlie feels bad for him.

"Because we've got him," Leo says. *"We've got him back and we're gonna take care of him."*

Leo shuts the video off. The silence rings louder than ever through the classroom. Leo lets them sit and stew in it. The air conditioning rattles and kicks on, and Charlie shivers. She resists the urge to look around at her classmates, not willing to risk reprimand at a time like this.

"Desperate people do desperate things. Do you know why Colson did this?" Leo asks to complete silence. Charlie realizes that in the hundreds of times she'd watched this fight, she'd never stopped to ask why. Not once.

"Does it even *matter?*" Charlie exclaims.

"*Yes, it matters,*" Leo says with the most feeling that Charlie's ever seen from him. It's fierce, and Charlie is startled by it. "Did you notice the only damage done was to the city and not a single civilian was harmed?"

"What about the damage to *Honor?*" Charlie's startled protest is out of her mouth before she can stop it.

"Honor has forgiven Colson and it is not your place to be angry on her behalf," Leo says. His voice is low and level, almost cold. Leo has never spoken to them this way, and it makes the top of Charlie's spine tingle. "Nor do you have to forgive him, but if you think your forgiveness is the one way ticket to reform, then you are sorely mistaken. No one needs your approval to be better tomorrow than they are today. No one needs your permission. And if you try to stop someone from becoming better then I regret to inform you that you've grossly misjudged this profession and it just might be better off without you.

"Good. Bad. It doesn't matter. It doesn't matter what he is. What *you* deem him to be. He's a person. What matters is what you are," Leo says. "Are *you* a good person? If you answer yes, then you should really think long and hard about what makes a good person and whether or not judgment to the point of death is one of those things.

"Heroes save anyone who needs saving. That's the job."

The silence that follows is agonizing. He's said what he needed to say and now it's their turn. Except no one has anything to say. Not Charlie. Not Jack. Not Malia. The Honor versus Incendiary fight is the stuff of legends even though it's not even two years old yet. They'd destroyed half the city in that fight, and Leo had said there were *no injuries?*

It seems impossible. Charlie can't wrap her mind around it. She's watched that fight a hundred times from fifty different angles and not once did she ever consider that—that what? She doesn't even know what it is that she's supposed to be considering.

She knew that Honor and Colson had been friends, everyone did. Vaguely, because the news would mention that they were in the same graduating class from Marvelous so of course they knew each other. Leo would too, and Verity and their other sister Grace. Then a piece of the puzzle clicks into place. Leo had used the big teacher words and used this to teach them a lesson about being a hero but he launched straight into an impassioned tirade without pausing to ask any of them what they thought. Leo never does that. He always gives them room to be wrong and to learn on their own but not with this. This was personal. Emotional. Leo was defending his friend.

Charlie glances over at Lochlan. She couldn't imagine what it would be like to have to fight him for whatever reason. But she doesn't *have* to because Lochlan would never do anything like that!

The silence is deafening. Not a single one of them wants to say anything, especially not when Leo's like this. Anything they have to say in opposition would no doubt be rebuked without kindness or compunction. Leo always has an air of sleepiness around him, like he's ready to take a nap at any given moment, too tired to really care much about the superfluous things in life, but he's wide awake now and the full weight of his attention is almost overbearing.

They sit like that, no one saying a word until Leo dismisses them and leaves the room. They have ten minutes before their next class.

"That was you, right?" Jack asks Malia, breaking the silence.

"Yeah," she says and sits back in her chair.

"So that's why you got in," he says, and Charlie pushes to her feet immediately.

"Do we need to fight again?" she asks, but Malia just shakes her head.

"Bold words for the poster boy of nepotism," she says.

Jack's neck flushes red, and Charlie sits back down, satisfied with his verbal smackdown instead of the physical one she's ready to deliver on a moment's notice. Some of the others start to murmur to their deskmates or across aisles.

"Well, I've been wrong before but this is…" Lochlan trails off, looking down at his page of notes. He hadn't written anything besides the date.

"This is a load of bullshit," Charlie hisses. "There needs to be consequences for actions or people will just do whatever they want."

"He's in Ameliora," Malia turns around to talk to them. "That's the consequence."

"A hero saves anyone who needs saving," Tommy says behind Charlie. She turns half way around to see him. "That's… is that not what everyone wrote for their entrance exams?"

"Is that what *you* wrote for your essay?" Charlie asks.

"Well, yeah," Tommy says, earnest and innocent. Charlie never pictured herself hating Tommy before that moment.

"Then it's a miracle that anyone besides Tommy got in," Lochlan mutters. Charlie never read Lochlan's essay, but she knows they had similar viewpoints. Heroes use their abilities to save those who can't save themselves. She vaguely remembers Leo saying something about how there's no one right answer, but there are wrong answers. So maybe they weren't wrong in the strongest sense of the words. But Tommy seems to be ahead of them by a mile. Yet another way Charlie is falling behind.

"Boy Wonder," Charlie calls across the classroom. Everyone else stops what they're doing to watch the exchange.

"What?"

"What did you write for the essay?" She asks. Jack just glares at her, unwilling to answer and especially in front of the whole class but then she tacks on, "Tommy wants to know." Tommy didn't explicitly say as much but because he actually does want to know, he doesn't contradict Charlie.

"I wrote that heroes protect people," he answers, which is vague and ambiguous and not good enough in Charlie's opinion, but she doesn't press him.

"So, what? Are we supposed to just… forgive Incendiary?" Ethan cuts into the conversation.

"I don't think we have to forgive anyone," Tommy says diplomatically. "I think the point was to challenge the way we see rogues and our perception of what it means to be a hero."

"You don't sound very challenged," Charlie accused. Tommy just shrugs. "That dude that kidnapped you," she starts and watches him tense. "Do you forgive him?"

Tommy looks at his desk, twirls his pens between his fingers, "No," he answers quietly.

"Do you think he needed to be saved?"

"Yes," he answers, immediate and solemn. "If someone had saved him when he needed it most, I wouldn't have needed saving at all."

"Well, fuck," Charlie says, simultaneously impressed with his emotional intelligence and irritated with her own lack thereof. Tommy offers her a smile and she can't help but smile back because Tommy's smiles are contagious and beautiful. No one else gets a chance to comment because Teddy comes in a few minutes early to get ready for their history class.

Charlie turns back around and kicks Malia's chair before she does the same. "Good job, *hero*," she says with a grin. Malia blushes and fights off her own smile. What Charlie wouldn't give for Honor to call her *hero*.

She doesn't pay attention at all during history. Still stuck on the Incendiary—*Colson,* Honor and Leo only ever call him Colson—fight. She doesn't understand how Colson could do something like that, attack his supposed best friend until she was beaten and bloody in the middle of the street, and still pretend that he's a good person.

Then she remembers the end of the video, the exclusive. The part the general public never saw. Aurora's cameras are so good that Colson's expression was clear as day on screen, so much anguish and guilt that even Charlie could see it. As much as Charlie wants to condemn rogues for their actions, she can't quite reconcile the villainous Incendiary in her head with Honor's supposed best friend, crying on a stranger's lawn and trying to blow himself up.

Charlie glances at Lochlan next to her. She thinks about it again—if he ever tried anything like that, hurting himself in front of her with her powerless to help… her chest seizes at the mere thought. She can't even imagine it, not really, because Lochlan would never do that. But that's probably what Honor thought too.

It's all so complicated. With so many moving parts. Charlie can't possibly know everything about everyone. She's finding she knows less than she thought too. Heroes fight bad guys. But if all bad guys are just hurt people who need to be saved then why do heroes fight? *Are* all bad guys just hurt people who need to be saved? If not, how is Charlie supposed to tell the difference? Surely, the ones rotting away in the Matchbox don't need to be saved.

Above all else, Charlie trusts Honor. Honor has never done anything except put herself on the line to help others. If Charlie wants to be a hero like Honor, then she's going to have to save anyone who needs saving too. But how is she supposed to tell who needs saving and who needs a good old fashion ass-whooping? Does Honor have a system? Maybe Charlie should ask. Maybe it's not save *anyone* who needs saving, but the people who meet certain criteria. That would make the most sense, Charlie thinks.

For the first time, Charlie is glad that she has so much time between now and becoming a full-fledged pro. This must be why a hero course takes six years. At least she has time to figure it out.

16

"Attempted Prison Break Foiled by Justice and Team"
—*Titan Daily*

"The kids are coming along," Verity says as she takes a seat next to Honor. They're high up in the bleachers to avoid the violent shaking of the stadium floor for the earthquake simulation. Honor hums her agreement. Some are coming along much quicker than others but they've all come so far in a relatively short amount of time.

Jack, as she suspected, is ahead of the bunch when it comes to physical prowess. His strategy is also decent, judging from his papers, but he struggles to implement them in practical situations when he has to work with even a single other person. Honor can't figure out if it's a leadership issue, if he's just shy, or if he thinks he can lone wolf his way to the top like his dad. If it's the last one, they may have a problem. But the first two are easy. Jack will grow more confident and eventually come out of his shell on his own with the right encouragement, which Honor and the others are sure to provide. Once he realizes his natural leadership and learns to use it? He'll be just fine.

Kids like Ethan, on the other hand, Honor is a little worried about. Honor knows he's got a great mind for hero work, especially when it comes to search and rescue. She's seen his videos, and he's got great insight even when he doesn't have all of the facts. Honor can recall a video he made about a job she and Leo did—a sinkhole in Pennsylvania. He critiqued their technique, claiming that Leo could have just used his shields to stabilize the sink hole while Honor and the other heroes on site got the victims out. His plan is a good one, and on a good day, it's probably something they would have considered doing, but he couldn't have known the extent of Leo's power on a good day, let alone that day. Honor and Leo had apprehended a fugitive who had put up quite the fight just that morning and neither of them were at full strength. So he didn't have all the facts, but the video was rife with facts he *did* have. Honor now knows more about sinkholes than she ever wanted to. Ethan, though, struggles with application, period. His analyses are usually close to flawless, some of the best in the class, but he freezes during practicals. Hard.

Malia has recused herself from triage duties, which Honor understands is a point of pride for her. Just because she has a healing marvel doesn't mean she should be stuck in triage *every* time. Honor appreciates the way she's utilized her marvel to heal otherwise immovable victims on site, it's very effective and lessens the burden on the triage team, but she'll have to do triage at some point.

Lochlan has yet to use his marvel during practicals at all. Honor will admit that his marvel isn't one especially equipped for search and rescue sims, but she's gone out of her way to give him openings that he either doesn't see or deliberately doesn't take.

Honor has detailed reviews of each of the students, complete with video footage. She plans to track their progress and give it to them at the end of the year so they can see for themselves just how far they've come. She knows that it can be tough to work so hard and think you have nothing to show for it because progress like this, the kind that can't be measured in neat little numbers like a lifting max weight, is hard to see in oneself.

Whenever Honor starts to feel the stress of *it's not enough, we have to do more, we have to win the tournament* she takes a deep breath to calm herself down. She can't let her school be like Marvelous. She can't. She *won't*. Her mind starts to spiral now, while she's supposed to be supervising an earthquake sim. She feels the cool rush of Verity's marvel wash over her skin and she relaxes in her seat.

"What's got your panties in a twist?" Verity asks, keeping her eyes on the sim. Jack thrives in this setting, moving the torn-up pieces of earth aside to free the bots trapped underneath. But there's a lack of cohesive work from his teammates, the others aren't sure who should be doing what and they're all over the place to the point where Jack almost sets a large slab of rock directly on top of Cora.

"Just thinking," Honor sighs.

"That'll do it," Verity says, and Honor huffs a laugh.

Jack's group finishes up, and Honor writes down their scores. The arena resets for Charlie and her group. Charlie really is just like Honor in the best and worst ways. She's quick to throw hands, confident, loud, and not afraid to take charge. She's a natural leader, already informing her group of their game plan before the sim is even set. She has an excellent grasp of not only her classmates' marvels, but also their personalities, what they excel at, what they're afraid of, and she's able to take it all into account.

Honor had listened to her figure out some of the locations of their tiles during the midnight drill. It had taken her all of three seconds to deduce that the tiles weren't randomly strewn around the district. She hadn't quite figured out where all of them were or the exact pattern Honor had used, but that's just because she's young and inexperienced. She'll only get better, smarter. But Honor is worried that along with those things, her fuse will grow shorter and her tolerance will lessen.

Charlie is already so full of conviction, and it's a good thing, but if she continues like this, that conviction could easily morph into something ugly like insularity. Honor has slipped down that slope, and it's a muddy climb back up. But Charlie is so many things that Honor isn't. She's kind and desperate to prove herself in a way Honor never was because Honor had been up to her ears in her own bullshit.

Charlie gets up early every morning to do extra training with Tommy. She helps Kai study. She sticks up for her friends even if it's *to* her friends. Honor constantly has to remind herself that though Charlie may remind her of herself to a frightening degree, she is her own person. As her teacher, Honor can only guide her. Charlie has to make the decisions for herself.

She makes the decisions now, breaking up the larger slabs of concrete from underneath with her marvel and letting her team pull the victims out. She's careful about how much force to use, but her marvel is still too unpredictable and some of the rubble ends up crushing the legs of a dummy. Charlie swears, loud and colorful.

"Swearing in a situation like this is ill-advised," Honor shouts down to her. "You're only making the victim feel worse, possibly panic. Shit happens, keep working."

"Yes, ma'am," Charlie says with a salute. She's coachable too, which is more than Honor could say about her younger self.

"That behavior gets docked in the tournament," Honor says to Verity.

"I know," she says with a scoff, probably remembering how Honor had cursed out a patient who had run back into the water during the flood sim they'd been assigned their first year at Marvelous. They just wanted to go back for their dog, which Honor understands, but she also understands to let the pros handle it. It was part of the test, and Honor had paid for it dearly, nearly costing them the win.

That was a win that Honor didn't need, didn't care about. This tournament is different and Honor won't be able to do anything except sit on the sidelines. All she can do now is teach her kids to the best of her ability and hope it sticks, because if it doesn't—

"Honor, in all seriousness, when have we ever, together, lost a fight?"

"Never."

"And we're not about to fuckin' start!"

17

Charlie has never been this stressed about finals in her entire life. She's always coasted through, never really having to study because school had always been easy and she hadn't really cared all that much. Now Christmas is right around the corner, and she would usually spend most of her time shopping instead of studying. But now she cares more than ever before, and school is *harder* than ever before.

They have an essay due in hero theory, which is essentially an entire field guide, language arts, history, and *Korean* that has to be written *in Korean*. Charlie thought Korean would be a fun language to learn and picked up on speaking it pretty quickly too. But then she found out that there are six different levels of politeness that she has to be able to use and match to the occasion, as well as learn a whole different form for writing! Her brain feels like it's going to melt out of her ears.

On top of all of the essays, they have practicals for tech with Aurora in which they have to fly an actual helicopter without crashing. Charlie doesn't even have a driver's license, yet how are they going to trust her to fly a whole *helicopter?*

Then there's the practical rescue exam, which they'll all have to work together on to test their large-scale cooperation on a large-scale disaster. They don't know what disaster it will be when they get there, but it will be one they did during first semester for sure, which only provides a minimal amount of relief. It will mimic the layout for the year end tournament, though, and Charlie is looking forward to seeing how they all work as a team so they can get their shit together. Preferably before the tournament.

She looks across the room to one of the photos tacked up on the wall. They'd been adding photos throughout the year, but there were a few already hanging to get them started, courtesy of their teachers. One of those photos is Honor and her sisters standing on a hastily crafted podium on the grass in front of a demolished stadium from their third tournament, the only year where there are individual winners. They're all standing together on the top level but Charlie's watched that footage too. She knows that Honor won. Barely.

Charlie wants to stand on that podium.

For now, she sits down on the floor of the common room with Lochlan and Kai, trying to figure out their topics for the tech essay. Malia comes in and puts a hand on Charlie's shoulder, healing all the aches and pains from the extra training she's doing. She breathes a sigh of relief and leans on Malia's shoulder while she joins the conversation. Luna comes over to help them with biology at some point, and then everything starts to devolve after that.

What started as a productive group study session turns into a hero debate that even shy and reserved Kai gets worked up about. What makes it even better, or worse depending on who's asked, is that they're not just a bunch of kids arguing about their favorite heroes anymore. They're hero students who have extensive knowledge of the pros in the current rotation and even some who aren't.

"I heard there's a graduate from Marvelous who can manipulate the bone structure of themselves and anyone they touch," Kai says.

"I remember him!" Charlie exclaims. "In his third year he had these huge bone spikes on his arms and legs."

Lochlan gives a full body shudder. "Isn't Marvelous' graduation rate at an all time low?"

"Only eight percent," Malia confirms. "They started off with eight hundred students and there are only sixty-four in their graduating class now."

"Could you imagine if only eight percent of our class graduated?" Charlie asks. "That's only one person!"

"Two if you round up," Lochlan adds.

"I bet we'll be the first school to have a one hundred percent success rate," Charlie says with the utmost confidence. "I don't see anyone in our class failing out."

"That's the advantage of having a smaller student to teacher ratio," Lochlan points out.

"What if someone decides they don't want to be a hero anymore?" Luna asks. "That doesn't mean they failed out, but it would mean we don't have a hundred percent pass rate anymore."

"Who would go through all of this and then decide they don't want to do it?" Charlie asks. "At this point you just have to see it through."

"I don't know," Kai says. "Someone could quit halfway through the year while it's still early. Like me. Contemplating dropping out just so I don't have to write this *goddamn essay!*"

They dissolve into easy laughter and go back to discussing essay topics. Luna is already set on doing her history paper on Spectra. Kai is already halfway through his field guide on flood rescues. Lochlan is the big surprise, at least to Charlie, when he says he's going to do his history essay on Incendiary.

"That happened like, a year ago," Luna points out. "Is it considered history?"

"I asked Leo," he says with a mouthful of chips. "He said 'history' and 'old' aren't synonymous, and since the Honor vs. Incendiary fight has already enacted major change in the justice system, I'm more than welcome to write about it."

"What are you going to say?" Kai asks before Charlie can. It's probably for the best. Kai's curious tone is much more inviting to answer than whatever would have come out of Charlie's mouth.

"Well, I was thinking about rogue reform and how even someone like Incendiary can be rehabilitated, but he hasn't been released yet so I don't think it has enough evidence," he says with a shrug.

"Maybe you could write about all the damage to the district he did," Charlie suggests, and judging by the look on Lochlan's face it's entirely too bitter, so she tacks on, "And how the entire district rebuilt bigger and more sustainable."

"Is *that* history?" Kai asks.

"Sounds more like urban planning," Malia says.

"It's gotta be history if it changed the face of the city forever," Charlie insists, ignoring the look Lochlan is giving her.

"I'll figure it out," Lochlan says, finally dragging his gaze away from Charlie and back to his paper where he scribbles down some notes.

"I heard he's being released in a few months, though," Malia keeps going. "Think it'll be weird? He's, like, famous but for being a criminal, and he's going to be just walking around."

"He's got Honor on his side," Kai says dismissively. "He'll be fine."

"Who said I was worried about him?" Malia asks, and Charlie feels a little relieved.

"Yeah," she says. "What if he goes back to whatever he was doing before?"

"*And* I heard that his mom is the leader of Paragon," Malia adds.

"What the heck is Paragon?" Kai asks.

"A gang," Malia tells him.

"His *mom* is a gang leader?" Kai asks dubiously. "The only thing my mom ever leads is a prayer circle."

"That's nice," Luna assures him.

"But what I'm saying is, if he did it once, then he can definitely do it again," Malia says.

"Then Honor will be going to the Matchbox with him," Lochlan says, still looking at his paper.

"WHAT?!" the rest of them exclaim. Lochlan looks up.

"Yeah," he goes on. "Leo told me that no one can graduate from Ameliora without a pro hero sponsor and that sponsor agrees to go to prison for whatever crimes the graduate commits as an accomplice or something. Honor is sponsoring Incendiary."

"She must have faith that he's not going to go rogue again," Luna says.

"Or that she can kick his ass before he even so much as thinks about it," Charlie points out. But that information sits heavy in her mind. If Honor is putting her whole life on the line for Incendiary, who is Charlie to question that? She's definitely not writing her essay on it, that's for sure.

"Hey, guys?" Ethan shuffles into the common room. "Can I use the TV?"

"Sure, for what?" Charlie says and welcomes the change in topic.

"I finally got my hands on the old tournament tapes from Honor's first year," he says.

Then everyone within listening distance is clamoring for a seat.

"Shut up, how did you find these?" Charlie asks as she settles into her seat on the couch, homework abandoned on the floor. Even though the tournament is broadcast live every year, all of the tournaments in which Honor and her sisters participated are regularly scrubbed from the internet. Charlie even heard rumors of peoples' personal hard drives being wiped by viruses when they tried to save it for themselves.

"I have a few friends," Ethan says cryptically and pushes his glasses up his nose while he plugs his computer into the television. Charlie couldn't care less about how he got them, she's just stoked that he has them. She's never seen any of Honor's tournaments in their entirety, only stolen clips and gifs online that never stay up long.

The tape starts to play, and Charlie does a quick headcount and finds nearly their entire class is there. Jack lingers by the back tables with Alex and Anthony, papers in front of them forgotten. Tommy sits on the floor in front of Charlie and Lochlan while Cora and Rose cram themselves into one of the armchairs.

There's the opening ceremonies where each of the classes and their assignments are announced. There's a wild commotion when Honor and her sisters come up on screen.

"They're so *young*," Malia says.

"They're *our age*," Lochlan says with the same amount of awe. Honor is bright and her smile is vicious. She looks more identical to Verity and Grace here, they all have the same length hair and no distinctive body art or styles since they're all in Marvelous uniform. Charlie has seen grainy gifs of this scene before but this is the first time that she can pick out a young Incendiary and a young Leo standing just behind them.

"Oh, he looks so emo," Ethan observes, and everyone busts up laughing because it's true. Leo's hair is long and falls into his face and they see his nails are painted black when he lifts his hand to rub at tired eyes.

The Triumvirate's class is assigned the flash flood emergency, and as soon as the buzzer sounds off to begin, their whole class is moving like a well-oiled machine. The de Mora sisters spread out, appearing to be leading three separate teams. Verity is on triage, and Honor and Grace divide up their section into quadrants for their teams to search. Since it's an old broadcast, it cuts away frequently to other teams and their class collectively groans whenever they leave their teachers, but they all cheer again when they cut back.

The water level is steadily rising and half their team is on boats. Without a water marvel, it makes their job a bit more difficult, but the triplets seem to take everything in stride. They're hauling volunteer victims out of the water, and Honor and Grace are diving in to pull out *animals*. There are animals in the test too?! Charlie never would have thought about that.

"See how they never put too many people in the red zone at a time?" Ethan points out. Charlie's mouth quirks.

"Yes, Mr. Wells," she sings like a kindergartener. Ethan scowls at her.

"If we're going to win, then we need to work together," says Ethan. "We spend a lot of time competing and not a lot cooperating." He looks at Charlie when he says it, and she looks at him with a hand on her chest, affronted.

"Well, it is a competition," Lochlan points out.

"Us against them," Ethan agrees. "We'll all be working together in the final, so we'll see how we all work together then."

"Your confidence in us as a class is inspiring," Malia drawls, and Charlie smothers a laugh in her hand.

There's a scream on screen and everyone's attention is drawn back to the television. Honor jumps out of the rescue boat she's in, accidentally ripping a hole through it in the process. Her teammates shout at her as they scramble to stay afloat, and someone else with a mending marvel patches it up before they can sink, but Honor never looks back once, confident in her teammates.

She lands on the roof of a house, sprints across it, then jumps to another, then runs off *that* and does a perfect dive into the water to rescue someone that none of them had seen. They've all been warned that doing water rescues without equipment is dangerous because the patient could drown you as well as themselves in their panic, but Honor doesn't hesitate.

She goes under, and then Grace is right behind her, lingering on the rooftop for backup which she gives when Honor surfaces again. She uses her baton, which lengthens into a whip, and wraps it around Honor's arm to pull her and the patient out of the water. The Triumvirate was a major factor in why classes are no longer allowed to bring outside support weapons unless necessary for marvel use. The

Triumvirate's already powerful marvels paired with additional support was unanimously deemed unfair by the tournament committee.

Honor and the patient soar through the air and all the way back to the triage station set up on the little patch of land they have left. Honor lands on her own two feet. She keeps the patient cradled in one arm and lifts the other in victory as the buzzer sounds.

Emotion swells in Charlie. Pride and admiration crest and flood through her system and the *desire* creates a current so powerful it pushes her to her feet. The desire to win, to make Honor proud, to carry on her legacy in the Academy name. All eyes are on her after the movement but all Charlie can say, with every ounce of her hard earned confidence, is;

"We can do this."

They cannot do this.

Well, they can. They did. But barely.

The practical was a *mess*. Turns out throwing all twenty of them together makes for quite the shit show. Especially since not all of them have been in a group before, as was made painfully clear when neither Charlie nor Jack could forfeit control and neither of them listened to Ethan who, objectively, had the best game plan for their tornado simulation. Something Charlie can only admit in hindsight because she wanted *her* plan to be the one that won the day.

Tommy was their only saving grace. He came up with a plan that included all of their major ideas, but nothing was cohesive. They weren't working together, they weren't communicating. They were competing, desperate to show off in an attempt to earn a higher score. Not even Lochlan was exempt, accidentally unleashing a storm into the Aurora-made tornado that nearly took them all out. Even Cora snatched up some dummies that Jayne had been sent to rescue because she thought it might earn her some extra points. Their ensuing shouting match probably lost them all points.

Charlie and Jack arguing isn't anything new, but during a sim was so horrendously stupid that Charlie cringes just thinking about. They'd never been in the same sim group before, but she has a hunch they'll be paired up a lot during the next semester.

They passed by the skin of their teeth, and that's only because none of the dummies were marked for death. Honor reamed them afterward and Charlie couldn't look her in the eye. It was *humiliating* and not at all how she wanted to start winter break. Her other grades come back exemplary, which is her only silver lining. Charlie is worried this performance is going to haunt her forever. If they act like this during the tournament, they can kiss that podium goodbye. There's no way Marvelous or Broadly will be that sloppy.

So Charlie assigns herself more training and studying over the break. She even ropes her siblings into being her rescue patients. She studies procedures. She watches training videos. Charlie doesn't do anything half way and she's not about to start now.

18

Honor waits with Verity in the sand dunes outside Las Vegas. They sit on the edge of one, their car parked back at the side of the road with the hazards on, and wait. Verity hums the Christmas song they'd been listening to on the radio. It's off-key, but Verity isn't known for her musical prowess. The sun sets behind them and paints the sand orange, shimmering in the dusk light and almost looking like gemstones. Vegas is far enough away that the light pollution doesn't reach them, and as the sun disappears, the stars start to wink down at them. Verity starts to slide through the smooth sand, and before she can catch herself, Honor extends a leg and kicks her down.

Verity swears at her as she goes tumbling down into the ditch, coughing up sand, and Honor howls with laughter so hearty she has to clutch at her sides. It reminds her of the nights they'd spend together as teenagers, just hanging out and doing dumb shit.

"Bitch!" Verity shouts up at her when she finally gets her feet under her. She hadn't really been trying, Honor knows because Verity can only be taken so far off guard. But it's more fun this way. Verity launches back up the dune at her with a single jump, and Honor scrambles to get out of the way.

Honor's scramble is still faster than the world record holder for hundred meter dash without a marvel, but her sister is the same and she's hot on her heels. She grabs Honor's ankle and pulls them both back down in the dune. Honor shouts out when her sweatshirt pulls up and sand gets into her clothes. She tries to swear at her sister but she's laughing too hard.

They sit there for a moment in the sand under the stars, just laughing. It reminds of Honor of when they were younger, three triplets and their mom shoved into a small two bedroom apartment in the Blade District, jumping off of secondhand furniture and breaking dollar store decorations and sometimes bones. Honor's heart gives a faint twinge at the thought of her mother. It always does that. She doesn't think it'll ever stop.

"Don't think I didn't notice that that's Leo's sweatshirt," Verity says once she catches her breath.

Honor's smile quickly morphs into a scowl. "It was by the door."

"Right next to your bullshit," Verity says. "Yeah, I saw it."

The portal lights up before Honor can say anything else. A circle of deep green light in the ground that shoots up toward the night sky, painting an out-of-season and unnatural aurora that will be gone before anyone really notices it. Honor has only seen a portal in person once before, when Grace went back to Viasyre. It had been gold, then. Honor isn't sure if it's the placement of the portal or the person who opens it that changes the signal color, she'll have to ask.

Or maybe she won't. Honor figures that the less she knows about portals, the better. She already has enough classified information living in her brain, and she doesn't like to think what would become of these portals or the worlds they lead to if their world at large were to find out about them. So they keep it a secret between sisters. It isn't their first and it certainly won't be the last.

The portal lights up, a brilliant and beautiful lilac color. It reaches up toward the night sky until it's swallowed by darkness. That's new. Honor and Verity are both on their feet in an instant.

An unfamiliar man walks through. He looks human, but both of them know better. He could shape shift or glamour himself into fitting in. That's how all the other Titans have done it. Well, most of them. The others make for good ghost stories.

"Hello!" he says as though he's greeting old friends. Honor isn't fooled into relaxing, but she feigns it anyway. Verity does the same beside her.

"Who are you?" Verity asks, taking him in. He's average height, average build, a full head of brown hair and some stubble on a regular jawline. He's spectacularly average all around.

"My name is Soat," he introduces himself with a small smile. "This is Earth, yes?"

"Sure is," Honor says. "Where are you coming from?"

"Far away," he says with a dismissive wave of his hand. He tilts his head back and looks toward the sky, turning in a slow circle to take in the desert around them as well. He's wearing slacks and a white button down, also average but deliberately human, too. "I've never been to Earth before. It's more beautiful than people give it credit for."

"Thanks," Verity says slowly, still unsure of what to make of their visitor.

"You know, it's not safe to leave your portals unguarded like this," he tells them. "Anyone can come through whenever they want."

"Clearly," Honor deadpans.

"Where I come from, there are guards around every portal," he tells them.

"How do you know we're not guards?" Verity asks.

"You are de Mora sisters, are you not?" he asks and looks them over. "You look just like her."

"Grace?" Honor asks. "Are you from Viasyre?"

"No, no," he says with a placating smile. "But I should be on my way."

"Meeting somebody?" Verity asks. He just laughs.

"You have a lovely evening!" he says over his shoulder as he begins to walk away toward the road.

"You too," Honor calls back. He disappears entirely before his foot hits the asphalt.

"Should we have… stopped him?" Verity asks after a moment of silence.

"We haven't stopped anyone else coming through," Honor says. "Can't stop everyone, either."

"Well, if he causes problems, we'll find him," Verity says, and that's really all that can be done about that at the moment. Verity punches Honor's shoulder. "Mood check. It's Christmas! None of this maudlin shit."

Honor punches her back. "You're right. Should we sing some carols?"

"Fuck off," Verity laughs.

The portal lights up again, a deep emerald color that tells them Cal activated the portal. When Grace comes through,

Honor and Verity jump on her. They sandwich her between them in a tight hug. Grace's laugh is musical.

"I missed you guys!" she says and extracts herself. "You remember Cal."

"Ah, yes, Cal, your half Titan husband from another world that you tried to con back when your memories were erased by dear old Dad and you helped him defend his world against a Titan seeking power, making you the strongest sister, and he helped *you* regain your memories and brought you back to us just in time to defend *our* world from a different Titan. How could we forget?" Verity says and embraces an awkward-looking Cal. He looks to Grace for help, but Grace can't help him when it comes to Verity.

"We're not married," Cal points out.

"Yeah, well, Grace chose to live with you instead of us and that means in her head you're married," Verity tells him and awkwardly slings an arm around his much taller shoulders to lead him to the car. "How does one propose on Viasyre? I'm interested."

"Oh no," Grace says with a laugh. She and Honor trail not far behind. Cal glances over his shoulder at Grace, equal parts frightened and amused. As he should be. It's cute. They're cute. "Is she going to give him the shovel talk next?"

"We already did," Honor tells her.

"You what?"

"Yeah, long time ago," she says, snickering at Grace's shocked expression. "Probably way scarier than it had any right to be, honestly. We were fresh out the fight, still covered in blood and running on adrenalin dregs. I think he saw his life flash before his eyes when I made you appear and you were crying because he broke your heart, and then Verity narrated in great detail what we would do to him if he made you cry like that while I provided visual aids."

"You did *what?*" Grace says again, much closer to screeching. "You're the worst. Also? Using your marvel to supplement the shovel talk? Genius. I'll be using it."

Honor snorts and slings an arm around Grace's shoulders, ruffling her hair like they're fourteen again and Grace hasn't hit her growth spurt that made them the same height. "Not any time soon, you won't."

"Are you sure about that?" Grace asks with a pointed look to her chest. Which would be a weird place to look, but Honor knows that Grace's sight works similarly to Verity's. She also knows from experience that names close to the heart tend to appear in close proximity to the actual heart. Honor isn't even sure whose name Grace is seeing.

She doesn't ask, either, just hooks her arm harder around Grace's neck and drags her down. Grace, slippery as always, manages to slide free, laughing.

"I'm here if you want to talk about it," she says.

"I know," Honor replies and wraps her arm around her again.

The next day, Honor knocks on the door to Colson's room. Bobby is stationed at the end of the hall, and Honor gives him a mock salute that he returns. Colson answers the door, surprised to find Honor there.

"What's going on?" Colson asks as he rubs his eyes.

"Were you asleep?" Honor asks, ignoring how adorable she finds it. She grabs his hand and tugs him down the hall. Colson provides no resistance.

"I sleep when I'm bored," he admits. It's not ridiculously early for someone to be sleeping but still early in the evening. "What are you doing here?"

"This," she says and proudly opens the door to the common area.

"Happy Birthday!" everyone shouts. Everyone consists of Honor's sisters, Cal, Aurora, Rae, Teddy and his husband, and Torro, an Ameliora graduate, with his two-year-old son.

Colson turns around and walks back out.

"BOOO!" Verity's shout follows them into the hall, but she's only teasing. Colson stops, not far but far enough to compose himself, lifting a hand to cover his eyes like it'll stop the tears, but it never does.

"You can cry inside your party, you know," Honor says. She grabs his free hand, and he holds it back tight.

"Fuck," he whispers. "I don't know if I can."

Historically, Honor has never been a patient person. It's a widely known fact mentioned in every interview she's ever done and on all her little fan profiles that litter the internet. But she's trying to be better. So instead of assuring Colson that *of course he can*, she waits. It's hard because everything in her wants to reassure him, because he can, she knows he can, but rushing him isn't going to help. If anything, it just makes Colson more resistant.

"Leo's not there," he says eventually. It surprises Honor. She hadn't expected him to say anything about it, even if she knew he'd notice.

"He's on shift," she tells him truthfully. She doesn't tell him that Leo had looked more relieved than anything when he received the shift. Colson wouldn't believe her when she says that it's because Leo is nervous to see him again, not because he hates him. Which Colson seems determined to believe. "V and I are both on call. You know how it goes."

"Yeah," he says, and it's clear he doesn't buy it. Then he puts on a brave face and smiles at her. "Thank you, for this."

"You're welcome," she says softly.

They head back inside the party, and Verity is perched on top of the table, eating Colson's cake with a fork straight off the platter.

"Oh shit, he came back," Verity says with a mouthful of frosting.

"Of course he came back," Grace says and hits her shoulder. "It's his party!"

"Your cake is really good," Verity says and swallows. "You're welcome."

"It's fine," he says with a small laugh. Grace gets up from the table and hugs Colson tight. He hugs her back.

"I missed you," Colson says.

"I missed you too," Grace says. She looks him up and down, getting an eyeful, and Honor watches carefully for a reaction. Grace is remarkably hard to read when she wants to be. Even to Honor, who's shared a face with her their whole life. "You look good."

"Yeah?" Colson asks, not fishing for compliments but genuinely asking if what Grace sees with her marvel is good. Grace has always had a special smile, one that's so kind and reassuring that it's been known to make people burst into tears when it's been aimed at them. Colson, already on edge, nods tearfully when Grace smiles at him.

Grace's marvel allows her to see the past, present, and sometimes even the future all layered over a single person, place, or thing. She can see where a person has come from, the choices they've made, the people they're closest to.

Grace knows practically everything about a person from a single glance.

"Yeah," she promises.

"I remember when we used to be fun at parties," Verity says through a mouthful of cake.

"We were *menaces*," Honor reminds her.

Verity, without missing a beat, fires back, "That's what I said." She hops off the table with one last bite of cake. "Let's open presents!"

"There are presents?" Colson asks. Honor takes him by the hand and leads him to the couches where the Christmas tree is set up.

"Birthday and Christmas," she says and pointedly ignores the way Verity squints at their joined hands. "We're all doing presents now since most of us work on Christmas this year." Colson breathes a sigh of relief that he won't be the center of attention during present opening.

Verity's eyes light up blue while she passes out presents to everyone, but Honor doesn't hear anything which means she's only talking to Grace. Honor's own eyes take on a pink glow when she cuts them off—*Don't make me hurt you on Christmas.*

Like that's ever stopped you before, Verity returns. *We weren't even talking about you, you narcissistic asshole.* Honor drops it because they start to get funny looks from those in the know, like Colson and Cal. It's not like the de Mora sisters to be quiet for very long.

Despite not buying her sisters' bullshit and knowing their eyes are on her, she can't help the way she leans into Colson's side, just a bit to remind them both that they're there together. Honor pulls the sleeves of her sweatshirt over her hands, Leo's sweatshirt. Colson curls her fingers around the cuff and opens his first present one-handed.

Triumvirate merchandise. Verity cackles at his face, equal parts amused and resigned and genuinely touched. The majority of his presents is merch from all their friends, and somehow it only gets funnier every time. Honor did make sure to throw in two new suits and a designer sweatshirt, but the first thing he pulls on is his Triumvirate hoodie with three eyes on the back in their respective colors.

The night progresses with more cake, more presents, and a healthy helping of good cheer. Out-of-tune singing and lots of laughter. For a brief flash, Honor sees Colson as his old self when he chases Verity across the room to get his last cookie back. His smile is wide and bright. Honor's chest aches. She wants to live in this moment for as long as she can.

Grace comes up beside her, rests her head on Honor's shoulder and says, "Me too."

19

School is back in session and Charlie feels like she's ready to take the world by storm. So what if they hadn't aced their group final? They *passed*. A new semester is a new start. She'd had a great holiday break, and their first Saturday back, she's out with her friends at Rizzo's for pizza and garlic bread. It's a double-floor restaurant, and the top floor has a great view of the Academy, but it's full for the night so they take to a downstairs table. They're in a corner booth made of red vinyl with a stained table top, eating and laughing too loud while arguing about the tournament.

"The Triumvirate's record is three consecutive wins by *a single class*," Charlie tells Kai, who is woefully out of touch with his hero trivia.

"Marvelous is known for stacking their classes," Malia points out.

"True," Charlie says, "The fact that all three de Mora sisters were in the same class meant no one ever stood a fighting chance."

Marvelous isn't subtle about putting their strongest and brightest students all in one class together. Two, if there's a particularly gifted year. But Marvelous holds the record for most tournament wins ever and they battle for it tooth and nail every year. They don't even care how the other classes finish as long as their top classes place in the top three.

"No one knew they were half Titan back then," Lochlan adds. "No one knew until the Titan Battle which was way after the tournaments."

"Yeah, but Honor let slip in an interview when she was like fifteen or sixteen that their mom had been training them since they could walk, practically," Charlie says. "Besides, the knowledge of the fact that they're half Titan shouldn't have made a difference. Looking at them and the way they work together and the way they fight? No competition. Zero. None. *We* need to look like that to other people."

"Okay, but none of us are half Titan," Ethan points out.

"I know," Charlie says, getting louder in her excitement. "But that's not the part that matters. It's the prowess. The confidence. The aura of power that we need to emulate. Not the Titan part."

"But those things come from being a Titan!" Ethan cries.

"Not necessarily!" Charlie argues. "Even if we can't do it to the *extent* that they can, we can still do it! Gravitas isn't a Titan but he's still intimidating as shit."

"That's because the dude's like seven feet tall," Malia says.

"Do you think Jack will get that tall?" Lochlan asks.

"Oh god, I hope not," Charlie says and sucks air through her straw.

"His mom is like 6'3" too, isn't she?" Kai asks.

"Yes, and a total babe," Charlie says.

"Agree," Ethan says and fist bumps her across the table. "But then it's likely that Jack will outgrow all of us."

"Never say never," Charlie says, "I have a brother who's 6'7". It's in my genes."

"*Six foot seven?*" Malia asks, eyes bulging out of her head. "Is he cute? Is he single? How old is he?"

"He's nineteen and doesn't know how to wash his own underwear so don't get your hopes up."

"I'll get my hopes up six feet and seven inches," Malia says and Charlie snorts.

"I need a refill. Anyone else?"

She ends up piling eight cups into her two hands and takes them over to the soda fountain. She manages to get them just fine, putting a bit of orange soda into Kai's cola because she thinks she's funny. When she turns around, she doesn't realize someone is standing right there and ends up spilling six of the eight drinks on her.

"Oh shit, sorry," Charlie says.

"What the hell is your problem?" the girl snaps. She looks like she's about Charlie's age, and Charlie bristles at her tone. She's sorry she dumped half the drinks on her, but it was an *accident*.

"I said I was sorry, damn," Charlie says, trying to salvage the last of the cups. "It's just soda. Chill."

"I will not fucking chill, what kind of idiot are you? Why are you trying to carry ten cups at a time anyway?" she says, voice rising. She pulls her sticky, ratted flannel away from her skin. She glares at Charlie and the bags under her eyes really cut into the intimidation factor.

"It was *eight* and it was a fucking accident! You don't need to be such a bitch about it!" Charlie's voice draws more attention to them because she's *loud,* okay? Lochlan's halfway out of his seat to come and try to diffuse the situation.

"You don't know *shit*!" the girl shouts with so much raw emotion that Charlie's taken aback. "You don't know *anything*! I just needed to pick up some goddamn pizza and here you are! Ruining my only fucking clothes!"

"Shit, dude, I can give—"

"I don't want you to give me anything!"

"If you need help then fucking ask for it instead of screaming at strangers!" Charlie shouts back.

"Girls," the manager comes over to them, and Charlie steels herself, but the girl? She fucking *loses* it. Her hands light up with brilliant blue fire. Charlie sees her life flash before her eyes.

Suddenly she's five again. Alone in the apartment when she smells smoke. She ventures outside her room to investigate and finds that the floor is too hot, there's black smoke curling in every corner of the house, and she's alone. She tries to open the door, but it's too hot to touch. She didn't know what to do then and she doesn't know what to do now.

Honor scrubs her hands over her face. She'd just gotten off a long shift and now this?

"Run that by me one more time," she says to Verity. Honor braces her elbows on her knees where she sits in one of the armchairs and watches Verity pace.

"I'm telling you, these things look like mini Krewas," she says. "Nothing like what came out of the Pulse the first time around, according to Maia."

"Fuck, so the Pulse really is another portal?" Honor asks. The Ocean Pulse had been a problem for the coastline and

Hawaii almost a decade ago. Maia's sentient surfboard, affectionately nicknamed Raven, had come through and attached itself to Maia as a defense against whatever the hell it was that came out of the Pulse the first time around. Maia had undergone two years of intensive private training and took her license test on recommendation to become the youngest pro in the country. The Pulse hasn't been a problem since. Until now, apparently.

It's just Honor and Verity in the teachers' dorm. Honor stares out of the window at the city and wonders how many portals there are on Earth and how many different places they lead. She really wishes she had paid more attention to Grace when she explained how the portals work, but she had written them off as not her problem.

Apparently not.

"Looks like it," Verity says. "Maia's keeping an eye on it for now. We think it was a scout, because only one came through and Maia took care of it on her own easily enough."

"Fuck," Honor sighs. "How's Maia feeling? Any different?"

"No, not from what I can tell," Verity says. "I thought that if they were Titans, that maybe she would be feeling it, but I didn't ask. I didn't think we wanted that getting out, not that I don't trust Maia."

"No, no, you're right," Honor says. When a Titan kills another Titan, they inherit their power, raw. So the specific powers of a Titan don't transfer but the sheer energetic power enters the victorious Titan

After they killed Krewa, the effects were immediately noticeable. They were stronger, faster, and their marvels were misfiring for weeks until they got them back under control. Grace said she felt something similar after she killed the Titan on Viasyre. But that power transfer had been stronger then since she was alone. Krewa's residuals had been split between the three of them. But if Maia didn't receive a similar boost in power, then it's either because whatever's coming through the portal isn't a Titan or Titan power only transfers to other Titans. They have no way of knowing, for sure.

"Did you tell Grace?" Honor asks.

"She must be sleeping, I didn't get a response," Verity tells her. "I'll try again in a bit, though. If there's a way to close it…"

"Then we need to close it," Honor agrees. "There's the Pulse, and the Dunes, that we know of. How many other portals are there?"

"Grace said most planets have at least four," Verity answers. "But given how close the Pulse and the Dunes are, it's probably more."

"Fuck," Honor says again, this time with more feeling, because that raises another, much worse question. How many Titans have already made their way to earth? Soat, the person who came through in December, is one. Whether or not he stayed is another question entirely and they have no way of knowing. Honor scrubs her hands over her face and glances out the window again.

Blue fire ignites just across the street, licking up toward the night sky and filling the street with midnight colored smoke. Honor pushes to her feet out of reflex. That fire isn't natural, that much is clear. It must be a marvel. But she isn't on duty, and there are plenty of capable pros in the Titan District who will be able to take care of it.

Then, Verity says, "Aren't the kids at Rizzo's?"

Honor, barefoot and in her sweats, is out the door in the blink of an eye with Verity right behind her. Rizzo's is only two blocks away so they're the first on scene.

"You get the kids, I'll get the civilians," Verity says, and somewhere in the back of Honor's head, she knows those two things shouldn't be separate categories, but they are. She heads inside.

"Charlie?!" Honor shouts. She gets a weird sense of deja vu before she gets a shout back.

"Honor!" It's Lochlan, not Charlie. They're stuck behind a collapsed wall that Honor throws out of the way. They stare at her with wide eyes and soot covered faces. Charlie is staring toward the stairs, pale.

She takes quick stock of the rest of them and after noting that none of them are seriously injured, probably due to Malia, she shouts, "Get back to campus!"

"What about—"

"GO NOW!" Honor shouts and heads deeper into the blaze, having no choice but to trust that her students will follow her orders.

This fire is blue, unnaturally so, and Honor knows it's the result of a marvel. It's hot, too. Hot enough that Honor knows it'll seriously hurt her if she gets too close or stays too long and that means no one else is getting in. She can only hope that they get enough water marvels on scene to stop the spread before this can get even more out of hand.

Honor's concern is finding the person who started the fire. She's in street clothes and laments the fact that she never has her goddamn suit on when there's a fire happening. She always has her gauntlets, though. She hits the thin bands on her wrists together twice until they expand to cover her hands and forearms. It's not much but they're all she has. She ducks under a half-fallen doorway and continues her search. The smoke isn't her biggest concern because she knows her lungs have withstood worse.

The soles of her feet singe as she runs up the stairs, but they're callused and used to less than ideal walking conditions so Honor is able to shove it in the back of her mind. She gets to the second floor and spots the culprit. A teenage girl, probably the same age as her kids. The look on Charlie's face starts to make a little more sense.

"Hey." Honor has to raise her voice a little to be heard over the roar of the flames, and the girl instantly panics.

"Stay away!"she screams and throws another line of fire, aimed at Honor this time. Honor puts her hands up to block the blast and swallows a curse when her gauntlets fucking *melt*. Aurora is not going to be happy when she finds out about this.

"Wait!" Honor shouts when the girl makes to throw another line of fire. She pauses when Honor lowers her arms. Recognition passes over her face, and Honor doesn't have time to wait and see if it's a good or bad thing. "I'm here to help you."

"Help me?" she repeats, voice wet but her tears are steam before they hit her cheeks. "*You? Help me?*"

If rogues keep sounding so surprised when she says she's there to help, she's going to have to reevaluate how she does things. They should be relieved, not shocked and incredulous.

"What's your name?" Honor tries, hands out, half-melted gauntlets embedded in her palms.

"It doesn't matter," she says.

"It does."

"I know yours." It's only years of training and experience that keeps her disappointment and frustration from showing on her face. "*Honor de Mora.*" The girl says it like a curse, with so much disdain that Honor's heart hurts.

The fire around them doesn't come any closer. Honor wonders if she's doing it on purpose or if the fire is repelled from her once it's released. Either way, Honor knows she has to stay inside this very small, safe circle and manage not to make it smaller by pissing her off or upsetting her more. It looks like that's going to be difficult since Honor's mere presence seems to upset her.

Leo has you contained. You good? Verity's voice in her head.

Fire marvel, she answers, relieved that the fire won't be spreading any further. *Upset kid.*

"What are you doing?" she demands, noting the way Honor's eyes glow.

"If I tell you, can you keep it a secret?" Honor asks.

"What? Why?" she asks and Honor takes a hesitant step forward.

"No one knows why my eyes glow and I'm trying to keep it that way. If I tell you, will you keep it a secret for me?"

"You're talking to one of your sisters," she says. "What are you saying?"

"What makes you think I'm talking to my sister?"

"Colson told me."

Sweat rolls down Honor's back and her wrists ache where the gauntlets are melted in.

Fuck.

"How do you know Colson?" Honor asks.

"I knew him before you *took him,*" she accuses, voice still shaking. Honor's brain kicks into overdrive. The building won't hold much longer and they're on the second floor which means they'll both go crashing down in a second. A fall Honor will survive, but she's not sure the girl will. She can't risk talking to Verity again or she'll upset her further and expedite the whole shitty process.

Before you took him. She must be talking about when Colson was with Ravenna, which means she's probably a part of Paragon. That would explain her immediate disdain for Honor. Honor's brain runs through every possibility in a matter of seconds. Since Colson had outed her telepathy with her sisters, it's safe to say he'd done so with her illusions too and if she tries to throw a trick now, she'll destroy any chance of building trust with this girl. She can't be older than seventeen.

"I didn't take Colson," she says. "He came home."

"No!" she shouts and the flames around them flare up. "You *took him.* He—he was the *only one* who cared about me in that place and now he's gone and it's your fault!"

"Do you want to see him?" Honor asks quickly, feeling the temperature rise. Her eyes go wide with the possibility, and Honor knows the answer is yes, but the real question is whether or not she'll accept the offer. "I'll bring you to him."

"You're lying," she accuses, voice thick. The floor beneath them creaks and Honor has to work faster.

"I'm not," she promises. "You can see Colson, but you have to come with me."

"Of course I do," she sneers. "She said you'll say anything to convince us to do what you want just like you did with *him*."

Honor's out of time and out of patience. "Look, kid, I haven't lied to you yet and I'm not about to start, so believe me when I say that Ravenna's a fucking manipulative bitch, I *love* Colson, and you and I need to get out of here because this building is about to collapse."

"And if I don't go?" she asks, steely resolve showing through, and Honor is simultaneously impressed and exasperated.

"I'm gonna have to make you," she admits, still truthful.

"Oh yeah?" she asks with all the bravado of infallible youth. She reminds Honor of her students. Of herself.

"Yeah."

They move at the same time, but Honor's infinitely faster. She throws another line of fire and Honor dodges, diving for the girl and tackling her to the ground. She grabs her hands and holds them in one of her own and hopes that's enough to stop her from activating her marvel. In the same motion, she's rolling them both over so she can get her feet under her, lifting the girl with ease. The kid screams and Honor throws them both out the window just as the roof caves in.

Honor twists midair, prepared to land on her feet, but the girl lights her palms up. Honor swears, thrown off balance. She only has enough time to twist so she's the one who hits the ground instead of the girl.

"Let me go!" she screams, crying openly now in the fresh night air. Honor does not let her go, just holds steadfast while she tries to burn Honor to get free. It hurts like a mother-fucking *bitch,* but Honor does not let go, even though she's still struggling to pull air into her lungs after landing flat on her back in the street.

"Honor!" That's Verity's voice. Outside her head. Which means she's close.

"Stay away from me!" the kid screams and throws enough fire to burn the entire district to the ground. It just leaps out of her without aim or purpose. Honor watches in horror as it lights up down the block, ripping through the emergency vehicles lined up. She doesn't have to use her hands. She can throw it from any part of her body. Ridiculously hot and powerful. It should be impossible that Honor's never even heard of this marvel before.

Then Honor sees the telltale shimmer of Leo's shields and realizes that there's a shield around every single person down the street. Every last one of them, safe. The kid hasn't noticed, judging by the way she starts to sob. Honor still has hold of her wrists in one hand, arms seared worse than when she fought Colson, and the other catches the nullifiers launched at them from the side.

The kids' eyes go wide when she sees them and the way Honor caught them without looking. She fastens them tightly around her wrists and the kid stops struggling, realizing that even though she burnt Honor halfway to hell, she's not letting go.

"Honor!" Leo runs up, sleeve torn. Honor knows that the fire tore through his big shield and that's why he had used the smaller ones. He looks at her with poorly concealed horror, the most expressive she's seen him in days. The kid closes her eyes like maybe she can pretend this isn't happening. The tears are free to stream down her face now, but she doesn't make a sound as she cries.

"Holy fuck," Verity says, appearing at her side. She takes the kid from Honor and gets a look at her arms. The rest of her is burnt up pretty bad but her hands and arms are the worst.

"Take her straight to Ameliora," Honor says. Verity and Leo look at her incredulously. "Don't do that. I promised."

"Promised *what?*" Verity asks.

"That she could see Colson," Honor says. The kid's eyes fly open to stare at Honor. She dredges up the last of her energy to appear strong for her. "I told you, I wasn't lying and I'm not going to."

The kid looks so lost in that moment, but Honor is tapped out and Verity can tell, so she hauls the kid away. Honor trusts her sister to get her to Ameliora and as soon as she loads her into transport, Honor collapses to the ground.

"Oh fuck, holy shit," she gasps.

"We need a medic marvel," Leo says into his comms. He kneels next to her but his hands hover, hesitant to touch. "Honor…"

"Bet it looks worse than it is," she says and tries to grin, but it comes out more of a grimace.

"You're not funny," he says.

"You should see the other guy?"

"There's not a fucking scratch on that kid."

"Then—"

"Stop! Just—stop," he says. "You don't—you don't need to put on a show for me, Honor. I know it hurts. Let it hurt."

Honor isn't used to hurting. Not physically, at least, and certainly not like this. Especially not since they killed Krewa. Honor's tolerance for pain and her sturdiness shot up exponentially after it had been astronomically high already. She's even been through literal fire before, and it hadn't burned anywhere close to this level. If anyone other than Honor or Verity had tried to bring her in, this would have gone much differently. She nods and even *that* hurts.

"I'm gonna… lay down then," she says.

"Okay, okay," Leo says and cradles her head as she lowers herself back to the asphalt. "Adrian's on his way. You're gonna be okay." She hums faintly because it hurts to do much else. "Honor? You still with me?" She hums again.

She's not sure how long she lays there, Leo's presence steady and strong beside her, but she hears Adrian running up with someone else. Aurora, maybe? Not Verity, for sure. Honor can't be bothered to open her eyes and check.

"Honor? Can you hear me?" Adrian asks. She hums again. She hears his screens clink open as he surveys her damage. "Okay, we need to get you to the hospital. We can't heal you until we get these gauntlets out."

Honor takes a deep breath that *burns*, then pushes herself into a sitting position fast. Too fast. Leo has to catch her when she starts to fall sideways. She hisses in pain but doesn't move. Adrian's hands hover over the burns he can heal for now and the tingly sensation she gets when Adrian activates his marvel is a welcome change from the constant throbbing. It's like her body is waking back up with fresh blood flow after sitting for too long.

Her arms had taken the brunt of it and it shows in a mess of blood and color, but her pants are a goner for sure and she's grateful to see the soft, smooth skin of her shins again instead of the charred blackness. As the adrenalin wears off, she realizes for the first time that the acrid smell permeating the air isn't the building burning; it's *her.*

Honor's stomach rolls as the stench gets stuck in her nostrils and she's unable to shake it. She doesn't dare open her eyes to look at her arms, but it doesn't matter, it doesn't help.

"I'm gonna be sick," she says thickly.

Leo, the angel he is, gathers her hair and holds it while she vomits in the street.

20

"Blue Fire Blazes Through Titan District"
—Titan Daily

Fire emergencies are one of the most common they get in the city, and Honor has handled more than her fair share. So today's simulation is imperative. The gym is set up to emulate a city block filled with apartment high rises and residences. Even though there are no actual people involved in the sim, it's easy to imagine what kind of families would live here. What kind of young professionals spill coffee on the sidewalk in the morning and joggers avoiding foot traffic and dogs tangling leashes around their owners' ankles. Half of their kids probably come from a neighborhood that looks just like this one.

Everyone knows this is going to be a tough one for Charlie after what happened at Rizzo's. Honor knows that it's going to be tough for different reasons. Charlie is one of the first people that Honor had ever saved as a pro. Well, a trainee with a provisional license, but the work is the same. Honor can remember most of her cases with quality clarity but there are always a few that stand out. The first save is one of them.

Sixteen-year-old Honor walks the street with a fresh provisional license burning a hole in her pocket and a smug smile on her face. Everyone thought she'd fail her first test but she'd nearly gotten a perfect score. Sure, she'd had to beat back some of her basic instincts with a baseball bat, but it worked.

Her phone vibrates and a message from Leo pops up, telling her where to meet the rest of them for lunch. Honor changes directions and jogs to the crosswalk before the blinking light settles on red. The sun is no longer in the sky, has sunk low enough behind skyscrapers to give the illusion of night, but some light still peaks through the cracks and reflects off of high rise windows.

It's one of Honor's favorite times of day. Late enough to be considered night but still light. The smell of summer on the air makes her inhale deeply. She's a little chilly in just her t-shirt and jeans, but the jogging helps a bit. Besides, Bucky's is always warm, so she'll be just fine once she gets there.

A gust of wind blows her hair forward and she hunches against the sudden rush of cold that slips under her shirt. She shoves her hands in her pockets and walks a little faster, turning down a street lined with town homes and engineered cherry blossom trees that wouldn't grow here otherwise. Then, the breeze changes from cold to hot in an instant, too sudden to be anything natural. Honor starts to sweat.

She turns around and sees the smoke rising one street over. It's no longer Honor's place to think, let the pros take care of it. *Not that she ever had, really, but she's one of the pros now, so she runs over.*

There are already two fire trucks on scene, and Honor can hear another siren wailing in the distance. The fire's already eaten through three buildings and it looks ready to jump to another one. The firefighters and heroes already on site are evacuating the nearby buildings and every available hose is aimed at the fire.

"Keep it from spreading! I want the next truck on the neighbors for protection!" The fire chief barks out orders. "Did we clear this building?" He points to the building directly in front of Honor, only half on fire but it's not going to stay that way for much longer.

"NO!" someone screams at him, clearly in distress. Panicking civilians make it almost impossible to do your job, so Honor pulls the girl out of the way of the fire chief and he orders more firefighters inside to sweep again. "My sister is in there! She's still in there!"

"Calm down, the firefighters will get her," Honor says. The girl can't be older than thirteen, probably babysitting since there are no parents in sight, and she doesn't seem concerned for them, only the sister.

"I can't! She's still in there! I just came out to get the mail and they wouldn't let me back in for her!" She's still staring up at the building like everything is hopeless. Honor takes her by the shoulders and spins her around so she has her full attention.

"Which room was your sister last in?" Honor asks.

"Her bedroom," she sniffs and the tears start. "The window on the left of the fourth floor."

"Okay, I'll—fuck," Honor swears when the second story of the townhouse collapses. The girl screams. The ceiling collapse means the firefighters can't get in through the door and the fire is spreading too quickly to set up a ladder.

"Charlie!" the girl screams. "Oh my god! CHARLIE!"

It's general protocol on fires and other disasters to follow the first responders' lead, but Honor has never been one to sit around and wait to be told to do something. So she jumps. She launches herself up to the fourth floor and grabs onto the ornate molding above the window with one hand and punches the window in with the other.

Honor swings herself inside and is immediately dripping sweat. It slides down between her shoulder blades and down to the small of her back.

"Charlie!" she calls out. Smoke curls around the roof, and Charlie's room is devoid of the girl in question. Had the firefighters already gotten her out? Did Honor jump the gun again? Spectra is going to have her ass.

She picks up the bed to make sure the kid isn't hiding under it and calls her name again. There's an answering cry—"Help!"— followed by fierce coughing.

Honor tears into the hallway and ducks under the flames that try to catch her. "Charlie!" she shouts again. She feels the smoke settle in her lungs but that's a problem for later. Honor already knows she can withstand a little oxygen deprivation.

"Help!" She sounds panicked.

"Where are you?" Honor shouts.

"In here!" she shouts back. Which. Great. Super helpful. She's probably, like, five. Honor tears through the top floor of the townhouse trying to follow the sound of Charlie's little voice. Honor nearly sobs with relief when she finds the girl huddled under the burning roof of a set of bunk beds. Honor snatches her up into her arms, and Charlie clings to her like a trauma- tized koala.

Honor heads for the nearest window and punches it out. She doesn't even give Charlie a warning before she jumps, which she's been told she should do but time is of the essence and fire licks at her heels. She lands on the street and manages not to make a dent this time.

"Charlie!" the sister cries out, full on sobbing now.

"Kimmie!" Charlie starts crying even though she'd been a trooper in the actual fire. She reaches for her sister and Honor relinquishes her without a fight.

"Get her checked out by paramedics," Honor tells the older sister. "She inhaled a lot of smoke."

"I will, thank you, oh my god, thank you!" Kimmie says, trying, and failing, to hold back her tears. Charlie coughs something fierce into her sister's neck and Honor pats her on the back.

With the building cleared, there isn't much left for Honor to do. She doesn't know if she has to be dismissed or anything, either. This part had probably been covered in one of her classes and for the first time, Honor finds herself wishing she had paid attention.

She's about to slip away when little Charlie's parents pull up, barreling past the safety lines to get to their daughter in the back of an ambulance. She sits on the edge with her legs dangling and swinging back and forth, a slightly too big oxygen mask strapped to her face. Both parents pull both daughters into a hug. The older sister starts crying again, probably because the dad is also crying, but Charlie just seems happy to see her parents.

Her mom pulls back to say something, smoothing soot covered hair out of her face. Charlie lifts a hand and points at Honor. Her mom turns and Honor waves awkwardly. She marches right up to her and hugs her like she's one of her daughters too.

"Thank you," she says, voice choked with emotion. Ridiculously, Honor feels her own eyes start to tear up.

"Just doing my job," she tries to brush it off. She releases Honor and then the dad is right there, throwing himself at Honor so hard that it would have knocked anyone else over. The dad is saying something, but Honor can't quite make it out because he's *still crying and then he's pulling Honor over to the ambulance where Charlie still sits.*

She gets to her feet when Honor comes over and holds her arms out for a hug. Who is Honor to reject a five-year-old kid's hug? She wraps the kid up tight, letting her feel just a hint of how strong Honor is. She hears a camera shutter but ignores it.

"What do you say?" Charlie's dad sniffs.

"Thank you," Charlie says, sounding much less hoarse.

"You're very welcome," she says and lets her go. "You were very brave in there, Charlie. You should be proud."

"What's your name?" Charlie's mom asks.

"Oh, uh, Trick," she answers, remembering the call sign printed on her license.

"Trick!" Charlie repeats and hugs her again. Honor laughs, taken off guard.

"Okay, Charlie," her mom says, sniffing hard. "You have to let Trick go now. She has to go save other people."

"Okay," she says and does even as she pouts. "Save lots of people!"

"I will," Honor promises.

From up in the stands, Honor watches that little girl now. The girl who had told her to save lots of people all those years ago, to do her absolute best to save people herself. She's been quieter since the incident with Monroe, the girl with the blue fire, at Rizzo's. It wasn't her fault, not really, and if anything it was better this way because Honor got to her first. Monroe was bound to blow at some point but Charlie makes a better catalyst than most.

It's eating away at Charlie. Honor can see it but she doesn't know what to do about it. She can't just tell her it's okay because it's not but she also doesn't want Charlie blaming herself like this, either. These things happen. Lord knows Honor has set off her own fair share of rogues, but dwelling on it, carrying it with you to the next job? That's dangerous.

Honor can see it happening right in front of her. No matter who's in her group, Charlie won't hesitate to take charge in a sim. Her classmates know it too. Even when she tried to take a back seat, to let someone else take the lead, everyone just looked to her.

That's a lot of pressure for a teenager, Honor knows first hand. But it's not necessarily the bad kind of pressure, either. This is the kind of pressure that makes a leader and alone, it's not an issue. But now Honor's starting to see the cracks from all of the other pressure that Charlie is putting on herself, and all of it together could prove catastrophic.

Honor would know.

Charlie thought that the fire rescue simulation would be like any other exercise they've done all year.

She thought she could do this, but now, facing down a burning building that somehow looks nothing and exactly like her old townhouse, she realizes how wrong she was. Her hands still have a phantom ache from where that girl burned them even though Malia healed them. She clenches them into fists now.

She grits her teeth. Investigate. Fast Attack. Command. She runs through what little she remembers from class about fire procedures even though she knows she aced that exam. "Since we don't have a water marvel, we're going to have to—uh, we'll have to focus on evacuation and containment.

Rosie, you can kick the tops of the hydrants and shape them to aim, right?"

"Well enough," she says with a shrug.

"Okay, Alex, send your copies into the building to clear it," she says. "Simon, you evacuate the block and I'll administer the first aid to anyone you bring out. Sound good?"

"Yeah, yeah, let's go," Simon says and pushes his glasses up his nose. His marvel isn't really helpful for search and rescue but he's always up to whatever task he's given. When he turns to run off, Charlie can faintly see the bulk of the porcupine spikes that grow out of his back. Several Alexes run out of Alex herself and into the burning building. Charlie fidgets while she waits, flinching when some of the spray from the hydrant across the street hits her cheek.

"Hey, are you okay?" Rose asks after she's done her job, wetting the alleys between the houses to help prevent the spread of fires. As soon as all the Alexes are out, she'll redirect the spray at the actual house.

"I'm fine," Charlie says and she doesn't sound convincing in the slightest. But Rose doesn't press further. Charlie stares at the burning building and feels, with uncomfortable clarity, a bead of sweat roll down the back of her neck and between her shoulder blades. Aurora had assured them that their uniforms were fire resistant, but that doesn't mean fire *proof* and Charlie can still feel the heat of the blaze through the fabric.

She tries to review fire procedure in her head, but it won't come, like her own brain has locked that information up in a vault and refuses to give her the key. She knows this, she knows that she knows this, and that makes it all the more frustrating.

"Uh, guys?" Alex's voice comes over the in-ears that Aurora provides them with. It also records their communications for playback later, so they can watch and listen to see what they did right or wrong during an exercise. "There are some gas canisters in the basement, the kind for a barbecue? We can't leave them here, can we?"

"No," Charlie answers as she searches through her brain for what to do. She knows she doesn't have much time, but that pressure only pushes the information further out of her mind. She can't find it and no one else is answering—*why is no one else answering?*

"Should I move them?" Alex asks.

"Yeah," Charlie says without thinking. With thinking but not anything useful. Then her whole body seizes when she realizes the mistake she's made. "Wait, *no*—"

It's too late.

The heat reaches the canisters and they explode.

Charlie ducks out of reflex, but she doesn't even feel the influx of heat from the explosion. She still hears it, though, rattling in her ear canal. She lifts her head from the protective cage of her arms and sees the fire climbing a shield. She collapses on her butt on the street, staring at the flame so close and fuck, *Alex*—

Alex comes out of the house next door, leaning onto Simon for support because it wasn't her inside the house, it was one of her copies. Charlie's chest breaks open with relief. She puts her forehead to the pavement and collapses there.

Honor is down in the sim in a flash with Leo right behind her, making sure everyone's all right. The simulation breaks around them, and they're left exposed in the middle of the arena. All eyes are on Charlie, but she doesn't look up, not until Honor crouches down in front of her.

Charlie is vaguely aware of Alex being carted off to the infirmary by Leo, but she can only focus on Honor in front of her, on her arms that have fresh ink because her old tattoos burned off. Because of Charlie. Even her boots look disappointed.

Charlie knows that Honor has to say it even though she knows that Charlie is well aware. She has to say it because that's what makes her a good teacher.

"If that were a real person, they'd be dead," she says. Charlie flinches.

"I know," she says, voice weak. Honor claps her on the shoulder. It's just more weight there.

"But, hey, that's why we train," she says. "You're fifteen. You're only gonna get better, okay?"

"Okay," Charlie says and shrugs her hand off. "Can I—can I be excused?"

"Sure, kid," Honor says. "I'll check on you later, yeah?"

"Okay," Charlie says. She keeps her head down as she goes to the locker room where she has plans to cry in the shower until class is over.

21

"Gravitas Saves Hundreds on Plummeting Plane"
—*The Independent Pro*

Honor gets the call before the fire simulation is over so she leaves the kids to Verity and heads straight to Ameliora.

"Are you okay?" Honor demands as she stalks into the infirmary, Adrian on her heels. The infirmary is built much like a hospital but still keeps to the theme of Ameliora in general; two beds to a room, the beds and the sheets are still white because apparently that's out of medical necessity and not style choice, like Honor had previously thought. But each blanket is equipped with a soft, navy blanket and the walls are a pale blue so any bodily fluids or chemicals or marvel residuals will still be easily visible.

"I'm fine," Colson insists, and it sounds like it's his hundredth time saying it. He doesn't *look* fine where he sits in the first bed with nasty second degree burns on his left cheek and shoulder and both hands. The injuries are no doubt from when he tried to shield himself after Monroe had somehow managed to override her nullifiers during the meeting Honor promised. His hair is wet, likely freshly washed after they cleaned his wounds on the back of his neck, and it falls into his eyes.

"You are *not* fine," she snaps as Adrian rounds his bed and taps his fingers together. Ameliora has healers on hand, but none that can repair damage like this as well as Adrian can. Honor had even briefly considered bringing Malia, but that would be grossly inappropriate so she refrained. Besides, Adrian will do a fine job.

She rounds on Lisa. "How did this happen? Isn't she wearing nullifiers? This is unacceptable."

"Honor, calm down," Colson pleads.

"I will *not*," she says.

"You're scaring them," he tells her softly. That pulls Honor up short. She looks at the others in the room. Lisa, Yancey, and Bobby, all of whom had been injured in the attack. Yancy is still bedridden like Colson and Adrian moves to help him, next. Lisa is clutching a clipboard to her chest, hands bandaged. Bobby has shifted his stance like he has to gear up for a fight.

Like he has to gear up for a fight *with Honor.*

Colson's right. They hide it well because they're good at their jobs, but Honor forgets, sometimes, that she's not entirely human.

Titan blood runs hot and vengeful. Her mother used to say that. *Power with a proclivity for violence.* She'd always warned Honor and her sisters to be careful, that they could cause unimaginable damage should they lose control. Honor had been a menace when she was younger, the worst of the three of them at controlling her temper, and would instill fear in seasoned pros decades older than her when she was in school.

Leo once told her that she doesn't even have to do anything specific. She doesn't have to scream or yell or wind up for a hit. As soon as she lets the anger take over, the air around her shifts. He'd likened it to a natural disaster, the moment in an earthquake when the world tilts under your feet and your stomach drops because you know something bad is coming and there's nothing you can do to stop it. There's no way to tell how big or bad or long it will be, and there's no way to properly defend against it either. You're entirely at the mercy of nature. *It's like that*, he'd said, *like a survival instinct that lets people know they're immediately and helplessly at your mercy.*

Honor doesn't like that about herself. It's worse now too, since she and her sisters killed Krewa. Honor split Krewa's power three ways with her sisters, but she still feels the new rush of it sometimes, hot and frightening.

She takes a deep breath through her nose to calm herself down. She's not actually angry at anyone, but that makes it worse. Where did all this anger come from, if not from Honor? She's just worried about Colson, about Monroe, about Bobby. When did that turn into anger?

"She was wearing nullifiers," Colson tells her as she keeps her breathing even. It's surprising to hear, but Honor forces down all emotions lest something turn into anger again. "She even surprised herself. She wasn't trying to hurt me."

"What was she trying to do, then?" Honor asks, voice low. Colson doesn't answer right away which means Honor isn't going to like the answer. Honor covers her face with both hands. "Colson."

"She just… didn't react well. To seeing me… again."

"Why? Did you do something to her?" Honor asks, dropping her hands. He frowns at her reaction. "What is it?"

"I just thought you—" he stops to think and this is another new facet of Colson. He thinks before he speaks.

Sometimes too much. "I know Monroe. I didn't think you'd react well to that."

"I already knew that," she tells him. "She was very vocal about how I took you away from her while putting up a stellar effort to burn the Titan District to the ground. Which is why I'm confused because I thought she'd be *happy* to see you again."

"It's… complicated," he says. "She really did a number on her, even before I got there."

When Colson says 'she,' Honor knows he means his mother, Ravenna. Honor is staunchly against the death penalty and firmly believes that heroes should never take another life given literally any other option. But to her own hypocritical chagrin, the only thing Honor regrets in her life is not killing Ravenna when she had the chance.

"Okay," Honor sighs. "We'll figure this out."

After making sure that Colson was all right and then pestering him until he became annoyed, Honor makes her way to Monroe's bedroom. Honor was told she had sequestered herself after the incident and refused to let anyone in or come out. She knocks on the door.

"*God*, won't you people leave me alone?" she shouts through the door.

"It's me," Honor says through the door, then winces when she realizes that Monroe might not recognize her voice. "Honor."

There's a long silence. Honor waits her out.

"What?"

She takes that as permission to come in. It's a fairly standard room. White walls and wood floors with a plush navy rug under the full bed made up in soft gray sheets and a matching duvet. There are nightstands on either side of it, but there's nothing on them, no personal effects or touches to the room at large. The lighting is soft and warm from the automatic LEDs tucked into the upper corners of the room. Honor sits on the edge of her bed and sighs. Then makes a face at herself for sighing. What is she? A mom?

"Are you here to take me to the Matchbox?" Monroe asks.

"What?" Honor whips around to look at her, where she's folded her legs in front of her like a shield with her arms wrapped around them. She resists the urge to sigh again.

"I'm sorry," Monroe barrels on. Tears start to leak out of the inner corners of her eyes, and she wipes at them furiously. "I'm sorry. I didn't mean to. It was an accident."

"Hey, hey, you don't have anything to be sorry for," Honor assures her.

"I *hurt* him!" She sniffs, hard, and Honor heroically suppresses her grimace.

"Then, I forgive you," she says. "And so does Colson."

"Really?" Her voice is small and Honor's heart hurts.

"Have I lied to you yet?"

Monroe shakes her head.

"You are not going to the Matchbox. Ever. What happened today was an accident. No one blames you and you're not in trouble."

Monroe buries her face in her knees. "Is Colson okay?"

"We brought a medic marvel in and he's like new. You don't have to worry about him, but he is worried about you."

"If he was so worried, why did he leave me there?" she asks, voice thick with tears again. Honor sighs and puts her hand on Monroe's knee.

"When we first brought Colson in and he went through questioning, he gave us the location of Ravenna's bases, and he told us that most of you were kids who needed saving and not villains that needed beating. But by the time we'd gotten there, everything had been moved. Colson did what he could with what he had. I'm sure if he was allowed out of here, he would have gone for you, himself."

"Sure," Monroe says with a disbelieving scoff. Honor resists the urge to convince her right now that it's true because Colson cares about her, cares about everyone, he's a hero at heart and always will be. But now is not the time or place.

"Tomorrow, if you're feeling up to it, Candor will come by again and ask you some questions about Ravenna's gang, Paragon," Honor tells her. "Now, I'm sorry about this, but I have to put new nullifiers on you."

"I didn't mean to break the other ones. I didn't even know I *could*."

"It's alright," Honor promises. "You have an incredible marvel and we'll test it and get it classified eventually but for now I'm gonna give you Class Ones, okay?" Monroe nods and holds her hands out. As gently as she can, Honor puts the new nullifiers on. "If you experience any extreme fatigue or sluggishness let someone know, okay?"

"Okay," she says meekly, eyeing the cuffs warily.

"I know they suck."

"You've had to wear them?" she asks dubiously.

"I have to test them," Honor answers honestly. "They're currently designing special Titan Class nullifiers and they suck *extra* hard. But I promise we're gonna get you out of these as soon as possible." Monroe doesn't say anything but she doesn't look like she doesn't believe what Honor's saying so she'll consider it a win. "If you want, tomorrow, Colson can sit in with you when you meet Candor."

"You won't be there?" Monroe asks, and Honor is already thinking about moving her entire schedule around to be there.

"Do you want me there?"

Monroe thinks for a long moment. Then nods.

"Then, I'll be there."

When the day finally comes, Charlie doesn't hesitate before knocking on the door to the teacher's dorm because if she does, she won't knock at all.

The door swings open and Honor doesn't look at all surprised to see her. Or Jack, who is standing right next to her with two fingers on the bottle like a weirdo. She's barefoot in the black Titan Academy sweatpants and a white Divine Knights t-shirt. Charlie tries, and fails, not to stare at her tattoos. Charlie wonders if the tattoos hide the scars on her skin or if there are no scars at all.

"Happy Birthday!" Charlie says and shoves the very expensive bottle of whiskey at her. There's a pink bow on the neck. Now Honor does look surprised.

"This is… really nice whiskey, wow, thank you," she says, reading the label. "How did you even get this?"

"Don't worry about it," Jack says with a little wave like he did something.

"That makes me very worried about it," says Honor. So Charlie technically stole this, but it was from her own parents' stash and they probably won't even notice. If they do, Charlie will just work off however much it costs, no big deal. Or, even better, shake Jack down for the money. Honor likes it and that alone makes it worth it.

"It's from everyone," Charlie adds. "The whole class."

"Well, tell everyone I said thank you," Honor says with a bright smile. Charlie thinks her brain goes offline for a millisecond.

"We, uh, Tommy and Cora have something for Verity, but she's on patrol right now," Jack adds helpfully.

"Yeah, pulling the night shift," Honor confirms.

"And we don't know Grace, but we wish her happy birthday too!" Charlie adds some more.

"I'll pass the message along," Honor promises. Charlie yawns but is reluctant to leave. "Tired? It's only like six."

"I'm fine," Charlie waves her off. "But what about you? Any fun birthday plans?"

"Just me and my whiskey," she says and holds up the bottle, with a little grin.

"We're having movie night," Charlie blurts. "If you wanna come."

"Movie night, huh?" Honor says and turns the bottle of whiskey over in her hands. She glances back into the teachers' dorm, but it looks dark. "What are you guys watching?"

Charlie immediately grabs Honor's free hand and tugs her across the hallway before she can change her mind. Jack explains their voting process and how everyone who wants to gets to nominate a movie to watch. Then they fight it out bracket style until they have a winner. The movie choosing process generally takes longer than the actual movie, but it's so fun that no one wants to come up with a better system.

Honor's presence in the student common room sends the rest of their classmates into a frenzy, and they scramble to rearrange their unspoken seating chart. All twenty of them cram into the top floor common room together and the stragglers usually have to sit at the tables behind the couches and chairs and the makeshift fort Charlie sometimes constructs.

Honor gets the seat of honor, front row center. It's on the good couch right in front of the television, and Charlie snags the seat on her right while Jack elbows Malia out of the way on her other side, but no one wants to really fight in front of Honor so Malia steals a pillow to sit on the floor in front of Charlie.

Charlie won last movie night and the rules say that she can't nominate another film this time, but she can still argue and vote. Under their normal rules, the runner-up from last time, Ethan, gets a bye for the first round, but since they add in Honor's nomination, they have a full bracket.

Tommy, as usual, nominates a horror movie that loses immediately in the first round. One of the classic cartoon films from their collective childhood makes it pretty far before getting beat by Lochlan's choice of a newer animated film they haven't seen. Honor's choice of a sci-fi hero flick sails straight through to the final round and goes head-to-head with Jack's romcom which he, hilariously, doesn't argue for. His face goes pink and he sinks into the couch with a pillow clutched against his chest.

"A romcom would be fun," Honor says because she's amazing.

"No, no, don't do that," Charlie says and gets up on her knees to hit Jack with a pillow across Honor. "Boy Wonder can tell everyone how he wants to watch his little gay romcom because he has a crush on the lead and wants to see that shirtless scene."

"Shut *up*," Jack snaps at her but doesn't correct her because she isn't wrong.

"Double feature?" Ethan pipes up helpfully. "Honor's first and then we end with the romcom?"

"Bet," says Charlie and pulls up the movie.

Charlie is absolutely buzzing the entire time. She's not really focusing on the plot but how Honor seems to run hotter than the average person and how they're close enough to touch, but Charlie is careful not to. She doesn't want Honor to feel like she has to move.

If someone had said to her a year ago that she'd be having a movie night with her favorite hero on said hero's birthday, Charlie would have lost her shit. She's losing it now, internally. She gets to release some excess energy by launching her last pillow at Kai when he pulls out his phone which is against the rules of movie night. But then she loses it some *more* when she spots Leo walking by their window and he doubles back to peer inside after he sees Honor.

He pauses for only a second before coming inside, still dressed in his three-piece suit that acts as his hero uniform. Some of Charlie's classmates say hi in hushed tones, and Leo ducks down low to sit on the floor in front of Honor. Honor pats his head in hello, and he leans back against her legs. Malia nudges Charlie's leg and Charlie nudges back with her foot, but there's nothing else they can really do to communicate with Honor and Leo *right next to them.*

Charlie gets restless halfway through like she always does, so she starts to braid Malia's hair, warmed by the fact that Malia just… lets her. Doesn't even flinch when Charlie's fingers start to untangle her hair. Charlie thinks she sees Honor glance at her out of the corner of her eye, but it's so fast she can't be sure she's not imagining things.

Charlie ends up falling asleep twenty minutes into Jack's romcom, and when she wakes up she's in her own bed.

22

"The Rankings Are In!
See What Heroes Cracked the Top Ten"

—*Super Citizen*

Charlie feels her exhaustion in her bones and, unfortunately, Malia's marvel doesn't fix that. It fixed the bruises she'd gotten from Tommy's new staff and the finger she'd broken during weightlifting, but Charlie is on her own when it comes to her heavy eyelids and brain fog.

She only half watches the group ahead of her during the hurricane sim. Kai is in his element, surrounded by water after they flooded a portion of the Arena to simulate hurricane conditions. Jack is in charge of driving the rescue boat, but he's already thrown up once, citing sea sickness. There's nowhere else for him to go, though, since the floods have reached the second story of every simulated house in their radius.

If Charlie wasn't too busy focusing all of her willpower into staying upright, then she would have found it amusing. As it is, she misses most of it, and is startled half awake when Honor calls her and her group mates up for their turn.

The terrain changes slightly. They're still dealing with high waters after a hurricane, but they're in a more urban area with more damage to buildings which means more debris to be wary of. Charlie is in a group with Rose, Anthony, and Ethan. Ethan volunteers to dive so he can light up the darker places below the surface because part of their job is also to recover the bodies of those who didn't make it.

Rose controls the boat with her marvel, which frees them all up to help survivors and continue the search. Anthony and Charlie's marvels aren't well-suited for this, so they're limited to what they can do physically, which is just provide first aid and such to the dummies.

After the incident with the fire simulation, Ethan takes point in this sim. Charlie is grateful. She's so tired, she can't deal with thinking for too long. She'll just do what she's told and get through this simulation so she can go back to her room and sleep.

She leans over the edge of the rescue boat to pull a dummy up and onboard. She hooks her hands under the dummy's armpits and tries to haul it up, but it's *heavy*. Charlie's still sore from her extra workout that morning, and even Malia's marvels couldn't fully take that away. Charlie sags over the side of the boat, catches her breath, and lets the dummy float for a moment, careful to keep its head above water.

Then she takes a deep breath and tries to pull again. She still can't do it. The dummy falls back into the water and Charlie falls over the side with it. She doesn't even feel the splash of the water, but she does hear someone shout her name.

Charlie wakes up in the Titan Academy infirmary and groans, immediately piecing together what happened. She feels thick and groggy and like she slept for too long but still needs to sleep longer. She raises heavy arms to her face and rubs at her eyes.

"Hey, hero," her mom says from her chair beside the bed. "How do you feel?"

"Like shit," she says which is true, but she's more embarrassed than anything. Did she really collapse in the middle of a simulation? She must have. She doesn't remember finishing, and there's only one way she'd end up in here. "What happened?"

"You collapsed during a training exercise," her mom tells her. "Your teacher said you were out before you hit the water. One of your classmates pulled you out with his marvel, the water one."

"Kai?" she asks, surprised and confused as to why she's surprised that Kai would help her. He's best suited to, and they're all there to be heroes after all, of course they would jump to save each other. Charlie would, if it were anyone else. Her mom nods.

"Charlie," her mom begins. Charlie groans again. She knows that tone. That's the 'lecture incoming' tone. She heard it when she gave that bully a black eye in the third grade and she heard it when she blew out a wall in the house with her marvel. She's too tired and sore and achy to hear it now.

Charlie thinks she's saved when someone knocks on the door. They don't wait to be told to come in to open the door. It's Honor and Leo and Adrian, and Charlie's stomach sinks even further. The grim and serious looks on their faces tell her that this isn't just a friendly check-in. They didn't even bring flowers.

"Hey, kid," Honor greets her as Adrian clicks his fingers together and checks her vitals on the small yellow screen that appears between his hands. "We need to talk."

Charlie's eyes bug out of her head and she starts to panic. "I'm not being expelled, am I? I'm sorry. I didn't—"

"Woah, woah," Honor says, taken aback. "You're not being expelled. You're not even really in trouble, Charlie. We're just worried about you." Charlie wills her heart rate to slow back down.

"You've been overdoing it," her mom says, matter-of-fact. "Your friend told us that she's been healing you almost every morning."

"Malia's marvel doesn't work like my marvel," Adrian tells her and his screen disappears. "Her marvel draws from *your* energy which means she's been inadvertently draining you daily on top of the training you do for class and whatever extra training you've been putting yourself through. It's too much. Your body gave out from sheer exhaustion, not because anything is wrong."

"We knew you were training extra hours," Honor says with an apologetic glance at Charlie's mom. "But we didn't know that you were training so hard that you required extra healing on a daily basis. Added to the stress of school, and the tournament coming, and with what happened with Monroe—we should have been keeping a closer eye on you, and I'm sorry that we weren't."

Charlie gapes like a fish for a moment. "You—you don't have to apologize to *me*," she says.

"We do," Honor insists. "It's our responsibility to take care of you and we failed."

"You didn't fail!" Charlie insists. "I'm *fine*."

"Charlie," her mom says sternly. "Your teachers have recommended that you be pulled from training for two weeks to recover, and I agree."

"Wait, what?" Charlie asks, looking around the room for confirmation. "No. You *can't*. I'll fall behind! The Earthquake sims are next week and if I don't get to do those and we get them in the tournament, then I'll be useless—"

"No, you won't," Leo interrupts. "I've already graded your paper for the land disasters unit and even if all you did was stand there and direct people during a sim, you'd be far from useless. You'll also be able to make up any missed exercises, including the one from yesterday. Several of your classmates have already volunteered to help."

"Yesterday?" Charlie's face burns at the implication of her classmates pitying her. She's just giving them extra work they didn't ask for now.

"You slept for twenty-two hours," Adrian tells her. "Your body needed that rest and it needs even more."

"You're coming home for the weekend," her mom tells her with a pat to her foot.

"But I—"

"Nonnegotiable," her mom says. "You're coming home to rest where I can keep an eye on you and you'll be back on campus Monday morning for class."

"This isn't a punishment, Charlie," Honor reminds her.

"Sure feels like one," she mumbles and looks down at the blankets.

"Mm, Lydia made her chocolate peanut butter cup cupcakes," her mom says. Charlie resists the excitement that threatens to swell up inside her. She wants to be *mad*, damn it! But Lydia's cupcakes are so freaking good, and the chocolate peanut butter cup ones are her favorites. She settles for scowling at her mom who grins in response. "C'mon hero, let's get you home."

"Fine," Charlie says and throws the blankets off. She stands up on her own just to prove that she can, but she does it too fast and the head rush makes her sway. Honor is the one to catch and steady her despite being the furthest away. "Thanks," she mutters and looks away, embarrassed again.

"Anytime, kid," she says with a reassuring smile. Charlie's kind of annoyed that it works.

23

"Honor de Mora Becomes Small Business Owner,
Buys Local Pizza Joint"

—*Titan Tribune*

The committee conference room has a long table made of the same dark wood that fills Ameliora. There's abstract art on the wall that Verity picked out herself in cool blues and grays, and Honor has spent a lot of time squinting at them, trying to make sense of the strokes. The chairs are soft vegan leather and ergonomic and don't squeak in the slightest when the last person takes their seat.

It's Colson's hearing, but he isn't allowed to be present for the majority of the meeting, so it's Honor, Ursula, Colson's doctors, Terence Jones, and a bunch of suits that Honor would love to chew up and spit back out. They'd been assigned to Ameliora by the Justice Department. Among them is Peter Nim, the Director of the Federal Bureau of Prisons.

"Let's begin," says Terence, the superintendent of Ameliora. He runs the joint, mostly from behind the scenes, and deals with the majority of the liasing with the government. Even though they're a private facility, they still need government approval to house people who are legally considered prisoners. "Today, we are discussing the graduation of Colson Cappelletti. His proposed sponsor is Honor de Mora, present here. We will hear testimony from his doctors and then from Colson himself, provided by Ursula Knight, also known as Candor, with the use of her marvel: compulsive truth telling. Any questions before we begin?"

There shouldn't be. There have been several other graduation hearings prior to Colson's and the staff hasn't changed once. They all know how this goes, but then Peter Nim sits back in his seat and steeples his fingers together.

"I think having Miss de Mora as the proposed sponsor presents a conflict of interest," he says. "It's well-documented that they have a history, and if we set a precedent of friends sponsoring friends, then anyone will be able to graduate."

"That's the point," Honor says. Next to her, Michelle Granger stiffens. Michelle is one of the lawyers on the Ameliora team and Honor's personal lawyer, so she's best prepared for what's about to happen to one Peter Nim.

People think they know heroes because they serve the public and their work is captured in real time, but most of the time they fail to see through the carefully crafted personas that all heroes wear. Honor especially, since she had deliberately placed herself in the spotlight as part of a plan, not because she wanted it. The more people who like you, the more people who see you, the easier it is to make money as a hero. The government stipend is hardly enough, and Honor knew from the jump that she'd need money to do all of the things she wanted to do and keep *control* over them too.

Peter Nim knows Honor's work. He knows that she's half Titan and she's got an attitude and she wins most fights through brute force. But he doesn't know *Honor*. Doesn't know that she was at the top of her class at Marvelous when she wasn't suspended. Doesn't know that she was team leader at Homeland Hero Division because of her brain, not her strength. Doesn't know that every move she's made since the Titan Battle has been thought out and calculated down to the decimal. But he's about to learn.

"What is the point then?" he asks as though she's just given him the upper hand.

"Everyone who enrolls in Ameliora should graduate, that is the point," she reiterates. "This is not a prison, this is a reform program. *Prisons* are meant to be reform programs as well, but I digress. To imply that someone, anyone, shouldn't graduate for whatever reason is a gross misinterpretation of our goals here, and if that's how you see it, I recommend you remove yourself from this committee immediately."

He looks slightly taken aback and opens his mouth to respond, but Honor doesn't allow it.

"The standards for sponsorship have been established, and I meet each and every criteria without fault. Nowhere does it state that a graduate cannot have a prior relationship with a sponsor. In fact, when establishing the standards for sponsorship, it was openly discussed that graduates would likely benefit from being sponsored by someone they already know and trust. However, given that one of the criteria for sponsorship is also being a licensed pro hero, that's been difficult to implement.

"As Colson's friend, I'm already aware of the events that led to the incident of his arrest. You'll learn of them shortly when you hear what his doctors have to say. They'll give you as much information as they're able, considering a large portion of it is still under active investigation that you do not have clearance for. And it is as Colson's friend that I am fully prepared to continue to support him post graduation.

"As for your point about setting a precedent of friends sponsoring friends, I feel compelled to point out that the vast majority of pros do not have friends who are also rogues by virtue of their profession alone. Colson's case is unique and cannot be considered a precedent for anything, let alone future graduate and sponsor relationships.

"Moreover, the point of having a licensed pro as a sponsor is so that the pro agrees to take on the responsibility of the graduate. That responsibility includes, but is not limited to, preemptively preventing any more crimes committed by the graduate. *Which,* we've proven, is statistically unlikely anyway, given the nature and purpose of the program. Any pro who accepts these terms is fully prepared to put their own reputation and career on the line because if a crime *is* committed, they will be charged as an accomplice.

"I am fully aware of these responsibilities. I have accepted these responsibilities, and it's already been proven that just about any other hero would be woefully inadequate in subduing Colson in the unlikely event of a relapse. Colson was classified as a Class Two Marvel when he was *eleven*. After graduating from Marvelous and further post-academic training, he has earned a Class One ranking. There are three other Class One Marvels in the state of California. Myself, my sister, Verity, and Gravitas. Verity also has a prior relationship with Colson, and Gravitas' son attends my academy, so a relationship could be construed through that connection as well, if we want to split hairs.

"So please, tell me whom you'd rather have sponsor Colson. If your point in raising this so-called concern was to have *no one* sponsor him and prevent his hard-earned gradu-ation from this program, I'll say it again: remove yourself from this committee immediately, because you've completely failed to understand the purpose of this program."

Nim gapes at her while Honor waits for his answer. She even managed to keep her cool. Verity will be so proud when she finds out. She knows there's going to be pushback about Colson's graduation. Honor is fully prepared to push back harder.

"Well," Terence prompts after a moment of tense silence. "Have your concerns been addressed, Mr. Nim?"

"I suppose," he says. Honor doesn't smile.

"Then let's proceed," says Terence. The doctors present testimony, detailing how he'll be closely monitored with monthly physical checkups for his marvel and blood transfusions, as well as continue counseling weekly. Colson's incident, Honor already knows, was caused by trauma sustained from his mother's abuse built up over years and years in his childhood and through high school as she attempted to kidnap him more than once, even going so far as murdering his father and attempting to murder Honor to get him to go with her.

An undisclosed event led to his mother finding him and using his vulnerability to manipulate him into finally joining her. That undisclosed event being a huge fight with Honor just before she released a Titan but no one on the committee needs to know that. Joining Ravenna in what, exactly, is classified and isn't discussed in the meeting. But the majority of them already know about Ravenna and Paragon, especially after Monroe's enrollment at Ameliora.

On the day of the incident, seeing Honor caused a break in the hold his mother had over him, and that break incited immediate panic. Over the past twenty-three months, Colson has demonstrated an incredibly fierce desire to improve himself and heal from his childhood trauma that he left untreated for so long. The doctors emphasize that he has a long way to go, but that progress can and should be made outside of Ameliora's carefully curated environment.

Then, Colson is called in.

He comes in wearing the white shirt and gray slacks Honor had given him for Christmas. His sleeves are rolled up and reveal his scarred forearms and slightly untanned wrists from when he used to wear nullifiers. Honor had almost forgotten how handsome he could be when he isn't hunched over and drowning in baggy sweats. Although, she kind of thought he was handsome then, too.

"Hi, Colson," Ursula says warmly. He can't quite return her smile as he takes a seat next to Honor. "I'm going to ask you some questions and you will be compelled to answer in the most honest way possible. Say yes if you understand."

"Yes," he says, clear and steady.

"Good, how are you?"

"I'm alright," he answers, startled by the simple question and possibly by his answer.

"Can you elaborate for me?"

"I'm a little nervous, but I know that I've done all that I can up to this point and now it's out of my control," he says. "I'll make the best of whatever the outcome of today is." Ursula smiles, proud, and Honor fights back a similar expression. She feels Nim's eyes on her instead of Colson, and she very purposely keeps her eyes on Colson.

"Very good," Ursula says. "The next few questions will be about your quality of life upon release. Do you have reliable housing upon release?"

"Yes," he answers without hesitation, partly because that's how Ursula's marvel works and partly because he knows he's welcome at Honor's for as long as he needs.

"Do you have reliable transportation that will be able to pick you up upon release?"

"Yes."

"Good," she says and glances down at the questions in front of her. If the answers to these questions are no, then it is the responsibility of Ameliora to help provide. "Do you have any employment opportunities or ideas?"

"No," Colson answers immediately, but this one is choked. He closes his eyes briefly and his hands curl into fists on his knees. Honor doesn't think twice before reaching out and taking hold of one, gently unfurling his fingers and threading them with hers. He holds on tight enough to hurt.

"Why not?" Ursula asks because she's required to.

"My whole life," he starts, and it's strangled like he doesn't want to, but he has no choice, "I only ever wanted to be a hero. It's the only thing I ever even considered being, and I know I fucked that up and I can't go back to it, but I haven't been able to process the idea of doing something else with my life because it—because it hurts and I haven't confronted that consequence to my actions yet."

"How do you expect to provide food, clothing, and other essentials for yourself if you are unemployed?"

"Honor said she would help," he says meekly. The back of his neck is flushed, but Honor doesn't think he has any reason to be embarrassed.

"And how long do you plan on providing that assistance?" Ursula directs the question at Honor before she's really ready for it, but that's on her. She should have expected it. Sponsors get interviewed by Ursula, too.

"As long as he needs," Honor answers, raw and honest. Ursula's marvel doesn't quite hurt, but it's close. It's uncomfortable, like the words are being pulled directly from her lungs, not up through her throat, but out through her chest, and they bang on her ribs on their way out.

"Alright, Colson, now it's time for the harder questions," she says to prepare him, prepare Colson and Honor, really. Honor hadn't been expecting the sudden question aimed at her, and now her heart is pounding.

"Okay," Colson says softly. He takes a deep breath, squeezes Honor's hand.

"In reference to the incident that preceded your hospitalization and arrest; why did you take those actions that day?"

"I saw Honor and I just *panicked*. We hadn't seen each other or spoken in a year and I knew the second she saw me she wasn't going to let me get away, so I panicked and ran. But Honor's faster than me, so I knew I'd have to use my marvel to try and get away, but it obviously didn't work. I was confused and scared and I didn't know what to do and I did the wrong thing. It's not an excuse, but I never wanted to hurt anyone."

"You didn't," Ursula tells him because she and Honor both know that Colson only caused structural damage. Honor made sure that Colson knew that when he woke up in the hospital.

"I hurt Honor," he whispers.

Honor isn't going to insult them both by lying and saying that he didn't. Colson did hurt her, in more than just a physical way, but more than anything else, she hurt *for* him because even before she knew what happened, she knew he had been through so much, too much.

She squeezes his hand. "I forgive you."

"I'm sorry," he wheezes out anyway.

"I know," Honor says gently. He uses his free hand to cover his face while he composes himself. Three more questions.

"Whenever you're ready, Colson," Ursula says like the angel she is.

"I'm ready," he says and sounds anything but. Ursula still takes him at his word.

"Do you regret what you did?" She asks.

"Yes."

"Do you want to be better?"

"Yes."

"Are you ready and willing to commit to being better in the world outside of Ameliora?"

"Yes," he says and heaves a sigh in relief like he'd been worried that wouldn't be his answer.

"Good," Ursula says. "That's all the questions I have for you. You did well, Colson."

"Thank you," he says meekly. His eyes are fixed on their hands under the table.

Honor breathes a sigh of relief. Colson is coming home.

24

"Disgraced Hero Incendiary to be
Released from Rogue Program"
—*The Marvel Spectator*

Honor's grateful to be alone in the apartment, and even then she heads to the added privacy of her own room. She'd gotten another message from Monroe's doctor saying that the social worker assigned to her case isn't as active as she should be in Monroe's recovery, which means Honor will have to find someone who *will* be active.

Her first thought is herself. Honor's first thought is always herself. If something needs to be done, then she'll do it herself. She doesn't need to ask anyone else to do it for her. Except, she's starting to crumble. On top of being a pro hero and sponsoring Colson, the kids' numbers are falling in sims on the heels of Charlie's spiral and collapse because Honor isn't there to train them as often as she should be. How can she help Monroe if she can't even help the kids she has now?

She knew Charlie was putting in extra hours and she didn't stop it, didn't even address it because she assumed that Charlie would take care of herself and that she was just working a bit harder than everyone else. She didn't know about the ramifications of long term, frequent use of Malia's marvel. She didn't even know Charlie was asking Malia to heal her on a near-daily basis, and she should have.

Honor is split too many ways, too thin, she's not doing anything as well as she should, even with the abundance of help she has. Maybe the Academy should be shut down. Maybe this was all a terrible pipe dream of an idea. If the school shuts down, at least Honor will be a failure instead of a quitter. No one could really blame her for not being able to reach the unreasonable standards set forth for her and only her.

Why is it so fucking hard to try and be better? Honor's been working nonstop for years to be better, and she can't ever remember having a goal she didn't meet head on. Why was it so much easier before? When she was brash and hard-headed and violent? Why is it easier to be the way she doesn't want to be?

"*Woah!*"

Honor can hear Verity shout through the wall, and then her door is being kicked in so hard that a hinge breaks. Honor startles and tries to arrange herself to make it look like she wasn't spiraling into her emotions just moments before, but it's no use, not with Verity.

"What was *that*?"

Ridiculously, Honor feels tears well in her eyes. She cuts her gaze away from her sister and leans back against her headboard, resisting the urge to pull her knees to her chest and make herself smaller. Verity comes to the other side of the bed and sits down next to her. She keeps her gaze forward, but she doesn't need to read Honor's expression to know what she's feeling.

The fact that Verity is willing to get so close, risking overwhelm due to Honor's overflowing emotions, means Honor must be worse off than even she realizes. Verity sits in silence with her for a moment, probably parsing through the influx she's receiving from Honor to try and pinpoint exactly what's wrong.

Thanks to her impeccable control and grasp of her marvel, Verity appears clairvoyant to a lot of people. She's just so experienced and talented in reading emotions and the way they mix and interact in a specific situation that she can usually parse out a source from feeling alone. But Honor also knows that it's hard, because in order to sort through all of those feelings, she has to feel them herself in addition to her own emotions. Honor doesn't know how she does it.

"Okay, spit it out," Verity says. Honor remembers some people saying that Verity should become a counselor to truly use her marvel for good. Anyone who actually knew Verity as a person would know that she's not even kind of suited for that line of work. Not a single ounce of tact to be found. Verity always said it was because she couldn't be bothered to expend the extra energy it would take to make herself more palatable. Honor's always admired that about her.

"I don't know," she says. Verity sighs like she's frustrated, and Honor isn't sure if that frustration is aimed at her or not.

"Okay, come on." Verity grabs her arm, not really giving her the choice unless she wants to pick a fight, and drags her out of her room, all the way to the Arena.

Verity punches a special code into the control panel, one Aurora had programmed specifically because they requested it, and the floor parts to reveal the biggest trampoline in the world, probably. Then she enters another code to open up the ceiling. Verity all but throws Honor onto the trampoline, and Honor lets her, lets her body fall into the canvas and bounce back up into the air.

For a split second she feels weightless. Everything she's been carrying on her shoulders disappears for one blissful moment. Then she goes crashing back to earth, but instead of shattering, she's caught and lifted back up.

After the second bounce she lands back on her feet and faces Verity, who's got her knees bent, ready to take off. Honor can't help but grin and bend her knees too. There's a split second where they both load up, far enough apart that they don't affect the other's jump, and then they both launch.

Honor reaches so much higher when she's trying to jump instead of letting herself fall. They both clear the Arena roof, reaching toward the clear night sky. An airplane blinks as it passes and Honor wonders if anyone can see them from their window seat. She reaches her hand up as high as she can, reaching for the stars and Verity does the same. Then, they're both falling.

"I totally got higher than you," Verity says as she lands on her feet, jumping up again but not nearly as high.

"You have never, and will never, reach higher than me," Honor says. The banter is comforting in its familiarity. But she's still stressed and freaked out, and those feelings start to creep back in. Her knees buckle, landing and bouncing softly on the trampoline.

"You still freaked out over what happened with Charlie?" Verity asks as she sits down next to her.

"With her. With Monroe. With just—all of them. Those kids deserve better," she says and barrels on before Verity can counter that. "They're falling behind and they don't even realize it because they're starstruck. They look at us and think we're the greatest thing in the world and don't think that they'd be better of somewhere else but they *would* and they *will* because we're gonna get fucking shut down anyway!"

"What's your weakness?" Verity asks out of the blue. Honor is startled enough to look over at her. Verity waits for her answer.

"What a weird way to kick me when I'm down," she says.

"Just fucking answer," Verity says, unamused.

"I…" Honor trails off. Not because she's not fully aware of her weak points, but admitting to them out loud feels too much like admitting to defeat. Still, her sister had asked, so she forces the words out even if they taste like bile.

"I'm too pushy. I'm too reckless. I risk myself to the point of carelessness. I don't ask for help enough. I try to do everything at once by myself—shit."

"Okay, let's unpack," Verity says in a mock serious voice. It's Honor's turn to look unamused. "First of all, the next time some shit like this worms its way into your brain, you talk to me or Leo or Aurora, *somebody*. You got it? If I have to feel a flare of self-loathing like that come from you ever again, I'm gonna skip straight to the ass-kicking portion of the evening." Honor snorts at that, knowing full well that Verity means it.

"Second, if we get shut down, then we get shut down and we'll deal with it when it comes, but you obsessing over it and everything you should be doing differently instead of, I don't know, actually *doing* those things? I'll ask you to refer back to the ass-kicking clause of number one.

"Third—I'll agree with you when you say the kids are too starstruck by us. They think we're invincible and that's a problem because it makes them believe that there will come a time, if they work hard enough, that they won't have any weaknesses. They might not even think they have any now and we can't raise them like that. You have to be aware of your weaknesses, especially as a hero, and while you can work on them and make them stronger or compensate in other ways, there will never come a day when someone doesn't have a weakness of some sort. Ever.

"The fact that you know yours and can say them out loud is a sign that you've already changed so much. The old Honor would have never admitted to weakness, and the old Honor wouldn't have been suited to teaching these kids. But who you are now? There's no one better.

"Not a single hero course in the *entire world* has a one hundred percent pass rate. Not Marvelous, not Monarch, or White Water, or Bangtan, or Storm Coast, *or anyone else*. For a reason," she says. "Not everyone is cut out for it and *that's okay*. You're gonna have to accept that as a possibility and stop framing it as the worst thing in the world. Our class started out with three hundred and twelve students. Only twenty eight graduated. *You* of all people should know that."

"That's different," Honor tries to interject.

"It's not," Verity insists. "The school system that's already in place failed you. It failed all of us in more ways than one, and what we're trying to do here? It's important. So don't go giving up now. These kids need us and I think we need them, too. The world sure as fuck will one day. That all being said! I say we take a fucking vacation!"

"What?" Honor half laughs. If she hadn't known Verity her whole life, she might've gotten whiplash from the sudden shift from motivational pep talk to travel agent.

"Yeah, this summer, whether we get shut down or not, let's go on vacation. A week off in the middle of nowhere, where no one can reach us."

Honor wipes away the residual wetness from her eyes and the next smile comes easy. "We could go see Grace. There's no cell reception on Viasyre."

Verity snaps her fingers and points at Honor. "You're a genius. We'll go visit Grace for a week. Something to look forward to no matter what, and a break from the shit show that is real life on Earth." Then, Verity pulls her into a hug that would misalign the spine of anyone else. Honor laughs, feeling lighter than she has in weeks.

"I love you a lot," she says.

"I love you too, bitch, let's get some food, I'm starving," she says and drags Honor up by the hand.

Verity's right. Honor has been stressing over things she can't control rather than doing the things she knows she *can* control. She'll talk to Charlie. Monroe is in good hands at Ameliora. Her kids are resilient and eager to learn, and Honor will be there to teach them all she knows for as long as she can. That's really all she can do.

Charlie is effectively put on bedrest. Her dad is a classic worrier and has brought her three glasses of water, all of which have condensed three water rings on her nightstand, a plate of Lydia's cupcakes, four of which Charlie ate in one go, and a book he thought she'd like in case she gets bored.

The book is starting to look like her best option as she exits yet another dumb daytime show. Her television screen zooms out to show her all of the thumbnails of the broadcasts currently happening. She clicks on another one at random and regrets it almost immediately.

"Titans are essentially aliens," the weirdo host says. He's got a backwards baseball cap and a wrinkled short sleeve button-up on, so Charlie is already opposed to whatever he has to say on principle alone. "There are definitely more out there. Who's to say that they're not gonna pay Earth a little visit?"

"That's why we have the Triumvirate," his guest or co-host or whatever says. She's also got a backwards baseball cap on, and if that's their uniform, they need to do some serious rebranding. At least her Gravitas shirt has been ironed.

"Who even named them that?" he asks, and then without pausing to allow for an answer, goes on, "Besides, who says we can depend on them when *more* Titans show up?"

"Their track record says we can," she points out. "That's the whole point of heroes anyway. To depend on them! Even if there are other aliens or Titans out there, maybe they're friendly! Maybe we should get into the intergalactic tourist trade now before it booms."

What a load of bullshit. Charlie's puts on Ethan's video channel to cleanse her palate from listening to the only people who don't have complete and utter faith in their top heroes. She would put good money on that guy having a dumb marvel and he's just bitter that he can't be a hero.

Having binged all of Ethan's videos with Lochlan and Malia in the dorms, she mostly zones out. But then she sees that he's posted a new video in the past week, and she clicks to listen to him analyze a tsunami rescue that hit Japan. Going directly from an older video to a current one, Charlie can clearly see a difference in Ethan. Not just the fact that he's filming in the dorms now instead of his room at home, but he sits up straighter and he fills out his t-shirts more and his skin is tanned from working out in the sun so often. He speaks with a different confidence now, too, the kind that can only come from first hand experience.

There's a knock on her door and it cracks open. Her mom peeks inside to make sure she's not sleeping. Or make sure she is. Charlie should probably be sleeping.

"How're you feeling?" her mom asks as she opens the door all the way.

"I'm fine," Charlie says and flops dramatically back onto her pillows. She will admit that her bed here is *much* comfier than her bed on campus. "Just like I was the last twelve times you asked."

"Hey, I'm your mom," she says and comes fully into the room to sit on the edge of her bed. "I get to ask as many times as I want."

"Well, the answer will be the same every time," Charlie tells her. Her mom does that thing then, where she just *looks* at Charlie. She's gearing up to say something, but Charlie feels like she needs to confess to a crime she didn't commit before she does. She looks down at her hands. "Do you remember when I used to get in fights at school?"

"You mean like when you fought Jack last semester?"

Charlie grimaces. "You know about that?"

"Of course I know about that," her mom scoffs. She lays a reassuring hand on Charlie's knee. "Go on."

"Okay, well." She pauses, trying to sort through her entire vocabulary to find the words to adequately explain something she hasn't really confronted on her own yet. "Every time I got into a fight, it was because I thought I was defending my friends." Her mom nods. "But now… now I wonder if I was only hurting those people more instead of just saving my friends."

Her mom hums in acknowledgment. "What makes you think that?"

"Something Leo said," she mumbles. A few things, actually, his comments at the seminar and after they studied the Honor vs. Incendiary fight. Charlie realizes she hasn't said anything about this to anyone, not even Lochlan, and now it's like the vault that is her chest is being picked open and spilling all her treasured secrets. "I just! What else was I supposed to do? *Nothing*?"

"You could never do nothing," her mom says fondly. "You've always been all or nothing, and maybe that's the issue. You weren't *wrong* to stand up for your friends, but you weren't a hundred percent right in the way you went about it. Not everything is black and white. In fact, most things aren't."

"Well," Charlie flounders for a second. "Why not?!"

Her mom smiles at her, and Charlie feels comforted by the sight alone. She's no less confused, but at least she's less stressed out about it.

"Life is made of nuance," her mom tells her, which sounds either like a quote from a dead famous person or something she made up on the spot right now. "First, you learn to see it. Then, you learn from it. Now, you see it."

"But aren't there some people who don't deserve to be saved?!" she bursts. Her mom doesn't seem fazed by the sudden pivot in conversation. "Some people deserve to be punched in the face!"

"Are those two things mutually exclusive?"

"How can punching someone in the face be saving them?"

"Ask Honor," her mom says with a shrug. "She's the pro."

"This is so confusing," Charlie groans and puts her head in her hands. Her mom rubs her back.

"You're only fifteen. Not everything has to make sense right now."

"Okay, but I would *like* it to make sense right now," she mutters.

"It might make a little more sense after you've rested some more and you've got your head on right." Charlie rolls her eyes.

"I told you, I'm *fine*," she insists.

"I know you are," her mom says. "But don't work yourself to death, okay? You have time. No one becomes a pro overnight and you don't need to become one tomorrow. Your teachers train you enough, and part of that training is knowing when to rest. Treat your body kindly now so it will be able to defend you later."

"Yeah, okay," Charlie mumbles, looking at her hands again. Her mom lingers, sensing that she has something else she wants to say, and Charlie feels the words in her throat but they don't know how to take shape. "Leo said that 'Heroes save anyone who needs saving'…" She pauses, unsure of how to proceed.

"Leo said that?" Her mom asks.

"Yeah, why?" Charlie finally looks up at her.

"Honor said that," she said. "When she petitioned to open the school. She said that's how she wants to raise the next generation of heroes."

"Well," Charlie exhales when the weight of that settles on her. "Fuck."

Her mom just laughs at her foul mouth. Charlie will do anything, *anything*, to be more like Honor, and that's not a secret. But Charlie thought she *was*. Honor used to be the type to kick ass first and ask questions later, and Charlie admired her for that, for her take charge attitude and the ability to stand up in the face of anyone, *anything*, and win in the name of defending others.

But if she really thinks about it, she can't recall a time in recent years when Honor hasn't tried to talk a rogue down before resorting to fighting them. Of course, Charlie noticed that she talked more than she used to in fights. Verity was more known for her running color commentary on the job, and when Honor started doing it more, Charlie thought she was just adopting some of the same mannerisms as her sister, especially because it's one of the things that makes Verity wildly popular.

Honor wasn't talking shit, though. She was always trying to reason with them. Even with Incendiary. *Especially* with him because they were friends. They are friends. Again, Charlie tries to picture what she would do if Lochlan went rogue like that. It's almost laughable because Lochlan would *never,* but if he did, then Charlie would try to save him, too.

Charlie's almost embarrassed to compare the way she's been acting to Honor in any capacity. She's not a hero. Not even close.

Charlie buries her face in her hands when her eyes start to sting and her mom rubs soothing circles on her back. "You're a good kid, Charlie," her mom says, and right now, Charlie isn't quite inclined to believe her, filing this compliment away in the 'You're Just Saying That Because You're My Mom And You Have To' pile, but then she adds. "But you can always be better."

25

"Human Converter, AKA Mr. Khalid Johnson of Marvelous, awarded Teacher of the Year Award"
—*Los Angeles Star*

Honor had made sure that the Ameliora facility had a press room. If her graduates are going to have to answer to the public, they're at least going to do it on what hopefully feels like home turf. No dumb step and repeat. No harsh fluorescent lighting. And security standing by to throw out any assholes. Honor waits with Leo by her side for Colson to come out. They're both in their hero suits, but since Leo's is a literal three piece, bulletproof suit, Honor feels under-dressed. She thinks it may be misplaced nerves about this press conference because her suit is like a second skin.

Colson had agreed to be the poster boy of rogue reform, and logically, Honor knows it's a great idea. He's the perfect candidate, having been very publicly arrested by Honor herself, and she has the utmost confidence in his ability to reintegrate into society. But as a friend, Honor just wants Colson to be okay, and she's not sure that putting him in the spotlight and under intense scrutiny like this is the best idea.

But it's not her choice. It's Colson's and he's made it.

Colson comes down the hallway, wearing the same dress shirt and slacks he'd worn to his hearing. Colson freezes when he spots Leo. Honor told him time and time again that Leo is busy because it's *true,* but Colson never really bought it. But that's something they have to work out between themselves.

But they might need a little nudge, she thinks, after two minutes go by and neither of them have moved. Leo's closer to Honor, so he gets the shove, and as soon as he takes a stumbling step toward Colson, Colson lurches forward and pulls him into the tightest hug Leo's ever received since he came out of his mother's birth canal, probably. Honor swears she hears his spine crack. But Leo gives as good as he gets, and then Colson is sniffing hard.

"Don't cry," Leo murmurs into his shoulder.

"You can cry," Honor says. "For the usual reasons, but also because it makes you relatable to the general public." Colson's laugh is wet, but his face is dry when he finally pulls back.

"Thanks for coming," he says softly. Honor sees Leo forcibly *not* react to the new tenor of his voice. Nothing to make Colson insecure or uncomfortable, especially not now, but it's hard to reconcile the Colson they used to know and the Colson in front of them now.

"Of course, man," Leo says and claps a hand on his shoulder. Colson takes a deep breath and looks at Honor.

"Should we go?"

"Whenever you're ready," she tells him.

"Aren't they waiting?"

"They can keep waiting," she says with an unconcerned shrug. Honor's never been the biggest fan of press anyway. A few extra minutes in a nicely air conditioned conference room won't kill them.

"I'm ready," Colson says. Honor doesn't question him, just opens the door for him to walk through first.

There's a table set up with three chairs and three microphones. Colson sits in the middle with Honor on one side and Ursula on the other. Leo waits off to the side. Flashes go off to a nearly blinding degree, and Honor is used to it, but Colson isn't. He squints a bit, then ducks his head.

"Good afternoon, everyone," Honor kicks them off. "On behalf of Ameliora, I'd like to thank you so much for coming today. You guys are all playing a big part in helping your fellow citizens get back on their feet and we really, truly appreciate it. As you all know, your questions were prepared beforehand and have been given to Candor who will be mediating the conference today. Is everyone ready?"

"Then let's begin," Ursula says after a vague chorus of confirmation. She looks down at the questions she's been given. "Colson, how are you?"

"I'm—nervous," he answers, surprised again by Ursula's simple question. If the press could ask themselves, they might've tried to hit him with a hardball straight out the gates, but Ursula has never and will never throw any graduate to the wolves like that. It's part of the reason why Honor has her do this. The press has no issue with it because they get guaranteed honest answers. "But pretty okay."

"Nervous about what?" Ursula prods gently.

"Saying the wrong thing."

"What would you like to say?"

"That I'm very grateful to be given this second chance, and I'm going to do my best to make it worth it," he says. Ursula smiles at him and continues with her questions. Most are simple.

"I don't know what I'm going to do for work just yet."

"I'll be staying with my sponsor, Honor."

"I get blood transfusions that prevent me from using my marvel so I don't have to wear nullifiers."

"Cooking is one of my hobbies. Did someone really want to know that?"

"Yes, I'm single. Did someone really want to know *that?*"

Honor only has to nudge him a couple times to remind him to look up at the reporters and their cameras and not down at his hands where he digs his thumbs in nervously. His gaze flickers to Leo every so often after that instead of looking down. Leo nods at him encouragingly each time.

"Everyone saw the infamous fight that led to your arrest and enrollment in Ameliora," Ursula begins and Colson stiffens. "What was that conversation like?"

"Painful," Colson says, honest and rough. After the initial response, he has a second to collect himself. "I woke up in the hospital and Honor and—and Leo were there. They said they forgave me, but I didn't feel like I deserved it. I still don't, really." His eyes get a little misty, and Honor reaches out to hold his hand again. He grasps it tightly under the table.

"Would you still do all of this, if you didn't have that forgiveness?" Honor has a feeling that that is one of Ursula's questions.

"I would," he answers without hesitation. Honor feels the pride swell in her chest as he continues, "Because I know that not everyone will forgive me, and that's okay. I'm doing it to be better, not forgiven."

"That's all the questions I have for you, Colson," Ursula says. "Congratulations on your graduation."

Colson huffs a laugh. "Thanks."

"Honor! Will you be answering any questions?" Someone shouts from the sea of reporters. Honor turns to look at them from where she's half turned toward Colson and leaning one arm on the table.

"You got a question?"

"Yes!"

"Go for it," Honor says, half sure she's going to regret this.

"What is your relationship with Colson?"

"Real hard hitting stuff," she says with narrowed eyes. "Candor?"

"What is your relationship with Colson?" she repeats for Honor with the weight of her marvel behind it.

"He's one of my best friends and I love him dearly," she says with the ease of honesty. Doesn't even have to try and fight it. "Sorry, I know you were looking for a juicy scoop or whatever, but some of us really are just trying to help people with no ulterior motives. I know that can be a foreign concept to some of you, but I strongly encourage you to try."

Several more hands go up.

"I'll give you one more question," Honor says benevolently. "Who wants it most?"

People strain in their seats like eager elementary school students. Honor ends up picking a reporter she recognizes and knows pretty well. Favors her even though she can't really remember her name. She asks good questions and that's what matters.

"Do you think that Ameliora will set a precedent for the prison system in the United States?"

"That's the goal," Honor says with a short head tilt. "The world too, if we can swing it."

26

"Summer Swim Safety: Sky Rider
Won't Always Be There to Save You"
—*Los Angeles Star*

"**O**kay, you remember where everything is?" Honor asks, looking around like she missed something. Colson's been in this apartment before. Spent the whole summer there one time after his dad died, before he could live on his own. She had just spent the last twenty minutes reminding him of where everything is.

It's small and cluttered, with the items accumulated by her and her sisters and their mom over decades of living there. Honor's been in charge of keeping up the apartment even though none of them live there anymore. It looks like none of them had left. They'd all bought new things when they moved out, when they tried to move on, after the accident that wasn't an accident.

Honor glances at a picture on the wall, one of her mom. Grace had taken it, a candid of her putting fresh flowers into a vase. Honor had stolen those flowers from campus, but her mom either didn't know or didn't care. She looks away when it begins to hurt too much.

"Yes," Colson says, faintly amused and not at all annoyed where he sits on the couch. It's purple velvet and kind of ugly if Honor's being honest, but she loves that couch. She thinks about taking it back to campus. But then she'd have to buy a new couch for Colson. Colson will have to buy a new couch, anyway, when he moves out. Whenever that is. She doesn't like the idea of it being soon.

"Good, good," she says. "I'm taking the kids on a field trip today for some sims with Maia in Blueside, but if you need anything I'm only a call away. Leo's on duty so he can't answer, but in case of emergencies, Aurora's on campus."

"Honor, I'll be fine," he promises and stands up. The curtains are drawn over the windows. They're relatively large, on adjacent walls in their corner apartment. She hasn't told him not to open the windows, would sound paranoid if she did, but she thinks he knows anyway. Just because Colson has graduated from Ameliora and is moving on doesn't mean other people are willing to trust him yet. Especially not in the Blade District. *Especially* when they don't know where Ravenna is. "I'm just gonna stay here and take some— aptitude tests or whatever so I can start looking for jobs. I know where everything is and I'm a big boy, you don't have to worry about me."

"Are you sure you don't want to stay on campus?" she asks.

"That sounds like one of your worst ideas," he says, not for the first time. "I'm sure none of your parents would be happy to find out that a rogue, reformed or not, is sleeping one floor away from their child."

"You could stay in Aurora's bunker in the arena," she says. He slates her with a look. "Okay, okay, fine. I'm gonna trick the door when I leave and obviously you're allowed to come and go as you please, but if you leave and try to come back the door won't appear for you. So."

"Honor."

"It's—I just… don't want you to disappear on me again," she whispers.

He pulls her into a hug. "I won't. I promise."

Honor ends up having to meet the kids at the simulation site after delaying so long, and Maia has already run through introductions and the ins and outs of the simulator. Everything is real, unlike in the arena, and they're even going to use volunteer victims for this exercise, real people so the kids can truly get a feel for it before the tournament.

"Glad you could join us," Verity says as she comes to stand beside her on the sand. The early morning haze has mostly cleared up, and Honor can see the man made island that they use for rescue simulations just like this one. They'll take the small boats to the barge to be closer to the sims that are already set up. The sun warms her cheeks, and she realizes she forgot to put sunscreen on, but at least it's warm, the promise of summer heavy in the air. The kids haven't noticed her yet, still entranced by Maia's demonstration of Raven.

"How's your ward?" Verity asks.

"Oh, shut the hell up. He's fine."

"How many times did you show him where the bathroom is in our two bedroom apartment?"

"Don't make me hit you in front of the kids."

"Honor!" Charlie cries in excitement. "You made it."

"'Course I did," she says. "Gather round, Verity has your groups for the shipwreck sims."

Verity divides them into their groups. Kai is bouncing on his toes in excitement while Jack already looks seasick and they're still on land. Only two groups will go at a time, each accompanied by Honor and Verity, while the other two will wait on Ol' Reliable, an ancient and rickety barge, while Maia keeps an eye on all of them from the sky. Honor's first group is Charlie, Cora, Anthony, Tommy, and Ethan. Honor steers them out to the arranged wreck, and Charlie tries to shove Anthony's head into the sea spray that comes up along the side to mess up his hair, but he warps away. He pops back up next to Honor, laughing. It brings a smile to Honor's face.

"Here we are!" Honor announces as they pull up alongside their sim, a slowly sinking factory trawler with a crew of twenty-two. There's a burst pipe and a hole in the hull from where they hit a coral reef. Someone is trapped under a broken bunk and the captain is unconscious. Honor knows all of this going in, especially since these are real people, not dummies. She knows each of their locations in case the kids miss something, but she has the utmost faith in her kids and lets them loose.

"Go for it," she says.

Charlie immediately takes charge. "Anthony and Ethan should sweep the lower decks and work their way up."

Honor smiles. That's good. She picked the two marvels best-suited for the job, too.

"Cora, you should stay up top and help people who are too injured to evac on their own with your claws," Charlie continues. "Tommy, you're in charge of first aid here."

"What are you gonna do?" Anthony asks her.

"We're too deep to anchor and since I'm assuming Honor isn't going to help with the sim, someone has to make sure we don't start to drift too far and keep an eye on any outside variables such as sudden turns in weather or outside attacks," she explains. Honor is truly impressed because she had purposely left the rudder turned so they would start to drift away. "And, if this were a real rescue, then we'd have to keep in contact with the GMDSS."

Good. Honor moves back and lets the kids get to work. It's not entirely seamless, but it's pretty damn good. Anthony learns the layout of the boat quick enough and gets comfortable enough to warp between levels. With her aura claws, Cora gently maneuvers the injured crew from the deck of the sinking ship to Tommy where he starts to administer the necessary first aid. It's a little slower than it should be in this sort of situation because the ship is taking on water faster than anticipated, but Honor has an eye on the situation. She's confident her kids will pass.

She keeps one eye on the sim nearest her too, Verity's group of Kai, Malia, Luna, Simon, and Rose. Kai gets a little overexcited and conjures up a wave that is far too large for whatever purpose he intended. Honor can't even think of a reason he would *need* to conjure up a fresh wave, but it grows and grows and then it's headed right for them. Honor braces for a mess she'll have to clean up, but then Charlie is jumping out of the wheelhouse and clapping her hands together.

Her marvel rips out of her and collides with the wave. It's quite the sight, Honor thinks, especially since she's never seen Charlie use her marvel versus water before. Clouds, shields, walls, the occasional person, but it splits through the water until it's raining down around them in a light mist, disaster averted.

"Well done," Honor can't help but say. Charlie doesn't hide her pleased grin very well as she climbs back into the wheelhouse.

Maia zooms by on Raven in her full case, leaving her group of kids on their own. Her board will coat her in the same stuff it's made of, there's no name for it, but it absorbs energy from anything that hits her and allows her to fire it back through Raven. The kids don't even notice. But if Maia is abandoning her post in full case, something is wrong. Slowly, without the urgency Honor starts to feel build in her gut, she exits the wheelhouse and heads to the bow. She crosses her arms and looks around at the kids, then turns her attention to where she can faintly see the outline of Maia on the horizon.

"What's going on?" she asks in a low voice into her comm.

"Ocean Pulse," Maia answers shortly. Shit.

Honor thinks back to January, when the Ocean Pulse was behaving erratically. If their suspicions were correct and the mini Krewa that came through the portal really was a scout, that means more are sure to follow. It also means that she, her kids, and her volunteers are double fucked. They all signed up for shipwreck sims today, not a Titan attack.

Honor's worst fears are confirmed. The portal opens fully. Seafoam green light toward the blue sky. It's not the same green as when Grace comes through with Cal. It's lighter and brighter. The same color of the eyes that Honor still sees in her sleep.

"Should we get the kids out?" Verity asks Honor over comms. She glances back toward shore. It's not too far, but it's far enough, and they wouldn't be able to evacuate the kids in a reasonable amount of time.

"Yes," Maia answers her. Honor's head snaps back toward the horizon and Maia. She can see the water bubbling under her. Whatever is coming is coming now.

Honor hears the faintest splash and looks down. There's one of them in the water and holy shit, Verity wasn't kidding, they really do look like mini Krewas. Titan genes are strong. Their eyes are one color, iridescent even before they break through the surface, and trained on Honor. The tips of their fingers glow, too, as they wrap around the edge of the boat to haul themselves up. The deep blue fabric they cloak themselves in is dry as soon as they hit their air, and they are light and just as nimble out of the water as they are in it.

Honor's baton is in her hand in an instant and she lengthens it to her sword. The sound gets the attention of her students, who pause in their activities.

"Space Daughter," comes the hiss, and it's garbled, as though they're still underwater, just as Krewa's voice had been. The kids stare, but don't scream which is a better reaction than Honor would have expected.

"Is that…" Charlie starts to ask, but Honor cuts her off.

"Get everyone off that boat and onto Ol' Reliable," Honor orders. She kicks the thing back into the water and jumps off the boat. The creature follows her, and Honor winces at her own choice in terminology. This is probably a person, or a person equivalent, looking for revenge for a dead mother. Honor really, truly sympathizes with that, but now her kids are in danger and that is *unacceptable*.

Honor doesn't land in the water, but in the now-empty speedboat Verity drives. She's likely given her group the same orders, and Honor can only hope that they follow through. In the meantime, it looks like Honor and Verity are the targets. Rightfully so, since they were the ones who killed Krewa, so the further away they get from the kids, the safer they'll be.

She hacks at the mini Krewa and her green blood seeps into the ocean water. She remains standing in the boat while

Verity steers. The Krewa offspring come straight for them. One leaps out of the water and Honor slices her clean in half. The dark green blood spatters across her and Verity.

"Ugh! *Gross,*" Verity spits. Her baton is in hand, blade already out, prepared in case one of them makes a move for her while she's driving.

Maia fights them off at the surface after coming out of the Ocean Pulse, but some of them head straight for Honor and Verity without surfacing first. Honor slices through them easily enough until three jump out at her at once. Verity throws her baton and knocks two back into the water and then the weapon flies back into her hand.

"What even are these things?" Verity snaps as she spits out blood.

"Krewa's... kids?" Honor tries to supply. "So other Titans? Half Titans?"

"Is there a better word for half Titan?"

"I believe the word is typically god," Maia supplies.

"Yeah, that's not gonna work for me," Verity mutters.

"Is there a way to close the portal?" Maia asks.

"Not that I know of," Honor answers. Verity's eyes glow blue while she asks Grace, the only person they can contact who might have an answer to that question.

"We have two dozen hostiles," Maia says. "No more are coming through from what I can see, but better safe than sorry."

Honor stands on the edge of the speedboat and it rocks with her weight, but she maintains her balance, and Verity evens them out. It's hard, fighting from the boat with her opponent in the water, but she knows the second she gets in the water, she gives them the advantage.

They don't give her much of a choice, though, when she's busy handling one of Krewa's kids, another grabbing her by the ankle and pulling her in. Honor curses into bubbles when her head hits the edge of the boat. She kicks out blindly with a boot to dislodge the bitch that pulled her under.

Honor can cut through water with more ease than the average person, but Krewa's offspring seem to be in their element. Wherever they come from must be entirely water. Does that make them merpeople? Honor supposes that doesn't really matter right now. Four of them swarm her at once. Sensing the trouble Honor is in, Verity dives in after her. They fend them off, green blood flooding through the water and limiting their visibility, but Maia swoops down into the water to pull them both out.

Honor holds onto Raven and kicks at the half Titan holding onto her ankle, but they hold fast. From atop Raven with Maia, Verity throws her staff and it slices clean through the Krewa look alike and they fall back into the ocean. The staff soars back into Verity's hand as she helps pull Honor fully onto the board.

"Sky Rider," Honor uses her call sign and it somehow adds gravity to the situation. She almost regrets using it. "What kind of advantage can you give us?"

"Raven can expand up to one hundred square feet," she tells them. "Think that'll work?"

"Better than the seven we're working with now," Verity quips back.

Maia dips the board so Raven is skimming the water, then they stop so abruptly that Honor stumbles a few steps forward, right to Raven's expanded edge and brings herself face to face with another offspring.

It's been a long time since Honor's used her sword. She only brings it out in life or death situations, and now, faced with the vengeful children of the Titan she killed? She'd say it's one of those situations.

"Space Daughter," one of the offspring hisses from somewhere behind Honor, but she knows it's directed at Verity. Verity grunts and there's a sickening squelch while Honor is focused on decapitating the opponent in front of her. The head with the weird, perpetually floating neon hair rolls into the water. Honor grimaces at the thought that some poor diver is probably going to have to fish that out later.

"What the fuck was that?" Verity asks, and Honor knows she's talking about the moniker. Behind them, Maia has some spear-claw thing attached to her hand via Raven, but none of the offspring are targeting her, so she swoops in to grab one that had been diving for Honor's back.

"They called me that, too," Honor says. "Think it probably has to do with Mom."

"You don't fucking say?" Verity snaps while she drives the blunt end of her staff into a skull hard enough to dent it. "They didn't say *time* daughter."

"I don't think now is the time to hash out our collective parental issues," Honor says.

"You know what?" Verity stabs another offspring through the chest and turns to face Honor, who's fending off two at a time. "That reminds me, I still want to hunt that bastard sperm donor down."

"Can we talk about this later?" Honor asks and then grunts when she takes a glowing claw in the back of her shoulder. Verity whips her staff around behind her to block a similar attack. "Preferably with a licensed professional."

"Fine," Verity says and dispatches her final opponent.

Krewa's offspring came woefully unprepared, and Honor doesn't know enough about them or where they came from to have the slightest idea as to why. They don't seem to have any offensive marvels from what she can tell, but then again, neither did Krewa. She was just unreasonably big and fast and recovered quickly.

But if this was motivated purely out of emotion and revenge, then Honor understands.

"What if they have something to say?" Maia asks.

"Then they should have fucking said it," Verity snaps.

"What do you want?" Maia asks one of the offspring, backing up as it advances, hands up in surrender.

"Dead Space Daughters," they hiss. Verity runs it through from behind.

"That's what they want," she says to Maia as the corpse falls onto Raven. The impact doesn't make a sound, the force absorbed by Raven.

"In that case," Maia starts. Power surges up from Raven, through the case that she's wearing and out of her palms, aimed at the last of the offspring just behind Verity. Whatever comes out of Raven and channels through Maia is pure energy. There's no blood and no mark. They just fall, also without a sound.

The ocean rocks under them, natural this time, and Raven bobs with the ebbs and flows of the water. Honor twirls her sword around her wrist and it shrinks back down to a baton. She holsters it on her thigh. Verity leans on her staff while Maia surveys the water for any more hostiles.

"Did they know we were here?" Verity asks. "Or was it coincidence?"

"I don't believe in coincidences," Honor says, but she also has no answers to offer. So instead, she just says, "Let's get back to the kids."

The kids have all made it and Honor breathes a sigh of relief after she does a headcount. Maia makes sure all of the volunteer victims are here, but only the ones that had been in the active simulations had made it back. The others are still waiting on their respective vessels. Since the threat is neutralized, they're not in immediate danger.

Then Charlie speaks the number one cursed phrase in their line of work.

"That wasn't so bad," Charlie says. All of the pros groan. Verity swears up a storm that has even Charlie gaping at her. Sure, they'd taken a bit of a beating, but everyone's in one piece.

"She's just a kid, maybe it won't take—" Maia says right before the ground starts to rumble. It feels like an earthquake, and the water starts to rise in waves, building higher and higher toward the sky with each rock of the ocean floor. Charlie loses her balance and stumbles before she falls to her knees, hard. Honor and Verity remain upright, eyes on the horizon.

A *monster* stands from under water, creating a vacuum of water that sucks all of the wrecks and rescue boats toward it. It lifts up a large pointed head and screeches out a roar. It's easily the size of an entire island, covered in magma and water and glowing the same seafoam color as the other things that had come out of the ocean. Charlie freezes to the spot, fear locking her limbs in place.

"Yeah, that looks about right," Verity says, sounding resigned and on the edge of whining. She takes a deep breath and then jumps, the force of it rocking the boat behind her. She draws her staff midair, aiming for the monster's eye with the blade at the end. The monster raises one giant claw-shaped hand and bats her out of the air like a fly. Verity crashes into the side of one of the already-sinking ships with a sickening crunch.

"Oh shit," Charlie says. It's one thing to watch Honor and Verity take those kinds of hits when it's through the television, but it's another entirely to witness it in person. Almost as if Charlie can feel the force of the impact reverberate through the air. All of a sudden, everything is so much *worse*.

"I'll draw it away from the island," Maia says and races off on Raven. She flies low on the water until she gets close enough to the monster to pull up and fly straight up towards its head. It tries to bat her away too, but she's already seen it pull that move and she's ready, buzzing around until it turns around to follow her.

"Charlie, listen very carefully," says Honor. She puts a hand on Charlie's arm, but her eyes are fixed on Sky Rider and the monster. "This is now a very real rescue mission, do you understand? You're in charge of your classmates and you need to get everyone safely onto the barge and start sailing back to the coast." Honor looks at her then, the full weight of her gaze landing on Charlie.

Charlie's chest seizes and panic starts to claw up her throat, but she can, *she can*. She swallows thickly and nods once, firmly. Honor looks proud for a split second, then she's gone too, but that split second of a fierce smile from her favorite hero is enough to bring the strength and confidence back to Charlie's bones.

"Alright, let's fuckin' go!" she shouts as she runs back up the stairs to the bridge.

Charlie dishes out more orders to her classmates. Kai is still in charge of pulling the boats closer to them with the tide and Jayne is scouting the other ships for stragglers. There are twenty students and about sixty volunteer victims. The barge is long and flat, too, previously used for slow boat tours, so there's nowhere to take cover or hide.

Ethan and Jack help unload a lifeboat that Jack had driven back from his simulation. A lifeboat from one of the other sims is already on the way, being guided as quickly as possible by Kai. After he's finished with that, Charlie will have him redirect all of his energy to getting this slow-ass barge to shore as fast as possible.

Charlie gets distracted for a moment watching the pros in action. She still can't quite believe what she's seeing with her own two eyes. A whole *monster* from another world. Maybe that guy she watched when she was at home recovering had been onto something. Maybe this is going to be their new normal. Titans and monsters and god knows what else.

Honor holds onto a spike in the monster's back while it thrashes, trying to throw her off. Verity climbs onto Sky Rider's board, wet and livid. She throws her staff this time, but the monster hits that out of the air, too. Instead of hitting the water, though, it flies back to Verity's hand. Honor is dislodged and falls into the water. It's a mess. How can they possibly bring down something so big? Charlie doesn't know how forming the giant Triumvirate works, but she's pretty sure Grace has to be there. Is there any way they can call Grace?

No. Charlie has a job to do, and she trusts Honor and the others to take care of this. They have before and they can again. Charlie directs more of her classmates to triage and makes sure everyone knows the plan of attack if for some reason they do have to face the monster. After seeing the fear in her classmates' faces at the mere idea of it, she rushes to assure them that it's just in case, there's no way that thing is getting past Honor and the others. They're totally fine.

It's not the first time Charlie is wrong.

Probably not the last, either.

"Oh my god!" Rose shouts. Charlie whips around and finds the monster closing in on them. The waves from the movement of a single leg is nearly enough to tip the barge over, and Charlie stumbles while Kai levels them out.

"Holy shit! It's gaining fast!" Ethan shouts.

"I can take it—" Kai starts, but Charlie cuts him off.

"No! Keep the boat steady!"

The monster is closer now, reaching for the barge like a child reaches for a toy ship in the bathtub. Its hand casts a shadow over the entire ship and blocks out sun and sky. Webbed fingers stretch wide. It's close, too close.

"Oh god, what do we do? *What do we do?*" Ethan nearly screams, on the edge of panic.

Charlie does the only thing she can do, she claps her hands together and then spreads them as wide as she can reach, pushing all she can into it.

The wave of her power knocks the monster's hand back. She forces her hands back together before the recoil has time to fully fade and does it again, this time aiming for the body. It feels like she's trying to tear her own arms off her body, but it works. It stumbles backwards, taking the water with it and nearly pulling the ship, too, but Kai pulls the current back. It's slow and almost doesn't work. Charlie knows he's almost spent.

But her blast wasn't enough to knock it over. The monster rights itself with an angry screech and starts forward again, faster. Charlie tries to force her hands back together, but she can't. The recoil won't budge. A tail whips around and hits Charlie—*it has a tail?*

Charlie's never been hit by a car before, but she imagines it would feel a lot like this. The wind is punched out of her, and she goes soaring through the air with no clue as to which way is up and which is down. She can only cover her head, close her eyes, and hope for the best.

She grunts and nearly chokes when her uniform shirt catches around her neck. The seams break as her progress is slowed, but Jayne is quick to wrap an arm around her and keep her from falling again. It hurts and her ribs are probably fractured at the very least. But it hurts less than dying, Charlie supposes. She just hangs there for a moment, thankful that Jayne had taken weightlifting seriously throughout the year and isn't having any trouble holding her up. She watches the scene below.

A few others had been caught by the tail and are in the water. Kai is trying to fish them out. The monster screeches again, and Charlie shouts, "Look out!" She reacts before she even really thinks about it, slapping her hand against the side of her leg where her uniform is torn from the rough skin of the tail and blasts the monster's hand that's reaching for her and Jayne.

It's not nearly as big as before but combined with Jayne's evasive maneuver, it's enough. Jayne flies them back to the barge and then starts to help the others in the water.

Charlie watches in horror as the monster gets closer and closer. None of the other pros are in sight. None of them have a marvel that can go against this thing. Kai is too spent and has to prioritize rescues. Jack can't do shit in water. Tommy can't even void the damn thing. *Where is Honor?*

They're going to lose.

And losing means death.

Spikes shoot past Charlie's ear, clipping the shell of it. She dives to the side.

"Sorry!" Simon calls. He's got his shirt off and he's running backwards toward the monster, shooting off every spike he has. The monster doesn't react to the spikes landing, it just keeps coming. Luna sweeps up some nearby seaweed. It's not a lot, but she aims for the eyes.

The monster screeches again and claws at its own eyes. In her peripherals, Charlie can see Cora reaching for the remaining people in the water. That's the last of them. If only they could *get away*—

The monster reaches them again, this time reaching with the claw hand and Charlie brings her hands together. The blast she lets out is just as big as the first two but now that the monster is expecting it, it doesn't push it back, at all.

The claw opens and some of her classmates scream.

It hits a wall.

Charlie can see the rainbow fractals that scatter out from the point of contact that tell Charlie and everyone else that it's *Leo.*

Charlie looks up to the sky and sees a black helicopter. A figure leaps out of it, and Leo lands on the boat just in front of Charlie. The monster child hits the barrier, and Leo slides a foot back to steady himself. He has one hand up to support the shield, something he only does when they're close to breaking, Charlie knows from Ethan's videos. His other hand draws back and pushes forward, slowly, like there's resistance.

The shield pushes back even as the monster child bangs on it, trying to get through. Leo flinches, but keeps pushing.

Charlie's never been on this side of a barrier when Leo moves it. There's some sort of recoil here, too, some force working against Leo from pushing it forward. He grunts as he pushes his hand forward a little more and the recoil force whips and tears at his sleeve. Charlie has just enough foresight to grab Luna and pull her down on the deck next to her before that force hits her, too.

The more Leo pushes forward, the more his sleeve tears, and Charlie can see each muscle straining forward.

"Kai!" he shouts. "Lift the ship onto the island!"

"I'm—" Kai starts

"DO IT NOW!" Leo shouts as the monster breaks through his barrier. It shatters in a million rainbow fractals with a sound like glass breaking, but Leo puts up another one just as quick.

The ship starts to rock violently, and Luna clings to Charlie. Charlie grips a ring on the ground with one hand to keep them from flying and wraps the other around Luna. Kai builds the water up under them while Leo puts up another shield when the second shatters.

The wave under them grows and grows and then suddenly they're all hurtled violently to the left, towards land. The ship clips one of the practice fields and they turn so they're flying point first toward the beach.

"Oh fuck oh fuck oh fuck," Charlie hears herself chant.

They crash onto land *hard*. The ship creaks and groans as it slides across sand and up to the tree line. It throws them all sideways, except for Charlie who has a grip on the ring and Luna, who has a grip on Charlie that makes her ribs scream. Leo drops the shield from in front of the monster child and puts a new one up to the side that the boat slams into instead of the trees.

The monster screeches again and moves to change direction, toward the island now, with its tail swishing behind it like it might lash out with it again. But another figure dives out of the helicopter, too far for Charlie to see, and dives into the water. There's a split second where Charlie panics because she doesn't know what's happening, but Leo doesn't seem worried and she trusts him, she trusts all of her teachers.

The ocean lights up.

Blue and green volts leap from the water and the monster child screeches at a new frequency that has them all covering their ears. It's being electrocuted.

Voltage.

"Wait— " Charlie gasps.

"Sky Rider got them out of the water," Leo says, reading her mind.

"Oh good," she says mildly as the monster collapses into the ocean, dead, or out for the count at the very least. The crash creates a tsunami heading straight for them, but Leo's barrier holds up against that no problem, protecting them and the island.

The water reflects the rainbow fractals of Leo's barrier and it's beautiful. Charlie sinks more of her weight to lean on Luna and she does the same. Charlie raises a hand to her comm.

"Is everyone okay?" she asks.

"Everyone is accounted for and in one piece," Tommy answers her. "Kai passed out, but he's breathing and his heart rate is fine. Probably just exhaustion." Charlie nods even though he can't see her.

Leo's shadow provides a cool respite from the sun as he kneels in front of Charlie. He claps a hand on her shoulder.

"Good job, kid," he says with a smile. Charlie's own exhaustion catches up with her as the adrenaline wears off, but the importance of this moment does not pass her by.

"He smiled! Leo smiled at me! I win!" she cries. Her classmates groan in chorus in her ear.

"Just when I thought today couldn't get *any worse*!" Anthony cries.

The laughter in her ear is weak and breathless. But it's there. They're all there.

PART THREE

VICTORY

27

"Marvelous Graduation Rates at an All Time Low"

—*Hero Review*

Six of her kids end up in the hospital. No one has any life threatening injuries for which Honor will be eternally grateful, and most of them, like Kai, are from exhaustion. But it doesn't make it any easier seeing her kids laid up in sterile, all white rooms in hospital gowns. Honor makes sure to visit all of them every day until they're discharged, which thankfully isn't very long. Once everyone is back on campus, she calls them to meet in the downstairs common room.

The media is having a field day with the attack. There were so many witnesses that there was never a chance in hell of keeping this quiet. Most of them are vilifying Honor and rightfully so. It's her fault that her kids were hospitalized. It's her fault that they were even in danger in the first place. This attack was personal. It's not the first time and it's definitely not the last. Honor was foolish to think that she could keep her work as a pro from bleeding into the Academy and onto her kids. She might as well have painted a big, pink target on them.

She's fresh off patrol in some sweats she hastily threw on at the agency and half jogging onto campus so she won't be late to her own meeting. They still haven't found a way to close the portal, but Grace and Cal are researching for them back on Viasyre. In the meantime, they've assigned patrols around the Pulse from Maia's agency until they can build some sort of monitoring outpost like the towers they have on Viasyre.

Ethan meets her out on the lawn before she can get to the common room. He wrings his hands together and glances around nervously. "I—I wanted to talk to you about something. I already told Leo, but I wanted to tell you myself."

"Okay," she says in the most neutral tone she can manage. But Ethan's kind of starting to make her worry.

"I'm—I'm not coming back," he says in a rush. It takes Honor a moment to parse it out, but then she understands.

Her world doesn't fall apart. Mostly because she's on her way to excuse the kids from the tournament and there won't be a school to come back *to,* but this moment is still what Honor had been fearing from the very beginning when she had been picking twenty names out of hundreds. What if she fails them? What if they don't make it to graduation?

She claps a heavy hand on his shoulder. "What do you want to do?"

"I—you're okay with this?" he asks dubiously.

"Ethan, I want to help you do whatever it is that you want to do. If that isn't Titan Academy and becoming a pro, that's more than fine."

"I… don't really know. I just know that being a hero isn't right for me. We only got a little taste of what it's really like and it just—it was too much for me."

Honor doesn't want to tell him that there's a very good chance that he would grow and adapt because she wouldn't want to sound like she's trying to reel him back in, but she also doesn't want Ethan doubting himself.

"I was thinking maybe going to regular high school and then becoming a paramedic?"

"Is that a question?" she teases. Ethan flushes. "What about Bangtan?"

"In Korea? What about it?"

"You still want to do rescue work, right?" she asks. He nods. "Bangtan has the best rescue program in the world adjacent to their hero program, so you still get the best training but you won't be on the front lines with the pro heroes. AND! You already learned Korean! You're welcome."

"I—uh, I… there's no way I could get in," he says. "It's like you said it's the best program in *the world*. I couldn't—"

"I'm gonna stop you right there, kid," she says. "I picked you myself. I know exactly what you're capable of. At minimum, at least. I'd love to see you soar above and beyond expectations, but that's not the point. I know you could get into Bangtan. I also know, that as Korea's number one favorite foreign hero, a personal recommendation from me would do wonders."

"Really?" His eyes go wide.

"I don't know if you're surprised that I'm Korea's number one favorite foreign hero or at the fact that I would write you a glowing recommendation. Both are hurtful," she teases. Ethan swallows.

"Um. Okay. I guess it couldn't hurt to apply. You're not… mad?"

"I'm not mad. I'm not disappointed. I'm a little sad to see you go, but that's only because I'll miss you," she tells him.

She slings her arm all the way over his shoulder and steers them toward the dorms. "Who knows? Maybe I'll come visit you in Seoul."

Honor walks into the common room with Ethan and lets him take a seat amongst his classmates for the final time. Ethan knows it's his final time, but no one else does. They're still a little bruised, but they're bright and alive and Honor loves each and every one of them, and that's why she gathered them all to tell them that they've been excused from the year end tournament. What she doesn't expect is the immediate protest.

"That's not fair!"

"Says who? Them or you?"

"We've prepared for this *all year*!"

"We *want* to do it."

"Screw that, we want to *win*."

"We executed an actual, real life, rescue but we can't do this dumb tournament?"

Honor looks to Verity for help, but she looks just as surprised at the outburst as Honor feels. Verity meets her gaze and her eyes flash blue.

Don't look at me. If someone had told me I didn't have to do this stupid tournament I would have jumped at the chance.

Honor thinks back to high school and what this tournament had meant for them then. It was a final grade. Nothing more. They went to Marvelous at the height of its tenure. They had been expected to win. It had been drilled into them every day all year that they would win. Failure was so far from an option that it had been laughable. Honor thinks they hadn't really taken it seriously. She and her sisters had been so young, so full of confidence and overbrimming with inflated egos, it was nothing to them.

But this tournament means so much more to these kids. They have worked all year for it. They've overcome what no other class has or would be expected to. They chose to compete with each other and the other schools in the beginning to prove their worth and the Academy's, and now they want to choose to participate when they are being given a pass.

Honor wonders if maybe the intense desire to prove themselves has stemmed from that same burning need in Honor herself. She's been desperate all year, and she thought she'd been careful to hide it from the kids. Maybe she wasn't careful enough. This tournament is the opportunity to prove themselves on one of the nation's biggest stages. But then, Honor thinks about Kai hitting his limit and going past it to save strangers. Jayne nearly tearing out a wing to save Charlie. Charlie going head-to-head with a Titan. She knows that these kids have absolutely nothing to prove to anyone.

They could do it. Honor never once questioned their ability and they've trained so hard all year, learning from their mistakes and striving to be better. It's Honor's own ability she questions. Her ability to teach and to lead the next generation of heroes. Honor has shouldered a lot of weight in her short lifetime, but this, this feels like too much. If something, *anything*, were to happen to one of these kids, it would be entirely her fault and she doesn't know if she could live with that.

"This is not a discussion," Honor cuts in sharply. It startles the kids into silence. Honor hardly ever snaps at them, and she doesn't know how to explain to them that this is only because she cares about them. Knows they won't understand what it's like to see one of your kids laid up in a hospital because they weren't there in time, because they weren't good enough. They deserve to rest, even if it's not what they want. "You will take your final A grades and go home for the summer and you will be happy about it."

She doesn't tell them there won't be any coming back. She has a feeling that would go over even worse. So, she'll send them home and contact the parents later to let them know they need to enroll their children elsewhere because Titan Academy is closing for good.

28

"What's Next for Colson Cappelletti?
All the Details From His Graduation"

—Titan Tribune

Charlie sits in her favorite spot on the couch at home and watches the video she'd been gifted of her progress. Honor was right, she didn't realize how much she had improved over the course of the school year. She cringes a little at the beginning, seeing her run headfirst into situations when she should have stopped to analyze. As if watching herself on film wasn't awkward enough on a good day, she also gets to watch all her bad days, from her broken leg to her failed fire simulation. But she also gets to see her make it up with a crew of her friends who volunteered to help her and made her better. She is better.

Looking back at the simulations, Charlie did so much better than she thought at the time. She reads the tags of notes Honor had left. They're the same notes she'd given after the exercises, but it's different to see them side-by-side with the events themselves. At the end of the video, she finds a highlight reel.

It's just random little moments caught throughout the year, mostly in the arena because the cameras are always rolling in there. Charlie high-fiving her teammates after a good run in a sim, goofing around on the bus on the way to a field trip, even her early morning training sessions with Tommy that she didn't think anyone knew about.

Charlie watches herself scream in victory when she manages to snatch a new record, throwing the heavy bar to the ground and fist pump into the air. Then she watches the way she cheers for Lochlan when he manages to pull a storm under his control. She sees, from an outsider's perspective, how she wraps her arm around Jack's neck and messes up his hair and how it looks like they don't hate each other even a little bit. She gets to see what she looks like doubled over in laughter after Jayne takes flight with a screaming Anthony wrapped up in a vice-like hug and how he warps back to the safety of the ground.

Charlie has always known that she goes through life like it's a competitive sport, but seeing it in action is an odd mix of embarrassing and empowering. She used to be worried that she's too loud, too pushy, too over the top in a way that would make people think she's an asshole. But Charlie likes the way she is. She may make mistakes, but everyone does. She'll apologize, learn, move on, and continue to live her life out loud.

"We're going to have to decide where you're going next year," her mom says when she comes into the living room, off hand, like it isn't a big deal.

"What?" Charlie asks and pauses the video. "I'm going to Titan Academy."

Her mother pauses and looks over at Charlie, grim. "So Honor didn't tell you, then."

"Tell me what?" Charlie asks, dread opening up a pit in her stomach. What hadn't Honor told her? Them? Any of them, because if one of her classmates knew something then they all would. They had their differences, but at the end of the day they're a team.

"Titan Academy is closing," her mom tells her.

"Closing? What do you mean 'closing'?" Charlie demands and pushes to her feet.

Her mom sighs. "The school board gave her an ultimatum at the beginning of the school year. They weren't happy about the fact that she found a loophole and was able to establish her academy without any oversight, so they threatened to take away her accreditation unless she either won the end of the year tournament or allowed three board members to sit on the administrative board. She chose the tournament then, rather than allow the board members onto her board."

"What?" Charlie shouts. "And you didn't stop them?"

"I was outvoted," her mom says calmly.

"We can't let this happen!" Charlie says and starts pacing the living room. "I have to do something. We have to do something. What should I do?"

"Fight," her mom says simply.

"I'll need help."

"Yes, you will."

"Can you do the adult paperwork things?" she asks. "Please, Mom? Like make sure we still have a slot in the tournament?"

"I think I can do that," her mom says with a small, proud smile.

"Okay, okay," Charlie says and tries to make sense of the whirlwind of thoughts in her head. She pulls out her phone and calls Jack. He doesn't pick up. She calls him again. He picks up on the third ring.

"What do you want, Charlie?"

"Did you know that the Academy is closing?"

"It's *what?*"

Jack is, rightfully so, just as stunned by the news as she is. He's immediately on board for rounding up the rest of their classmates. They divide the list into two and start making calls, telling everyone to meet them back at Jack's house. The only problem is Ethan, who dodges both of their calls.

Jack agrees to pick her up and go by Ethan's house on his way home from his dad's agency. When he pulls up to the curb in a ridiculously expensive luxury car that she doesn't know the name of, Charlie doesn't know whether to laugh or cry. He opens the butterfly door from the inside and Charlie can see that all of the details on and in the glossy black car are neon pink. That's the only thing that stops her from making fun of him.

"Do you even have a driver's license?" Charlie asks him as she buckles up.

Jack rolls his eyes at her as he pulls onto the street. Charlie has a permit but she doesn't turn sixteen until late July. She's also sure she isn't getting a car unless she manages to pay for one with the job she doesn't have. Even if she was, she's certain it wouldn't cost anywhere near what this car does.

"Of course I have a license," he says. He drives with both hands on the wheel like a responsible nerd. After a full school year getting to know Jack, she knows why he avoids the media so much. He's not nearly as cool as everyone thinks he is.

"He's either dead or asleep," Charlie says when they pull up to Ethan's house. All of their other friends had already agreed to the plan, worked up halfway into a rage and ready for action. Ethan's the only odd man out.

They get out and walk up the narrow walkway through a perfectly manicured lawn, up onto a porch decorated with creepy little gnomes. Ethan's got a nice, if a bit average, house, and Charlie realizes for the first time she doesn't know much more about Ethan other than his work at school and his videos. Does he have siblings? Does he live with his parents? Grandparents? Does he have a room dedicated to filming his videos? Charlie kind of wants to see it.

Jack knocks on the door three times. Then, they wait. Charlie stares at Jack.

"What?"

"Of course you knock like a cop," is all she says.

"What does that even mean?" Jack asks, exasperated.

Ethan answers the door, barefoot and still in his pajamas. He looks surprised to see them as if this wasn't the only outcome after he avoided both of their calls.

"Emergency Class Alpha meeting," Charlie says by way of explanation. "Let's go."

"Um, okay, so listen," he says and Charlie already knows that whatever he's about to say is going to piss her off. "I'm not actually… in Class Alpha anymore."

"Yeah, none of us are," Charlie says. "That's what we're trying to fix."

"Wait, what?" he looks between the two of them. "What are you talking about?"

"What are *you* talking about?" Charlie fires back with narrowed eyes.

"Um, well," he says, then laughs nervously. "I'm actually transferring."

"What?" Jack scoffs. "Why? *Where?*" His tone heavily implies that there is no place better than Titan Academy. A sentiment with which Charlie wholeheartedly agrees, but now is not the time.

"Listen, Litebrite," she says and Ethan frowns. "I don't care where you go next year. You're still a part of our class now and this year isn't over yet."

"Compelling," Ethan says.

"Look, *Ethan*," Charlie tries again. "We need to do this and we need your help. First years in the tournament get search and rescue sims and that's your wheelhouse. We can't do it without you." Ethan looks at Jack who backs her up by nodding. They must make quite the compelling sight, the two class rivals willingly working together toward a single goal. "If you don't want to do it for yourself, I get it. You don't really have anything to gain or lose in this situation. But Honor does. All of the teachers, Leo, Teddy, Verity, Aurora, and Rae—all of *us* and all of the people who come after us who deserve to learn from the best of the best. This isn't just about winning the tournament for bragging rights or kicking Marvelous' ass—"

"Well," Jack starts, but Charlie holds a finger up in front of him.

"I will give you a signal when it's your turn to speak," she says and turns back to Ethan. "If you don't want to do it for yourself, do it for them." Ethan looks between them for a beat longer, and Charlie thinks she should have scripted out a better speech beforehand, but she honestly hadn't expected that Ethan truly needed to be convinced.

"Okay, let's go," he says. Charlie heaves a sigh of relief and claps him on the shoulder hard enough to make him flinch. Charlie still isn't used to how strong she's gotten in such a short span of time. She apologizes sheepishly and tows Ethan to Jack's car before he can change his mind.

Knowing who Jack is and who his parents are, Charlie is already expecting a mansion. But nothing could have prepared her for the sprawling acres of land in the hills, safely tucked away from the general public behind gothic wrought iron gates. It's not a mansion. It's a *castle*.

Charlie doesn't even try to pretend that she isn't gaping and Ethan practically has his face pressed to the window behind her. She'd pictured something sleek and modern with lots of glass windows. Maybe one of those flat, angled roofs. But this looks like someone plucked it straight out of a storybook.

Jack chews on his cheek while he pulls past the other, regular people cars in the circular driveway, into the garage next to several other very expensive foreign cars. Charlie steps out of the car and onto a shiny custom floor that twinkles like it has stars in it.

"Holy shit, Boy Wonder," is all she can say. Jack gets out of the other side of the car.

"Yeah," is all he says. Charlie and Ethan follow him inside. The garage leads into a mudroom where Jack takes off his shoes so they follow suit. Jack seems to be growing more tense by the moment, so Charlie brings her hands down on his shoulders from behind. He jumps a bit at first, but then she violently massages him until the tension drops and whatever weird emotion he was feeling turns into irritation.

"Gonna give us a tour?" she asks.

"Don't we have something more important to do?" Jack replies. He leads them out of the mudroom and into a kitchen that is probably half the size of Charlie's whole house. This room is an example of the modern luxury Charlie had been picturing. The walls are the same beautiful creamy stone as the exterior, but the counters and the *two* islands are all marble. The cabinets are all black with gold handles, and one of them probably hides the refrigerator. There's even an artsy bubble chandelier. Two, actually. One over each island.

"You're right, a two-day tour would probably cut into our planning time," she says.

"Two-day tour?"

"Yeah, I assume that's how long it takes to see all five hundred rooms."

"It's not five hundred," he mutters.

Gina comes into the kitchen as they're heading out through the big archway. She's holding an empty tray, barefoot and beaming in her casual clothes of jeans and a Titan Academy t-shirt.

"Oh good, you're here!" she says and kisses Jack on the cheek. "The rest of your friends are in the lounge."

"Your home is gorgeous," Charlie gushes.

"Thank you, sweetheart," Gina smiles at her. "I'm glad you're all here. Jack's never invited friends over before."

"Mom!"

"Well, you're never getting rid of us now," Charlie says. Gina laughs and ushers them out of the kitchen. Jack leads them down a hall lined with paintings that each have their own little spotlight above them. Ethan gets stuck looking at one abstract painting of the Earth from space, and Charlie has to double back to tug him along.

Their classmates are strewn about the lounge. There's the biggest screen that Charlie has ever seen outside of a movie theater mounted on the far wall, and there are sliding glass doors that lead to the backyard on the adjacent wall. Charlie can see a row of deckchairs and an Olympic-sized swimming pool through them. There's a black leather sectional that most of their friends are piled onto, but some are in the big emerald armchairs, and a few people are on the carpeted floor which honestly looks plush and comfortable. There's a large ottoman that matches the sectional and it has a tray with a bunch of snacks and drinks on it. Charlie snags one of the cookies on her way to stand in the front of the room with Jack while Ethan sits on the arm of the couch.

"Jack! You've been holding out on us, man!" Anthony jeers. "Can we sleep over? Is your dad here?"

"Is your pool heated?" Alex asks, looking out of the sliding glass doors.

"Your mom said there was a game room," Lochlan adds. "Is it, like, an arcade?"

"Uh," Jack falters, and Charlie thinks he's more lost than uncomfortable. Especially after Gina told them that Jack's never invited anyone over before. She can't imagine never having friends over. Especially since Jack doesn't have any siblings. It's just him and his parents in this big castle.

"Slumber party plans later, guys, we have a problem," Charlie tells them, and the room sobers up immediately. Charlie and Jack deliver the news and suddenly everyone is shouting.

"How is that even possible?"

"Why wouldn't they tell us?"

"We *said* we would do it!"

"Maybe they *want* to close." It's Kai who says it.

"They don't want to close," Charlie snaps. "Not after all the work they did for us this year, if they wanted to close, they could have half-assed everything but they didn't. We got field trips and midnight drills and super special secret access to their missions. They wouldn't do that unless they were in it for the long run and they don't give up. So neither can we."

Silence rings out in the room. Everyone stares at Charlie.

"So what do we do?" Anthony asks.

"We compete," Charlie says. "My mom said she can make sure we're still registered and everything and then all we have to do is show up."

"So why are we all here?" Rose asks.

"Because the terms weren't just that we had to compete," Jack tells them. "We have to win."

"So, we're here to strategize," Charlie says. "We're going to review the top scores from each of the training exercises and formulate a plan for each scenario so we're prepared for anything and everything."

"I have all the scores," Jack says and pulls out his tablet from a secret drawer hidden in the wall beside the television. His ears go pink when everyone begins to rave about it.

"You have *everyone's* scores?" Malia asks dubiously.

"Yes, I like to stay on top of everything," he mumbles and ducks his head.

"More like stay on top of the class," Kai mutters.

"When he'd really like to stay on top of—" Anthony begins but Alex cuts him off.

"*Nerd!*" she jeers, throwings some of her snacks at Jack. He just scowls at her in an oddly thankful way. Honestly, it's a miracle Tommy hasn't figured out Jack has a massive crush on him yet. Charlie's half convinced that he has and he is much better at hiding it than Jack.

"Anyway," Jack says through gritted teeth. "I think we should follow the plans from the top scorers and implement the marvels of those who weren't in their group because we'll all be working together as a class instead of smaller groups."

"What are they?" Lochlan asks.

"Alex's team won the scavenger hunt, if we count that," he says. "My team scored highest in the rockslide and earthquake sims, Lochlan's team for the fire sim, Kai's for hurricane and flood rescue, and Charlie's for the building collapse search and rescue."

"Really?" Charlie asks, genuinely surprised.

"Yeah," he says like it's obvious. "I also think Charlie has the best decision-making skills under pressure, so she should be team leader regardless of the scenario we get. We wouldn't even be here without her, so."

Charlie opens her mouth, but no words come out.

One of these days she's going to have to admit that she and Jack Zelweger might make a pretty good team. But today is not that day.

"I agree," Lochlan announces.

"Are we voting?" Rose asks. "All those in favor?" She raises her hand and all of their classmates follow suit.

"I don't…" Charlie trails off.

"Yes, you do," Jack scoffs without knowing what she was even going to say because *Charlie* doesn't even know what she was going to say. She has to fight off a face-splitting smile because it feels inappropriate given the circumstances. But she's proud and honored and she's going to welcome this pressure and let it make her into a diamond.

"Let's get to work," she says.

"Life! Joy! Victory!" Jack cries their school words like the little nerd he is, and claps his hands together. There's a collective groan from the rest of the class, and Charlie hits herself in the forehead with her palm. Classic Boy Wonder. But she can get behind the sentiment.

It's unsettling to Honor to feel as though she's outgrown her childhood home. She sits in the living room on the purple velvet couch and looks around. There's a chip in the coffee table that Honor made with her tooth when she was nine. The photographs on the wall are still crooked because Grace insisted she could eyeball it. The hole in the wall from Verity throwing the toaster at her is a different color in the kitchen because they couldn't find the original paint color and their mom didn't want to repaint the whole place.

Honor and her sisters are stamped into every corner of this place and yet, it doesn't feel like hers anymore. Then, Colson walks into the living room from the hallway and suddenly the place feels a little bit homier.

"Any luck with the job hunt?" Honor asks and makes room for him to flop on the couch next to her.

"Not even a little," he groans and lets his head fall onto the back of the couch. "Maybe I should change my name."

Honor immediately hates that idea. "And your face?" She grins when he pouts because Colson likes his face, but he's so recognizable that changing his name alone won't do him much good.

"I can't even find a gym that will let me in," he says and covers his face with both hands. "Starting over fucking *sucks.*"

"You can work out at the Academy," she offers. He doesn't even have the excuse of the kids being there or parent protests since they're closing down. "I'm not selling it."

"Okay," Colson says and uncovers his face to look at her. A frown line pinches between his brows and Honor reaches out to poke it. "If you're not going to sell it, what are you going to do with it?"

Honor shrugs. "I'll figure it out."

"The tournament is tomorrow," he says as if Honor doesn't already know that. "Are your kids going still?"

"No," she says and looks down at her lap. "I excused them. They've been through enough." Colson's new phone vibrates in his pocket and he fishes it out. He looks at the screen and the corner of his mouth lifts. Honor heroically resists prying. Colson deserves some privacy after having every second of his outside communication monitored during his time at Ameliora.

"Leo wants me to make sure you're not moping," he offers on his own. Honor scowls.

"I'm not *moping*," she says. Colson doesn't comment on that, just types out a reply and hits send. Then, he puts his phone down and turns to face Honor on the couch, pulling his leg up onto the cushion between them. Honor watches him warily.

"So are you gonna tell me why you quit?" he asks. Anger flares up in Honor for a hot flash before she shoves it back down.

"I didn't *quit*," she says through clenched teeth. Colson's eyes flit over her person, assessing. Her anger doesn't scare him, but he still takes note of when it appears.

"Then what do you call excusing the kids from the tournament?" he asks.

"Compassion," she snaps. "They don't need to go through that circus to prove anything."

"So you don't think they could win."

"Of course they could win! They handled a *Titan-level threat*. They are perfectly capable of acing that tournament."

"Then they'd win and then the Academy could stay open," Colson says. "So you're quitting."

"*No,*" Honor snaps then sighs. "What are you doing?"

"Trying to understand."

Honor has been taking care of Colson since she found him again. He needed her support and she gave it freely, of course she did. But given what a whirlwind the past year has been, Honor almost forgot that this is a two-way street. Honor takes a deep breath to remind her body that this is neither a fight nor flight situation. She's safe here. She's safe with Colson.

To her horror, feeling safe also means an influx of tears.

"I'm tired," she admits in a whisper. "And scared." Colson reaches out and takes her hand and squeezes. She cracks a knuckle when she squeezes back him but he doesn't even flinch. "I'm so sick of being afraid to make the wrong decision. I've made so many just—fucking catastrophic choices. I couldn't have the kids be collateral."

Colson opens his mouth, closes it, then opens it again to speak. "Deciding to do nothing is still a decision. A dangerous one, at that."

"It's not *nothing,*" she says. "I *decided* to free them from the burdens of *my* mistakes!"

"What mistakes?" Colson asks, baffled. Honor doesn't have an answer. "Oh. The mistakes you haven't even made yet? Honor."

"What?" she snaps.

"Listen, I've never met your kids, but you picked them, so I feel confident in saying that they, and you, can handle making a few mistakes. Couldn't avoid it even if you wanted to. Making mistakes is a part of life and no one is exempt.

But I know you could handle the fallout of anything that comes your way. You have so far."

"That's exactly my point!" Honor exclaims and shoots to her feet. Colson follows, slower. "I made the mistake of freeing Krewa. I lost you in the process and people *died*. Because of me! Because of a decision that I, and I alone, made. Those kids were in harm's way because I chose to open this school. That was *my fault*. Every time I make a decision, someone gets hurt!"

"I think you're doing those kids a disservice to assume that they can't make their own decisions. Or, knowing what they know now, that they wouldn't choose to do it again given the chance. They're kids, but they're not stupid. I know they're not." Honor opens her mouth to argue more but Colson cuts her off. "I don't blame you for what happened between us because that was also a decision that *I* made. You are not the only person making decisions or afraid to make the wrong ones.

"I can, and will, forgive you a thousand times for what happened with us. But it's not going to make a difference if you don't forgive yourself too."

Honor is quiet for a long moment while those words struggle to find a way to penetrate her thick skin. She narrows her eyes at him.

"Did your therapist teach you that?"

He lifts his hand to the back of his head. "Maybe."

"Well, it's too late anyway," Honor says and wraps her arms around herself. "I already pulled out of the tournament and it's tomorrow."

"I think you can forgive yourself for that, too," he says. Kindly, as if he knows Honor already regrets it. That she made yet another wrong decision and she can't go back and fix it.

But she can go forward and be better. Honor de Mora isn't ruled by her fear. Colson is right, she can handle anything that gets thrown her way. Even if it is a boomerang of bad decisions.

"I'm gonna hug you now," she says, voice still a little tight with unshed tears.

"I'd be disappointed if you didn't," he says and holds his arms wide.

29

"Who Won? Who Lost? Who Died?
All the Tournament Stats from the Last Ten Years"
—*Los Angeles Star*

Honor wakes up early the morning of the tournament. She'd excused the kids from participating, but she and her staff aren't so lucky. They still have to attend to judge and provide security. They drive together, and it's an oddly somber trip to the Sapphire Stadium. They check in with the least amount of interaction possible and receive their posts for the day. Honor doesn't have one since she was originally supposed to chaperone her kids. Leo will be up in the security booth, watching from a safe distance and ready to step in should the need arise. Aurora will be in the security booth with him on the camera feeds and security system. Rae is assigned to the entrance along with Teddy, and Verity is—

"Announcing?" she asks as she squints at the paper. "Are they serious? Why do they want to give me a microphone?"

"That will be broadcast nationwide," Rae adds.

"What the fuck," she asks flatly.

"I don't think you're allowed to swear," Aurora says, hiding her giggles behind her hand.

"What. The. Fuck." Verity enunciates slowly. "I want a do-over."

"Oh, I can't wait to hear this," Honor says and wraps her arm around her sister's shoulders to walk her up to the booth. "Remember they're just kids, so be nice. No name calling."

"If they want me to announce, I'll call it like I see it," Verity says.

"Point out their highlights, not their lowlights," Honor goes on.

"I should've been security with Leo and Aurora," she complains. "If someone gets too into it, I can calm them down. I even have security experience from Opia! I have no announcing experience!"

They arrive at the doors to the booth and Honor shoves Verity inside after opening the door for her.

"Well, you won't be able to say that tomorrow," she says with a grin. Verity flips her off and sits down heavily in the chair in front of the microphones. There's a large glass pane with a clear view of the arena, and they're above the stands as well. Screens line the back wall for closer views of both. Aurora slips inside and touches her fingertips to the screen, and they whir to life.

"Is this fucking thing on?" Verity tests the microphone, and Honor can practically hear Rae cackling at the first security checkpoint. The stadium is still empty except for staff. A frazzled coordinator bolts between Honor and Leo to get into the room.

"Miss de Mora!" she cries. "We have to go over—"

"Miss de Mora?" Verity repeats, mic still hot. "Who *the fuck* is Miss de Mora?"

"And I was worried today was going to be boring," Fergus says as he ascends the steps.

"Are you announcing, too?" Honor asks. Fergus is another pro that they've worked with on occasion, but he primarily works in the Emerald district and in white collar crime so they don't cross paths often. His sleek, shoulder length blond hair is braided back, and Honor briefly wonders if he were to activate his marvel, would the strands pull themselves out? Or would he have to undo the braid himself? That seems awfully time consuming. Prehensile hair feels like it would be a cumbersome marvel.

"Indeed I am," he confirms. Verity catches sight of him filling the doorway with his gaudy red, white, and blue Hero Axis Agency shirt and viking braids.

"Oh great, fucking Cousin Itt is here," she groans. The coordinator scrambles to try and turn off the microphone, but Verity has strategically placed her hand over the switch.

"Would it kill you to call me by my real name?" Fergus asks as he sits down next to her.

"Your real name is *Fergus*," she says with obvious pity. "I'm doing you a favor."

"Have fun," Honor says to Leo and turns to leave.

"I'm sure I will," he says and takes his place in the booth.

Honor mostly wanders around while everyone else preps. She stops to look at the photos from her victorious year with her sisters, grinning at the memory of the three of them standing on the hastily-made podium with a demolished stadium behind them. Honor still has her copy of that photo. It's one of her favorites.

She laughs to herself while Verity shouts expletives into the microphone and pretends she doesn't know how to turn it off. Honor's sure she's trying to make sure she's never asked back again. She'll probably succeed too.

Honor is wandering through the team rooms, lingering outside of the one that had been marked for Titan Academy while people start to filter into the stadium mid morning when Soleil appears beside her. She doesn't say anything in greeting, just stands next to Honor and looks with her. Honor breaks the silence first.

"Are your kids ready?"

"We'll see," she says with a noncommittal shrug. Honor knows the drill. Soleil won't reveal anything about her kids, and that's a luxury she still has. Marvelous is known for keeping their classes under wraps. The whole world knows about Honor's kids, but they're not competing, anyway.

"*You all have assigned seats, what the hell are you fighting for? Read your goddamn ticket,*" Verity says, and Soleil snorts.

"*What Verity means is please ask an usher for help if you can't find your seat,*" Fergus's voice rings out next.

"*I meant what the fuck I said, Ferngully.*"

"*What's a ferngull—you know what, I don't want to know.*"

"They're going to be a fun pair," Soleil comments.

"If Verity's not thrown out of the booth by the second event, I owe Rae ten dollars," she says.

"I'll get in on that," Soleil says with a grin. "My money's on the finals."

"Bet," Honor says and they shake on it. Soleil's hand is a tad too warm against hers and she holds one for a split second too long. Honor knows she wants to say something. She doesn't know if she'll be able to wait her out like Verity can. But she has somewhere to be, and Honor doesn't.

"Incendiary was released," she says. It's not a question so Honor doesn't answer, but she does brace for whatever's coming next. She doesn't expect it to be: "He's all right?"

"He's… recovering," Honor says, unsure of how to answer or even what the truth is.

"Good," Soleil says, and Honor is surprised by her sincerity.

"Why do you care?" she asks before she can stop herself.

"When he came to Marvelous," she starts and then looks around because she's clearly not supposed to be talking about this, "Khalid could draw from him easily, deeply, and it worried him."

That's right, one of the many charges brought up against Colson. He and a group of rogues infiltrated the Marvelous dorms and the official charge was attempted kidnapping, even though they never got anywhere near the kids thanks to the teachers fending them off. But considering the dorm building was left intact and Colson hadn't used his marvel once, Honor was also inclined to believe that the attempt was all a show. Which was later confirmed during Colson's rigorous interrogation by Ursula.

"That sounds right," Honor mutters. "He's—I…"

"You'll take care of him," Soleil says. Honor doesn't know how she can say that with so much certainty, so much faith. Honor can only nod. Her phone starts to vibrate in her pocket and she can hear the opening ceremony beginning in the arena.

"Good luck today," Honor tells her when she starts to leave for her own team room.

"You too," she says.

"Oh, we're not competing this year," Honor tells her. "After everything—I let them go early."

"Oh?" is all Soleil says before she turns fully. Honor fumbles to answer her phone before it can go to voicemail. It's her home number.

"What is it? Are you okay? What's happening?" she answers in a rush.

"I'm fine," Colson promises immediately. "I don't remember you worrying this much."

"Yeah, well, that happens when you become a parent," she says. "What's up?"

"I'm watching the broadcast."

"Yeah? You hear Verity's very colorful color commentary? We have bets going on how long before they kick her out if you want in," she says and hears a ghost of a laugh in response. It makes her smile.

"I'm calling because you said your kids weren't competing," he says.

"We're not," she says for the second time in less than five minutes and her gut starts to twist. She looks in the direction of the arena even though she can't see it.

"Did you tell them that?"

"What are you talking about?" Without thinking about it, she starts to run toward the nearest tunnel to the arena, and then she hears Verity, not over the sound system, but in her head: *Where are you?* It's not worried, and that eases some of the tension that had started in Honor's muscles, but she sounds surprised and a little ... awed?

Honor gets to the tunnel that leads to the lowest seats in the arena. She skids to a halt in front of the railing there. There are her kids. Right there in the middle of the field, all dressed in Titan colors and looking ready for a fight.

Charlie stands at the head of the class with Jack and Tommy on either side of her and the rest of the class behind them. Even Ethan is there, next to Kai, wearing his uniform just like everyone else. The crowd is cheering at the introduction that Fergus is doing, because Verity has likely been shocked into silence like Honor.

"*… Against Titan Academy. The Titans are coming fresh off a fight for their lives, a real life taste of what it's actually like to be a pro. Defending our planet against another Titan invasion is the best experience a young hero could ask for. Arguably the most talented group of kids in the tri-state area, hand picked by Honor and Verity de Mora, Class One heroes and Earth's very own resident Titans. Verity, do you have anything you'd like to say to your students before their first tournament?*"

A mistake. A huge mistake. Unless Fergus knew exactly what he was doing and did it anyway, Honor wouldn't put it past him.

"*Yeah, if you're gonna compete after we said* no, *you'd better fucking win!*"

Most of the crowd is immediately put off by her vulgar language aimed at the kids, but the kids themselves start laughing.

Honor watches Cora fist bump Rock Buddy with one of her aura claws and Anthony warp out of Simon's hold before he can mess up his hair, carefully gelled and styled like always. Tommy turns to wave up at the booth and Charlie is grinning fiercely when she turns and catches Honor's eye.

"Smile, Honor." Colson's voice in her ear startles her. She forgot she was holding her phone. "You're on TV."

She looks up at the jumbotron and sees her own face staring back at her. She sees her stupidly big, proud smile and looks back at her kids. They wave excitedly at her. Honor's never been more in love.

30

"Volunteer Victims: Death is a Real Risk"

—*Marvels Today*

The Sapphire Stadium feels bigger than the Titan Arena with its open roof and full crowd and the giant spire of disasters spinning in a slow circle in the middle of the field. It's such an incredible feat of engineering, even Charlie can appreciate it. To have separate disasters that don't overlap but are all ongoing at the same time while keeping the students, spectators, and volunteer victims safe?

Seems like a huge shitshow, honestly.

Charlie watches this tournament on TV every year, but standing in the starting position on the field with hundreds of thousands of eyes on her at once is daunting. These people look like ants on screen at home, and they kind of look like ants now, all the way up to the top, but here their gaze carries weight as it all lands squarely on Charlie's shoulders. Not to mention the fact that they can't just do well if they want to save the school, they have to *win*.

"Broadly First Class: Hurricane."

She's secretly hoping for the earthquake or flood sims. They've got dead ringers with Jack and Kai when it comes to those, and if they get the fire rescue, Charlie may internally lose her shit, but they have a plan and she can stick to it, no problem.

There's a maximum of one thousand points possible, and classes with thirty kids have a steep advantage over their class with only twenty, but they can make it work. No one ever gets the full thousand anyway. They're aiming for nine hundred since Marvelous and Broadly typically score in the high eight hundreds. They all know it's a stretch. Charlie just has to focus on getting her points and doing her part. As long as they all do that, they can pull this off.

"Marvelous Class B: Fire," the announcer who isn't Verity goes on, listing all of the schools and their classes. There are multiple sims of each type, and every other school except Titan Academy has multiple classes. It just increases the odds of another school winning through sheer numbers.

Charlie's never cared much for odds.

"Titan Academy: Structural Collapse."

Charlie heaves a sigh of relief. Her best sim. It's arguably one of the harder ones for the tournament because the cause of the building collapse isn't revealed beforehand. If it's an earthquake, then aftershocks are likely. If it was a bomb, a secondary fire could start. If it's any other reason, there's a million more things that could go wrong, but they've prepared as best they could.

A buzzer sounds, and instead of taking off immediately like half of the other classes, they group together to finalize their plan. The giant clock over the top of the stadium begins to count down. They have one hour, and from past experience, Charlie knows that a single hour on the job will pass faster than a single-minute snooze.

"With no obvious cause for collapse, we have to go in with extra caution," Charlie says and her classmates nod along. "Jack and Luna will secure the outside of the building, and Cecily will clear away debris and obstacles with Rock Buddy. Rosie's lead on shoring, and take Kai with you, I can hear the broken pipes from here. Tommy's in charge of triage with Lochlan, Luc, Simon, Reese, and Dom. The rest of you are on scouting and extraction. Jayne's team will take the top ten floors, and Ethan's team the lower ten. Proceed slowly. Don't rush and don't panic. Everybody ready?"

"Let's get to work," Jack says. Jayne flies up to the top of the building with Malia in her grasp so she can heal those inside with substantial injuries to lower the risk of moving them. Tommy's team starts setting up the triage while Jack and Luna shore up the outside of the precariously leaning building to prevent further collapse.

They're a well-oiled machine and no one is without a job, but Charlie will admit that it's odd to be overseeing and giving orders rather than to be in the thick of the action. Some people start stumbling out of the building on their own when Rock Buddy clears the way, covered in dust and soot. Half of them are bleeding. Tommy ushers them to the space his team had cleared.

"Who's in charge here?!" someone shouts. Charlie goes immediately to the big burly man in an ill-fitting suit. Volunteer victims aren't used very often because the job is so high-risk, but the benefits are astronomically high and most have marvels that they can use to keep themselves safe if they absolutely have to. But they mostly let the trainees do their best to save them first.

"I am," she says and takes over so Tommy can focus on the others. "Sir, are you hurt?"

"No," he huffs.

"Sit down, have some water," she says and gets a water bottle off Reese. "Can you tell me what happened?"

"It was just a normal day, then all of a sudden the building just collapsed!" he cries. He takes the water bottle from Charlie but doesn't drink it. Her eyebrow twitches. This is a part of the training, she knows it is. How she responds to victims, no matter how unhelpful, will dictate her points. Most people would be in shock and so the inability to help isn't purposeful. She has to exercise patience and be able to get the most use out of the most useless information.

"Can you tell me how many people were inside at the time of collapse?" she asks. She opens the water bottle for him and gently urges him to drink.

"A hundred," he tells her. "It's an off day for most people, so it's a big building, but mostly empty."

"Okay," she says and quickly does a headcount of the people that were able to get out on their own. Twelve. Thirteen, now, as Jayne brings down a woman from the top floor. Eighty-seven people to go.

The man finally takes a sip of water, then, upon realizing he's parched, downs the entire thing.

"What can you tell me about the building layout?" she asks. He looks impressed for a flash before he's fumbling at his shirt pocket. He pulls out a holotile.

"I'm the building manager," he tells her. "These are the floor plans."

"Thank you," she says and takes it, waving down one of her classmates. "This is Simon, he's gonna take care of you, get that arm checked out."

"My arm is—" He looks down at his arm with a large but shallow gash from wrist to elbow. His shock is evident on his face, genuine. He looks back at Charlie. She grins and winks at him, taking the holotile to her mini command.

It's a folding table, one of the few things supplied to them by tournament officials. To keep everything fair, everyone in the same sims are given the same materials, and they're given everything that they need, even if some of it is a little outdated like the walkie talkies they're using instead of in-ear comms.

Jack's voice crackles over the walkie in Charlie's belt. "Integrity to Command. It looks like they were doing some construction around the back of the building, and they were doing a mediocre job. Some support beams were ill-placed and caused the collapse."

"Copy," Charlie says. "Command to Extraction. We have a total of one hundred patients. Thirteen have already been evacuated. That leaves eighty-seven unaccounted-for patients still in the building."

"Copy that, Captain," Jayne says.

Charlie fires up the holotile and gets a look at the building schematics. They're in-depth, not just the general layout of the floors and the major structures like stairs and elevators, but also the plumbing and electrical lines, too. Charlie's grateful she talked to that man and that she asked the right questions.

Touching the floors on the schematics can change the colors or the overlay of what she's looking at, so she has the teams relay to her which floors have already been clear so she can mark them green. She moves Kai from shoring with Rose to integrity with Jack when the downstairs flooding threatens further collapse of the lower floors. He moves outside to funnel the water, not just out of the building, but he gives the clean water to the triage team too.

Luna uses vines tied to strong redwoods to tether the front of the building to keep it from collapsing inward toward the side that Jack had secured, and Jayne's team keeps bringing more and more people out. No one seems seriously injured, but that could be because Malia got a hand on them before they were rescued. Having those people calm and largely uninjured is vital.

A blast of heat from next door distracts Charlie for a split second, and she looks over to the fire sim that the Marvelous kids are handling. A secondary fire has broken out, and they're scrambling. Without a water marvel among them, they're left with nothing but the hoses and hydrants provided for them. Noah is on triage, and Beck is there too, but Charlie doesn't look long enough to figure out what his job is.

Time's almost out. Charlie needs to focus on getting the remaining eight people out of the building. All the floors have been cleared which means they missed something somewhere. Charlie's starting to sweat.

Where they are right now, they'll pass. But passing isn't good enough. They have to *win*. Charlie can't control how other classes are doing, but she knows that to have any shot at winning, they have to clear the course, which means getting the remaining eight people out.

Seven. Two Alexes come out carrying an unconscious woman between them.

"Does anyone else smell gas?" Rose asks on the walkie. Charlie tenses.

"Not us," Jack says.

Charlie's eyes are drawn back to the fire sim going on a hundred feet away from her. The flames are licking up toward the sky, but are contained well within their course area on the platform. Charlie knows Leo and probably other heroes with defensive marvels are watching in case anything goes wrong, but her mind starts to spin out of control.

The smell of gas is familiar. Twice over. From her failed fire simulation and from the building fire that Honor had saved her from all those years ago. Charlie remembers being terrified that she was going to die. The black smoke and smell of gas sat thick on her tongue as she huddled under the table with her arms wrapped around her head.

Charlie?! Honor's voice was what pulled her out of her inner death spiral. Relief had immediately washed through her with just one word. Her own name. From the hero that would become her favorite for that moment and every moment on the job after.

Honor hadn't been in any kind of uniform, just jeans and a t-shirt, which meant she had gone out of her way, as a student not even a pro, to save Charlie because she needed saving. Charlie can remember, even as a kid, the swelling joy and admiration that filled her little body to the brim, to the point she thought she'd explode. She had to be a hero, she knew it right then. She had to.

"Extraction to command, how many patients left?" Ethan asks.

"Seven," she answers.

"Six," Tommy corrects because another one had been brought out by Anthony when she was distracted by the fire sim. The flames are getting even hotter, to the point where Charlie starts to sweat from it. The clock continues to count down. Two minutes and six patients left.

If that had been a real person, they would have died. Honor's voice and one of Charlie's worst moments forces its way to the forefront of her brain. A wall and a portion of the roof collapses as fire eats away at it in the Marvelous simulation.

Charlie sees the gas canisters that were hidden in the room. She wills Noah or Beck or *anyone* to notice but it doesn't look like they do. Or will.

"I've got a patient trapped under a stone wall in the first basement level," says Ethan.

"I'm on my way," Jack says, and Charlie trusts him to handle it.

"Charlie, where else do we look?" Rose asks, and she can hear the stress in her voice. They're running out of time.

These are real people in these sims. People *have* died in this tournament before despite all of the safety precautions taken, and they will again because that's how disasters work. But *someone* must know where those patients are, where the gas canisters are, how close they are to each other. Charlie can see across the line from where she is, in her own simulation. The patients are huddled under a table in what looks like a break room. The gas canisters are stacked together on a palette for easy moving. The building must be some sort of store.

Then, she remembers Leo saying he can't shield anyone he can't see and she realizes that from her vantage point, off to the side and far enough away to get a full scope of the situation—she's the only one who can see them. They're going to die.

Five-year-old Charlie's little lungs fill with acrid smoke and she coughs and coughs until she doubles over on the bed. It's so hot, the heat from the fire feels like a physical wall closing in on her. She doesn't know where to go or what to do. She tried to leave through the front door, but the metal knob had burned her hand. She cradles it gently against her chest now while she cries, tears evaporating before they hit her chin.

"Help!" she cries, desperate for someone, anyone, *to hear her. "Charlie!"*

That's her name. It's not a voice she knows. It's not mom or Kimmie but she shouts for help again anyway, hope filling her chest like fresh air. "I'm in here!"

Through the smoke, a hero crouches down in front of her. She's not wearing a cape, but that's okay. Charlie can tell she's a hero because she doesn't look scared. She reaches for Charlie, and Charlie flings herself into her arms, clinging to her, to her hero, with every ounce of strength in her little body. She's going to be saved.

No one is going to die today if Charlie has anything to say about it.

"What floor hasn't been double swept yet?" someone asks but Charlie's gone.

Heroes save anyone who needs saving. That's the job.

They're going to lose and the Academy will close, but Charlie isn't going to let anybody die in front of her. She abandons her post and sprints across the lines that mark the courses and into the fire sim with the Marvelous kids. She'd left her walkie behind so she only vaguely hears the shouting.

The fire is unbearably hot this close, and Charlie isn't a Titan so her skin overheats fast. The flames that do manage to lick her *hurt,* but she ignores them. She touches her fingers together to blast the debris out of the way to get to the patients nearest to the canisters. She pulls them both out from under a wooden table by the collars. She moves them forcibly, too rushed to be gentle or patient, yanks their arms over their heads.

"Tuck your bodies, protect your heads, and hang on tight," she orders, shouting to be heard over the flames. She ducks under the table and the metal floor sears her back but she has no choice; she has to get under the table so she can bring her hands together and blast it up through the hole in the collapsed roof and out of the danger zone.

The patients scream but are caught by someone with a flying marvel from Marvelous. The table crashes to the ground and splinters to pieces. Charlie can hear the whistling of the canisters. She doesn't have time to wait for the recoil to recede to get herself out of there.

She has to run.

She can't run fast enough.

The explosion sweeps her off her feet and launches her across the field. She feels the skin of her back and arms singe and she braces to hit the ground hard. But she's caught by a shield that still knocks the wind out of her. It is still a decidedly softer impact, and Leo lowers her gently to the ground. She coughs and closes her eyes against the spots that appear in her vision. The ringing in her ears hits her spine like a tuning fork, and her whole body sings with pain.

Fuck, fuck, fuck, shit, goddamn, fuck, she would say if she could speak, but the words get lost in her lungs while she still struggles to breathe.

Then, there's a hand on her, gentle and warm, and her whole body tingles.

Malia.

Charlie heaves a sigh of relief that's close to a sob, and she manages to open her eyes. She's met with the sight of a very worried Malia and Jayne hovering over her. She tries to muster up a smile for them.

"I'm okay," she says.

"Screw you!" Malia shouts, voice wet. "No you're not! You *scared* us, asshole!"

"Thank you," she says because she's not sorry, but she doesn't want her friends to worry about her. "Is everyone okay?"

"They're fucking *fine*." Malia is still shouting, and it hits Charlie's eardrums hard. She suppresses a flinch and lets Jayne pull her into a sitting position.

"Charlie!" Honor barks and shoves her way through the crowd that had gathered. Teachers aren't supposed to be on the field. But it doesn't really matter, Charlie supposes, since they didn't win and Honor technically isn't a teacher anymore.

Honor relaxes a fraction when she sees that Malia already got to her and she's freshly healed. She's definitely feeling the exhaustion seep in more than the pain had a chance to, which means that explosion really did a number on her. Thank god for Malia.

Honor hauls her to her feet and pulls her into a tight hug.

"I'm sorry," Charlie says, fighting off tears.

"What the hell are you apologizing for?" Honor asks.

"I—we didn't win," she says, hiccuping. "The school is gonna shut down and I abandoned my post and—"

"*Never* apologize to me for doing the right thing, do you hear me?" Honor cuts her off. Charlie nods against her shoulder. Then Honor spins her around so fast it makes her dizzy. "Besides. Look."

Up on the jumbotron are the points per individual student and the total points per class. Charlie fully expects to see Marvelous as the winner with their 870 points, but then she looks at the Titan Academy board.

TITAN ACADEMY: 899

"What? How…" She looks at their individual scores. Her scores should be low, close to zero because she hadn't actually gotten to do anything in their simulation, but then she sees next to her name;

CHARLIE WHITTAKER: 50

The largest sum of points allotted to a single person in tournament history.

Charlie lets out a wordless cry of astonished victory and her classmates roar around her. It's Jack who slams into her first, lifting her clear off her feet.

"We did it," he cries. "We fucking did it!"

It's chaos after that, with her classmates swarming them, and Verity shouting on the mic, and the deafening roar from the crowd at the last-minute save. Charlie's cheeks are wet, but she can't stop smiling. She looks for Honor again and finds her eyes shiny with tears and a grin to match Charlie's on her face.

Charlie launches herself at her hero for another hug. Honor catches her in impossibly strong arms and nearly crushes her.

"My hero," Honor says, and then Charlie really does start to cry.

They did it.

They fucking did it.

31

"Historic First Win for Titan Academy!"

—*Titan Tribune*

Charlie manages to convince Honor to let her visit Monroe about halfway through the summer. She waits in the sleek lobby of Ameliora, slightly uncomfortable, like if she touches anything she'll screw up the pristine interior design. The nice man behind the desk smiles and promises that Honor will be out in just a moment.

She comes through the automatic doors not ten seconds later, looking tanner and happier than Charlie remembers seeing her at the tournament. And she had been pretty damn happy at the tournament. Grace has been spotted with her sisters a lot recently, so maybe she has something to do with it.

"Hey, Charlie," Honor says, and sometimes it still rocks Charlie's whole world that she's on a first name basis with her favorite hero.

"Hey," she says, a little nervous. Honor grins because she definitely notices but doesn't comment. Just turns and gestures for Charlie to follow her back through the doors and not even halfway down the hallway to a visitation room. It's bare enough to not truly feel like a home, but it's pretty cozy considering it's technically a detention facility.

Monroe is the only other person in the room. Well, the only other rogue. She has her own personal guard, a pretty hulky dude who nods at Honor when they walk in. Monroe glances up at them, then she crosses her arms over her chest and looks away. Well. Charlie supposes she knew it would be difficult, and Monroe doesn't owe it to her to make it any easier. Charlie takes the seat across the table from her and the guard walks over to Honor on the other side of the room to give them the illusion of privacy.

"Hi, I'm Charlie," she starts. Monroe doesn't respond with her name, but Charlie already knows it. Should she pretend like she doesn't until Monroe says it? Ugh, this is too fucking complicated. Charlie needs to cut to the chase. "I, uh, I wanted to apologize."

"For what?" Monroe asks, a little meaner than necessary, Charlie thinks, but she doesn't really have the room to talk. Monroe looks better now than Charlie remembers. The bags under her eyes are practically gone, and her hair is washed. She looks better in the slightly too-baggy Ameliora sweats that don't have any holes in them.

"For, you know, the shit I said, at Rizzo's," Charlie goes on. "It wasn't cool."

"You weren't wrong," Monroe says like she's trying to prove something. Charlie's still too tired from summer training to match it. She shrugs.

"Doesn't mean I should have said it," she insists. "So I'm sorry. I didn't mean to hurt you, but I know that I did."

Monroe looks at her like she's grown another head. "Don't apologize to me." Charlie winces a bit at that, and yeah, okay, Honor had warned her that Monroe might not forgive her right away or at all, but that shouldn't discourage her from doing it. Doesn't mean it doesn't sting. But then she adds, "I should apologize to *you*."

"What? Why?" Charlie asks, surprised. She glances over at Honor, who is talking to the security guard and doing a well-enough job of pretending not to listen.

"I hurt you!" Monroe says, louder now. Honor's eyes do cut over to them at that, and Monroe sinks lower in her seat. "I hurt you and I hurt *her* and I hurt Colson. All I do is hurt people and everyone is apologizing to *me*."

"Oh," is all Charlie can say for the moment. She can only assume that the *her* Monroe's talking about is Honor, and Charlie had no idea that she hurt Colson, so she definitely can't speak on that. She almost tells Monroe that she doesn't have to apologize, but then remembers how infuriating that had been for her to hear not even five minutes ago, so she refrains. Says instead, "I forgive you."

Monroe's eyes go wide then narrow immediately, landing on Honor.

"She told you to say that, didn't she," she says.

Charlie is so, so lost.

"No? Honor didn't tell me shit. I forgive you because I want to."

"*Why?*"

"Uh," Charlie is at a loss once again. She resists the urge to look at Honor again. "I guess because I've done some stupid shit and hurt some people too, on accident even, and I was forgiven. I think it takes a good person to forgive someone for hurting them, and I'm trying to be a good person."

"'On accident even?' What the hell is that supposed to mean?" Monroe demands, blowing right past the part about being a good person. Charlie was proud of that one.

"Well," she rubs the back of her head. "Some of them were definitely on purpose. Like I said, I've done some stupid shit, and I was lucky enough to be forgiven, so."

"So, what?" Monroe asks.

"*So* I forgive you! Damn."

"What now? We just become best friends?" Monroe scoffs.

"Sure, why not?" Charlie says with a shrug. Monroe looks taken aback by her nonchalant answer, which is how a lot of people react to her declaring their friendship. Charlie's used to it, and it's worked out so far.

"So," Monroe says and looks away from Charlie, back toward Honor, "if I went to your school… you wouldn't hate me."

"Dude, *dude*, are you gonna go to Titan Academy when you get out of here?" Charlie asks. She's not even fully sure how she would feel about that yet but not because Monroe is a rogue, she's sure. More on the side of *oh shit more competition.* But after this year? Charlie welcomes the competition. It makes her stronger. It already has.

"I might," Monroe says, eyeing Charlie carefully to gauge her reaction. "I don't know."

"You totally should!" Charlie says with honest enthusiasm. She launches into her recap of the tournament they just won despite Monroe telling her that she already saw it on television. She doesn't know everything, and Charlie graciously fills her in on all the behind the scenes details.

Pride swells in Charlie's chest when Monroe looks genuinely impressed. She glances over at Honor every so often, and Charlie desperately wants to know the story there, but she's not going to pry. At least, not so soon. For now, she's happy to gush about her friends to her new friend.

32

"Another Titan Attack: Are We Safe?"
—*The Marvel Spectator*

Portals are officially the worst thing in the universe, Honor decides. Sure, intergalactic travel is cool in *theory*. But having to organize defenses around the universal pathways hidden all over the planet is, to no one's surprise, turning out to be a huge pain in the ass.

"You look like a princess!" Honor exclaims with childish delight when Grace comes through the portal. Yet another new one that Grace has found. It's easier to find them when you're coming rather than going, and Grace's help has been crucial to this process despite several protests from high-ranking government officials that she could be a spy from Viasyre. Luckily, it's not up to them, but to the International Heroes Council.

On the few occasions that Grace has come home to visit, she's always changed back into her old clothes. 'Earth' clothes, she calls them. But now they're short on time, so she'd come straight through without delay, and she's wearing a green velvet gown with a black shawl around her shoulders and a golden circlet on her head.

"*Are* you a princess?" Verity asks, eyeing her up and down. She looks toward the portal, lit up a soft gold color, a beacon in the middle of the Apostle Islands in Wisconsin of all places. The color dies out slowly until it's a faint glimmer against clear blue skies. The caves are right below them, and it doesn't seem like the portal extends down, only up.

"Technically," Grace says, surveying the area around the portal. That should honestly come as less of a surprise.

"We will be coming back to that," Honor says because right now they have a more pressing issue. "Is there a way to close the portals?"

"Not that we could find," Grace answers. "Cal is still looking into it, but no one has ever even attempted to close a portal on Viasyre. But that visitor was right, having so many portals unattended is dangerous."

"These portals have always been here, though," Verity points out. A breeze blows her hair into her face. "We've never had a problem before."

"That was before humans posed any threat or interest to outsiders," Grace points out. "Now you're on the map, passage has to be monitored somehow."

"First of all, I don't like that you said 'you' instead of 'us,'" Verity says, and Honor snorts softly. "Second, how do they manage to do that on Viasyre?"

"There are towers built around the portals," she explains. "Like border patrol. If you come through the portal, you're met with a kind of customs process."

"Thanks, I hate it," Verity says.

Honor sighs. "The IHC is already developing the process for Earth. All we have to do is find the portals."

"Speaking of which," Grace says and turns away from the portal, toward them. "We've mapped a dozen portals already, and you guys are already here when I come through every time. How do you know where I'm going to come out?"

"I just thought it was a triplet thing," Verity says with a shrug.

"Well, you give us a general area beforehand," Honor adds. "Once we get here it's easy to just… walk to you, I guess?"

"Extra easy when the portal lights up," Verity says, and Honor points at her. That's true, they'd been about hundred feet away when the portal first lit up, but they'd made it over by the time Grace actually came through.

"Okay, then I think the next question is: are you sensing me or are you sensing the portals?" Grace asks.

"You," Honor and Verity answer at the same time. No doubt about it. They've always been able to find each other in a crowd, even when they were little, without so much as a shout. It makes coordinating in battle seamless too.

"We only find the portals that you come through," Verity adds. "There's no draw from them. Oh, another thing, the portals carry auras."

"They do?" Grace sounds surprised at that and turns to look at the portal even though it's gone dark. "What do they look like?"

"They carry the residuals of the auras of people that passed through, and I can only see it when they're active," Verity tells them. "As far as I can tell, only you've come through this portal. At least, recently."

"Can you see anything?" Honor asks Grace.

"Just where they go," Grace says. It's another reason why she is uniquely equipped to map out all of the portals. She could probably make a killing if she charged for this galaxy-wide. "So you can tell *who* has passed through a portal?"

"Yeah, why?" Verity and Honor can both sense that Grace's mind is turning in a different direction now.

"I might have you look at some portals when you guys come to Viasyre," she says.

"Only if I get to do it in a pretty gown," Verity says. "Hey, if you're a princess and we're your sisters, does that also make us princesses?"

"I'm a princess through Cal," she explains.

"So you *are* married," Verity says like an accusation.

"Engaged," she clarifies with a cheeky little grin then holds up her hand. Honor and Verity shout for joy at the same time and scramble to look at the ring on her hand. It's very clearly handmade, with a large, rectangular emerald stone inlaid in a gold band that looks like ivy where it wraps around her finger all the way up to her knuckle. Verity whistles. "He even looked up human customs."

"What are Viasyre customs for engagement?" Honor asks.

"Blood," Grace says.

"That's enough details for me!" Verity says. "So when's the wedding?"

"You think I didn't plan it for when you're visiting?" Grace says. She's glowing with how happy she is. Verity squeals with joy, and Honor beams at both of her sisters. She wishes her mom were here. Grace glances at her and her smile turns soft, having seen that longing.

"Do we get to go to a Viasyrian dressmaker?" Verity asks, clapping her hands together.

"Viasyrian?" Honor echoes.

"That's right, actually," Grace says, clearly surprised.

"I know stuff," Verity says, jokingly defensive.

"Of course you can," Grace says and slings an arm around both their shoulders. "Only the best for my sisters."

Honor lets the simple joy of this moment sink in. She's with her sisters, Grace is getting married, they're all alive and well. They'll deal with whatever comes their way just like they always have. Well, maybe a little better than before. Honor likes to think she's learned a few things on her way here.

Acknowledgments

It truly takes a village to raise a child and this book is my baby. I'd like to thank everyone for their endless support and encouragement in my writing journey. Special shoutout to everyone who never asked me when I was getting a 'real' job. Thank you to my parents for supporting my dreams from day one and an extra thank you to my mom for being my manager. Thanks to my siblings, too, for keeping me humble. I'd like to thank my editor, Frankie, without whom I'd be utterly and totally lost, and so would a lot of commas. If there's anything "wrong" in this book, it's entirely my fault and probably on purpose. Thank you to my beta readers, Becca, Ryan, and Rue. Your early feedback and enthusiasm was a bedrock for this series and I'll never forget it. And thank you to my writer friends whom I've never met in person but have been ceaselessly kind and supportive. I love you all dearly.

And you, reading this now, thank you. If you've made it this far, you've made it to the end of this story and I hope to see you in the next.

About the Author

McKenna Ashton Lumley was born and raised in Southern California and still lives there in her mom's house because the cost of living is ridiculously high, so she'd really appreciate it if you'd buy her books. McKenna loves to consume content across all mediums and genres and frequents her local movie theaters, bookstores, and theme parks.

McKenna spends her days in a hostage negotiation with her ADHD to release her dopamine and get some sort of work done but usually ends up daydreaming with enough zeal to bring those dreams to life through sheer force of will.

Find her on social media @McKenna_Lumley or at mckennalumley.com

Made in United States
Orlando, FL
08 February 2024

43465961R00226